CAPITOL MURDER

Shepherd & Associates Series — Book 1

JUDITH ERWIN

Emerald Cat Press

Jacksonville, FL

Judith Erwin / Emerald Cat Press
Jacksonville, Florida
www.juditherwinofficialwebsite.com

Book Layout © 2017 BookDesignTemplates.com

Cover Image: licensed by Adobe Stock
Dog image (on Jake's card): Amelia Erwin
Cover Design: Marigrace Doran and Judith Erwin
Editor: John C. Boles

Capitol Murder / Judith Erwin. -- 1st ed.
ISBN 978-0-9997056-2-9 - Trade Paperback
ISBN 978-0-9997056-3-6 - eBook

Library of Congress Control Number: 2021900966

Dedicated to

NANCY H. DUTY

*There is no possession more valuable
than a good and faithful friend.*

—Socrates

Novels by Judith Erwin

Shadow of Silence

Shadow of Doubt

Shadows from the Past

Shadow of Dance Series

The Ballroom

The Ballet

The Studio

ACKNOWLEDGEMENTS

Once again, I give thanks to all those who played a role in the creation of my seventh novel, *Capitol Murder*. Specifically, sincere thanks to my brilliant editor, John C. Boles, for his sharp eye and vigilant guidance. Thanks to Julie Delegal, a dear friend and outstanding writer, for her support, plus valued comments and suggestions.

I, again, thank the incredibly talented Marigrace Doran for her amazing expertise in technology and design. She patiently endures my fickle mind and makes sure my covers and content are the best.

With every book, questions arise that even Google can't answer. It's then that a writer must seek expert input. With *Capitol Murder*, Rhonda Hullender was kind enough to read and provide excellent feedback on an important scene in this book for which I am extremely grateful; and Jean-Ellen DeSpain shared valuable input on Oklahoma and Native Americans.

To my granddaughters, Mary Caroline Erwin and Amelia Erwin, I express thanks for their wonderful photography. Also, a huge thank you to my daughter-in-law, Lynda Erwin, for serving as a beta reader; my grandson, Trevor Norton, for his graphic art; my grandson, Judson Norton, for his marketing contribution; and my new marketing expert, Katie Crain of Urban Sherpa. Not to be overlooked, a big thank you to my magnificent grand dog, George, for playing the role of Jake's K-9, Kai.

Finally, words cannot express how grateful I am for the support and love of the rest of my family—Bill, Allison, Marshall, Keri, Sarah, John, and Brooks. As I've said before, they give meaning and purpose to my life.

CHAPTER ONE

Jake stood outside the Federal courtroom in a black suit that predated his tenure with the FBI. Lila Stonebridge, VP in charge of fraud investigations for industry giant Washburn and Batson Insurance, flipped through a file from her seat on a nearby bench. A discarded newspaper next to Lila caught Jake's eye as he shifted impatiently from foot to foot.

SENATOR FOUND DEAD!

Jake's cop mentality kicked in. *Foul play?* However, professional responsibility quickly returned his attention to his assignment. Although thoroughly familiar with the halls of justice, he would have preferred to be most anywhere else. But he was on the clock, and thirteen-year-old Sabrina wanted to attend an expensive summer dance program.

Lila made a note before closing and stuffing the file into her Ferragamo briefcase. Rising, she gave him a flick of her head, which he recognized as her intention to take a break. Jake nodded, his eyes following the perfectly tailored Armani suit and Louboutin pumps walk away.

With a smirky smile on his face, he thought, *Great ass for a corporate cougar.*

Lila kept herself in shape. A savvy and somewhat ruthless career woman, she had climbed the corporate ladder at warp speed with a focus on claiming the CEO chair. Her prospects appeared favorable. As usual with their cases, she insisted Jake stay until the jury came in, despite the lack of a valid reason other than liking to have him around. The two were not involved romantically. Lila had no room for the encumbrance of a relationship in her master plan, but it did not prevent her from indulging in carnal pleasures when the desire struck. Likewise, Jake, a divorced father, eschewed the formation of any ties and had no problem accommodating the executive. He believed their first encounter had been his audition for the position of number-one-investigator.

Lila was barely out of sight when Jake's cell vibrated. Glancing down, he read a text from his assistant.

Potential, high-profile case $$$$$. Madison called. Wants you to see client TODAY—on Gray MacGregor's dime.

He was about to respond when a door to the courtroom opened, and an assistant prosecutor came out.

"The jury's ready. Thought you would like to know."

"What about the judge?" Jake asked.

"They have to find him. So, it'll be a few minutes."

Jake hastily typed in:

Almost done here. Set it for—

He turned his wrist over and glanced at his watch.

four.

Following the text to Liz Glover, Jake sent one to Lila, alerting her of the forthcoming event and then waited outside the tall, double doors for Lila to return.

When she arrived, he held the door for her as she asked, "So, what do you think it will be?"

"I've already told you. The guy is as guilty as I'm an Oklahoma cowboy."

"But did the jury get that?"

He gave an affirmative nod.

"Are you ever wrong?"

"No."

"That's what I like about you, Shepherd—your stupendous humility."

Jake smiled.

As the pair slid onto the bench at the rear of the courtroom, the defendant, accompanied by his team of lawyers, entered and proceeded toward the defense table. Not far behind, a man and woman, both wearing black suits, entered. As they passed, Jake tipped his head, and the male gave him a thumbs-up sign.

Lila raised an eyebrow. "Miss the Bureau?"

Jake stifled a snicker. "I'll take the Fifth on that one."

"You could have stayed."

"And lose all the private bounty you guys toss my way? Why would I want to miss that?"

"Because money doesn't mean a damn thing to you, Shepherd, and you know it."

"Yeah. Well it does to my thirteen-year-old daughter. She's a high-maintenance kid."

Before Lila could respond, the gavel sounded, and everyone in the room stood.

After the judge took the bench and instructed the assembly to be seated, he said, "Deputy, would you please invite the jurors into the courtroom?"

While the panel filed into the jury box, Jake studied each face. Lila followed suit. As the men and women took their seats, Lila turned to Jake, seeking his opinion without speaking.

He nodded, maintaining a stoic expression, and raised a thumb out of sight of all others present. He noticed Lila's fingers were crossed. *Since when does a world-class, hard-boiled pragmatist engage in superstition?*

Judge Reicher spoke. "Let the record reflect that all members of the jury and alternates have joined us. Good afternoon, ladies and gentlemen."

After hearing the simultaneous response, he asked for the sealed verdict forms, which the deputy took and passed to the bench. The judge opened the envelopes, reviewed the documents for proper form, and then handed them back to the deputy for delivery to the foreperson.

As the judge recited each count of the indictment, asking for a verdict, the foreperson responded. Jake watched Lila's face, amused that she seemed to be holding her breath as though in doubt about his prediction.

When the final verdict, "Guilty of arson in the first degree," was read, the judge ordered the defendant into custody, thanked and dismissed the jurors, and adjourned the proceedings. Lila turned to Jake, all grins.

"Told you," he said.

"You are so damned pompous, Shepherd."

"Probably, but if I don't know it, I won't say it."

"Whatever. On behalf of Washburn and Batson, I personally thank you for saving us two-mil."

"You mean on behalf of Lila Stonebridge's campaign for top dog, don't you?"

She grinned. "Your blatant honesty will get you in trouble one day."

"Wouldn't be the first time. But I've gotta run. New billable hours calling. Give me a ring whenever you need me"—he hesitated, raising an eyebrow with a twinkle in his seductive hazel eyes—"for a new case."

As he turned his back to leave, she called out, "Consider buying a new suit with the fat check we'll be sending your way."

Jake glanced over his shoulder. "Damn, you're hard to please. I bought a new tie for this gig."

As he exited the courtroom, he rubbed shoulders with Special Agent Deke Weston, a former colleague at the FBI. The Fed grabbed Jake's hand and shook, simultaneously patting his shoulder.

"Good work, Shepherd. How about a drink next week?"

"You're on. Give me a call."

Walking out of the building, Jake pondered the potential case. *What politician has been caught in the wrong bed this time, and what's MacGregor's connection?*

CHAPTER TWO

Scarlett Kavanagh stepped out of the Uber and stood in front of the Arlington, Virginia, office, reeling from the shock of why she was there and trying to understand how she became her twin sister's savior. She paused to read the wooden sign.

SHEPHERD & ASSOCIATES
Investigation and Security

A quick once-over of the facility did not impress Scarlett or heighten her confidence in the investigator's skill. The trim on the one-story, brick building cried out for fresh paint. The landscaping lacked design—in sharp contrast to Scarlett's pristine law office in Atlanta. The only redeeming feature was a potted hydrangea in full bloom by the entrance. *Poor flower. It looks embarrassed by the surroundings. I hope you knew what you were doing sending me here, Gray MacGregor.* Shaking her head, she proceeded up the walkway.

If there had been another option, Scarlett would have tapped the Uber icon and headed back to the hotel where Savannah was cloistered. *Here goes.* Reaching the entry, she rang the bell and then heard the familiar click of an electronically controlled lock.

A rosy-faced, silver-haired woman, sitting behind a cluttered desk, looked up and smiled. "Good afternoon. Welcome to Shepherd and Associates." The nameplate in front of her read "Elizabeth Glover."

"I'm Scarlett Kavanagh. I have a four o'clock appointment with Jake Shepherd." Scarlett glanced around the room. *I'm not impressed.* The sparse furnishings screamed Goodwill store. Plaques and frames with certificates and news clippings hung on two walls, adding little aesthetic relief. The only semblance of decor was a small vase of fresh flowers on Glover's desk and a large oil painting of a dog on the back wall, which held Scarlett's attention for several seconds.

Obviously noticing Scarlett's interest in the art, Elizabeth said, "It was a gift from a client."

"Oh."

"Jake's not back from court, but I expect him any minute. Please have a seat, Ms. Kavanagh." She motioned toward a pair of chairs on the side of the room. "May I offer you something to drink? A soda or a water? You don't want to drink our coffee. Jake likes it strong enough to support a high-rise."

"I'm fine. But do you have any idea how long he will be?"

"I don't, but he always rings in when on the way."

Out of the corner of her eye, Scarlett detected motion in the hallway to her left. "Can I speak to his associate? I really don't have much—" The subject of her distraction strolled into the reception area.

"Only if you're a dog whisperer." Elizabeth pointed to the one-hundred-pound German shepherd staring at Scarlett.

Scarlett glanced at the dog, up at the painting, and then back toward the woman. "You're not saying—"

"Meet Jake's partner, Kai. K-9 Certified."

Scarlett's eyebrows scrunched together. "Certified?"

"A certified arms sniffer and security K-9—with a few bonus skills."

"I hope people-friendly is in his catalog of tricks?" Scarlett eyed the animal with apprehension. "Or should I be nervous?"

"You're fine unless you're armed—" Her cell phone pinged, signaling receipt of a text. "Excuse me."

As Elizabeth read and responded to the message, Kai sauntered past Scarlett and lay down beside the desk as if to say, "Here's the line. Don't cross."

"Jake's five minutes away. He said to have you wait in his office. It's the door at the end of the hall." She pointed in the direction the dog had come from.

Relieved to get away from the intimidating animal, Scarlett walked briskly, looking over her shoulder to see if Kai followed. When she reached a closed door with a brass plate, bearing the PI's name, she entered, leaving it open. Finding the one chair, out of three, free of boxes, notebooks, and manila folders, she sat, took a deep breath, and gazed around the messy office. A guitar stood in one corner; a narrow bookcase held a number of trophies, validating unknown skills, plus several photographs of a young female. Nearly obscured on the desk, Scarlett could see a portrait of a stately man, dressed in a navy-blue suit, with a small pin in the shape of a star on his lapel. He wore a ten-gallon hat and stood beside an American flag. *Is that Shepherd? No, he wouldn't have his own photo on his desk.* As she contemplated what the investigator would look like, she noticed one photo of the girl included a man. *Shepherd? His daughter?*

Before Scarlett had time to take in more, she heard Kai give off a subtle bark as the front door opened. *That must be him.*

"How'd it go?" Scarlett heard Elizabeth Glover ask.

"Signed and sealed. Guilty as charged." A trace of a Southern accent mellowed the husky baritone of the private investigator, producing a cross between Matthew McConaughey's sexy drawl and Blake Shelton's.

"Lila must be happy. That's … what? Two million you saved the company?"

"Less my fee, but yeah. I think she was pleased."

"Your four o'clock is waiting."

Scarlett strained to hear the rest of the conversation, but the woman had lowered her voice.

Within seconds, Jake took over the office, pulling off his coat as he entered. "Sorry. Had to wait for the jury verdict in one of my cases." He hung the jacket on a hall tree and then yanked off his tie. After tossing it on his desk, he proceeded to unbutton his shirt as the dog settled in front of the bookcase.

Scarlett watched, a perplexed expression on her face. "No problem, but I hope you don't plan to remove your trousers."

Jake laughed, stopping halfway down the line of buttons. "Not today. At least not until we exchange names—mine's on the door. You're Ms. Kavanagh, right?"

"Right." She watched as he rolled up his sleeves, reached across the desk for a manila folder, and took a seat on the edge of the ancient but sturdy piece of furniture. Kai stationed himself at his master's heel.

Jake opened the file and quickly perused the contents. "So, you're the late Senator Kingsley's sister-in-law. Saw the headline. I'm sorry for your loss."

"Thank you." Scarlett stared at the weapon at Jake's waist.

Her gaze caught his eye, and he patted the Glock. "Don't let it freak you. Old habits die hard. So, what can I do for you, Ms. Kavanagh?"

"I'm here on behalf of my sister. Although it's not official, Savannah believes Scott was murdered, and she is afraid the FBI is looking at her as the prime suspect."

"In a homicide investigation, it is pretty standard to look at the spouse. Rule her out first. Cause of death hasn't been announced?"

"It hasn't. But apparently Savannah was interrogated by a team of agents."

"If she's innocent, shouldn't be too much to worry about. Is she?"

"You don't bother with being subtle, do you?"

"That's not an answer to my question."

"I don't have an answer other than she's innocent until proven guilty."

He closed the folder and laid it on the desk. "You need to know before we proceed, I'll go the limit to prove a client is innocent, and I'll succeed. But if I find they're not, I'm out."

"Isn't it true that one can have committed the crime but not be legally guilty?"

He studied her face for a second. "Let me be clear. I'm expensive but not for sale. Even Gray MacGregor's bottomless bank account isn't enough to tempt me to work for a guilty party. I understand his money is backing you. What's your connection to MacGregor?"

"Friends. And for the record, my family will pay him back every penny."

"Not my business. Friends? Or friends with benefits?"

Scarlett winced. "I beg your pardon! If you're inferring I'm sleeping with Gray, back off. His wife, Fury, is one of my best friends."

"Don't get your feathers caught in a fan. I'm just trying to see how deep the quicksand I'm stepping into might be. Glad to hear Gray isn't fooling around. But back to my question. Do *you* believe your sister had anything to do with the death of her husband?"

"She says she didn't. What you won't find in that file you're holding is I hardly know my twin. We haven't spoken in something like twelve years. If I had to answer your question, the best I could say is she's a narcissistic sociopath but not smart enough, or evil enough, to commit murder."

"Looks like I'm not the only one who dispenses with subtleties. What did she do, steal your favorite doll when you were kids?"

Scarlett cocked an eyebrow. "More like favorite fiancé."

"Uuuuh, oh." He frowned, giving a thumbs down sign. "Not the late senator?"

She pointed at him with a tight-lipped smile and a wink. "Nailed it."

"That must make Thanksgiving dinner fun."

"We don't attend the same ones."

"Touché. But you're here, and she's not."

"Believe me, that question is on my mind as well. But as for Savannah, let's just say between the fact she's an emotional disaster and my legal opinion that she stay on the down-low until we can sort things out, she's on a leave of absence." One of the certificates on the wall caught Scarlett's eye as she spoke. "Is that a law degree?" She pointed to the diploma.

"That's what it says."

Scarlett stood and walked closer to the wall. "Yale law degree? Why aren't you practicing? Failed the bar or disbarred for rudeness?"

Jake burst out laughing. Catching his breath, he said, "And you think I'm sharp-tongued? I think you're a match for me any day."

"I'm sure of it. For the record. I'm Harvard Law."

"No wonder I can't get a straight answer out of you. So, will you represent her in the event of a problem?"

"Absolutely not me. And don't give me that look. It has nothing to do with past issues. I'm a family law attorney, licensed to practice in Georgia, plus my knowledge of criminal court is limited to domestic violence."

"Family law, huh. How's that working for you?"

She stared at him for nearly a minute. "Fine. If you like seeing the best people at their worst."

"Why am I detecting a little note of cynicism?"

"I'm sure I don't know." *Not quite true.* "But I do not see the relevance of my career to my sister's case, Mr. Shepherd. Getting back to Savannah. Gray arranged for Phillip Madison to represent her."

"Right. Slipped my mind. It'll take Gray's money to keep Phil on the case, but he is as good as it gets."

"So, you know Madison?"

"I'm his investigator, which puts this meeting protected under the work-product umbrella. They probably taught you that at Harvard."

"Cute."

"Sorry. Cheap shot."

She nodded, giving him a dirty look.

"Phil's office is where MacGregor and I met. We both clerked for Phil back in the day. Guess you two have Harvard in common. Does he think your sister's innocent of any foul play?"

"Gray doesn't know Savannah. I called him for help because Savannah doesn't trust anyone in DC, and I knew he had connections everywhere."

"Savannah. A Southern belle no doubt."

"She plays the part, like our mother. They can pour a proper cup of tea, make a mean mint julep, and whip out a credit card at the mall with the speed of a gunslinger. But neither can balance a checkbook, kill a spider, or boot up a computer."

"And you're the polar opposite"—he gave her a once over—"I can see."

"God, I hope so."

He glanced up at the ceiling and then back to Scarlett. "Okay, Ms. Kavanagh, or may I call you Scarlett?"

She nodded.

"Scarlett, how about I meet your sister? That is if I haven't totally offended you."

"If you have, it wouldn't matter. I trust Gray. He says you're the best, and you seem to agree. Besides, you're my only option at the moment."

"Understood." He grinned and stood, extending his hand to assist Scarlett. "I have a few questions for her, and we'll see where it goes from there."

CHAPTER THREE

Scarlett stood, watching Kai while Jake tucked Savannah's skinny folder into a leather portfolio and gathered his discarded clothing. Questions churned in her head. Should she trust the investigator or kick him to the curb? With the stakes high, there was no margin for error. While ill feelings toward her twin lingered, they were blood—plus, there were two fatherless children to consider.

"Mark me off as with Ms. Kavanagh the rest of the day," Jake said, as they passed Elizabeth Glover's desk on the way out. "If you don't mind, give Kai a ride home, and I'll see you in the morning."

He talks like the freakin' animal is human. Scarlett wanted to ask if the canine had a key but decided to dial back on the barbs. However, as Jake held the door for her to exit, she imagined the dog bounding from the car and trotting to the door like a latchkey kid. Her willpower failed. "Does she just let him out at the door?"

The remark drew a belly laugh from Jake. "He's not quite that smart. Liz has a key and knows his routine. In my line of work, regular hours do not exist."

"So, she's your office wife?"

"Could say."

"Is there one at home?"

"Nope. Not anymore. Got the pink slip several years ago."

No mystery why, Scarlett thought as he led her to a recent model, black Lexus SUV. To her surprise, the vehicle was immaculate inside and out.

"Nice wheels." Scarlett had expected a cheap, beat-up car with empty drink containers in the cup holders, debris on the floorboards, and worn upholstery matching his office décor.

"It's reliable—serves the purpose."

"But pricey."

"No comment." As he slid behind the wheel, he asked for their destination, plugged it into the GPS, and turned on a pocket recorder. "Tell me everything you can about your sister and the senator."

Scarlett glanced down at the device and back at him. "Since I'm being recorded, I'll be careful what I say."

"Relax. No intent to trap you. I just want the facts. No editorials."

"Where do you want me to start? The playpen?"

"If you think it's important. I need a feel for who she is and who he was."

"Like I told you in the office, Savannah is my opposite. In school, she was a prom queen; I was on the debate team."

"Not surprised. Bet you annihilated the competition."

Scarlett cut her eyes around at him and grinned. "So, you keep a charming mode as well as an offensive one in your arsenal."

"I try to keep it under the radar. Tell me more. Is she docile, short-tempered, vindictive, mean-spirited? You called her a narcissistic sociopath. Describe that for me."

"She's all about Savannah. No—she's not vindictive, probably not mean-spirited. Just me-spirited. Believes she's entitled to take whatever. Growing up, if she wanted to wear something of mine, she helped herself."

"Kind of like she took your fiancé?"

"Exactly. Our mother treats it like she got makeup on my favorite blouse. With her helpless-little-me attitude, Savannah could convince a homeless man to contribute to a GoFundMe campaign for Jeff Bezos. In high school, I even did her homework when she had a hot date." Scarlett took a deep breath and focused on the passing scenery for a minute. "Mom made excuses for her and told me I had to protect her because I was stronger. Here I am—back in the role."

"How did Scott Kingsley come into the picture? I assume you met him first."

"Sophomore year at Agnes Scott. He was a junior at Georgia Tech. We met at a fraternity dance and started dating. I pushed through and graduated the year he did. He proposed the night of my graduation."

"Where was Savannah?"

"University of Georgia. God only knows how she got in."

"When did the wheels fall off the wagon?"

Scarlett took a deep breath. "From the beginning, Scott aimed for a career in politics with a plan to attend Harvard Law. He liked my ambition. We both applied. The agenda included mutual degrees, marriage, a joint law practice, and the rise to POTUS and FLOTUS—Bill and Hillary style."

"I see a picture developing. You made it to Cambridge—he didn't."

"Bingo. He ended up at Georgia. Savannah was still in Athens, finishing her degree in society wife with a minor in table setting. The rest is history. The week of one-L finals, I got a call. Offering a feeble apology, he informs me they are married. Seems like she's pregnant. He actually said it was my fault. I chose Harvard over him."

"Paints a clear picture for me of Senator Scott Kingsley. No less than the week of your first law school exams? Wonder if he planned it." He tipped his chin, frowning. "The guy's a class act. Must have been brutal for you."

"I don't remember taking the Civ Pro exam. Don't know how I passed. So, anything from then on about the two of them is strictly hearsay. I've managed to keep my distance."

"I'll bet the upside is the betrayal fueled your fire to succeed."

She looked at him for a second. "I'm impressed. You are perceptive."

Ignoring her comment, he said, "Tell me about the hearsay. Any talk of trouble in paradise?"

"No. I don't think so. Sounded like a family designed by Walt Disney and Martha Stewart, according to Mom. Dad respected my feelings and didn't talk about them, nor did our younger sister."

As he made a right turn, his tone changed. "Scarlett, I don't need to tell you murder is the top of the chart. Granted, some of the most unlikely people kill, but more often there are signs ahead of time." With one hand on the wheel, he reached down to the recorder. "I'm turning this off. Do you believe your sister has the mettle to take a person's life?"

After thinking for a minute, she took a deep breath and said, "This whole thing is surreal. I've had so many thoughts and feelings since it happened—disbelief, nausea, you name it. My intellect says—no. Savannah is a shallow person but not a vicious one. I was sarcastic when I said she doesn't have the intelligence to concoct a murder plan and carry it out. But there's a shred of truth in the statement. She lives life in a clueless vacuum. Or at least she always did. But I wouldn't be honest if I didn't admit tiny little seeds of doubt creep in, making me ask—could she?" Scarlett caught herself. "I shouldn't have said that. You'll probably bail."

He smiled. "No. I would be more likely to bail if you lied. It's only human to have doubts. Your doubts don't make her guilty."

He pulled the vehicle into the entrance of a hotel, located about six miles from the Ronald Reagan Airport. "How have you avoided the media? I assume the two of you look alike. I have to admit, I don't have a mental image of her."

"Kinda but we're not identical. Savannah's a blonde. Doesn't it fit? We're the same height and general body type, but I got dark hair from Dad. Savannah's a carbon copy of Mom."

"That helps. How is the room registered?"

"In my name, using an old ID with her maiden name. Apparently, they didn't look closely. She wore a scarf and dark glasses when she checked in."

"Her car?"

"Parked at another hotel. She took a cab with cash, following my instructions."

"Clever thinking. You're pretty good for a divorce lawyer. Done this before?"

"Actually, I have. Volunteered at a battered women's shelter where evasive measures were required to protect the victims from the abusers."

"Makes sense. And how are the two of you communicating?"

"Since I arrived, with TracFones I bought with cash in Atlanta."

"Impressive. See why you got into Harvard."

She smiled. "Did you apply?"

"You don't want to know."

"*Au Contraire*. Give, Shepherd. Did you apply?"

"I'll tell you when I know you better."

"I hope that doesn't mean I have to sleep with you to find out."

He laughed. "There's an idea."

When they reached the room, Scarlett knocked once, paused, and knocked twice.

"Don't you have a key card?"

"Yeah. But even though I texted her from the car, she might be indisposed. I'll wait for her to let us in."

A woman in disheveled clothing, with the desperate expression of a trapped bird, opened the door. "Thank God, you're back," Savannah said as she threw her arms around her sister. "I've been going crazy. What took you so long? I'm starved." She glanced at Jake with a puzzled look.

Careful to avoid calling Savannah by name in the hall, Scarlett said, "This is Jake Shepherd. Gray and your attorney think he can help." Glancing back to the investigator, she said, "Jake—my sister."

Jake wore his jacket, concealing his weapon, but his shirt remained half-open. Savannah took a few seconds to assess him before responding. "Pleased to meet you, Mr. Shepherd." She offered her hand for a powder-puff handshake and then turned to Scarlett. In a stage whisper, she said, "He's very attractive."

"He can hear you, Goldilocks." Scarlett looked at Jake and gave a weak shrug. "Excuse her. She's distraught."

Jake restrained the grin battling to escape. "Understandable."

"I know I must appear a mess. I've been crying for hours." She reached up to smooth her hair back. "I'm sure you know—"

Scarlett frowned and put her finger to her lips in an effort to shush Savannah. *Same old Savannah.* "You want to let us in, or would you rather go public?"

Savannah stepped aside. "Maybe I should freshen—"

"Oh, please. Don't go there. We don't give a fig whether your makeup is perfect," Scarlett said.

Savannah's appearance suggested she had been through a rough time. With no makeup, her pale features were next to invisible. Eyeliner conceded to red-rimmed orbs, and her hair fell flat and limp in contrast to its usual coifed perfection.

As the door closed, Scarlett continued, "Jake is a private investigator. He needs to ask you questions, and I'm sure he doesn't have all night."

"Oh."

Scarlett took a deep breath, walked over to one of a pair of upholstered chairs in the far corner of the room, and gave a wave of presentation. "She's all yours. Good luck."

Jake directed Savannah to the matching seat and then pulled the desk chair out to sit in front of her.

"First, I'm very sorry for your loss, Mrs. Kingsley. I know this is a bad time, but I need some information from you before I agree to take on your matter."

Savannah turned to Scarlett, a frown on her face.

"Just answer his questions. You need this man's help."

"You told me not to talk to anyone without the lawyer present."

Emitting a patronizing sigh, Scarlett said, "Well, there are two lawyers present, so I think you can talk. You are a lawyer, aren't you, Mr. Shepherd?"

"New York, DC, and Virginia—last time I checked." Jake smiled again. "And both of you"—he glanced from Scarlett to Savannah—"I answer to Jake."

Scarlett threw her hands up. "See? Talk."

"You don't have to be so hateful, Scarlett." A tear ran down Savannah's pale face.

Spare me, Savannah. You're probably grieving because your dream of being the first lady vaporized.

"She hates me, Mr. Shepherd."

"Jake."

"Right. Jake. She thinks I ruined her life, but I didn't."

"Savannah. Jake doesn't need to hear about our family skeletons. He needs to know about Scott."

"Actually, I would like to know why she believes she didn't ruin your life. Is there a specific reason, Savannah? You don't mind me calling you Savannah, do you?"

"No, Savannah's fine." She looked back toward Scarlett while speaking to Jake. "Just ask your questions."

"Is there a reason you don't believe you ruined—"

"No. I shouldn't have said that." She turned attention toward her hands.

Jake studied her for a second. After making a note on his legal pad, he resumed his focus on Savannah. "How long were you and the senator married?"

"We celebrated our twelfth anniversary in April." Savannah raised her head, the tension in her body appearing to relax as she took a breath and re-crossed her legs.

"How did you celebrate?"

Her face softened. "Scott arranged a fabulous dinner party at the Hay-Adams. So many important people came." Her eyes projected a dreamy state. "I thought we were just going to dinner and spending a night in the Luxury Suite."

Jake leaned slightly forward as if intent on hearing her every word.

"But he invited ninety guests and even had a string quartet play."

"Sounds like an exciting evening." He tipped his head, maintaining a steady gaze on her face. "What did you wear?"

What the? Scarlett's brow furrowed. *Why is he wasting time asking such irrelevant questions?*

An elated grin broke out on Savannah's face. "A fabulous Zac Posen. You're a man and probably don't know designers. I found it at Neiman's. Surely you've heard of Neiman's."

"I have, but I couldn't afford a walk-through. Your dress must have been expensive."

Savannah covered a smug smile with her hand, shrugging her shoulders. "Outrageous, but I looked fantastic. It accentuated my best features. Wish I could show you the pictures."

Good gosh, Savannah. How shallow can you be? Scarlett rolled her eyes.

"I'd like that, but let's move on to what you know about your husband's death. I'm sorry if it's painful, but it is necessary, as I said earlier."

Savannah nodded, dropping a veil of gloom over her face but dodging eye contact. She lowered her voice to barely more than a whisper. "I don't know much. They found him in his office. They said there were signs of a struggle."

"Hold it. I need you to stop with the pronouns. Who are they? Who found him, and who informed you?"

Savannah shifted her gaze toward Jake. "One of his assistants found him when he came into work. I think his name is Jack or Joe, maybe it was Clyde Yes, it was Clyde Register, Scott's Chief of Staff. Two FBI agents came to the house and told me. I don't remember their names. They weren't very nice. One was a woman. They said the medical examiner would have to determine the cause of death."

"The agents gave you notification, but did they ask you questions?"

She nodded. "They asked when I last saw Scott."

"And you said?"

"Sunday night."

"Sunday? He wasn't found until Wednesday. How is it you didn't see him for, what, two—two and a half—days before he was found?"

"Because I didn't." She broke eye contact, squirming on her chair. "Because I just didn't." Her volume increased with each word, and she continued to fidget. "What do you want me to say?"

"Let me simplify it. Where were you during the two and a half days before Senator Kingsley was found?"

"They asked me that."

"I'm sure the Feds did. What did you tell them?"

Scarlett watched Jake intently. *Savannah is taxing his patience.*

"Home. I was home with Colin and Victoria."

"Colin and Victoria? Your children?"

She nodded.

"Did you leave at any time during that period?"

She shook her head. "I had a migraine."

"Was anyone there with you besides your children?"

She stared at him for several seconds as though searching for her words. "Most of the time. We have a live-in nanny, well semi-live-in. She's taking care of Colin and Victoria now."

"What are their ages?"

Savannah appeared to relax. "Victoria's eleven, almost twelve; Colin is seven."

"And what is the nanny's name?"

"Manuela. Manuela Garcia."

"How long has she worked for you?"

"Since a month after we came to Washington—almost two years. What's she got to do with this?"

"I'll need her address and phone number. Is she married? Have a boyfriend?"

"I don't think so. I don't know. She stays with her sister when she's not with us."

With a no-nonsense tone, Jake asserted control of the exchange by locking her in direct eye contact. "Savannah, why didn't you see your husband on Monday morning?"

Disconcerted, she turned her focus to the floor before answering. "He always left before I woke up. He liked to get to his office before the phone began ringing and people came for meetings."

"Where was he Monday and Tuesday nights?"

She stared toward the window, taking time to answer. "I don't know. He didn't come home, but it wasn't unusual. Whenever he was working on a project, he would stay at the office. He kept clothes there and could sleep on his couch. At least, that's what he told me."

"Did he call or touch base in any way?"

"No."

"You didn't call him?"

"No." She stared at the wall to Jake's left.

"If you don't mind, please look toward me while we're talking."

Savannah snapped her face in his direction.

"You're sure you were home alone with your children?"

"I was. I told you."

"Did anyone call you or drop by? Any service people, deliveries—pizza?"

She shook her head.

Jake paused to make several notes on his pad.

"Did your husband have any health problems? High blood pressure? Heart issues? Diabetes?"

She shook her head.

"What about his state of mind? Was he depressed? Suffer from anxiety?"

"They asked me all that."

"The FBI?"

"Yeah." She gave him a hard look.

"Again, what did you tell them?"

"No. I said none that I know. I don't know. He never threatened suicide or anything. He was stressed a lot of times, but isn't everyone? I take Prozac."

Scarlett perked up at Savannah's last answer. *She's on Prozac? So, it wasn't Disneyland in the Kingsley household.*

"Did the senator use any mind-altering substances?"

Savannah stared at him, a puzzled expression on her face.

"Alcohol, drugs—prescription or recreational?"

Again, Savannah focused on the window. "Everyone has a glass of wine or a cocktail, especially here. But he didn't use any drugs that I know."

As Jake covered his mouth with a hand, observing Savannah, he appeared to penetrate her façade. Breaking the momentary silence, he asked, "Did your husband have any enemies you are aware of?"

"I guess. He was a politician. No one likes politicians."

The corner of Jake's mouth strained to break into a smile. "Anyone specific?"

She briefly glanced in his direction, settling her focus on his pad. "I don't know any names. Scott sometimes got ugly letters. He didn't pay much attention to them. He said all the legislators got them. 'You can't please them all,' he always said. 'You have to step on a few toes to get ahead.'"

"And the young, charismatic Senator Kingsley moved ahead quite fast, didn't he?"

"I suppose," she said, lifting her chin.

"Let's move on to the delicate questions. How was your marriage, Savannah?"

Savannah peered at him, her eyes going vacant as if she didn't understand—or she feigned a lack of comprehension to avoid answering.

Jake tossed a hand up in a gesture suggesting it was a simple question. "How was your marriage?"

"That's personal."

"There are going to be a lot of personal questions—from me, from the press, from the authorities. You'd better get used to it."

"My marriage was fine. It was great." She stared at the ceiling.

"Was your husband cheating?"

She popped her head back in his direction, frowning. "I just told you the marriage was perfect. We were planning a trip to Paris."

Ignoring her response, he pushed harder. "Were you playing around?"

Savannah turned to her sister. "Scarlett, this man is rude."

"If you think I'm rude, wait until the FBI comes back. Worse yet, wait until you're in front of a grand jury, being grilled by a seasoned U.S. attorney. I repeat, do you have a lover?"

"No, I—"

"Stop. Let's start over." He dropped his pen in the fold of his portfolio. "I'd prefer you not lie to me. You're not good at it."

Scarlett's eyes grew large. *Wow, Shepherd. You don't pussyfoot around.*

"You have a lot of nerve saying that." Savannah again turned to her sister. "Scarlett?"

Scarlett shrugged. "Don't look at me. He's here to help you."

"He's rude."

"Yeah. But do you have anyone else? You're in the crosshairs of a nasty gun, Savannah, and important people say this is the go-to guy."

"Tell you what, ladies. I'm going to take a break, get a drink, and we'll start over. However, when I come back, I'm going to ask the same questions and expect to hear the truth. Otherwise"—Jake glared at Savannah—"I'll let Scarlett explain the otherwise to you." He stood. "Either of you want anything from vending?"

Both shook their heads.

CHAPTER FOUR

When the door closed, Savannah turned to Scarlett. "He's rude. Mean and rude. I don't like him. How could he treat me like that? I just lost my husband."

"I didn't like him either; however, I'm changing my mind."

"How could you? Why didn't you say something? Speak up for me?"

"Savannah, if you want someone to pamper you, protect you, and tell you everything is okay, you've got the wrong Kavanagh. You need Mom. Listen to me. This is damned scary. You've always talked your way out of everything. But, if this one goes sideways, your Prada purses vanish. And orange is not your color. Shepherd comes with credentials you've only read about. He's abrasive, arrogant, and ir-reverent. But he knows what he's doing. You'd better suck it up and cooperate."

Savannah leered at her sister, speechless.

Jake was gone less than three minutes. When he returned, Scarlett let him in and sat back in her chair.

"Okay. Here's the deal. I fold up my notebook, wish you good luck, and leave. Or, we start over with the truth. Your choice." He set his can of soda on the desk.

The room echoed silence as Savannah peered around toward Scarlett, took a deep breath, and said, "Stay."

"I'm not sure I heard you."

Savannah snapped her head around with sparks shooting from her eyes. "Now who's lying?"

Jake burst out laughing. "Good response." He sat down, opened his portfolio, and clicked his roller ball into action.

"How was your marriage?"

Silence.

"How was it?"

Savannah heaved a sigh. "It was good—"

Jake glanced up with a cautionary squint in one eye.

"And not so good."

He nodded. "That's better."

"We had ups and downs. All couples do."

"He was a rotten husband, wasn't he?"

Scarlett gasped. Shock covered her countenance.

"He cheated on you, neglected you, treated you like chattel, abused you mentally—maybe physically—and he ran the show. Right?"

Savannah nodded. "But he loved me." Her lips quivered.

"You didn't ruin Scarlett's life. You inadvertently saved her misery. Right?"

"Right."

"Who is your lover?"

"I don't have a lover."

"Are we going to start this again? Who is he?"

"Scarlett?" Savannah's eyes bore panic as she reached for support.

Jake's fierce expression relayed his disgust. "Don't look at Scarlett. Talk to me. Who is he?"

"My security guy." Panic changed to hostility. From the sparks flying from her eyes and the tightening of her hands into fists, she appeared on the edge of attacking him.

Her outrage had no visible effect on Jake. "Now, we're getting somewhere. His name?"

"Darren. Darren Warner."

Oh, my, Scarlett thought.

"Did you stand to benefit financially from your husband's death?"

Savannah gave him a dumbfounded look.

"Don't go back there. It's a simple question. Are there assets? Is there insurance? What will you inherit from your husband?"

"You're suggesting I killed him."

"Don't try to dodge or play games with me. I'm not suggesting you killed him. I'm asking if you had a reason to kill him."

"That's the same thing."

With a look of disgust, he started to close his portfolio. "I don't engage in arguments with clients. Either you answer my questions, or I walk."

"No. Wait. I'll tell you. I don't know how much for sure, but Scott had money and he had life insurance. But I didn't kill him."

Jake paused, stared at her for several seconds, and then nodded. "Okay. Did you have any other reason to want your husband dead?"

Her color paled as she looked away for a second before snapping her head back and looking Jake in the eye. In a defeated tone, she said, "You're cruel. Yes. He was a forking *jackass*."

Savannah's choice of words gave her twin a jolt. *Goldilocks using unladylike language?* Scarlett blinked and pinched her eyebrows together, not believing her ears. *God, he is good. How does he do it?*

"Did you kill him?"

Scarlett held her breath. For several seconds, the only sound she heard came from the street below.

Without warning, Savannah collapsed into hysterical sobs. "I told you. No. I didn't. I didn't do anything to Scott. He was a horrible *ass,* but I didn't do anything. I needed him."

"Don't oversell it. I believe you." Approval replaced his fierce expression.

Scarlett sat back in her chair, processing the previous nineteen minutes. *He believes her? Is he kidding? Hell, no. The guy's cunning as a fox.*

While he appeared to join Savannah's team, Jake offered no tea and sympathy. "If you can pull yourself together, Savannah, I have just one more question for now."

She sniffled, grabbed a tissue from the table next to her, and blew her nose. "What?"

"How much of what you just told me did you tell my former colleagues?"

She shrugged as if she didn't understand.

"The agents—FBI."

Scarlett flinched. *No wonder he's so good. He's former FBI.*

Savannah tightened her lips, took a deep breath in through her nose, and said, "I don't remember. Most of it, but I didn't tell the stuff about Darren and how Scott really was. I told them we were happy, and *they* believed me."

With a tight smile, he said, "So they let you think." He made several check marks on his notes and then said to Savannah, "Are you a barbeque fan?"

The tension in Savannah subsided as she said, "Why do you ask?"

Where is he going with that? Scarlett twisted her mouth to the side and furrowed her brow.

"I heard you mention being starved earlier. I happen to know a small place not far from here, owned by a Texan. He serves the real deal. What say Scarlett and I make a run for food? What's your preference? Beef? Pork?"

"That sounds scrumptious. I can freshen up and go with you."

He raised a palm. "Not so fast. You need to stay put."

"But—"

"Not up for debate. One person recognizes you, and the onslaught of paparazzi will look like a swarm of vultures on roadkill. The last thing we need is you in a CNN soundbite."

Scarlett perked up. "What about her children, Jake? They've been with the nanny since Wednesday."

"I recommend we get them out of the District."

Savannah looked at Scarlett. "Should I call Mama and ask her to come for them?"

Scarlett shook her head. "Have you forgotten? The folks don't know. They're on one of those Viking cruises in Europe and won't be back until the middle of next week. Plus, I don't think you want to get them involved any sooner than necessary. You know Mom will go apoplectic."

Savannah's face fell. "I forgot about their trip. I wondered why she hadn't called my cell."

"You don't have it."

"Yeah, I do. It's right here." She reached in the pocket of her slacks and pulled out a leather phone pouch on a gold chain.

"Savannah!" Scarlett rolled her eyes. "You've got to be kidding. It isn't on, is it?"

"Yes, but I haven't made a call."

"I told you to turn it off and get rid of it. That's why I bought you the prepaid phone."

"I couldn't. I needed to know what was going on at home."

"Savannah. If the damn thing is on, it can be tracked." Scarlett sighed and shook her head. "See what you're dealing with, Jake?"

"Give me the phone, Savannah." He extended his open palm. "I'll take care of it."

She leaned forward to hand him the phone and then pulled it back. "You don't need my case." Her hand shook as she pulled the device from its container. "I'll put the other one in it."

When she handed it over, the case slid to the floor.

Scarlett scooped it up, reading the gold designer inscription before passing it to Savannah. "I'll bet that's the first prepaid ever carried in Givenchy," Scarlett said. "What did that little luxury cost?"

Savannah gave her a dirty look.

"You two can debate fashion statements another time." Jake took a set of papers out of his portfolio. "For now, Savannah, while Scarlett and I go for the food, read over my engagement contract and releases, and then pack up the room. You can sign them, and Scarlett can witness, when we come back. I'll relocate you to a safe location after dinner. If we're not back when you finish, begin a list of where all electronics, including computers, tablets, cell phones, cameras are stored—yours and Senator Kingsley's. I want you to include those in active use and those abandoned. Also, provide the location of any paper records, including credit card statements, old phone bills, bank records, and the location of any safe deposit boxes, storage units, or other off-site storage. Finally, list your passwords for all devices, computers, social media, financial accounts, and website subscriptions, plus any you have access to for your late husband."

Savannah took in what Jake was saying until his final instruction at which time her interest turned to indignation. "No. I certainly will not give you my passwords. That's personal information. Don't you know about privacy laws?"

"Whoops! I guess I missed that class in law school." He shook his head, his gaze sharp enough to pierce steel. "Didn't we cover this before? In the legal system, privacy stops at the courthouse door. If you're extremely lucky, you might be able to keep out what you told your psychiatrist, your spouse, me, and your lawyers—nothing else."

Savannah sat back as though dodging his words.

Jake continued, "Having your passwords is non-negotiable. I won't run an investigation in the dark. Further, I need to see what the Feds will find when they take over. They won't need your passwords. They have tech people who can break into any file. *Capiche?*"

She took a second, staring at him, her blue eyes seething with resentment. "You sure are bossy."

Jake broke out in a belly laugh. "I'm just starting. Get used to it." Taking the legal pad out of his portfolio, he tore off the notes made earlier and stuck them inside a folder. Handing the blank pad to Savannah, he said, "In addition, make lists of all your family members, friends, lovers, employees, service providers, accountants, lawyers, financial planners, insurance agents—even your dry cleaner. In short, everyone you know. I want full names, phone numbers, addresses, relationship, and a brief summary of what they know about your personal life. I'll also need a list of your memberships to country clubs, civic and charitable organizations, religious institutions, schools, gym, resorts, etc."

Savannah's eyes looked as though they might pop out of their sockets. "I can't possibly do all that."

She is lost, Scarlett thought. *I'm lost. My client questionnaire and document request is paltry compared to his.*

"I don't expect you to do it all tonight, but it is essential I have a complete picture. Don't leave anyone off. If the ME declares a homicide, which is likely, the Feds will converge on you like Crazy Horse and company on Custer. Don't think you can hide anything. They'll know whether you install your toilet paper rolls over or under and the brand of food your cat prefers."

"We don't have a cat."

With a roll of her eyes and a sigh of impatience, Scarlett said, "He's trying to impress on you how invasive the investigation will be, Savannah."

Jake gave Scarlett a nod of affirmation. "I have a narrow window of opportunity to get ahead of the authorities and the potential of their locking me out on some fronts. We're already down approximately thirty-six hours. As for your children,"—he turned toward Scarlett—"didn't I hear you mention another sister?"

"Grace."

"Could she help? Where does she live?"

"Why can't Colin and Victoria stay with me? I couldn't ask Grace—"

"I could," Scarlett said. "She and her husband live a little south of Atlanta."

"At this point, you don't need the burden of trying to shield your children from the press. If the worst happens, the Feds will want to talk to them. I assume you'll have the funeral in Georgia," Jake said.

Savannah's expression took on a look of confusion. "I haven't thought about it. I don't know how to do a funeral."

Annoyed with Savannah for what Scarlett considered another helpless-me ploy, she wanted to say, "It's like a wedding, only you wear black," but stifled the impulse.

"If I'm not mistaken, Savannah, the senate has a protocol for the service of members passing away while in office," Jake said. "As his widow, you'll have the right of choice as to the location. Scarlett, check with your other sister about the children. I'll start arrangements for getting them out of DC."

"Couldn't we have Grace come up here?" Scarlett asked.

"No time for that. I need access to the house without them present. Having both the children and the nanny out of easy reach of the media is vital. I'll send a car to pick up the three of them. Savannah, you'll need to use the disposable phone to call Manuela and explain the plan. Make up a code word for my guy to give her when he gets there so she'll know she can trust him. No packing—no leaving the house with luggage."

Savannah looked befuddled.

Jake noticed her confusion. "If the house is being watched, I want it to appear they are just going out—not traveling. I'll interview Manuela in Atlanta. I hope she's legal and has a valid ID."

"She's legal," Savannah said. "Scott made sure. He didn't want his political enemies to have ammunition to use against him. Can Scarlett stay here with me while you go? I can't remember all that stuff you want."

"No. You'll just have to do your best. Start with where the electronics and records are in your home. I'll go over the lists again when I come back. As for Scarlett, I need to talk to her."

Scarlett stood. "Savannah, write down on separate sheets of paper a heading for each category you remember. I'll help you later."

CHAPTER FIVE

Once Jake and Scarlett were in his vehicle, he said, "You are right. The two of you couldn't be more different. However, I differ with you on her IQ. She's smarter than you think but working with her will be a challenge."

"You saw how dumb she was in keeping the cell." Scarlett buckled her seatbelt.

"I see she's not good at following directions, but keeping the cell wasn't entirely a mistake. I need to review her texts."

Scarlett raised her eyebrows. "You're right. Where is my head?"

"Not as engaged as it would be with an arm's-length client. Don't beat yourself up. Here." He handed her his phone. "Call your other sister. Tell her we're sending the children down on the first flight and will forward details. If she can't accommodate them, ask for hotel references close to her home."

Scarlett was still talking to Grace when Jake pulled into the entrance of the Holiday Inn National, only three miles from where they left Savannah. She looked at him, her eyebrows pinched in a frown. "I'll let you know details as soon as plans are confirmed," she said into the phone and then turned it off. "Why are you stopping here? This isn't the restaurant; is it?"

"First priority is to secure Savannah for the night. We'll register, obtain keys, and bring her back after dinner. That way she can enter through a side door and not risk recognition. Tomorrow, we'll drive her to Richmond for a flight south."

"My knowledge of criminal law is sketchy. Is it legal for her to leave the jurisdiction?" She handed him his phone.

"Although investigators like to bluff suspects by saying 'don't leave town,' it's legal until an arrest warrant is issued. Phil will handle the authorities. How did it go with the other sister?" With one hand on the wheel, he slid the cell back into his pocket.

"She's got no problem with keeping them. She can even accommodate the nanny for a couple of days. I knew she would. Grace could mother the universe with homemade chicken soup and apple pie."

"Three sisters, three personalities."

"Yep. One sister short of *Little Women*."

"I'll text Liz to put the travel in motion. Are you up for a little game of amateur sleuth?"

Scarlett felt an adrenaline rush course through her veins. "What do you have in mind?"

He pulled the Lexus into a parking place and killed the engine. Turning toward her, he said, "You heard me list what I need to examine; time is short. I'm going to do a little legal B and E and could use some help. You onboard?"

A smile broke out on Scarlett's face. "I can't believe I'm saying this, but it sounds like the most exhilarating thing to come my way in a long time."

"Okay, Harvard. Let's go check Mr. and Mrs. Shepherd into the inn."

She looked at him, a blood rush stimulating her nerve endings.

Once at the reception desk, Jake texted Liz Glover while the desk clerk ran his credit card and assigned their rooms.

Once Jake had the plastic keys to adjoining rooms, the pair headed to the barbeque restaurant.

"I didn't want to say anything in front of the desk clerk, but why did you book two rooms?" Scarlett asked.

"You'll see."

"Do you ever give a straight answer?"

"Not if I can help it."

Watching him drive, the thought zipped through Scarlett's mind of what it would be like to share a room with Jake. *What the hell am I thinking?* "Do you believe Savannah's safer in Atlanta than DC?"

"She's not going to her Georgia home. I'm a little more creative than that."

Surprised, Scarlett said, "Where is she going?"

"As I recall, Gray MacGregor has a mountain place in North Carolina within driving distance of Atlanta and Greenville, South Carolina. Ever been there?"

"No. But I've heard about the house. How do you know about it?"

"He had me down once when we worked for Phil. If memory serves me right, it's located close to the top of the mountain with only a narrow road for access. Easy to monitor. However, best no one else has knowledge of where she is, including your family, until I have a chance to investigate. She'll have to appear for the funeral. Phil can speak for her until then, explaining that she is in seclusion for grief recovery."

"That's a stretch. After your interrogation, I don't see that she's grieving so much. I've got to ask. How did you know Scott was such a bastard—and she had a lover?"

He glanced over at her with a smirky smile. "Simple. Deductive reasoning. Didn't they teach that at Harvard?"

"Yeah. But I took basket weaving instead, you smart-ass Yalie."

"Sorry, I couldn't resist. It wasn't astrophysics. Look at the facts. He cheated on you. He's a politician—natural-born egotist and liar. He slept over at the office—didn't check in with his wife. Come on, Scarlett, you're a divorce attorney. Do you need a pair of crotchless panties under the seat of his car to follow the map?"

Scarlett pursed her lips, frowning.

"She let an important clue slip when she said she didn't ruin your life. It was easy to read between the lines. Life with Senator Scott Kingsley was no day at the spa."

She twisted in the seatbelt toward him. "Okay, I concede on Scott. But, Savannah? My empty-headed sister cheating?"

"You described her as a narcissistic princess, accustomed to holding court, not to mention she cheated on you. She marries another narcissist, who is probably a sociopath. He neglects and betrays her—ego-bending for the prom queen. Just a matter of time until she sticks her hand in the cookie jar of carnal delights for a little pleasure and a boost in self-esteem. *Voila!*"

"Oh, yeah. But then, why do you believe her? You could see how easily she lies. I'm her sister, and I'm not sure I believe her."

"She's telling the truth. She didn't kill him, but my gut tells me someone did. Her feelings about his death are conflicted, but she didn't have anything to do with it. I wouldn't send her away for life for playing his game and raising him one. Plus, if she didn't do him in, there's a killer out there. Without knowing who or why, we have to consider she might be in jeopardy as well."

"She's a good actress and could fake the tears."

"You weren't paying attention. When she lied, she would wiggle a little in her chair, glance away, play dumb, or try to avoid answering. When she told the truth, she was confident, focused, and in direct eye contact. The tears didn't affect my opinion one way or the other."

"So human polygraph is also in your inventory of skills?"

He made a sharp turn, jolting Scarlett.

"I see they didn't have driver's ed at Yale."

He chuckled. "And I can see this case is going to be a challenge. A featherweight suspect and a smart-ass Harvard lawyer. You need to study Paul Ekman, nonverbal communications expert. Might help in your divorce work. Changing the subject. How does Mister Kavanagh feel about you playing the fixer?"

"My father?"

"I was thinking husband."

"I've managed quite nicely without one of those."

He glanced around at her. "Surprising. With your looks, I'm sure there's been no lack of applicants. Did you chew them all up and spit them out?"

"If that was meant as a perverted compliment, thank you. But no thank you. After Scott Kingsley and years in the divorce business, marriage is not for me. By the turn of the next century, it won't be in the dictionary."

He gave a quick tick of his head, his eyebrows pinched together. "Ouch. That's pretty cynical even for a feminazi."

"I'm a nonbeliever not a man-hater, but you're a lawyer. Look at the evidence—divorce and cohabitation are statistically tipping the scale. I spend fifty hours a week with dysfunctional couples, many wanting to kill one another."

"In my field, they do. At least in your realm, the clients take time to go to court. In mine, they go to the gun show."

She laughed. "I know it isn't funny. You see much homicide with PI work?"

"In the private sector, it usually turns up in a life insurance claim." He pulled into a parking place in front of a small strip of stores, the restaurant on the end.

"So, you were FBI?"

"Guilty."

"How long?"

"A few years."

"What's 'a few' in Yale time?"

"Enough to learn about human nature." He turned off the motor and began unfastening his seat belt.

"Mind if I ask why you left?"

"I don't mind you asking if you don't mind me not answering."

Her eyebrows pinched together, but undaunted, she fielded his dismissal. "That bad, huh?"

"No comment. Let's just say your profession factored in." His cell pinged, and he took it out of his pocket.

"That's interesting. Divorce caused your exit? Did you get caught with a badge bunny?"

Reading the new text, he said without looking up, "Let's say I might have been married to one, and she found a bigger, shinier badge."

"Wow! That's heavy." She leaned her head against the headrest. "I dated an FBI wannabe in law school."

He turned off his device and slid it back in his pocket. "How did that go?"

Turning toward him, she said, "With me or the FBI?"

"Obviously, you dumped him, but did he make it into the Bureau?"

"I don't know. He was full of himself—a showboat. Wanted to be on the HRT, whatever that is."

Jake's head moved up and down in assent. "Hostage Rescue Team." He clicked his tongue. "The guy aimed high."

"Yeah. He liked to tell me it was the equivalent of Navy SEALs and Army Delta Force. Were you an Indian or a chief?"

He pulled the door handle and pushed it open. "Strictly an Indian—in more ways than one."

She opened her door, grabbing her purse as it was about to slide off her lap. "Where did you work?"

"All over." He gave her the coy smile, accompanied by a sexy twinkle in his eyes, she was beginning to recognize as his signature.

"I mean, where were you based?"

"Quantico—mostly. Last assignment was DC. Let's get the food."

As she walked in front of Jake into the restaurant, Scarlett found herself wondering what his wife had been like.

Jake opened the rear of the three-ton LX 570 and dropped the take-out bag of barbeque into a Yeti Tundra. The tan cooler stood conspicuously between assorted black cases and a metal, three-drawer cabinet. Combination locks secured all the storage units. When Scarlett passed by him on her way to the passenger door, her Creed fragrance caught Jake's attention. He slammed the tailgate closed and watched her enter the vehicle. *Having her around should make this case interesting.*

Once they were on the way back to Savannah's hotel, he set his phone in a holder on the dash and hit a speed-dial number with the device on speaker.

"Coop. Shepherd here. Couple of things. Do we have a guy by the name of Warner on the payroll?"

"I don't think so. What's the first name?"

"David . . . Da—" He looked at Scarlett.

"Darren."

"Darren Warner."

"No. Never heard the name."

Jake gave Scarlett a thumbs-up. "Good. I'll explain later. Next thing. I need about four guys—three at a minimum—to travel tonight. Can we make that happen?"

There were a few seconds of silence on the phone before Pete Cooper responded. "I can give you three, but four might be a problem. How important is a fourth?"

"I can coast on three. Are Sonny and Brenda available?"

"Let me check." The phone went silent for several seconds. "I can switch up a job and make them available."

"Ten-four. I'll text the details."

He terminated the call as he pulled into the parking lot.

"Should I ask, who is Coop?"

With his signature look, exposing a trace of teeth and twinkling eyes, he said, "Wouldn't have made the call on speaker if it were confidential. Coop, Peter Cooper, and I have a security company. He runs the day-to-day. Have to admit, I am relieved your sister's paramour isn't one of ours."

"That would have been awkward, but who is traveling tonight? I thought you were just sending the nanny and kids to Georgia."

"Revised plan. I want the widow out of range. Let's collect her and make the transfer."

"We aren't going to eat here?"

He shook his head. "The sooner Savannah's out of the DC area, the better. I doubt any tracking of her phone has taken place, but there is the possibility."

When they reached the second hotel, Jake carried Scarlett's suitcase and a small duffle bag of his to the rooms, leaving Savannah's bag to be transferred to her security team. In the room, he scarfed down a sandwich and then drew his cell out while Savannah and Scarlett continued eating. Out of the corner of his eye, he watched Savannah gingerly nibble on French fries and her sandwich, which she had cut into four pieces. *A quintessential dumb-acting blonde who knows exactly what she's doing. Bet she set out to ensnarl the wannabe bigshot but wasn't quite smart enough to see him for whom he really was.*

Moving into the adjoining room, he closed the door and called Phil Madison. After filling the lawyer in on his progress and confirming his belief in Savannah's innocence, Jake said, "Any word from the ME?"

"No. Still quiet. I've served formal notice of representation to the FBI and the U.S. Attorney's office."

"It'll be a surprise to me if it's ruled anything but homicide, and from what I'm seeing, the pool of suspects could fill a stadium. Can you get in touch with MacGregor and arrange for use of his mountain home?" Jake ducked into the bathroom for added privacy. "I'm sending the client south with a two-man security team and need a safe house."

"Consider it done. Are you making the trip with her?"

"No. My plan is to toss her Georgetown home tonight and head down tomorrow with the sister. It'll give me a chance to cover the hometown connections. Looks like she wants the funeral held at an Episcopal church in Atlanta."

"If you're sure, I'll make the appropriate notifications once the body is released. In any event, I'll be down before the service. I don't want her loose in public without me," Madison said.

"Judging from my time with her, I would mark that imperative. At least the sister is a savvy soul. Trust me; you're going to need all the client-control tricks in your kit for this one. I'll stay in touch."

"Jake. Before we hang up, the last time we talked, Gray mentioned his father-in-law is a retired Atlanta cop. Might keep it in mind if you need any extra help down south."

"Noted."

By nine thirty, Scarlett and Jake had changed to casual attire and were en route to Georgetown while the Kingsley family headed south. Savannah and her security team were on the way to Greenville, South Carolina, where she would stay in a hotel until Scarlett and Jake arrived. A third bodyguard was escorting the nanny and children to Atlanta via a commercial airliner. As Jake drove into the Kingsley neighborhood, he let out a low whistle. "Pretty swanky for a $174,000-a-year government employee. Where did the gold come from?"

"Don't look at me. I hardly know these people. But it didn't come from Savannah. I don't remember Scott's family being wealthy. They lived comfortably—in a small town in North Georgia. About like my family."

"Well, in this market, you need your name on a string of oil wells or a chunk of Silicone Valley to buy an average house. This one is anything but average."

"What are you thinking?"

"Opens up a whole new set of questions. There are congressmen who don't have a residence in DC. Some sleep in their offices when in session and regularly commute to their home district."

"Are you kidding? How do you know so much about the politicians?"

"I've been on a few fixer assignments. No congressional murders, but a share of indiscretions and financial scandals. Uh-oh."

"What?"

"The Bureau has eyes on your sister's house—as I expected."

"How do you know?"

He pointed forward. "See the SUV on the left, trying to blend into the shadows?"

"How do you know it's FBI?"

"Trust me. I know. Let's have some fun." A mischievous grin lit his face.

"What are you going to do?"

He ignored her, pulled his vehicle up extremely close to the other one, and rolled his window down. "Hi, fellows. Enjoying the view?"

"What the fuck are you doing here, Shepherd?" the driver said.

"Might ask you the same question, but I probably know."

The agent gave Jake's Lexus a once over. "Mighty nice wheels, you've got there. Private sector must be paying well."

"More money, less risk."

"So, are you trolling for business or on a job?"

"Just escorting Mrs. Kingsley's sister into the house to pick up some things for the widow."

The female agent in the passenger seat leaned forward for a better view of Jake. "Who the hell is this guy, Deke?" she asked.

"My apologies, Sylvia. You haven't met Former SA Jake Shepherd, ex-husband of our ASAC's wife, and a legend in his own mind. Where is the senator's widow, Shepherd?"

"You know I couldn't tell you if I knew. You'll have to check with her attorney."

"I hope I don't have to remind you to be careful about what you tamper with in there."

"I know the rules. Not going to remove or contaminate a single piece of evidence."

"Don't we need proof he's got a right to enter the house?" the female agent said.

Deke Weston shook his head. "Waste of time. He does. He's too smart not to." Turning back to Jake, he said, "And I'm guessing whatever you come up with is work product, right?"

"You've got it. But if your partner wants proof, I've got the engagement letter on my phone." Jake held up his cell.

"Don't bother. I know you're Madison's boy, and he's Mrs. Kingsley's rep."

Jake reached out and patted the FBI vehicle. "You guys have a good night. Give my regards to Kirby." With that, Jake turned the Lexus around and pulled up the driveway of the Georgian style, red-brick house.

Scarlett stared at him with a mesmerized expression. "You've certainly got *chutzpah*."

"I think you meant something a little less polite, but I get it. Weston's a good guy. We worked together for a while. Don't know the rookie."

"Translate ASAC for me."

"Assistant Special Agent in Charge. Their boss."

Scarlett gave him an incredulous look. "Did I hear right? Your ex is married to their supervisor?"

"Mrs. ASAC Hal Kirby. You heard right."

Scarlett's eyes grew so large the whites glowed in the beam of a streetlamp. "What does that do for Savannah's case?"

"Nothing—maybe even helps," he said as he drove up the drive toward the back of the house.

"I don't see how." She shook her head.

"It's complicated. I'll spell it out when I know you better." He hit the remote, opening the garage door.

"Why are we pulling into the garage?"

"You ask a lot of questions."

"Have you ever known a lawyer who didn't? As I recall, we're trained to avoid assumptions. Isn't the saying, 'Assume makes an ass out of *u* and me'?"

He snapped his fingers along with a slight twist of his head as the motor died. "Damn. You're right."

"Never mind. I should have known you don't want Scully and Mulder to know any more than necessary."

He grinned. "There's hope for you yet."

Motion sensor lights illuminated the area as Scarlett and Jake exited the vehicle. Although a three-car garage, the only other vehicle present was a Mercedes Benz S 550 coupe, which caught Jake's attention, evoking another low whistle. "That's a senator's annual salary on wheels."

"It looks like my sister left Atlanta and landed in Xanadu."

He opened the tailgate with his key. "But it appears Karma caught up."

"Funny you say that. When we were eating earlier, I looked at her and thought about how many nights I dreamed of an implosion of their marriage."

"And?"

"It's a total letdown—no jubilation at all. Just a—whiskey, tango, foxtrot?"

He clicked his tongue. "They just don't make Karma like they used to."

"I guess I should be ashamed."

"If evil thoughts could be prosecuted, we'd all be in prison." He scooted himself onto the floor of the cargo space and unlocked the metal cabinet. After taking a digital recording device, an electronic tablet, camera, portable scanner, scanner wand, and two backup drives from the largest of three drawers, he placed them in a duffle bag and then opened one of the smaller drawers. Removing a keyring of odd-shaped keys and a small leather case of lock-pick tools, he added them to the stash of equipment and relocked the unit.

"You are certainly prepared. This truck is a warehouse on wheels."

"A man is only as good as his stuff."

Her eyebrows came together in a dubious expression. "I'm not touching that. Are weapons stored in any of those containers?"

Jake chuckled. "No. Not unless I'm invited to a shootout. Too risky to leave them in a vehicle. Not good to have a gun stolen, and then it turns up later in a homicide." He opened one of the black cases and took out latex gloves, two small tactical flashlights, several pads of sticky notes, and two pens. "Put these on," he said, handing her a pair of gloves. When she had them in place, he shared the note-taking materials and one of the battery-powered lamps.

"That should do it," he said as he climbed out of the SUV and closed the tailgate. "You have the security code ready?"

She dropped the items he gave her into the pocket of her jacket, reached inside her handbag, and removed a folded sheet of paper and key. "Right here."

Entry from the garage put the pair in the laundry room. Scarlett disarmed the security system, while Jake began opening drawers, cabinet doors, and the appliances. "I'll cover this room and the kitchen; you take the living room and dining room. Check every drawer, bookcase, underneath furniture, and the cushions. Tag any suspicious items and be sure window coverings are closed before turning on any light. Our watch committee knows what we're doing, but I'd rather not provide photo ops."

"What am I looking for?"

"I wish I knew. As the esteemed Justice Potter Stewart said, 'I'll know it when I see it.'"

"Yeah, but he was talking about porn. Can you nail it down a little tighter?"

"Not really. Think courtroom—evidence. You're a lawyer."

"If you don't give me some clues, I may screw up."

"I have faith in you, Harvard. They didn't let you in because you're stupid. Keep in mind; most murders are triggered by money-slash-greed, sex, or revenge. Look for evidence of dicey financials, unusual correspondence, notes, cards, photos, anything appearing to be out of place. It's not so different from what you look for when nailing a husband in a divorce. And definitely tag any illicit activity in the erotic department, keeping in mind the latter might not be limited to an ordinary extramarital affair."

"What does that mean?"

"Kiddie porn, switch-hitter, trafficking, sex games—fodder for blackmail. You'd be surprised the hobbies some outwardly respectable people have. If it catches your eye, it's worth checking out. Right now, the playing field is wide open."

"Good gosh. Your mind has a broad scope."

"Have to start wide and narrow down. I need to know: Who benefits from his death? Who stood to lose if he lived? And is there an unaccounted-for money trail? When I finish in the kitchen, I'm going to head to his home office. According to the sketch your sister did, it's here on the first floor. After you cover the rooms I mentioned, check out the bedrooms."

"I don't need to cover the kids' rooms do I?"

"Don't skip anything—linen closets, trash cans, under all mattresses. Those trying to hide something become quite creative. If you finish before I do, turn all the containers in the medicine cabinet face

forward. Obviously, you wouldn't know if every"—he hesitated—
"scratch that. I'll take care of the medicine cabinet."

For twenty minutes, the only sound in the house was drawers and
cabinet doors opening and closing. As Jake headed to Scott Kingsley's
office, a yelp, followed by profanity, came from the direction of the
staircase.

"Are you all right?" he called out. "Scarlett?"

"Yeah. I just hit my shin on a brass elephant. The darn thing has
a lethal trunk. Where are you?" A beam of light hit her eyes. "Hey,
you're blinding me."

"Sorry."

Rubbing her leg, Scarlett hobbled toward the banister, almost losing her balance.

"Whoa. Steady there." Jake's hand went around her waist and sup-
ported her until she regained her balance.

"Sorry. I'm not known for my grace."

"No problem." His words bore a slight edge of pleasure.

As she regained her composure and started to pull away, he
grabbed her arm.

"What?"

"Shh! I heard something." Releasing her, he reached under his
jacket and drew his weapon from a holster inside his waistband.
"Turn off your light," he said, putting his on the hall console, beam
downward.

"God, I forgot you're armed."

"Drop to the floor and stay quiet."

He eased over to a tall window overlooking the side yard.

Ignoring his instructions, Scarlett followed. "What do you think it
is?" she whispered.

Pulling the drape back at the side, Jake looked outside without
responding.

"Do you see anyone?"

"There's someone in the shrubbery."

"One of the FBI guys?"

"No. They wouldn't pull a stunt like that with me." He held an arm out to prevent her from advancing. The muzzle of his revolver held the drape back, allowing him visual access to the yard. *What the?* He squatted, keeping only his head and the weapon above the window base.

"Can you see anything?" Scarlett asked.

Jake put his free hand up in a halt position.

"Is there more than one?"

Jake shook his head, clenching his teeth.

CHAPTER SEVEN

Suddenly, floodlights came on from the house next door, illuminating the Kingsley's yard. A shadowy figure sprang from the bushes and fled.

Jake lowered his arm. "Weston must have moved on. Whoever it is, he's on the run."

"Should you go after him or call those agents?"

"I don't think so."

"But he might be a burglar about to break in."

Ignoring her comment, he said, "You don't take directions much better than your sister."

"You could catch him," she continued.

"And what would I do with him?"

"I don't know—something."

"Yeah—and maybe get shot in the process."

"You have a gun."

"But not a badge. And he might have a friend. To say nothing of the possibility I could be shooting an unarmed, teenage prowler or an overzealous reporter looking for a headline. Let's just say, I apprehended him. What then? Lose what little time we have with the red tape that would entail. I'm entering this one in the no harm, no foul column." Jake holstered his gun, moved back to the desk, and picked up his flashlight.

"That was unnecessarily patronizing."

"If so, I apologize, but simmer down. He's gone, and we have a job to do."

"You always carry a weapon?"

"It's a hard habit to break."

"Glock 22?"

"Nope—19."

"Humph! I thought the 22 was the gun of choice with cops."

"The 19 is easier to conceal, but what's with the interrogation? You a weapons expert?"

"In a family of all girls, I was Dad's surrogate son—his skeet partner."

Laughing, he said, "Then, I'd better watch my back—nothing more dangerous than a beautiful woman with a gun."

The peripheral glow of his flashlight exposed a tiny smile on her lips.

"Let's get on with it; shall we?" he said.

Scarlett didn't move, a grimace overtaking her face and crinkling her nose. "I have to admit, I feel a little sleazy going through my sister's personal space."

Jake nodded. "Understandable, but it's got to be done. And don't be surprised if you find she has more secrets. She wasn't telling me everything."

Scarlett stared at him for several seconds, trying to decide what she should do. "I can't go through Savannah's intimate possessions, Jake—at least not the drawers in her dresser or chest. I could never look her in the face again." *This will tick him off.* She tensed and waited for him to assail her position. To her surprise, he smiled.

"I'll take the sensitive areas, but first, I want to check something in the office. Wait here for a second."

He walked down the hall to the side of the staircase, returning within a minute. "As I suspected, I need a locksmith to open Kingsley's safe."

"With all your tools, you can't compromise it?"

He took out his cell and began texting, his eyes on the screen as he spoke. "I can pick a standard lock, but never needed to learn safe-cracking. When I've had to break into one, destroying the mechanism worked. Here, I need a little more finesse." Tucking away the phone when done, he glanced up and said, "Let's rock and roll."

She turned and started up the stairs, the flashlight in one hand, her other on the banister for guidance and support. Jake trailed behind.

When they reached the second floor, moonlight shone through a second-floor window, providing moderate illumination. "The master suite is to the right at the end," he said, pointing toward the north end of the building.

"My gosh. How many rooms are there?"

"From Savannah's diagram, appears to be six to the left and two, plus the master to the right. I'm reasonably certain the guest rooms are clean. Too risky to hide incriminating evidence where a nosy guest might discover it."

When Scarlett opened the door to the Kingsley boudoir, it was pitch black.

"Turn on a light. The windows are covered in here," Jake said.

When the light unveiled the area, Scarlett gasped as she surveyed the suite. "My gosh." Her eyes expanded to take in the massive room, decorated in opulent, Louis VI style. "This is larger than my entire condo." In addition to the bed section with overstuffed chairs, the collective included a sitting room, two luxurious bathrooms, plus his and her dressing rooms, each as large as an average bedroom. "Come here and look at this," Scarlett said, pointing to Savannah's pink-marble soaking tub, set inside a carved wood surround.

"We don't have time for sightseeing on this trip." Jake had begun opening the drawers built into one side of Savannah's dressing room along with shelves for accessories. Hanging garments lined the opposite wall.

"Refresh my memory, what ticket did your brother-in-law run on?" he asked as Scarlett entered the area.

She took a few seconds to reply. "I'm pretty sure it was an independent."

"Yeah. Figures. I'll need to look at his list of contributors."

"What are you thinking?"

"Just collecting data. Go ahead and start in his closet."

"I am. But do you mind if I process all this for a second?" She gazed around Savannah's wardrobe. A subtle aroma of jasmine permeated the area. On the back wall, a six-foot mirror hung above a velvet-covered bench. Overhead, there was a chandelier of crystal prisms and gold-plated arms. "I'd hardly call these areas closets." When Jake continued without responding, Scarlett moved on to Scott's space.

Again, the only sound in the house emanated from the search until Scarlett returned to Savannah's dressing room. "Here, I forgot about Savannah's safe. You'll need this to open it." She handed him the slip of paper on which Savannah had provided the location and the combination. "Your guy won't have to crack hers."

"Which means she hasn't used it to hide her secrets—probably because the senator had the combination as well." Jake took the instructions and followed them to open a small safe, similar to those found in hotel rooms, as Scarlett watched. He found the safe, mounted in the wall, above the end of a shelf.

When the tumblers released the catch, the box was empty.

"There's one in his dressing room as well, but Savannah didn't give me the combination."

Jake chuckled under his breath before saying, "Are you really surprised?"

As Scarlett started back to Scott Kingsley's domain, Jake said, "Well, well, well. Here's the mother lode."

Scarlett swirled around and walked to the end of the room where Jake had a deep, lower drawer wide open. "I see nothing but junk. Threadbare towels, rags, old newspapers, magazines, paperbacks."

He pulled a layer of items back and flipped through the books. "Look closer." Between the pages were handwritten cards and notes— at the bottom, a trove of hidden items disguised as clutter.

She moved closer. "You're right."

"I'll catch you up later. Finish the rest of this floor, tagging or photographing anything you find suspicious, and meet me downstairs when you're done." With that, he stood, accompanied her out of the dressing room, and proceeded to set up the portable copy machine on a console table in the bedroom.

Scarlett's brow furrowed as she ambled back toward Scott's dressing room. *What did he find?*

CHAPTER EIGHT

When she reached the senator's area, nostalgia descended. *Damn him. He still wore Aramis.* The aroma of his cologne drifted through the air. *Stop thinking about him that way. He was a narcissistic sociopath.*

She went directly to the drawer in Scott's space corresponding to the one in Savannah's where Jake discovered items of interest. But Scott's contained only neatly folded tee shirts. She rushed through the remaining drawers and then turned to the hanging garments.

One by one, she rummaged through casual and formal clothing, checking pockets. Over and over, she came up empty. Halfway through the rack, the aroma of his fragrance, remnants of the man, and memories began to nauseate her. *He was a bastard. I shouldn't blame her.*

As Scarlett moved the jackets along the brass rod, sliding her hands into pockets, pessimism set in. *There's not going to be anything left in his clothes. He wasn't stupid.* Ramming a defiant hand in the pocket of a red UGA windbreaker, she felt a piece of paper. *Hmmm.* Jerking it out and unfolding it, she found it was from a hotel memo pad—the Salamander Resort & Spa.

"Jake, I found something," she said, walking to the doorway.

He stood over the copier, monitoring the function. "Let's see it." Taking the slip from her, he read it aloud.

"'I'm naked. Hurry.'"

"Whew. Talking about the big bucks—the Salamander is in the big leagues. Is that Savannah's handwriting?"

Scarlett shook her head. "No. Absolutely not."

"Then it looks like this may lead to something the senator had going on the side." He took it to the machine and made a copy. "Here, put it back where you found it and snap a photo with enough showing to ID it." As Scarlett left him, he said, "We need a name to go with the invite."

He had hardly finished speaking when his cell buzzed.

Scarlett stopped and listened as he answered, "Drive to the back and let him out. I'll open the patio door."

"Your safecracker?" Scarlett asked.

"We prefer locksmith, if you please. That was Liz. She's dropping him off."

"He doesn't drive?"

"Why would I want to give my friends out in front the identity of my locksmith? They have nothing by tracing Liz's tag."

"Oh. Your *locksmith* wouldn't by any chance have a record, would he?"

"Only a very small one." He smiled. "Finish up. I expect our work is cut out for us in Senator Kingsley's office."

As Scarlett passed the bed on her way back to Scott's dressing room, a landline on the night table rang, causing her to jump. Instinctively, her hand reached toward it.

"Hold it."

His harsh tone startled Scarlett as she pointed down to the phone. "But what if it's Savannah?"

"Call her on your phone."

As she pulled her hand back, she gave him a dirty look. When the ringing stopped, Scarlett said, "If it's important, she'll text my cell, but she's right. You are rude."

He laughed. "So I've been told. What would you rather have? Competence or courtesy?"

"Where I come from, they're not mutually exclusive."

"We're not at a cotillion, Harvard. Don't let it get around, but when I'm polite, you better watch your back."

Shaking her head, she took out her cell. "I don't see what it would have hurt for me to answer."

"Ever heard of wiretaps?"

She froze for a second. "You think that phone is bugged?"

"I'd bet my fee on it."

"They really think Savannah killed Scott?" Her eyes widened in dismay.

He took the last of the documents from the copier and packed his bag as he responded, "Until eliminated by alibi or evidence, she's at the top of the suspect list. But that's not the only reason for tapping the line. Someone killed the senator. Any call coming or going could offer a lead as to who or why. You bet they got a warrant ASAP. Same reason for the surveillance."

"Sitting out there for hours has got to be a tedious assignment."

"I've been on worse."

"Like what?"

"You do ask a lot of questions. Remind me to tell you later. Right now, I'm going down to let my guy in and then to the senator's office. Meet me when you finish up."

She shot him an unseen dirty look as he walked away.

When Scarlett made it to Scott Kingsley's study, Jake's locksmith was gone but had opened the office safe and the one in Scott's closet. A strongbox sat on the senator's desk next to an iPad and a MacBook Air. Jake sat in front of the black screen, tinkering with the keys to gain access.

"Find anything else of interest?" he asked as she entered.

"Just this key." She held out what appeared to be a door key. "It was in the inside pocket of one of Scott's overcoats. It's probably to his office or maybe one of their houses."

"Maybe. Maybe not." He took the key, turned it over, and took out his phone and tapped in a text.

Liz. Bring Joey back. Got another job for him.

When one of Jake's keys finally opened the strongbox, the contents revealed a large stash of cash.

"How much do you think is there?" Scarlett asked, pointing to the container.

"Looks like enough to fund a modest revolution."

"Good gosh. Where do you think it came from?"

"I think a lot of people are going to be asking that question. If I had to guess, I would say from nothing legal."

"Are you going to count it?"

"No. You can do that while I break the code to get into his electronics. Photograph the cash as you count."

She wanted to ask why he was bringing the locksmith back and how he thought he could get into the computer. *I'm not giving him another reason to accuse me of asking too many questions.*

Within minutes, Jake's phone pinged with an incoming text. Glancing over, he said, "Joey's back. Do you mind letting him in the kitchen door?"

"Amazing. You can be polite." She tucked a package of one-hundred-dollar bills back in the strongbox.

"Don't get used to it. It won't happen very often."

She rolled her eyes and started toward the rear of the house.

When Joey and Scarlett returned, Jake had the laptop booted up. Gazing at the screen, Scarlett said, "How did you get in? It *was* password protected, wasn't it?"

"Wasn't too hard."

"Did you override the password?"

"Nope," he said, shaking his head. "A narcissist like Kingsley is pretty transparent. Just plugged in a few permutations of his name along with POTUS and bingo!"

"Never underestimate Shepherd," Joey said. "What can I do for you, Jake?"

Jake held up the key Scarlett found. "Make a duplicate of this and then see if you can ID it."

"No problem with the duplication, but the identification will take me a little time. I'll take a copy and a photo back to the shop and let you know."

By the time Joey left, Jake had made mirror copies of Scott's iPad and laptop and done a final walk-through of the house. "I think we've covered it. Let's hit the road. Tomorrow's going to be a long day."

Back at the Lexus, Scarlett watched him methodically arrange his equipment and the files. "No offense, but your office doesn't reflect your organizational skills."

He glanced around at her. "It might surprise you to know that the mess you think you saw in my office is perfectly organized. There's not a slip of paper I can't lay my hands on in ten seconds."

"You could have fooled me. By the way, Joey doesn't seem like a felon."

He grinned. "He's not. Be a little hard for him to get a license, even though he doesn't need one in DC."

"I should have known that."

"Don't be too hard on yourself, Harvard," he said, closing the rear of the SUV. "You're family law. Your skill set should help when we examine the financials. Don't you comb through those in your practice?"

"Oh, yeah. What are you thinking after what you've seen tonight?"

He didn't answer until behind the wheel. "Way too early to form a theory. There are certainly shades of infidelity and corruption—domestic or worse. At this point, no telling what rats are going to crawl out of the ruins. Whatever or whoever is behind that wad of Franklins could pose a serious threat."

"Threat to who?"

"Whoever gets in the way—starting with your sister. I'll be having another conversation with her when we get her settled in the MacGregor house. Right now, we need to get some sleep. It's nearly midnight."

As the Lexus approached the hotel, Scarlett turned to Jake. "You can just drop me at the main entrance. What time do you plan to come back to the hotel tomorrow?"

"I'm staying here."

Her eyebrows shot up. "You're staying here? Why?"

He turned toward her, with one eyebrow cocked. "Just a precaution."

"That's not necessary. I'm fine."

"Maybe. But I won't take the risk."

"Seriously? I'm fine, Jake."

He swung the vehicle into a parking place on the side of the building, cut the engine, and faced Scarlett. "We need to get something straight. This relationship will work a whole lot better if you let me be in charge. I know you're a Type A personality and accustomed to calling the shots with your clients, but this is my territory. Believe it or not, I know what the hell I'm doing. You don't have to agree with me or like me, but if I'm going to do my job, you are going to have to trust me. *Capiche?*"

If the sparks flying from Scarlett's eyes had substance, Jake would have been riddled with holes. "Was arrogance a required course at Yale?"

"Actually, at Quantico. Now that you're completely pissed off, ask yourself, would you want an insecure, unskilled surgeon wielding the scalpel? Same principle. You're putting your sister's life, and by association yours, in my hands. I'd better be both competent and confident."

After glaring at him for about thirty seconds, she heaved a silent sigh and then said, "You win this one."

CHAPTER NINE

At four forty-five, Saturday morning, Scarlett lay awake, rehashing the events of the previous day, when a text came on her cell.

> *Going to the gym. Don't leave the room or open your door*
>
> *until I get back. Text if you need anything.*

Glancing toward the slightly ajar doors between their adjoining rooms, she recalled their arrival only hours earlier. Liz had been waiting with Jake's travel bag and Kai. The former, he informed Scarlett, stayed prepared for sudden departures. When she expressed surprise at the presence of the dog, Jake smiled and said, "Added security."

An awkward moment occurred when Scarlett attempted to close the doors between their rooms.

"Leave them partially open," Jake had said.

"Excuse me. I've known you what, eight or nine hours, and you expect me to share a hotel room?"

"Relax, counselor. You're a hell of an attractive woman, but I gave up rape for Lent."

"But it's not Lent."

"Yeah? Well, that's okay. I'm not Catholic. No more buts." He pointed to the passageway. "The doors stay open enough that the dog and I can hear trouble. For your peace of mind: 'Thou shall not fraternize with the subject of a security assignment' is the first commandment in the investigator bible. Your virtue is safer than it would be in church."

This is going to be a long day, she thought, flinching at the sound of his exit door closing. Rubbing her forehead, she pictured Jake on a treadmill. *OCD—gotta be. Working out before five a.m. after last night?* She punched her pillow and buried her face in the linen. *Did he take the dog? All this security is BS. I'm in no danger.*

She wanted to go back to sleep but knew it was an unavailable luxury. Rising, she paused for several seconds to collect her faculties and to assess the circumstances. *If he's gone, no point in leaving the door open.* Swinging her feet to the floor, she tiptoed across the room, not wanting to arouse the German shepherd if left behind. After easing the door shut, she returned to her bed to ponder her next move. *Who is this guy? Today, I'll spend all day in the car with him. I haven't been this up close and personal with a man since—damn, I can't even remember when.*

Shaking her head as if to clear it, she whispered to herself, "Stop wasting time. Take advantage of the privacy and shower while he's gone."

By the time Jake knocked on her door with coffee and muffins, Scarlett was not only dressed; she had her belongings neatly packed and ready to leave.

"I'm impressed, Harvard. I might have expected you to sleep in."

"Your radar is down, but I don't do predawn workouts."

He looked her up and down. "Judging from what I see, you do something to keep yourself in shape."

"Careful, Shepherd. I'm going to get the impression that you're a cowboy Casanova."

"You flatter me. I'm just an ole country boy from Oklahoma."

His eyes lingered on Scarlett long enough to make her self-conscious. *Keep your guard up, Kavanagh. He may have walked the line so far, but he is a man—and from what I see, an extremely healthy one.*

Once in the Lexus, Kai settled in a rear seat, a safety harness securing him. Scarlett checked her phone for messages while Jake began the nine-hour drive.

"No messages. If Savannah called, it must not have been important."

"I had a text from my guy. They are headed to Asheville this morning to meet us." He reached for a knob on his dash and turned on a playlist.

Scarlett recognized the melody of the 1980 hit, "Lady." When Jake began to sing, she turned. "So, Shepherd. What are you? A Glock-carrying James Corden?"

"I prefer Kenny."

"I stand corrected."

He smiled but continued without further comment.

As Scarlett stared at the man singing, her dubious expression mellowed. "You're actually good—excellent Kenny Rogers cover. If this PI gig doesn't pan out, maybe you could hit Nashville."

"It's crossed my mind, but they don't let you shoot people in the music business." He hit the advance button, and an instrumental of "Islands in the Stream" came on. "How about you join me? Makes the drive a whole lot less tedious."

"You've got to be kidding. You really do this carpool karaoke bit?"

"Of course. Loosen up, Harvard. Stir a little sugar in with the lemons." He hit replay.

By the time Jake finished the opening section, Scarlett found herself singing along. When the song ended, Jake gave her a quick glance, grinning. "See, Harvard. Music soothes the soul."

"How did you know I knew the lyrics to that song?"

His eyes danced mischievously. "Let's just call it a hunch."

"The kind that told you Savannah was lying?" She studied his face.

"Maybe."

"You're something else, Shepherd. Just when I think I have you figured out, you pop up with a new facet to your puzzling personality."

"Do I now?"

"Yeah. For your information, I had a text from Fury. Seems Gray said to tell me not to underestimate you."

"Good advice. Haven't seen MacGregor in quite a while."

Scarlett rolled her eyes along with a slight shake of her head. "Well, you'll see him in Atlanta. I'm sure they'll attend Scott's funeral even though they didn't know him."

"I thought you and MacGregor's wife went back to college days."

"We do. But were only acquaintances at Agnes Scott. We became close friends after she and Gray married."

"Your sister stole the wrong boyfriend. MacGregor swims in the financial pool with Bezos, Zuckerberg, and Gates."

"So, I've heard, but Gray and I were never lovers—strictly friends. I was in dumped-fiancée-mode—smarting from a wound too deep to allow interest in a new relationship. Gray was known as a one-date-wonder at the time and found it comfortable to socialize with a woman not trying to snag him. We worked together on a Harvard alumni project."

"So, you recovered?"

"Recovered from what?"

"The breakup."

"Oh, yeah. What choice did I have? You're divorced. How was that?"

"I've survived worse." His eyes didn't leave the road.

Scarlett studied his set jaw, wondering if she should follow up his declaration with a query. *When in doubt, don't.* The lawyers' sage mantra popped into her mind. *Never ask a question if you don't know the answer.*

Within seconds, Jake's hand went to the audio control and clicked on "Friends in Low Places." Turning to Scarlett, he asked, "Know this one?"

"Yeah. Garth Brooks. Who doesn't know it?"

"For a gal who has Groban and Brightman on her playlist, you have quite a country music repertoire."

"How do you know what I have in my iTunes library?"

He smiled. "Lucky guess."

"Somehow, I don't believe that."

For the next hour, they restricted verbal interaction to carpool karaoke. When they stopped at a rural gas station on I-81, Jake released Kai to take care of doggie business while Scarlett went in for cold drinks. When she returned with a water for herself and a Pepsi for Jake, he asked, "So, what was it with you in school besides debate team? Choir or musical theater?"

"What gives you the idea I was part of either?"

"Family law involves litigation. Litigators are performers—extraverts. You're a good singer, and you weren't a dancer because you don't walk or stand with your feet splayed."

"Being around you for long could be disarming, Shepherd. Do you have some sort of extrasensory powers?"

"Can't admit or deny," he said with a devilish expression.

"Should have expected that answer. Yes, I dabbled in theater." She took a gulp of water. "Changing the subject. What happens with all the documents we collected last night?"

"Liz will screen them and highlight the entries she knows I'll want to see."

"You trust a secretary to do that?"

"First of all, Liz is not a secretary. She's my office manager and research assistant."

"Okay. Got that. She seems like a surrogate wife or mother."

"She takes care of me. Liz worked for the Bureau for over twenty years."

"She was an agent?"

"Not in the field. Her husband was. Liz was an analyst. Retired when her husband died—heart attack."

"Is that why she retired?"

He nodded. "She wanted a change of scene and preferred not to charge into the lives of her adult kids. I'm her substitute project, but I couldn't run my business without her. I will review all the records, but she screens to help jumpstart the investigation."

"She left the Bureau the same time you did?"

"It worked out that way."

"Was leaving the FBI worse than the divorce? You said divorce wasn't your worst experience."

"A toss-up. But let's not rain on the sunshine. Stick around, and I might tell you the rest."

"You're good at asking questions but a master at dodging those thrown at you. I need to start a list of all you'll tell me later."

He grinned, crunched his empty can, and proceeded to take it to a trash receptacle. "All in due time, Harvard. All in due time. Right now, we've got miles to go, and time is not our friend."

"And you don't speed, I've noticed."

"Only if I'm in a hurry."

They arrived in Asheville at seven thirty and found Savannah, with her escorts, waiting in a small diner.

"Hey, buddy." Jake grabbed the outreached hand of the male security guard, tipped his head toward the female, and then turned toward Savannah. "Good evening, Ms. Kingsley. I hope your trip was pleasant."

A smile crept across Scarlett's face, which she turned away to hide. *Uh oh. Watch your back, Savannah. He's being polite.*

Savannah offered a lame nod.

"Sonny, Brenda, this is Ms. Kingsley's sister, Scarlett Kavanagh. Be nice. She's a lawyer. Scarlett, these are our two best operatives: Sonny Lassiter, former Special Agent, Federal Bureau of Investigation, and his wife, Brenda, former Baltimore PD."

As the couple exchanged handshakes with Scarlett, Jake asked, "Food any good here?"

"I think you'll like it, Shepherd," Sonny replied. "We are in your ancestral territory, right?"

Scarlett and Savannah both looked at Jake.

"Hey, you're right." Jake grabbed the sheet of specials from the table. "Fried trout, fry bread, a three sisters' casserole. I'm back home at my mother's table."

Scarlett's face scrunched in a puzzled look. "Your ancestral home? I thought you were from Oklahoma."

He raised a thumb, together with a nod. "My grandmother's people—the Cherokee—were driven from here on the Trail of Tears."

Scarlett's face tensed in a frown. "I'm sorry."

"We have to keep the tomahawks out of sight when Shepherd drops in," Sonny Lassiter said, grinning. "If we cross him, scalps might be involved."

"And don't forget it," Jake said, cocking an eyebrow.

Noting the comradery between the men, Scarlett surmised they had a history. *Must have worked together.*

Savannah failed to react, staring aimlessly around the room.

During dinner, Savannah remained quiet. The men exchanged friendly barbs while Scarlett and Brenda made small talk. Later, when they reached the MacGregor house, a caretaker met them with a key and showed Jake the ropes.

"You have my number. If you need help with anything, give me a call," Gray's man said as he left.

Looking around, Jake said, "I've only been here once, years ago, but it's pretty much as I remembered. To the left, there's a master suite, a smaller suite to the right, and three bedrooms upstairs. Scarlett, Savannah, and I will bunk upstairs. Sonny, you and Brenda cover this level."

Savannah stared at Kai as Scarlett walked over to the far wall, running the length of the living, dining, and kitchen. It consisted of floor-to-ceiling windows and rustic French doors opening onto the massive deck. Although nearly nine o'clock, the moonlight allowed her to see the outline of the mountains. "I see why Fury and Gray spend so much time up here."

"Was Gray the guy who caused Mom to be so upset when you didn't take him seriously?"

Scarlett looked at Savannah. "You knew about that?"

"Are you kidding? When you were seeing him, Mom was beside herself. I hadn't connected it until now. Every time I talked to her, she told me again and again how he was on the Fortune 500 list. Didn't his family own a marble factory?"

"Quarry."

"Hate to interrupt, ladies," Jake said, "but we need to get you settled in. I think everyone is tired, so, I'll wait to start work until morning—early."

Scarlett looked at Savannah. "When he says early, he means early Shepherd time, not Savannah time."

"Like nine o'clock?" Savannah said.

"More like six," Jake said.

Savannah heaved a sigh, closing her eyes, but didn't argue.

Sunday morning, Scarlett heard Jake and Kai go downstairs at five a.m. Like in the hotel, he insisted doors remain ajar. The sisters were in separate rooms with a bath that adjoined both. Scarlett showered and dressed before waking Savannah.

"What time is it?" Savannah asked, groaning.

"Time to get up. Jake wants to start interviewing potential witnesses in Atlanta. I hope you have the list ready. He'll talk to you first."

"I don't know if I can do all of this. Let me sleep a little longer."

"Did you take something?"

"Leave me alone."

"Damn it, Savannah. Get your you-know-what out of that bed. We're all here for you. The least you can do is cooperate."

"Okay, okay. You don't have to be so hateful. I need coffee."

Images of Savannah's extravagant lifestyle and her affair flashed across Scarlett's mind. "Well, there's no room service. I'm not even sure what we're going to do about eating. I get the feeling Jake isn't going to take the time or risk of going to restaurants three times a day, and I don't see deliveries coming here. Do you cook? Scratch that. I'm sure you don't after seeing your house, and I sure don't—at least not much."

Savannah cut her eyes around at Scarlett, furrowing her brow. "I don't like any of this."

Scarlett relaxed, a trace of sympathy softening her attitude. "Of course you don't. I don't either."

"Why do I have to be here? Why can't I stay with Grace? Does he think I'm going to be arrested?"

"From what I can tell, he doesn't know what is going to happen. The FBI was watching your house last night, but Jake said it didn't necessarily mean they are sure you are guilty. But since no one knows what happened to Scott, there's a chance you could be in danger. Jake is so paranoid that he wants all of us under protection."

"You're scaring me."

"Haven't you been scared? Your husband was probably murdered. Savannah, how many lovers did you have?"

"I'm getting up. Will you please see if there's any coffee in this house?"

CHAPTER TEN

At six fifteen, the aroma of bacon and coffee brought the sisters downstairs to find Jake and Kai in the kitchen area.

"Oh my god, coffee." Savannah rushed toward the counter where a Keurig stood.

"You kill, sing, and cook, Shepherd. Such a triple threat you are," Scarlett said.

Sonny burst out laughing from an easy chair by the enormous stone fireplace at the other end of the room. "She's got you pegged, Shepherd."

"Let's be clear. I don't kill—unless there's no other choice."

"I haven't seen that weapon out of your reach since I met you two days ago." She glanced over at Jake's Glock, lying at the end of the kitchen counter.

"You can take an agent out of the Bureau, but it's hard to take the gun out of his hand," Sonny said.

"Well, I feel like I'm living under martial law with all of you surrounding me with guns," Savannah said. "Next thing I know, Scarlett will be armed. She loves guns. Used to go target practicing with Dad when we were kids."

Sonny's eyebrows shot up. "Good god, Shepherd. You'd better stay on Ms. Kavanagh's good side."

"I've already figured that out, but much as I like the comedy routine, I've got a full day. There's the coffee, the bacon, and there's bread by the toaster. Eggs are in the fridge. You're on your own from here. While I talk with Ms. Kingsley, Brenda can make a run to the store for food supplies. When I'm done, Scarlett and I will leave for Atlanta."

"Where is Brenda?" Scarlett asked.

"On the deck, soaking up the view," Sonny said.

She glanced toward the windows and then back toward Jake. "Where did you go at the crack of dawn, if you don't mind me asking?"

"No problem. Gray's got a workout room and an office downstairs."

"Have we got that area secured?" Sonny asked. "I didn't realize there is another level."

"It's good. Be easier to breach Ft. Knox." He picked up a cup of coffee. "I'm going upstairs to shower and check in with Phil and Liz. Tell Brenda to use the company credit card and stock up with whatever she likes." With that, he headed up the stairs.

By the time Jake returned to the first floor, breakfast had been cleared away, and Brenda Lassiter was gone. Scarlett, Savannah, and Sonny were sitting around the fireplace in the living room.

"Email came in from Madison," Jake said. "The autopsy is done. The ME says cause of death was asphyxiation as a result of anaphylactic shock, but he hasn't tagged it homicide, yet. There was blunt force trauma to the head, which caused massive bleeding but was not lethal."

"Scott's allergy," Scarlett and Savannah said almost in unison.

"What kind of allergy?" He looked straight at Savannah.

"Peanuts. But he always had an EpiPen. He kept one everywhere."

"Sounds like there wasn't one around when he needed it." Jake glanced between Scarlett and Sonny. "Can you two give us the room?"

Sonny rose and went toward the suite he and Brenda shared. As Scarlett stood, Savannah grabbed her hand.

"Stay."

Scarlett looked at Jake, who shook his head.

"Not this time. I need a one on one."

Savannah looked at Scarlett with a silent plea on her face.

"You'll be fine. His bark is worse than his bite."

Jake dropped his legal pad on the table. "Want something to drink before we start?"

Savannah shook her head as she walked over to the long table between the living room area and the kitchen.

Pulling out a chair at the end of the long dining table, he pointed to the seat, waited for Savannah to come, and then helped her slide the chair in place. "Make yourself comfortable while I grab a water."

Returning to the table, he took a seat to her right and removed a pen from the pocket of his shirt. "I'll remind you of the ground rules. I need the candid truth—no embellishments, excuses, distortions, or spins. If I need you to elaborate, I'll ask. If you don't look at me when you answer, I'll assume you're playing fast and loose with veracity. Got it?"

She nodded.

"I'm not trying to set you up. I'm trying to unravel what happened, and who is responsible. Understand?"

She took a deep breath and agreed.

"In your opinion, is it possible that Senator Kingsley accidentally consumed the contraband?"

"No."

"Why?"

"He checked everything. He wouldn't allow anything in the house that contained peanuts, peanut butter, or peanut oil; and I'm sure he was the same way at the office. He nearly died when he was a little boy and was terrified of it."

"Did you have any peanuts in your home?"

"I just told you. No. Absolutely not."

"Keep in mind, a search warrant is likely to be issued for the house. If any peanuts are found, it will not look good for you."

"We didn't even have peanut butter for the kids."

"Where did he keep his EpiPen?"

"He always had one in a pocket—a jacket, shirt, whatever. It was standard—like his wallet, cell phone, and keys. He kept a backup in his desk drawer at the office. I know because he would have me pick them up when they expired. At home, he had one in his office, one in the dining room, and always put the one he carried in his pocket on his night table. He was afraid that if he came in contact with peanuts, or developed a new allergy, he might not have time to reach a pen."

"Who knew about his allergies?"

She shrugged her shoulders. "I don't know. Most people who knew him very well would have known."

"Are you aware of his allergy being mentioned in the media?"

"No. Yes. Maybe. I don't know. I didn't read every article written about Scott."

"Don't worry about it. I'll have my people research it. When we talked in the hotel, you admitted to having an affair with a security guard—Darren Warner. Is that affair still active?"

"Sorta." Savannah began to fidget. "I don't like talking about Darren."

Jake ignored her comment. "Why do you say sorta? Did one of you cool off?"

"No. I don't know." She began shredding a tissue she took from her pocket.

"You were seeing someone else, weren't you?"

Her eyes flashed. "Why do you say that?"

"Savannah. I searched your room—your cell." Jake maintained eye contact and a steady tone. "I found your little sexting stash. I suspect I'll find more on your computer."

Savannah's face turned red. "Did Scarlett—"

"No. She only saw some of your special wardrobe. Who is the other guy?"

"Please don't make me tell you that."

He dropped his pen and stood. "I'm not judging you. But I need to determine whether any of your lovers could have wanted to eliminate an obstacle. Who belongs to the explicit photos? Warner—the mystery man?"

Tears began flowing down her cheeks. "I can't tell you. Please don't make me. It was stupid. I can't believe I did it."

Before Jake could respond to Savannah, Kai rose from his position, struck his on-alert stance, and then started for the front door. Jake dropped his pen, his right hand instantly going to his weapon as the dog emitted a guttural growl. Jake signaled Savannah to stay put and with his left hand sent Sonny a 911 text from his Apple watch.

"Couldn't it be Brenda?" Savannah asked, panic dilating her pupils.

Jake shook his head. "Too soon."

When Sonny entered from the hall off the kitchen end of the room, gun drawn, Jake gave the bodyguard a signal and followed the canine. Savannah sat frozen, staring at the trio. Fear grew in her eyes, and the color drained from her face.

When Kai reached the entry, he started to bark, but Jake hushed him in German. *"Ruhig."* With a hand signal, he beckoned the animal to his side. Standing askew of glass sidelights bordering the door, he looked out and burst into laughter as he holstered the Glock. Sonny relaxed, following suit with a pinched frown of bewilderment.

"Relax, crew. It's only Yogi looking for honey." Addressing Sonny, he said, "You'd better alert Brenda to be on the lookout for fur-covered trespassers when she returns." He reached down and patted Kai. *"Lass es*, boy. You're tough but it wouldn't be smart to take on a four-hundred-pound opponent."

Savannah looked totally confused. "What was it?"

"A bear," Jake said with another chuckle.

"Shouldn't you shoot it?"

The two men exchanged glances before Jake answered. "No. He won't bother us if we don't bother him. Unlikely it's a dangerous mama bear because it's not cub season. But keep Kai inside. His protective instincts could get him killed."

"I'm not going near the door," Savannah said.

The ruckus had distracted her to the point of drying her tears. When Jake returned to the table and picked up his pen, she bristled.

"Where were we?" he said as if he had forgotten.

"I don't remember."

With a sardonic smile, Jake locked her in eye contact. *Like hell you don't.* "I don't have time to fight you this morning, but we will revisit this subject." *Don't think I won't get the truth.* "Do you have a list of witnesses for me?"

"It's upstairs." She made no move.

"Are you going to get it for me, or am I supposed to go up and dig it out?"

"I'll get it." She shot him a dirty look and bounded up the stairs with more energy than displayed all morning.

Returning, Savannah slapped several sheets of paper down on the table. "That's all I could think of."

"Am I to assume there will be more forthcoming?"

"Assume whatever you like. If I think of any others, I'll write them down."

Jake skimmed the list while Savannah watched. "Where is Darren Warner's contact info?"

"It isn't on there."

He glared at her. "Mind telling me why? I asked you to provide info for all friends and acquaintances, including lovers."

"I don't want you contacting him." She looked to the side.

"That's not an option."

She snapped her face around, giving him a sharp glare. "It's my personal life."

Jake's patience stretched the envelope as he fought the impulse to terminate the interview, possibly the case. "If you want to fire me, say the word. Otherwise, get yourself in gear and cooperate."

Savannah swallowed hard. "You're getting paid to help me. Why do you bully me like this?"

"I am doing *exactly* what I'm being paid to do. If you don't like my methods, I'll boot up a computer, and you can find someone else. I won't fight for you and *with you* simultaneously."

"I want to talk to Scarlett."

He shook his head. "She's not a part of this." He started to put his pen away in a gesture suggesting he was stopping the interview.

Savannah took a deep breath, squeezed her eyes shut for a moment, and then raised her hand. "Okay, okay." Her chin quivered, but her tone was defiant. "I didn't have an affair with Darren Warner."

Jake put pen back to paper with a skeptical expression on his face.

"I lied."

"Why should I believe you?"

"It's the truth. I can't tell you anything more. I can't."

He took a few seconds to contemplate his next move. "I'll accept that for now. An honest denial is better than a lie. Keep that in mind." He made a note at the top of her list, underling it with a flourish. "I see no names for your husband's paramours. Why is that?"

"I'm not withholding anything. I don't know her name—their names. I just know there have been illicit affairs. I didn't want to know who they were."

"Afraid you might have to admit they existed?"

She didn't respond.

"Since I have a lot of ground to cover, I'm going to give the extracurricular activities a rest for now. But I will come back to them. I know I asked you before, but I'm going to ask you again, were there any peanuts or peanut products in your house?"

"No."

"This is not something you can be squirrely about, Savannah. The investigators will obtain a search warrant for your house at some point soon. If you're lying, they'll find the evidence."

"Our chef did most of the grocery ordering. He knew not to use peanuts in our food, but I didn't check his grocery orders."

"I'll check with him." Jake glanced through his notes for several seconds. "Before I forget, in the email, Phil said to tell you a committee from the Senate will make all the funeral arrangements pursuant to your choice of time and place. The medical examiner is ready to release Senator Kingsley's remains. Should you choose cremation, you'll need to file for a clearance in DC, regardless of where it will be performed."

"No cremation. I told you I want the service in Atlanta, but it needs to be after my parents come back from the cruise on Tuesday."

"Have they been told?"

Savannah nodded. "My other sister got in touch with them. They wanted to make emergency arrangements to come home, but Grace convinced them to wait since it would only be a day or so difference. Thursday would probably be a good day for the funeral."

"Noted. Have you chosen a burial site?"

"Westview Cemetery in Atlanta. Asa Candler is buried there."

"Am I supposed to know who that is?"

"The founder of Coca-Cola."

"Ah. Guess I missed that one on *Jeopardy*. I'll forward your instructions to DC."

"Are we done?"

"One more question before we leave. Where does the money come from?"

She flinched. "What are you talking about?"

Jake gave her an intense stare. "Cut the BS. Haven't you caught on? I don't buy your lack of candor."

"Mr. Shepherd, I honestly don't know what money you mean."

He looked down at his pad, shaking his head. "It's getting tiresome, Mrs. Kingsley—Savannah." He looked her in the eye. "You live in a DC house that rocks multiple seven figures with high-end furnishings, drive luxury wheels, maintain what I suspect is a nice home in Atlanta, and from what I see, enjoy all the amenities of wealth. No way an annual salary under two hundred thousand can cover that." He dropped his pen in disgust. "Explain."

"I don't know what you want to know. Scott made the money and paid the bills. I never had anything to do with family finances. He gave me an allowance—extra when I asked."

"Is there a mortgage on the DC house?"

"It's not ours."

Jake cocked his head with a beady look on his face, picked up his pen, and made a note. "Now, that's interesting. Whose is it?"

Savannah took a deep breath, causing her shoulders to rise and then relax. "I don't know. Scott said a wealthy supporter owned it but wasn't using it. He let us live there with an option to buy."

"An open-ended option?"

"I don't know what that means. Can't you check who owns it?"

"I can and will, but I suspect it is going to be dicey. If it's what I think it is, a great deal of care has been taken to muddle the paper trail. Did it ever occur to you your husband might have been playing fast and loose with financials?"

"No. He was a successful lawyer and had lots of support when he ran for office. And, he inherited some money from an uncle."

"I bet he did. Did the two of you attend the uncle's funeral?"

"No. It was out of the country."

Bet it was.

Jake's phone pinged. "Brenda's back. Probably a good time to take a break." He stood and headed for the front door. The GMC Yukon pulled up as Jake started out. Sonny came from around the house, having exited through the laundry room, and the two men unloaded the groceries.

As the trio entered the house, Scarlett came down. "You guys finished with the interview?"

"For now."

"Fury called and wanted to know if we needed anything. When I mentioned we were coming to Atlanta today, she invited us to stay with them. I told her I would check with you. I can stay in my condo, but you could stay with the MacGregors."

"That's a good plan. We'll both stay there."

Scarlett looked toward Sonny and Brenda. "Isn't he paranoid? Do you guys think I need security?"

They both nodded. "Trust his instincts," Brenda said.

"Better safe than sorry," Sonny added.

CHAPTER ELEVEN

"What's your plan?" Scarlett asked as Jake drove down the mountain, headed toward Atlanta, having left Kai behind.

"Today, I plan to interview the children and the nanny—maybe your sister. That'll take most of the day. Tomorrow, I'm going to Kingsley's law firm. See what his partners and staff have to say. Depending on how long it takes, I'll consider visiting the senator's parents. I'm okay with you staying at the MacGregor house tomorrow."

Scarlett adjusted the air conditioning vent. "I'd like to go with you, but I'd also like to check in at my office and be sure my assistant has been able to get my pending cases covered."

"Not sure the subjects will be candid with the sister-in-law listening in."

"Don't tell them. I don't look that much like Savannah, and I don't know any of them. They do corporate work, insurance defense, and estate planning, I think. They certainly don't show up in family court. Couldn't we just pretend I'm your partner?"

He glanced around at her with a smirky smile. "Partner, Harvard?"

"Why not?"

"I'll think on it." He pulled out on the road, checking his GPS for directions.

The SUV remained silent for several miles before Scarlett spoke, "Not doing karaoke today?"

"Not today. Thinking through my strategy."

"My cue to shut up?"

"If that's possible for a Harvard lawyer."

"Very funny. I'll just read a book on my phone."

"Tell you what, Harvard. I'll introduce you as my assistant if you want the job, but I'm doing the law firm alone."

"I like partner better."

"Assistant's the best deal on the table."

"If I'm reading between the lines, that means I take orders."

His smile grew broader. "Can you handle it?"

"Of course I can, but don't expect to hear a 'Yes, sir.'"

"Damn. Thought I could corral that smart-ass spirit of yours."

"Good try, Sherlock."

He reached over and patted her knee. Scarlett's gaze followed his hand as it returned to the wheel. "First assignment: dig out a pad and pen. I may want to dictate a thought or two as we travel."

She leaned forward and retrieved the needed items from her purse. "Is bossing women around in your chauvinist's manual?"

He shook his head without taking his eyes off the road. "I'm not a chauvinist. I'm equally obnoxious—bullying men and women without discrimination when I'm running an investigation." Turning toward Scarlett, he raised his eyebrows. "That's why partner works only with the dog."

"Didn't you have to partner with a mere mortal in the FBI?"

"Someone was always the lead."

By the time they reached the entrance to US-23, Jake had given Scarlett multiple notes. "Looks like you needed me, Shepherd."

"I have a recorder, but having them written will be easier. Let's grab lunch, gas up, and then travel nonstop to Atlanta. Once we get there, I want to interview the nanny first, which might be complicated. I think she'll hold back if too many are present. Is your sister's home large enough that I can talk to the witness in private?"

"It is. Her husband has a home office you can use."

"Get either Fury or Gray on the phone. I want a security guard I can trust to meet us at your sister's. Gray's father-in-law can make that happen."

By the time Jake turned onto the long driveway leading to the Burton home, it was after two p.m.

"Nice neighborhood," he said as Scarlett put her phone away after alerting Grace to their arrival.

"It is. If we were *Little Women,* Grace would be Meg—the responsible, accommodating one."

"Sorry, Harvard. I never read *Little Women.*"

"Of course you didn't. What did you read when you were a kid? Sherlock Holmes?"

"One or two stories, but it was a little too literary. My tastes ran more along the lines of Wyatt Earp, Bat Masterson, Doc Holliday, Louis L'Amour books."

"Fan of the Old West I see."

"What would you expect of an Oklahoma boy?" He brought the vehicle to a stop close to the house—behind an SUV—and killed the engine.

Scarlett began collecting her purse and stowing her sunglasses. "Yeah. Makes sense."

He turned, lifted his Gatorz Magnums, and gave her his trademark smile.

Scarlett rolled her eyes. "Gunslingers were your role models?"

With a snap of his head, Jake said, "I like to think lawmen. Let's go meet the family and Consuela."

"Why do you do that?" Scarlett asked, exiting the vehicle.

"Do what?"

"Pretend you don't remember names. You know the nanny is Manuela. You don't forget anything, Shepherd."

"I don't? Really? I didn't know that," he said, slapping the side of an SUV parked in the drive when he passed and giving the driver a thumbs-up as Scarlett rang the doorbell.

"Your guy?"

"Yup."

She shook her head, stopping when Grace opened the door, an apron tied around her waist.

The sisters embraced before Scarlett could introduce Jake.

Grasping Scarlett's hand, Grace said, "Come in and make yourself at home. Can I get you something to eat or drink? How is Savannah?" As Grace fired off her questions, Rob Burton walked up behind his wife and then circled around her to embrace Scarlett.

"I'm glad you got back here okay," Rob said to Scarlett. "I know it's been hard on you."

"Not as hard as it's been on Savannah and the children, I'm sure." Scarlett looked around the area. "Where are the children?"

"They're out back," Grace said, pointing toward the opposite side of the room. "Colin is playing with my kids. Tori is reading. I'm worried about her, Scarlett. She won't talk much. Manuela is with them."

Jake stood by, observing the family dynamics with his portfolio in his left hand.

Noticing Jake, Rob extended a hand. "Rob Burton, here—"

"Oh, I'm sorry," Scarlett said. "Grace, Rob, this is Jake Shepherd. He works for Savannah's attorney, gathering evidence and ensuring the family's safety since no one knows what is going on."

"Is that your man outside in the vehicle?" Rob asked.

"It is. But he'll be heading back to DC. I'm picking up a local team."

Rob nodded, putting his hands on his wife's shoulders.

"As I said before"—Grace raised her hand for attention—"can I get you something to eat?"

"I think we're fine," Scarlett said. "We stopped for lunch, but I could use a water if it's not too much trouble."

"Of course. How about you, Mr. Shepherd?"

"Call me Jake. I'm fine." Before anyone could speak, he continued, "At the risk of being rude, I would like to get started with the nanny, if that's okay."

"Most certainly," Rob said. "That's what you're here for."

"Rob." Scarlett put her hand on her brother-in-law's arm. "Do you mind if Jake uses your office to meet privately with her?"

"Certainly. Follow me, Jake. Grace, can you call her in?"

CHAPTER TWELVE

"Should you go in there with them?" Grace said as the nanny entered her husband's office.

"No. Jake made it clear that he wanted to interview her one-on-one." Scarlett took a sip of her water. "For right now, I'll just get to know Tori and Colin."

Nodding, Grace motioned for Scarlett to follow her and said, "Don't you want to know what she says?"

"Of course, I'm curious, but at this point, I have to trust the experts. Gray MacGregor recommended the lawyer and Jake. You don't know Gray, but I can tell you, he is brilliant. I've had to swallow some of my apprehensions about Shepherd, but I truly believe he is better at what he does than he is at winning friends."

"He's very handsome." Grace tipped her chin, her eyebrows rising with a patronizing expression. "Surely you've noticed. Is he married?"

"Take off your matchmaker cap."

"I didn't say anything." Grace pulled back.

"You didn't have to. I know you and your Noah's ark mindset. You think everyone should be two-by-two, married, live in an ivy-covered cottage with a mortgage, have two-point-five children, two cars, and a dog."

Grace rolled her eyes as she opened a French door to her patio and allowed Scarlett to pass. "Make fun of me if you want to, but you're not getting any younger. You want to end up alone in your old age?"

"Alone isn't all bad. I'd rather be alone than in a miserable relationship—yours being the exception."

After calling the children over, Grace introduced the Kingsley siblings while the Burton children responded to their aunt with hugs.

After minimal chitchat, the younger children resumed their activity. Tori returned to a wooden loveseat suspended by chains from a large oak tree at the back corner of the yard. She immediately picked up an iPad and focused her attention on the screen. Grace and Scarlett took seats around a patio table.

Watching Savannah's daughter, Scarlett's face tensed. "Did Tori bring that tablet with her?"

"No. It's mine. I felt sorry for her not having her things, so I had her choose a few books on Amazon and downloaded them for her, plus some game apps."

Scarlett relaxed. "That's good. Has the nanny said anything you think might be important since she's been here?"

"Are you kidding? She has hardly spoken to anyone but the children and acts like a frightened rabbit. If I hadn't heard her talk to Tori, I would wonder if she speaks English."

Scarlett tipped her head toward the house. "Jake will probably traumatize her."

"Why do you say that?"

"He's a no-holds-barred personality—aggressive and impatient."

"That must have gone over well with Savannah."

"Are you kidding? He broke through her BS in less than ten minutes. Fortunately, he doesn't believe she had anything to do with what happened."

Her eyes squinting, Grace said, "You don't either, do you?"

Scarlett stared at her sister for nearly a minute. "No. No, I don't really think she is capable of that heinous an act, but she doesn't walk on water like Mom believes. Moving on. How are those children handling all this?"

"I'm not sure. Colin seems okay as you can see." She pointed to the slide where the children were taking turns. "My question is how are you and Savannah getting along?"

"Seeing her after so long has been bizarre."

"I can imagine, but the two of you have mended your fences, I take it."

"That's a good question." Scarlett nodded. "Probably. It's a bit weird."

"That will make the folks happy. Back to the kids, as I said, Colin's not showing stress. He may not completely understand. We don't talk about Savannah and Scott with him. I've just tried to show both of them that they are loved. He talks about a friend—a babysitter. I think he's a teenage neighbor. Colin wants to know if Kyle can come down to play video games with him."

"What about the daughter? You said she is quiet."

"Very. I'm almost afraid to talk to her. She talks to Manuela but not to us. Katie wants to interact with her, but Tori seems to stay in her shell."

"How old is Katie now?"

"She's just turned nine. I'm sure Tori, at eleven, considers her baby. Last night, I heard Tori crying. I went in to comfort her, but she immediately dried her eyes and tried to act like nothing was wrong. They might be happier, at least Tori might, at Mom and Dad's. They stayed over there a lot when Scott was campaigning, and Savannah traveled the state with him. Maybe the folks should move into Scott and Savannah's house until this is all over."

"You might be right, if Jake considers it safe."

"Is Savannah coming to Atlanta anytime soon?"

Scarlett shook her head. "I think Jake wants her to stay where she is. He's totally paranoid."

Grace's daughter emitted a yelp and both women turned. When the child continued playing, without sign of injury, Scarlett said, "Jake says until there is a better idea of who might have killed Scott, he has to consider everyone in danger."

"Where is Savannah?"

"I'm sorry." Scarlett took a sip of water. "It's better I don't say. Not that you would do anything to harm her, but Jake says the more people who know, the more likely someone will slip, and the wrong people will find out. I agree. All I can tell you is the house is nice, and she has heavy protection."

For the following fifty minutes, the sisters sat on the Burton patio, watching the boys and Katie Burton swing, slide, and run around the yard. They debated what might be ahead and how their parents would react. For the entire time, Savannah's daughter remained isolated with the tablet. Scarlett considered approaching Tori and inquiring what the child was doing on the device but refrained.

CHAPTER THIRTEEN

When Manuela Garcia walked into the office, Jake saw she was terrified. Hoping to mitigate her stress, he rolled Rob's desk chair out from behind the desk, positioning it in front of the nanny.

"Relax, Ms. Garcia. You have no reason to be nervous. I'm here to help find out what happened to Senator Kingsley."

"I don't know anything," she said with a heavy Spanish accent.

"Maybe not. But sometimes, a person knows more than they realize. You want to help Mrs. Kingsley, don't you?"

She nodded, looking down at her lap.

"Has anyone told you who I am?"

"You're like police."

"No, not police. *Privado, el investigador privado.*"

"*Privado, si?*"

"Yes, but the FBI, the police, will want to talk to you. What you tell me is confidential—*privado*. Understand? *Entiende usted?*"

She raised her chin, making direct eye contact with Jake. "*Si.* Yes."

"Okay, let's get started. If you don't understand something I say, please tell me, and I'll try to explain."

She nodded.

He opened his leather portfolio and extracted a pen from the center. "Where are you from, Manuela?"

"Colombia."

Jake made a note on his pad, paused for a second, and then underlined it. "What brought you to the states?"

"A big airplane."

Smart, Shepherd. "I mean, why did you come?"

Her eyes moved from Jake to her lap and back. "*Mi padre.* My father. He want my sister to come, and she not want to. So, he send us both."

Interesting. "Did your *padre* have a special reason for wanting your sister to come to America?"

She looked around the room, apparently not wanting to answer.

"Did you understand what I asked?"

"*Si.*"

When she didn't elaborate, Jake had to restrain his impatience. "Why did *Papá* want your sister to come?"

"She pretty. More pretty than me. He said the nice man wanted to help her have nicer life here in states. He give *Papá* money. We send money to *Papá*, so family have good house."

"Was the nice man, Senator Kingsley?"

"No."

Universal word. "Did Mr. Kingsley ever go to Colombia when you were there?"

She shook her head. "No."

"Do you see the nice man since you're here in the states?"

She took a deep breath. "*Si.* He come."

"To the Kingsley's house?"

She nodded. "But more to Maria's."

"Did Maria, your sister, and the nice man get married?"

"No."

Not surprised.

"She has many boyfriends. She went to school when we come to states."

"What kind of school?" Jake leaned forward, elbow on knee, chin in hand. "Cooking school? Business school?"

"No. School to learn how to make man happy."

Jake felt his pulse quicken but kept his stoic gaze on the nanny. *Trafficking!* "What is the nice man's name, Manuela?"

Her face registered immediate alarm. "I don't know. I say too much."

Jake weighed his options. Pushing her to answer sensitive questions could shut her down, he decided. *Better let it cool—maybe come back later.* "Let's go back to Senator and Mrs. Kingsley. Did anything bad ever happen in the Kingsley house that you would like to tell me about? Something that scared you?"

"No." She wriggled in place and broke eye contact.

"Was there ever anything that you don't want to tell me about?"

She seemed to freeze as her shoulders and jaw tightened.

"It's okay, Manuela. Senator Kingsley is dead, and Mrs. Kingsley wants you to help me figure it out."

She took another deep breath.

As he studied her face, Jake sensed she wanted to tell him something but needed a breather to collect her courage. "Do you want a drink? Maybe a soda? I could use one."

She turned her head away from him, cutting her eyes to the corner as if she wasn't sure what to say. "*Sí.* I would like Coke."

Jake took out his cell and texted Scarlett. Within a couple of minutes, a knock came at the door, and Grace entered with a tray of Coca-Colas, glasses with ice, and napkins.

"Scarlett said you prefer Pepsi, but this is Atlanta. Can I get you anything else?"

Jake smiled. "No. This will do fine." As Grace left, he handed Manuela a glass and a can and then popped a can open for himself.

"Where were we? Oh, yes. I was asking you about the Kingsley family. Describe Senator Kingsley for me. What was he like?"

"Nice."

An edge to her voice told Jake she wanted to say something different. He studied her face for a few seconds. "All the time, or just part of the time?"

Manuela looked toward the window, took a drink of the soda, and then said, "Part."

"Just part of the time? And the other times?"

She shrank back in her chair. "He could be mean—not to me."

Jake waited before asking the next question, wanting to make certain he didn't push the fragile woman too fast. "You stayed out of his way, right?"

She nodded.

"Who was he mean to, Manuela?"

She coughed, looked at him for a second, and said, "Mrs. Kingsley. . . ."

Jake waited, sure that she would say more. "And . . ."

"Maria, my sister."

"Describe *how* he was mean for me."

She shook her head. "No. I can't. I say too much."

Jake paused while she calmed down. "You haven't said too much. You need to tell me. What did he do to your sister? Was he one of her boyfriends?"

She remained silent.

"How was he mean?"

"I can't talk about. Don't make me."

"Then give me a hint. Did he yell at her?"

She shook her head.

"Did he hit her?"

She didn't answer.

"Did he make her do things she didn't want to do?"

The room was so still a flower bud could be heard opening.

"What did he make her do, Manuela?"

Her eyes grew glassy. "Things in the room where she sleep. Things they taught her, but she hated. I hurt for her."

"What would happen if she refused?"

Her eyes grew wide with panic. "They kill our family." Tears flooded down her face.

Kingsley was into something. But how deep? And who are the players? Jake leaned back, his head nodding. "It's okay. I've got it."

He gave her a few minutes to collect her emotions as he added notes to his pad. When she seemed to be in control, he said, "Manuela, do not tell anyone what you told me, other than the FBI if they ask you. Don't tell your sister. We don't want to chance it getting back to the *nice* man. Understand? *Entiende usted?*"

She took a swallow of her Coke and nodded.

Jake watched her for several seconds and then said, "Manuela, do you have a key to the apartment where Maria lives?"

She nodded.

"May I look at it?"

She frowned but reached into her purse and took out her key ring.

Jake immediately recognized the key she pointed out as the same type Scarlett found in the Kingsley house. He took out his phone and snapped several photos and then forwarded them to his locksmith for comparison. When done, he returned the keys to Manuela. "You should stay here for a while. If you do, do not contact Maria because we can't risk anyone discovering where the children are. Understand. *Si?*"

"*Si.*"

"I'll have someone check on her. Okay?"

"I'm scared."

"I know and will do what I can to help you and your sister. But I've got to know you fully understand how important it is that you speak to no one about this. *Entiende usted?*"

With her chin barely moving, she nodded and whispered, "*Entiendo.*"

Jake returned the nod. "Good. That's good. I'm going to stop now, but I will ask you a few more questions after I talk with the children."

As Jake opened the door for her to exit, the image of his daughter flashed across his mind. *What kind of bastard sells his child?*

When Manuela was out of the room, Jake returned to his seat and began making notes.

> Suspects: Nice Man? (Organized crime)   Maria Garcia? (Escape torture)
>
> Find out what the client knows about Garcia sisters.
>
> Touch base with the Bureau.
>
> Double down—

A soft knock came at the door, and it opened.

"Okay, if I come in?" Scarlett asked.

Jake slid his pen in his shirt pocket and closed his portfolio. "Sure. I was about to text you to bring the children."

Scarlett sat in the chair vacated by Manuela. "Did you get anything of interest from the nanny?"

"Possible lead. I think your sister should sit in when I talk with the children—mitigate their apprehension."

"I'll let her know." She paused, studying his face. "Are you going to tell me what you found out?"

"No."

Her eyes flashed. "Is there a problem trusting me?"

"Has nothing to do with it."

She cocked an eyebrow. "But you're not going to tell me."

"I'm not." He gave a quick twist of his head. "Sorry, Harvard. Right now, it's need to know only." His eyebrows shot up as his hazel eyes collided with hers. "Your turn to trust me."

"You don't make that easy, but what choice do I have?" She stood, hands on her hips. "Want the children now?"

He gave a thumbs-up and looked down at his watch. "It's almost half-past three. I estimate an hour with the children—another half hour or so with a nanny encore. How long will it take to drive to the MacGregor house?"

"It's about fifty miles. Considering light Sunday traffic, we should be able to drive it in about an hour. I'd like to swing by my condo and check on my cats, if you don't mind. My neighbor is taking care of them."

"Cats, huh? We can do that."

CHAPTER FOURTEEN

Colin, a handsome seven-year-old with his mother's blond hair, plus a sprinkle of freckles peppering his nose, led the small brigade entering the office. His blue eyes glistened with mischief and innocence. His sister, Tori, a serious eleven-year-old with chestnut hair and blue eyes, followed. She could have passed for Scarlett's daughter.

"Is your gun real?" Colin asked, his gaze glued to Jake's weapon.

"I'm afraid it is," Jake said, smiling at the child.

Trailing behind Grace and the children, Scarlett closed the door and moved to the corner of the room, wondering if Jake would dismiss her.

When he motioned for the children to take places on a leather loveseat and pulled his chair up to face them, Scarlett relaxed. Grace took a seat nearby.

"Hi, guys. I'm Jake, and I'd like to talk with the two of you for a few minutes. Are you enjoying the visit with your cousins?"

Tori nodded, but Colin responded with enthusiasm. "It's fun. Aunt Grace makes great cookies."

"Chocolate chip or peanut butter?" Jake asked.

Scarlett eyed Jake with the intensity of a cat stalking prey while Grace sat on the edge of her chair as if ready to come between man and child if things went sideways.

"Oatmeal."

"Boy, did I get that wrong. Guess I should turn in my detective license."

Colin laughed—pleased with himself. "Aunt Grace said you're a policeman. Why don't you have on a uniform?"

"I'm not a policeman. I'm a private investigator."

"What's a private investigator?"

"They solve problems for people. So, tell me, what have you been doing besides eating cookies?"

"Playing computer games!" Colin's exuberance overshadowed his quiet sister.

"How about you, Tori? Or do you prefer Victoria?"

She hesitated, looking toward Grace.

"It's okay, honey. Jake is trying to help your mom. You can talk to him."

The child turned her focus back to Jake. "Tori. Victoria is what Mom calls me when she's mad."

"Gotcha. When my mom called me Jacob, I knew I was in trouble."

A smile tried to escape but Tori curled her upper lip inward to suppress it.

"What have you been doing since you got here—was it yesterday?"

With a nonchalant expression, Tori said, "Watching TV and read—"

"Where is Mom?" Colin asked.

Jake smiled. "She's in a beautiful vacation house, enjoying a little relaxation."

"When can we see her?" Tori asked with the most animation she had released.

"Soon. She'll be coming to Atlanta this week."

As both children allowed their attention to switch between Jake and Grace, neither appeared aware of Scarlett's presence in the room.

"Can I see your gun?" Colin asked.

Now what are going to do with that, Shepherd? Scarlett thought, shifting her weight from one foot to the other as she leaned against the wall.

"How about I give you a rain check, Colin?" He tore a small piece of paper from his pad and scribbled a note across it. "Here. You can cash this in when you're a few years older."

Damn. Who is this guy? He's actually got a softer side.

"If you guys have the time, I'd like you to tell me about your life in Washington. Do you like it there?" He focused on Tori, managing to capture her in eye contact.

"It's okay. The house is big."

"I like it. I have a good friend." Colin fidgeted in place as if his energy would explode.

His sister's brow wrinkled. "Are you talking about Kyle?" Tori said, staring at her brother.

"Yes."

"He's not your friend. He's the babysitter."

"No, he's not. He's my friend. Mom said so. We play all the cool games on the computer, and he comes over when Mom's at home. Babysitters only come when your parents go somewhere."

"Tell me about Kyle," Jake said. "How old is he?"

"Old. He's in high school," said Tori. "I don't like him much."

"Why would that be, Tori?"

Scarlett stared at Jake. *Is that important, or is he just trying to act interested?* She wanted to say something but bit her tongue. Knowing Jake, as she had come to know him in two days, she knew he might kick her out of the room.

"Mom makes a big deal over anything he does for Colin."

"Does he come over a lot?" Jake asked.

Both children nodded. "He spends the night with us sometimes when Daddy's working," Colin said.

"Daddy died," Tori said, her face expressionless.

"Did you know that?" Colin asked.

Jake nodded. "I did know that, and I'm very sorry."

"Maybe Kyle will move into our house since we don't have a daddy," Colin said.

"Don't be dumb," Tori said, giving him a disgusted look. "He can't move into our house."

"Sure he can. His mom likes our mom. She would let him."

"What is Kyle's last name?" Jake asked.

"I don't know," Colin said.

"I do. It's McClellan—just like his mom. Her name is Regina McClellan. Mom calls her Reggie."

Jake made a note as Colin appeared to process his sister's comment.

"Do you know how Kyle became your babysitter?"

"Friends," Colin said.

"Friends?"

"His mom and our mom met at some women's club, or committee, or something," Tori said. "They play tennis together."

"And they live near us," Colin added.

"Makes sense. What's his father's name?" Jake asked. "Do either of you know?"

"I don't," Colin said.

Tori shrugged.

"Did you have many visitors come to your house in Washington?"

Both heads bobbed.

"Mostly people talking to Daddy," Colin said.

"Were they nice?"

Tori remained silent, allowing Colin to dominate the exchange.

"They didn't talk to us. We had to go upstairs. And sometimes, they went into Daddy's office."

"Do you know who they were?"

Colin shook his head.

Jake turned to Tori, inviting her contribution without speaking.

"Some were his staff. I don't know who the others were."

"Did any have unusual accents?"

Colin shook his head while Tori sat motionless.

"Tori? Did you ever notice anyone with an accent?"

She hesitated for several seconds. "Once. He was kinda of scary, but Daddy said for me to go to my room and watch TV."

Jake struck pen to paper with a flourish, underlining his last note.

After subtly quizzing the children about the relationship between the parents, Jake dismissed them.

"Thank you for your time, guys. I know your mom will be proud of you." He stood, and the children followed suit. "Give me five," Jake said to Colin, and the boy obliged, grinning from ear to ear. "Look me up when you're about twelve or thirteen, and I'll not only show you my gun, I'll take you out where you can shoot if your mom approves."

Colin appeared beside himself. "You would?"

"I would, but now I need to speak with Manuela again before your Aunt Scarlett and I head out."

As the family left, Scarlett paused in front of Jake. "What have you done with the real Jake Shepherd?"

He cocked an eyebrow.

"The one who chews people up and spits them out. I was concerned you might terrify them."

He chuckled. "Come on, Harvard. I'm a father. I don't traumatize children."

CHAPTER FIFTEEN

Waiting for Manuela to return to the office, Jake perused his notes, embellishing some and highlighting others. He underlined Kyle McKellen's name, put an asterisk beside Reggie, and double-underlined a notation referring to anonymous men with accents visiting the Kingsley home. *Out of the mouths of ba—*

A knock at the door interrupted Jake's thought. He considered calling out an invitation to enter but changed his mind and answered the door.

"Come in, Manuela. Take a seat and relax. I have just a couple of follow-up questions."

The timid woman gave him a wary look. "I say too much. I can't tell you anything else."

"I know you're nervous—a little frightened, right?"

She nodded, twisting the edge of her apron.

"I need you to believe me when I tell you I am going to use my resources to protect you." Jake's eyes locked with hers. He could see she wanted to look away, but something held her. "But in order to protect you, I need to know more. Do you understand?"

She didn't respond.

"I need you to tell me everything you remember about the nice man who brought you and Maria to the United States."

Silence filled the room. Her expression was that of a vulnerable victim coming face to face with her armed assailant in a dark alley.

Patience, Shepherd. Build confidence. "It's okay. I know you're afraid but trust me; I can protect you, Manuela."

She pointed to his holster.

He nodded. "I know what I'm doing. Can you believe that?"

Her gaze fixated on the Glock. "They will kill my family."

"I don't think so. They said that because they want you to be afraid. We have ways of dealing with them. But I need your help." Jake noted the nanny's fascination with his weapon.

"Would you shoot a person?"

Jake paused for several seconds. "Only if I had no choice."

Her eyes grew larger. "Have you?"

What is she thinking? Jake studied her face for several seconds, debating how to respond. "I carry a gun only to protect. Does my gun scare you?"

Continuing to stare at the weapon, she answered, her voice barely above a whisper, "Some." In a sudden shift of focus, she made eye contact with him, "Are you good?"

"With the gun?"

With a tip of her chin, she acknowledged the question.

"Very—better than good, and so are the people I have to protect you."

Manuela appeared relieved by his response.

"Now, what do you remember about the nice man? Did you ever hear anyone call him by name?" Jake flipped the page of his legal pad.

Manuela didn't answer.

She knows something.

"Did you ever see him in the United States?"

She flinched.

"You did, didn't you? Where, Manuela?"

She looked away.

"Manuela, I can't help you if you won't talk. Where did you see the man?"

She shook her head but in contradiction spoke, "My sister. Her *apartamento.*"

"Her apartment?"

She nodded.

"That's good. Thank you. How many times?"

"Not so much."

"Anywhere else?"

Her shoulders tightened, and she clasped her hands together—the knuckles losing color.

"Where else did you see him?"

She stared at Jake, her pupils nearly obliterating the color of her irises.

"Did he visit Senator Kingsley, Manuela?"

His question appeared to take her breath away as her chest heaved.

"He visited." Jake's head moved in a slight nod with one eyebrow arched, beckoning an answer. *You don't have to say it. The answer is written on your face.*

"Is the nice man Hispanic?"

She stared, devoid of expression, and then ever so slightly shook her head.

"American?"

Gaining a bit more confidence, she shook her head with more force.

"Italian?"

She frowned.

"Russian?"

Although she remained silent, Jake read her body language as her hands tightened, her knuckles whitened, and a stricken expression paralyzed her face.

Nailed it!

After identifying the general nationality of the anonymous sex-trafficking broker, Jake prodded Manuela further for a name and description. He managed to ascertain the man was middle age, with gray in his hair, several inches shorter than Jake, with pale, vicious eyes and a trim physique. The only name she provided was Boris—a man accompanying the recruiter who may have been a driver, bodyguard, or enforcer.

"I'm going to leave that subject and ask you about the McClellan family."

Manuela scrunched her face in an I-don't-know-what-you're-talking-about expression.

"Kyle? Mrs. Kingsley's friend, Mrs. McClellan?"

Recognition replaced confusion. "*Si*. Kyle. He takes care of children for Senora. She sends me home for break when Kyle comes."

"Is that when Senora and the senator are away?"

"No. Sometimes. She says Colin likes to have Kyle—he's good with Colin."

Jake made a note before continuing.

"That's good, Manuela. Moving on, I know I told you that whether you stay with the senora's family here in Georgia or return to Washington is your decision. However, the more thought I've given to the matter, the more I believe you should be with Colin and Tori until I can put things in place to protect you. I am equipped to keep you safe here."

"But my sister. She is there. I don't know these people."

Take your time, Shepherd—patience mode. She's fragile. "I appreciate that."

She looked down at her lap. Her hands were shaking.

"Look at me, Manuela. Look me in the eye."

Several seconds passed without her compliance.

"Why would I do anything to hurt you? Look at me."

Slowly her chin began to rise.

Jake said nothing but nodded ever so slightly. The sound of the children outside had ceased, leaving the office silent. Jake wanted to urge a response from Manuela as the day was slipping away and the trip to the MacGregors still lay ahead.

After several seconds of eye contact, Manuela spoke in a near whisper. "Can I think about it?"

Jake's usual style would have been to push—bully, but he sensed it would not work with the terrified woman. "You can. I'm going to assume for the time being you will stay here. You can let me know through Mrs. Burton if you change your mind. My man is returning to DC, but a new team of security will take over. They will be here for you and the children. *Comprendes?*"

"*Si.*"

After Manuela exited the office, Jake closed the door, secured the lock, took out his cell phone, and tapped a name.

When the contact answered, he said, "Jackie. Put Hal on the phone."

"Good afternoon, Jacob. And how are you? Why do you want Hal?"

"Can we dispense with the interrogation? It's business, okay?" He rolled his eyes.

"Your usual rude self, I see. Just a minute."

Jake could hear his former wife call out to her husband, "Hal. Jake's on the phone and wants to speak to you."

"By the way, before you give the phone to Hal," Jake said, "I'm not going to be able to take Sabrina this weekend."

"Damn it, Jake. Not again?"

"It can't be helped. I'm out of the area on a case. May be a slight chance I can get back by Sunday. Tell her I'll make it up."

"Did it ever occur to you, we might have—no, of course not. Your plans are always the most important. Here's Hal."

Jake could hear Hal Kirby asking, "What the hell does he want?" and could imagine Jackie shrugging.

"To what do I owe the pleasure, Shepherd?"

"Need you to look into something."

"Do you now? Since when does the Bureau serve at your bidding?"

"Come on, Kirby; cut the bullshit. You know I'm working the Kingsley murder, and I know you're running the investigation. Doubt it took your team more than two minutes to brief you."

"So, you're calling me on Sunday afternoon to discuss Kingsley?"

"I'm calling to give you a heads-up on something you need to look into."

"You've got to be kidding."

The fingers on Jake's free hand curled, but he harnessed his patience. "Hear me out. It's in our mutual interest."

"And what would that be? Your client confess, and you want to work a deal?"

"The wife didn't have anything to do with—" A knock interrupted him. "Hold on." Jake held out the phone, activated "mute" with his thumb, and then slid the device into his jeans pocket. Crossing to the office door, he opened it to face Scarlett. Before she could speak, he raised a palm and said, "Give me a few minutes." He closed the door without allowing her to respond.

Unmuting the device, he said, "Get a pen and paper. You'll need to make notes."

"How about a clue as to what this is about?"

"Think Brighton Beach."

"Brighton Beach? The Russians? What the hell do they have to do with Senator Kingsley?"

"That remains to be seen. For the moment, I need you to put eyes on a gal in the District and keep them on her. Her name is Maria Garcia. I'll text you the address. In the meantime, wake up your IT people and start running a check on her—known associates—the works. I repeat, lock down surveillance. If I'm right, it could be just a matter of time before she becomes dispensable to the wrong people."

"So, on an out-of-the-blue call from Jake Shepherd, I'm supposed to crank up a full-scale investigation and dispatch a detail to keep tabs on some woman because you say she's connected to Brighton Beach and maybe the dead senator? I'm sure the Director will think that's an efficient allocation of resources."

"Be as sarcastic as you like, but do you want to eat crow when you disregard me, and it goes south—especially when it comes out you had notice from a reputable source?"

"Reputable? Listen, Shepherd, I know you were a hotshot when you carried a badge, but that doesn't mean you're on an ask-and-ye-shall-receive basis for life."

"Forget our personal issues for a second, Kirby. Roll the dice. You'll end up thanking me."

"Just so we're clear, the IOU card you hold has an expiration date, Shepherd. But said personal issues aside, it might help if you could give me a little more."

"You need to trust me on this one. I trust you with my daughter. Are your people going to attend the funeral, or are you going to leave it in the hands of the Atlanta field office?"

"That's to be determined. We just got word final services will be in Georgia. Is that where you are?"

"Maybe."

"So, the widow is already there."

"Actually, she's not. However, she is safe. You'll see her at the funeral. Can I trust you to follow through on my request?"

After a moment of silence, Hal Kirby replied, "You'd better have something. If this is a blind alley, your name goes on my shit list."

"I'm pretty sure it's been there. Tell Sabrina I love her and will see her as soon as I can." Jake hung up without waiting for a response.

CHAPTER SIXTEEN

When the office door practically slammed in her face, Scarlett had fought a kneejerk reaction, but stifled it and walked away. *What was he doing? Why the secrecy?* The closer she came to the kitchen, an aroma of onions sautéing with bacon permeated the air. *Bet she bakes from scratch and cans her vegetables.*

"So, has Mr. Shepherd completed his interview?" Grace said as Scarlett slid onto a barstool at the counter.

"I think so. He's not generous with information."

As she emptied a can of tomatoes into the pan of bacon and onions, Grace appeared to miss the annoyance in Scarlett's tone. "Although he's not overly friendly, he seems to know what he's doing—a take-charge kinda guy."

"You can say that again. That smells phenomenal—Mom's perlo recipe?"

Grace nodded. "Why don't the two of you stay for dinner?"

"The MacGregors are expecting us to eat with them. But thanks for the offer."

"Savannah hasn't called the children." Grace paused stirring the food. "My heart is breaking for them."

"Jake won't let her. He's afraid all of our lines are vulnerable to tracking."

"Oh, my god. This is turning into a spy—"

"Sorry to interrupt, ladies, but Scarlett and I better be going." Jake crossed the family room and laid a cell phone on the counter dividing the rooms. "Mrs. Kingsley can call this number. Do not call her from your mobile or landline."

"Is that yours?" Scarlett asked.

"A disposable. I'll pick up another on the way." He turned toward Grace. "Manuela will stay with you for the time being. Let one of us know if she gets restless. I want her here." He shifted his focus to Scarlett. "The relief security just pulled up. While I brief him, you can wind up your visit with the family. Meet you at the truck."

A look of urgency swept across Grace's face. "What about Scarlett? Does she need security?"

Jake grinned. "She's got the best."

"Am I to assume you are my security?" Scarlett said as she buckled her seatbelt.

With a flick of his head, Jake said, "That's a fair assumption."

"If you think I'm in jeopardy, I'll pick up my gun when we stop at the condo."

"You can pick it up, but not a good idea to rely on it."

"Not a good idea? You believe I need protection, but you don't think my having a weapon is a good idea? That math doesn't work. I am completely competent with firearms."

"So you've told me. I'll give you a chance to prove it after I meet with the senator's law partners tomorrow. But knowing how to use a gun is only the first step, Harvard. You've also got to know when and who to shoot. I doubt your shooting range, gun club, or dad gave you that training."

That's not rocket science. You shoot the bad guy. Although she wanted to debate the issue, she adjusted her position and then brushed a stray lock of hair off her forehead without responding.

"You want to direct me to your place?" he asked.

"You don't want to plug the address into your GPS?"

"It's disabled. Likewise, my regular cell and my watch for today."

"Oh. You're thinking if someone wants to know where you are, GPS could give it away."

"You got it. I'll pick up another disposable if there's a store open on our route."

When they reached Scarlett's condo, Jake followed her in. As two Persians, one black and one white, took turns rubbing up against her legs, he said, "Pack up your cats. We'll take them with us."

As she leaned over to pet Casper, the white one, she glanced toward Jake. "Pack them up?"

"I think it best they don't stay here. We can take them to Gray's if you don't have someone to keep them."

She stood erect, the white cat in her arms. "What's going on, Jake? What are you not telling me?"

"I'm telling you under the present circumstances, I would not leave a pet alone in the apartment."

"That's not good enough."

"It is for now."

"What did you find out from the nanny that upped the stakes?" she said, glaring at him.

"Mind if I find something to drink in your kitchen?"

"You're not going to tell me, are you?"

He shook his head. "Not until I know more."

After putting the cat on a nearby chair, she faced Jake with fire in her eyes. "That's not fair. If there's a threat, I deserve to know."

Slowly massaging the back of his neck, he twisted his head around as though his neck was stiff and then looked her in the eye. "I'll tell you this much. If what I suspect is true, your brother-in-law played with heavy hitters. At this point, it's reasonable to assume anyone close to him could be in jeopardy."

"But I wasn't close to Scott."

"No. But the people in question don't know that. Without elaborating, you need to believe me when I say this is a criminal element capable of taking out everyone to be sure their tracks are covered. Get the cats ready and anything that can't be replaced."

"I can't barge into the MacGregors' with two cats and expect them to—"

"Do you have an alternative?"

Scarlett thought for several seconds. "I guess I don't."

By the time Jake and Scarlett stopped for Jake to buy a new phone and then reached the MacGregor home, it was seven forty-five but still light on the pleasant spring evening.

"Quite a place," Jake said as he drove up the drive of the massive two-story home after being admitted through the electronic security gate.

"It's been in the MacGregor family for over a hundred years. Wait until you see the inside. There's marble everywhere. His great-grandfather owned one of the largest quarries in the country, along with most of the town."

"Phil always said Gray could buy the city of New York with enough money left over to buy DC. So, MacGregor's family turned marble into gold."

"That was where it started, but from what I understand, Gray took it to a whole new level with his investment acumen."

As Jake brought the Lexus to a stop, Fury and Gray MacGregor appeared at the front door.

"I'm *so* glad you guys are here," Fury said, rushing down the stairs to embrace Scarlett as she exited the vehicle. "I'm so sorry for your loss."

Gray followed and grasped Jake's hand with a firm shake. "Long time, buddy. Good to see you."

"Likewise. Thanks for taking in a couple of fugitives." Jake swept an arm around toward the building, and said, "I thought your mountain house was impressive, but this one—what can I say?"

"Don't let it fool you. It's just a stack of stones. Come on in. You must be starved, and you've never met Fury." He turned toward the women. "Honey, this is Jake Shepherd."

"Oh, my gosh. Gray has told me so much about you." She extended her hand.

After Scarlett, Jake, and the cats settled into guest rooms and had an opportunity to freshen up, the pair joined their hosts for dinner where light conversation prevailed. When the group finished eating, they adjourned to a cozy sitting room for coffee.

"By your asking for a security detail, I take it the situation is dicey," Gray said as they took their seats.

"It could be." To adjust the holster at his waist, Jake set his cup on the coffee table situated between his leather chair and the matching sofa where Scarlett and Fury sat.

Fury's gaze followed his gesture, which Jake noticed.

"Does my being armed disturb you, Fury?"

Her face relaxed. "No. Not at all. Gray told you I grew up with a cop. Dad retired as a detective with the Atlanta PD. I'd just forgotten." She smiled. "Do you have any idea what happened to Scott Kingsley?"

Scarlett eyed Jake, wondering if he would give up any clues.

"Too soon to speculate."

Good dodge, Shepherd.

"When Scarlett called a few days ago, she seemed afraid her sister might be suspected of foul play. Gray said you were an FBI agent, right?" Fury asked.

"A while back." Jake paused for a sip of the beverage and then returned his focus to Fury. "I understand you're an author."

Before she could answer, Gray asked, "Have you talked to any of your old friends in the FBI about the senator's death?"

Swallowing several more gulps of his coffee, Jake took his time responding, which seized Scarlett's attention.

Is there something else I don't know? She held her breath, waiting for him to answer.

"Briefly. But it's getting late. If you folks don't mind, I'll excuse myself."

Damn you, Shepherd. What are you holding back?

"Of course we don't mind," Fury said. "We're rude to keep the two of you up after what you've been through the past few days. Maybe we can visit more tomorrow night. You're staying until the funeral, right?"

"If it's not too much trouble, we are," Jake said.

"It's absolutely no trouble. And Scarlett, we'd be happy to keep your cats for as long as you need a safe place for them. You know what a cat lover I am."

"That's an understatement," Gray said as he stood. "She's even won me over—to the chagrin of our dogs."

The others rose as well. After again thanking the MacGregors and exchanging social niceties, Jake escorted Scarlett upstairs toward their respective rooms.

"I would hate to have you on the stand for cross-examination, Shepherd. You have dodging questions down to a science."

"Is that a fact?" He reached for the doorknob to let her into her room.

"And that's all you're going to say?"

"I guess it is."

CHAPTER SEVENTEEN

On Monday morning, after working out in the MacGregor gym, Jake and Gray arrived in the breakfast room where Scarlett sat sipping tea. Gray still wore sweats, but Jake had showered, changed to street clothes, and carried his gym bag. Sunlight streamed through a large bay window overlooking the terraced backyard.

Both men headed for the Keurig coffee maker on the sideboard as Scarlett said, "Fury is helping the boys dress for preschool. She said for you to start breakfast without her."

"Do you know what time you can see Kingsley's former law partners?" Gray asked Jake.

"Not yet. I plan to crash the gate. Since it's a corporate firm, it's unlikely anyone will be in court."

"Wouldn't it be better to call for an appointment?" Gray asked.

"Waste of time. I'd be stonewalled. This is when a badge would come in handy."

"Am I going with you?" Scarlett asked.

Jake stood directly across from her. "No."

She started to protest, but he held up his free hand. "Before you go off on me, think about how difficult it will be to pry information out of lawyers. Your presence would add another reason for them to balk." He tipped his head down and raised his eyebrows.

"Why would that surprise me? If you won't let me go with you, I'll go into my office and work on clearing my calendar."

"Another bad idea. Hang out here." Jake turned to Gray. "You've got pretty tight security, don't you?"

"Unfortunately, it's necessary these days. The house has an electronic alarm, surveillance cameras, and one man on duty twenty-four hours a day. If you want more, Fury's dad, Mike O'Quinn, is sitting by the phone, waiting for an invitation to strap on a gun and flex his cop muscles again."

"I couldn't impose on him," Scarlett said.

Gray filled a plate from the chafing dishes on the sideboard. "You'd be doing both him and my mother a favor. Retirement drives Mike crazy, which spills over on her."

"Your mother?" Jake said.

"Scarlett didn't tell you?" Gray said, taking a seat at the table. "Mom and Fury's dad got married a year ago."

Jake smiled. "Interesting relationship. Father-in-law is your step-father." He put his coffee cup on the table. "I'm going to grab a couple of biscuits and sausage and take them with me if you don't mind."

"I'll get you something to put them in," Gray said, standing.

Scarlett checked the time on her phone as Gray left the room and then said to Jake, "What's the hurry? It's not even seven thirty. I doubt you'll find law partners in the office this early."

"I've got another stop to make." Leaning down to where he left his small duffle, he opened it, took out his gun, and said to Scarlett, "Do you mind dropping the bag in my room when you go upstairs?"

"No problem." When she didn't probe into his mystery, he gave her a sly glance. "Not asking where I plan to stop?"

"Why should I? You won't tell me."

He laughed. "Trying to keep you off balance, Harvard. I'm stopping by the Atlanta Field Office of the Bureau."

As he reentered the room, Gray apparently overheard Jake and asked, "Can you just drop by, unannounced?"

"Good question. Civilians can't walk in without advanced application and approval, but I still have contacts who will vouch for me." Jake took the paper goods offered and began putting his breakfast together as Gray took a seat at the table. "My team came here on a hostage incident back in the day. Got to know Dan Cameron. Thought I'd check in and see what role they plan to play at the funeral. Also, drill down on any unclassified info in their files on the senator. By the way, I need to leave my weapon here. I'm hoping you own a safe. I'm not comfortable leaving it unsecured with children in the house."

"Got you covered."

After closing the paper bag, Jake said to Scarlett, "I'll be back for you by two o'clock. Make an appointment at your favorite firing range for three, and I'll let you show me what you've got. We'll work in a visit to your office tomorrow."

As Scarlett watched Jake exit, Gray asked, "Aren't you having breakfast?"

"I'll wait for Fury, but you go ahead before yours gets cold." She took a sip of her tea as he began eating.

After several bites, he said, "How are you holding up under all the stress?"

"I think I'm fine. It's so surreal, I often remind myself of where I am. At the risk of prying, what can you tell me about Jake?"

A wide grin broke out on Gray's face. "Haven't figured him out, have you?"

"Hell, no. Every time I think I know what he's about, he does something to torpedo my theory."

"That's Jake. The only thing sharper than his brain is his intuition. He is damn good at what he does—better than good—and he knows it. While he may abuse social protocol, there's no one I would rather trust with my life. You've probably figured out that he has no patience with dishonesty, game-players, or phonies and no problem calling them out. Jake will never win a medal for diplomacy, but if I were in trouble, I'd want him on my side. "

"If he's so smart, why isn't he practicing law?"

"He doesn't want to. Phil would put him to work in an instant, but from your short exposure, can you imagine him stuck in business attire, behind a desk, or cajoling needy clients? Jake has the bedside manner of Simon Cowell and Gregory House combined."

With a nod, Scarlett put her mug down. "Good point."

"Jake's a born crime fighter. The cowboy in him thrives on the risk-taking; the genius in him feeds on the puzzle-solving."

"And he takes no nonsense from my sister."

"Nor from anyone else, I bet."

After draining his coffee cup, Gray stood, took a business card out of his wallet, wrote a number on the back, and then handed it to Scarlett before picking up Jake's handgun. "This is the combination to the safe in my study. Fury can open it for Jake, but in case she's not around when he needs it, this will get him in."

CHAPTER EIGHTEEN

After buckling his seat belt, but before cranking the Lexus, Jake made a call.

"What the—? How did you get my direct line, Shepherd?"

"I worked for you, or have you forgotten?"

"That would be impossible. I'll make a note to change the number."

"Did you follow up on what I asked?" Jake could hear Hal Kirby heave a sigh of disgust through the phone.

"I had a team at the building an hour after our conversation. Am I going to be forced to put up with constant harassment from you?"

"Maybe. Anything to report?"

"Nada. We managed to install our camera in the hall outside her unit. No sign of the woman. No record of car ownership or even a driver's license."

"I assume you pulled a photo from ICE?"

"I'm good at the job, Shepherd."

"No comment. I need you to do something else, Kirby."

"Try writing a letter to Santa Claus. I don't work for you."

"Very funny. I need you to call Atlanta. I'm going to run by there this morning and don't want a problem clearing the gate."

"Damn it, Shepherd. I'm not the only one you know in the Bureau. Why don't you call someone who likes you?"

"Because you're the highest-ranking name on my debtor list."

"Yeah? Well, for the record, I didn't break up your marriage. It crumbled long before I came along."

"As you've said. Make the call, Kirby; and keep me posted on the Garcia woman."

Jake didn't wait for an answer. He clicked off and smiled down at the phone, aware no matter how much he growled, Hal Kirby would follow through. After scanning emails and text messages on the device, Jake hit "Office" on his favorites list.

"Liz. Need you to do some digging. Probably will be time consuming."

"Does that mean you want me to pull off of the records you collected from the Kingsley computers?"

"For now. Has any new work come in?"

"Only a couple of background checks from the big bank HR. I can call Pete and hand them off if you think I should."

"Yeah. Do that. And if Lila has a case come up, see if Pete can do the preliminary. Got a pen?"

"I do. Fire away."

"I want you to search all our newspaper databases for images of Scott Kingsley. I'm sure there's going to be a large volume. What I'm looking for are photos of Kingsley with a Russian male, age forty or over. Also, and this is a tedious assignment, check through articles that mention the senator and any male Russians."

"How far back do you want me to go?"

"To the beginning of his law career. You can find the date on the membership roster of the Georgia Bar web site."

"My god, Jake—that could take the rest of my life."

"Use key words to narrow the search. The name 'Boris' should get priority, but it could be a pseudo. Also, pull his campaign contributor list and probe it for Russian names or companies with Russian affiliation."

"Do I get overtime?"

Jake chuckled. "You bet. Do what you can, and if you need help, I'll work on it. Not to overwhelm you, but I expect to be forwarding more files later. Leave those until I tell you different. I may put the client's sister on them here in Atlanta. She's anxious to be involved, but I haven't briefed her yet."

"You'll allow a civilian to work the case? What have you been drinking?"

"She's a Harvard lawyer and from what I'm seeing, pretty savvy. Needs a little grooming but I can handle it."

"If you're talking about the one I met, she's also a very attractive woman."

"Really? I hadn't noticed."

"Liar."

Jake laughed. "Buzz me if you find something."

Forty-five minutes later, Jake walked into the private office of Assistant Special Agent in Charge, Dan Cameron. "Shepherd, nice to see you. Sorry to learn you left the Bureau—our loss." Cameron walked around his desk and greeted Jake with a hearty handshake.

"What can I say? Congratulations on your position. You've moved up the chain since my last visit."

"Just a title. What brings you here today?"

"Since my exit from the Bureau, I do private investigations. Currently, I'm working for Senator Kingsley's widow. But I expect you've been briefed, considering I cleared this visit through DC."

"I'm not sure how I can be of any help, Jake. The Kingsley case falls under their division."

"True, but with the funeral scheduled for here in Atlanta, I thought I should check in to see when and how my security team will fit into the official plan. Plus, I need a favor. I don't have time to go through the official process for request of documents under the FOIA and hope you can put me on the fast track for obtaining open files the Bureau has on the senator and anyone close to him."

"Can do, but why didn't you ask DC to pull them for you? You obviously have connections there."

"Again, time, plus a few other reasons. I needed to get the widow out of the District and into safe seclusion."

Cameron appeared to think about it for a couple of seconds and then said, "Have a seat." He pointed to a chair beside his desk. "And bring me up to speed. Are your people covering Mrs. Kingsley?"

Jake sat as Cameron resumed his place behind the desk. "They are. I'll be candid, Dan. My gut is telling me Mrs. Kingsley could be in jeopardy. Until the cause of the senator's death is locked down, she needs protection and maybe other family members do as well. Did you know the senator?"

"Had I met him? Yes. Did I know him? Not really. Do you have a list ready of the files you want?"

Jake reached into his portfolio and withdrew a sheet of paper. "This is what I want to start. How long will it take?"

Cameron glanced over the list. "We should be able to put them together by this afternoon. Do you want to pick up hard copies or have us send them electronically?"

"Electronic will work." Jake took a card out of his wallet and laid it on the desk. "My email address is on the back."

As Cameron slipped the card into his desk drawer, he said, "To address the funeral security, the Capitol Police are charged with protecting congressmen and their families, but both our office and the Atlanta PD will be on site. I'm sure they will have it covered, but Mrs. Kingsley is certainly entitled to private bodyguards as well. I expect our DC office will send their team of investigators. Whether official or unofficial, I will attend."

Jake stood, gave Cameron's desk a slap, and said, "Appreciate your cooperation. Always a pleasure."

Within thirty minutes of leaving the FBI building, Jake arrived at the downtown high-rise location of Scott Kingsley's former law firm. As expected, the receptionist attempted to brush him off, stating the partners did not engage in meetings without an appointment.

"Tell you what"—Jake glanced down at the nameplate on the counter—"Ms. Armbruster, ring up a partner and tell him this is about the murder of Senator Scott Kingsley. I'm an investigator out of Washington, representing Mrs. Kingsley." He laid his card on the counter in front of her. "If this firm prefers, I'll take my questions to the press." The card identified Jake as both a private investigator and as an attorney.

The stench of old money permeated his nostrils as he glanced around the richly appointed waiting room. *This is not a firm that wants to show up in a six o'clock sound bite.*

"I'll take a seat over there." He pointed to a leather couch, flanked by matching, wingback chairs. "I'm in no hurry."

Jake hardly had time to open a magazine before a quintessential lawyer type entered the room. The forty-something attorney wore the classic, button-down oxford shirt with a conservative, blue-striped tie. The glimmers of silver in his immaculately groomed hair added to his silk-stocking image. His rolled-up shirtsleeves, revealing a gold Rolex, lent a casual touch to his appearance. The lawyer erroneously appeared superior to Jake, who sported a three-day stubble beard, medium-length bro flow hair, jeans, and a leather jacket.

"Mr. Shepherd, I'm Sutton Rhoades. What can I do for you? I understand you represent Senator Kingsley's widow. Such a horrendous shock. Please convey the condolences of our firm to Savannah and tell her we're available for anything she needs."

I'm sure you are, Jake thought, smiling. "I'll certainly tell her. I'm sure she'll appreciate your concern."

"Why don't you come back where we can be comfortable?" He turned to the receptionist. "Margaret, buzz Lisa and have her bring a tray of coffee to my office." Glancing back at Jake, he said, "Regular or decaf?"

"The real stuff, stronger the better."

Once in his office, Rhoades took a seat on one of a pair of chairs flanking the twelfth-floor window. He motioned for Jake to take the mate.

"What can I do for you, Mr. Shepherd, or should I say, what can I do for Savannah?"

"As you are aware, Senator Kingsley died under mysterious circumstances."

"Of course. We heard on the news the medical examiner has ruled the death a homicide. Surely, Savannah is not a suspect?"

Jake stared at the lawyer, locking him in eye contact. "Why would you say that?"

Rhoades appeared caught off guard by Jake's question. "Good question. I misspoke."

Jake continued to stare at him but didn't speak, which seemed to cause Rhoades discomfort.

"I mean, isn't it true the spouse is the first suspect in a murder? But of course, there's no way Savannah Kingsley had anything to do with Scott's death. Again, why are you here? Scott Kingsley hasn't been a part of this practice in several years."

"I'm here to learn as much as I can about the man."

"Isn't that the job of the authorities—the FBI?"

"It's their job, but depending on what happened and who was responsible, Mrs. Kingsley's interest needs attention. Describe the senator for me."

"I'm not sure what you want."

"Forget who I am, just describe the man you knew."

"Smart—ambitious. I would say completely focused on a career in politics. He came into this firm right out of law school and handled some very important clients during his tenure."

"Would you consider him a personal friend?"

Rhoades hesitated just long enough for Jake to discount his answer.

"We didn't socialize outside the office, if that's what you're asking."

"Did he socialize with anyone from the firm—outside the office?"

"I wouldn't know."

Oh, I think you do, counselor. "Should I remind you the dead can't be defamed?"

"Of course not. Look, Mr. Shepherd, my relationship with Scott Kingsley was strictly superficial. We worked in different departments of the firm. Scott headed our sports and entertainment law department. My area is construction law."

"Sports and entertainment? Are those practice areas in big demand in Atlanta?"

"The film industry is flourishing in Georgia since the legislature passed the tax credit. Of course, sports have always been popul—"

A knock came at the door and Rhoades' secretary entered with the tray of coffee. After pouring both men a mug, she left.

"Was Senator Kingsley ever involved in a scandal while working here?"

"Of course not. Anything of that nature would have come out during his campaign."

"Actually, it might not. I suspect the brotherhood of the club would have worked damned hard to keep it under the radar. Let's be honest, Rhoades, Kingsley's name may not be on the door, but your clients know this was his firm. I bet he appears in some of your literature—as a former partner, of course."

"What makes you suspect Scott Kingsley was involved in something off center?"

Jake chuckled. "In my experience—rarely is an innocent guy murdered outside a robbery or random drive-by. This was neither. For someone to plan and carry out a homicide requires a degree of hate, jealousy, fear, revenge, or greed. Since Mrs. Kingsley is the only one known to profit from his death, and I've ruled her out, that leaves the other four motives—all of which require some participation by the victim ninety-nine percent of the time."

"What were you? A criminal attorney?"

"Department of Justice and twelve years with the Bureau."

"Oh. Look, I don't know anything that can help you. Were there rumors? Yes. But I have no firsthand knowledge of his walking in the weeds."

"Who would?"

"Ford Costas. He worked with Kingsley and took over as head of the department."

Rhoades pushed a button on his desk phone. "Lisa, buzz Ford Costas and find out if he's free. If so, tell him I want to bring someone down to his office." Even though the secretary indicated she would follow through, when he punched off, Rhoades said to Jake, "She'll let us know."

Jake gave him an affirmative nod. "Appreciate it." *At least he didn't try to warn the guy, but this one knows more than he's admitting.*

It took only minutes for the secretary to respond, saying Costas was expecting the visit. Rhoades stood. "Come. I'll take you down and introduce you."

The Sports and Entertainment Department of the firm was on the other side of the sprawling office, past a large, glassed-in conference room. While Phil Madison probably billed at triple the hourly rate of the Atlanta lawyers, their facility equaled his in terms of the rich ambiance.

As the two men entered the office of Ford Costas, he stood.

"Ford, this is Jake Shepherd. He's a private investigator working for Savannah Kingsley and would like to talk to you about Scott."

The broad-shouldered lawyer had the look of a former athlete who kept in shape. Jake surmised he failed to make the pros and settled for a life representing them.

Costas walked from behind his desk with a hand extended toward Jake.

"Nice to meet you. We're all stunned and devastated by what happened to Scott."

"I'll pass that on to Mrs. Kingsley."

"I'll leave you two to chat," Rhoades said, backing toward the door. "It was a pleasure meeting you, Mr. Shepherd. And, again, please tell Savannah to let us know what we can do for her and the children."

Jake gave him a nod.

"Forgive me, Mr. Shepherd," Costas said, "if what I'm about to say comes across as rude or ignorant, but why does Mrs. Kingsley need a private investigator? Isn't Scott's death being investigated by the Washington police?"

"The FBI has the lead in a crime against a federal official. But there are potential aspects of the crime that could impact *Mrs.* Kingsley. Do you mind answering a few questions?"

The muscles in Costas' face tightened. "I'm not comfortable talking about a colleague and not sure why I should."

With a glance around the room, Jake gave Costas his signature look of impatient disdain. "I'll spell it out for you. A man is dead. Right now, it's my job to make sure a similar fate doesn't befall anyone else." Jake glared at Costas. "Do you want to help . . . or stand in my way?"

Costas studied Jake's face for several seconds. "I suppose I have no problem—as long as you're not planning on recording me."

"I'm interested in information, not evidence. I wouldn't attempt to record you without your permission."

"In that case, have a seat."

Jake sat, took a business card from a holder on the lawyer's desk, opened his portfolio, and tucked it into a pocket. Afterward, he glanced around the office. The first thing to catch his attention was a law school diploma hanging among autographed photographs of celebrity athletes. *Jock all right. This firm would never hire a fringe-school grad if he didn't have a rain-making name.*

"Where did you play?"

"How'd you know I played?" Costas appeared surprised.

"Lucky guess."

"State U."

"What happened?"

"You mean, why didn't I turn pro?"

"Something like that."

"I made fourth-round draft pick, but a drunk driver ended it for me before it started."

With a commiserating tip of his head, Jake said, "Bad break."

After asking several more ice-breaking questions about Costas' background in sports and his opinion as to the Braves' current season, Jake got to the point.

"Tell me about Scott Kingsley. This was his department, right?"

"Yeah, but Scott focused more on the entertainment side. They hired me about a year after he took over the department, and once I learned the ropes, Scott pointed the sports clients in my direction. He said I talked the talk. He hung with the film clients—production companies, a few actors—local TV celebs."

"At the risk of overstepping, how much does a department head in this firm make a year?"

"No secret. You can check it on the web. My salary as an equity partner is one twenty-five—plus profit sharing and bonuses. Scott's was the same."

"The extras double the salary?"

"Don't I wish. I guess it's possible, but I haven't seen it happen in the eight years I've been here." The lawyer toyed with the letter opener on his desk.

"I haven't been to the Kingsley home here in Atlanta, but the one in DC is what I would call a borderline mansion."

Costas grinned. "His home here is damn impressive. Scott lived large. Wish I knew his secret. My wife is a public defender, and we can't afford that lifestyle on two incomes."

"Think he had family money?"

"Not that I'm aware."

"How would you describe the man?"

"Smart. Competitive. Burning up with ambition. Willing to push the envelope. A typical politician—plastic smiles and hearty handshakes." He turned his head, breaking eye contact. "I shouldn't have said that."

Jake grinned. "Relax. You can't hurt him now. Tell me, would you describe your relationship as strictly professional, or did you have a personal relationship as well?"

Before speaking, Costas grimaced, squinting his eyes. "Personal? Scott wasn't a watercooler kind of guy. If the rest of us went for a drink after work, Scott made an obligatory appearance, shook everyone's hand, and disappeared. He never seemed interested in cultivating male relationships."

"Now that's an interesting comment. Care to elaborate?"

"Probably not. Anything I say would be rumor. I have no firsthand knowledge of his extracurricular activities, or if any of it is true. Why cause his widow grief?"

"Unfortunately, the circumstances of his death do not allow for social discretion. To sort this out, we need to know everything possible about the man. Who were his friends? Who were his potential enemies? Who had a reason to want him dead?"

"In a nutshell, Scott never missed a pretty face or figure. How far it went, I never wanted to know."

"I'm feeling you didn't like the guy."

"Let's just say people were either assets or liabilities to Scott. My worth to him was making sure his cases were covered and showing up for PR gigs. Of course, he wanted my endorsement when he ran for office. You know—the jock connection."

"And—"

"I gave it. It was good for the firm to launch a public figure. And let's not kid ourselves, I wanted his nod for this job. To our senior partner, the firm's founder, Scott was platinum. Whatever else the guy lacked, he made up for in charisma. He could charm a fix away from a junkie in withdrawal."

"Did any names ever come up in those rumors?"

Costas shook his head. "None that I recall. It was more like, 'Kingsley's cozying up to the new runner,' or 'Kingsley's got something going with a hot number on his campaign team.'"

"Is there anyone you can point me toward who would know more about potential women in his stable?"

Costas thought for a minute. "Not in this office. Maybe his campaign manager. They were law school buddies as far as I know. Can't remember his name but you should be able to find it. Fairly sure he made the move to DC with a fat government job in Scott's office."

Jake made a note on his legal pad, rose, and took a card from his pocket. "I'll leave you to your day for now. Take my card and give me a call if anything comes to mind you think might help."

When he settled into the driver's seat of the Lexus, Jake texted Liz Glover.

> *Find name of Kingsley's campaign manager and where*
> *currently located. Also, check his FEC filings for list of*
> *contributors with eye out for film people.*

Jake then called Scarlett. "Finished sooner than expected. I'll pick you up in thirty. We can grab a quick lunch, swing by the Kingsley house, and then the range. You have the key and security code, right?"

"I do. Did you have any luck with the lawyers?"

"I'll fill you in when I get there."

CHAPTER NINETEEN

Scarlett slid her phone into the pocket of her jeans and turned to Fury. "Looks like I'll need a rain check on lunch. I'm sorry. Sherlock Holmes is on his way."

"No problem. His schedule has to be your priority." Fury picked up the empty tea mugs and put them on a tray to be taken to the kitchen. "I'm just happy to have any time with you."

"It has been nice. While we were catching up, I actually forgot why I'm here and what has happened, but it's back on course for me now. I'd better run upstairs for my things. Can I take those"—she pointed to the tray—"to the kitchen?"

"You know Ella, our housekeeper. She would be insulted. You go ahead. I'll retrieve Jake's gun from the safe and meet you in the living room."

Scarlett made it downstairs with her purse and gun case minutes before Jake rang the doorbell. Fury greeted him.

"Why don't you and Scarlett stay for lunch?" Fury said as Jake entered. "Ella can whip it up in a hurry."

"I appreciate the offer, but we've got a full schedule."

"I understand, but you will be here for dinner, won't you?"

Jake smiled. "You bet. Promised Gray I would show him who's boss on the pool table."

Fury grinned. "That I can't wait to see." She handed him the pistol. "I assume you have the holster."

"In the vehicle."

After picking up hamburgers at a fast-food window, Jake and Scarlett drove to the Kingsley's home in the Buckhead section of Atlanta.

"You've never been here?" Jake asked as they drove past the Georgia governor's mansion on West Paces Ferry Road.

"Never."

"Come on, Harvard. Surely your curiosity had you do a drive-by of your sister's house."

She made a face. "Sorry to disappoint you, but nope. Never happened. Believe me; I know what it looks like. My mother described it often enough."

When they reached the two-story house, situated at least one hundred feet from the road, Jake whistled. "I gotta give it to Kingsley. He had the Midas touch."

"Exactly as Mom described."

When they reached the front door, Scarlett used her sister's remote to disarm the security system, and Jake unlocked the door. They were hardly inside the entry hall when Jake held an arm out. "Stop. We've got a crime scene."

"Oh, my gosh! How did this happen?" Scarlett said, looking around the entry. Drawers of a Louis XV bombe commode were open—the contents scattered about. In the living room, cushions were strewn around the floor. "Why didn't the alarm company call the police?"

Backing out of the house, Jake said, "My money is on the system being compromised. It was likely already disarmed when you hit the remote."

"How could anyone do that?"

Jake did not answer as he pulled out Dan Cameron's card, tapped in the number, and put the call on speaker. "Shepherd here. Glad you answered. We've got a situation at the Kingsley house. It's been tossed. You might want a team out here ahead of the Atlanta PD."

"Are you inside?"

"No. Mrs. Kingsley's sister and I opened the front door and stepped in. It was immediately apparent the house has been ransacked, so we backed out. We'll stay here in my vehicle until the perimeter is secured. Do you want to notify Atlanta—work out the jurisdictional issue?"

"Yeah. I'll take care of it. I'm on my way."

When he ended the call, Scarlett said, "Jake, is it possible the alarm went off, the police were called, and they couldn't reach Savannah?"

"If they had been called, there would be crime scene tape around the property."

"I wasn't thinking. Maybe it was just a burglary."

"Not likely, Harvard. Disarming a security system requires a pro."

Within fifteen minutes, Dan Cameron and his team arrived on the scene, closely followed by a unit from the Atlanta police department. "Thanks for holding the fort, Shepherd, and for not compromising the scene," Cameron said as Jake met him on the front walk.

"I think the only trace of us you'll find is my prints and DNA on the doorknob. Who's taking the lead here, you guys or Atlanta?"

"We'll work together. We've got a good relationship, and I don't think they want to deal with what happened in DC."

"I know you're bound by confidentiality in an ongoing investigation, but anything you can share would be appreciated. Is Kirby sending anyone down?"

"He is. Have to tell you, he uttered a few choice words when he heard you discovered the break-in."

"I'll bet he did." Jake grinned. "Ms. Kavanagh"—Jake pointed toward the Lexus—"and I will leave it in your very capable hands. Thanks, again, for help with the files."

"Are we leaving?" Scarlett asked as Jake slid into the driver's seat.

"No point in hanging around. We can't enter. I'll try to get an okay to go in before we head back to DC."

"What if they don't let you?"

"My guess is they're going to come to me to find out what I know, and we'll negotiate on sharing."

"I suspect it really helps that you were an agent. You understand the process."

Jake nodded as he cranked the motor.

Thirty minutes later, Jake and Scarlett were at a shooting range, which she and her father frequented.

"Okay, Harvard. Let's see what you've got."

Scarlett adjusted her ear protection muffs, put on safety glasses, removed her pistol from its case, and inserted a magazine.

"I'm hoping you clean your weapon regularly," Jake said.

"Believe it or not, I do. I told you, my father taught me everything I know about guns and shooting."

As she raised the compact Glock 42 and took aim, Jake watched.

"Good grip. I'm impressed. But relax your right hand. It'll give your trigger finger more flexibility."

"What do you mean? I need to make sure I have control."

"Trust me. You want about sixty percent of muscle strength in your right hand. Control the weapon with your left. If you don't believe me, try it both ways."

Scarlett took a deep breath and followed his suggestion, firing six rounds into the paper target at the end of the range. All six shots landed within the bullseye zone, albeit one hit the outline.

"Nice," Jake said.

"Your turn."

Aiming his larger Glock 19, Jake fired eight rounds in rapid succession. Most hit dead-on, but a couple struck slightly outside the primary zone.

Scarlett grinned. "Not bad, Shepherd, but I won that round."

"So you did."

He then turned and emptied the magazine, each shot finding its place within the bullseye.

"Wow! You're pretty good."

"Just got lucky. Reload and show me one more time what you can do. Tell you what. Let's make it interesting. We'll each fire twelve rounds. One who scores best gets to pick the music we play on the ride back to North Carolina."

"You're on. Watch and weep. You go first."

Jake fired six rounds—all perfectly placed.

"You're making it hard, but I think I can match you," Scarlett said. As opposed to Jake, who fired in rapid succession, Scarlett took her time aiming each shot and managed to do as well as he had.

Assuming his stance, Jake raised his Glock 19 and fired—his first five shots hitting the mark, the sixth straying a fraction of an inch.

"Seems like I've left the door open for you," he said.

"So, it does." She took her position, stretched her arms forward, and fired six times. Each bullet found a home in the target zone. She turned, lifted her glasses, and grinned. "Looks like we'll listen to Andre Bocelli and Il Divo."

"Damn." Jake squinted with an expression of disdain. "Who the hell are they?"

"It'll give you a taste of culture, Shepherd. So, are you satisfied I'm competent with a pistol?"

"I'll have to reluctantly agree. But don't get carried away. Like I told you, knowing how to fire a gun and knowing when to fire are discrete skills."

As they packed up their equipment, Scarlett said, "Are you ever going to give me a clue as to what you've found out—what is going on? I'm not a featherweight like my sister, Jake."

"I know. Let's get out of here, and I'll tell you a little more."

Once they were in the SUV, headed back to the MacGregors, Scarlett turned toward Jake, anticipation radiating from her eyes. "So?"

He backed the vehicle to the street and headed in the direction they came from. "It appears Senator Kingsley had connections to organized crime. His spending habits far exceed his known source of revenue. One of the witnesses mentioned a potential association with a foreign person of suspicious description. I'm not trying to hide the ball, but I don't want to give out information not yet proven."

"Mafia? That is scary. Can you tell me which witness gave you the information?"

"Not yet. As for the Mafia. It's a broad term in the vocabulary of the layman. The general population knows of only a fraction of the cartels, syndicates, brotherhoods, et cetera."

"Do you think an organized crime group had Scott killed?"

"I don't speculate. It undermines an investigation to form a conclusion too early. However, Kingsley's involvement with any crime chief could put Savannah and possibly others at risk. The bosses don't like loose ends."

"But you have your suspicions, don't you?"

"Maybe. And I'll be honest with you. Your sister knows more than she's shared. I have not pinpointed what she knows, but she's hiding something."

"You think Savannah was involved with the Mafia?"

"Did I say that? I don't think I did. I said she is hiding something." He made a sharp left turn northward. "I hope I'm not making a mistake trusting your discretion."

"I know. I know. 'Three can keep a secret if two are dead,' but I'll prove Ben wrong."

"I'm serious, Harvard. I don't usually work with civilians. No talking about what I've told you, which includes both of your sisters and your parents. I'm only sharing with you because I believe you are a pro."

"I understand. Thank you."

CHAPTER TWENTY

Monday evening, Mike O'Quinn and Gray's mother, Zaira O'Quinn, joined Scarlett and Jake for dinner at the MacGregor home. After the O'Quinns left, the two couples moved into the MacGregor game room.

"Your dad's all right, Fury," Jake said. "He may be old school, but he knows the territory."

"He loved talking shop with you and loved having a useful purpose."

Gray walked over to a wall rack and removed a cue stick. "Rack'em up, Shepherd. I want to show you how the game is played."

"Well, brace yourself to lose," Jake said.

"Never happen. I'm so confident that I'm going to let you break."

"Bring it on," Jake said and took a couple of sticks down, checking them out before making a choice. As he leaned over the table, poised to take his first shot, his cell phone buzzed. Halting his action, Jake took the device out of his pocket, read the caller ID, and laid the cue stick on the table.

It appeared the caller began talking before Jake could speak as his eyebrows pinched together, and his jaw tightened. He held a finger up to the group, requesting a pause.

Addressing the caller, Jake said, "I suggest you stop talking. I'm hanging up. You get one do-over, and an attitude adjustment is in your best interests." With that, he terminated the call.

When Jake's phone rang a second time, he glanced around the group, a scowl denoting his mood. Before opening the call, he said, "Excuse me for a minute," and then moved to the hallway.

"Before you say a word, Sabrina, remember who you're talking to."

"Mom said you're out of town until Sunday. You promised. You know how much I want to see the National Ballet. *You* gave me the tickets for my birthday. Did you forget, Dad?"

Jake took in a deep breath. "It looks like I might have, and I apologize, but it can't be helped. Can't your mother take you?"

"No. She can't. She and Hal have some big deal to go to for the hospital. You've got to take me. You promised."

"Sabrina, hold it. You know I don't always have control over my schedule. I'm on a case. There is no way I can get back before Sunday at the earliest. I'll call Liz and see if she can take you."

"What if she can't?"

"I'll do my best. That's all I can tell you. Give your phone to Hal and leave the room. I need to talk to him about business. Love you and promise to do my best to get you to the concert."

A minute later, Kirby came on the line. "You need to talk to me?"

"Any new developments with the Garcia woman?"

"Nada. If you don't give me something more, or I see some activity, I'm going to pull the surveillance. And by the way, Weston and Blake will be down there tomorrow. Try to cooperate, or stay out of the way. I understand you reported the invasion of the Kingsley home."

"Right. I'm always cooperative. What have you done to locate Garcia?"

"What do you mean? What have I done? You know I put round-the-clock surveillance on her apartment."

"Have you thought about calling the Metropolitan boys for a welfare check? See if she is in the apartment—maybe see if she's alive."

The phone went silent for several seconds.

"By your silence, I take it you haven't." The fingers of Jake's free hand began to curl as he fought his impatience. "Might be a good move. I'll check back with you tomorrow."

As he terminated the call, Jake could hear Kirby swearing. He then texted Liz Glover.

*Need a favor. I promised to take Sabrina to Kennedy Center
Friday night. Can you cover?*

He had hardly finished typing when his phone buzzed.

"Jake, I can't. My sister will be in town for just the night. I'm so sorry. Can't Jackie take her?"

"Apparently not. Don't worry. I'll figure it out."

When Jake returned to the game room, he snatched the cue stick with a vengeance.

"Got a problem?" Gray asked.

Jake shook his head—his eyebrows almost meeting in the center. "Minor issue."

"I'm reading more than minor. Want to share, or is it classified?"

"Damn. It's annoying being with a guy who knows how to read people."

Gray laughed. "Look who's talking."

Jake relaxed and nodded. "Touché. Just a slight father-daughter conflict of interest."

"Anything we can do to help?"

"Not unless you have cloning skills."

Gray tilted his head to one side. "If I'm reading you right, your daughter had plans that won't work for you."

Jake laid the stick back on the table, turned, and leaned back against it, arms folded across his chest, chin down. "Hazard of the job."

Scarlett stared at Jake with concern. "What is the conflict?"

He shook his head as if brushing off the question but then changed his mind. "There's a ballet at Kennedy Center Friday night. Three months ago, I gave her tickets for her birthday. Seems neither her mother, nor Liz, can fill in."

"Oh, Jake," Scarlett said.

"It's fine. She's thirteen—old enough to understand life doesn't always play out the way you want. I'll figure out how to make it up to her."

"Jake, it's not about what she wants," Gray said. "It's about your father-daughter relationship." All three turned their attention to him. "I've got this one covered."

"Yeah? What does that mean?" Jake asked. "You have a fairy godmother on the payroll in DC?"

"No. But I have a plane. I can get you there in under two hours. Fly up in time for the performance and back right after. You'll be gone six—maybe seven—hours and can sleep in the air."

"No way. I can't accept that."

"The hell you can't. You and I both know what it means to have a good father. Although for diametrically different reasons, we both lost out. Let me help make sure your daughter doesn't."

Jake shook his head. "Can't."

"You'd do the same for me."

Jake continued shaking his head.

"Let him pay it forward, Jake," Fury said. "It's nothing for Gray, and who knows? One day he may need you to get him off when he strangles me." She winked.

"True, but it would be a simple defense," Gray said, raising his eyebrows with a small grin, "justifiable homicide."

The quip caused all four to laugh, and then Gray refocused on Jake. "Kidding aside. You heard her. Get over yourself and accept my offer."

Jake faced away from the group, not responding. Silence hovered over the room. After a minute, he turned, swooped up his cue stick, tossed it from one hand to the other, and approached Gray. With a steely glare, he pointed a finger toward his host's chest. "Just as long as we're clear on one point. Your saving my ass won't stop me from running the table."

Gray grinned, slapped him on the shoulder, and said, "Take your best shot."

CHAPTER TWENTY-ONE

Tuesday morning, Scarlett came downstairs as Jake poured coffee into a Yeti cup.

"Are you leaving now?" she asked.

"Jammed-up schedule."

Scarlett joined him at the buffet and took an empty cup.

"Liz dug up the names of a couple of major contributors to Kingsley's campaign here in Atlanta for me to interview. The senator's political office in town is closed, according to the outgoing phone message, but I'm going to ride by there. Anything new from your family?"

"I talked to Savannah and told her about the break-in."

"What was her reaction?"

"More concerned about damage to the house and what to wear for the funeral. I promised to shop today for her. It'll probably max out my AmEx card."

"Did you ask about electronics in the house?"

"I did. She said there were none. They took them all to Washington."

"Good to know." Jake frowned. "You're not shopping alone."

"I knew you would say that. Fury, her dad, and one of his retired friends from the Atlanta PD are going with me. Is that enough security for you, or do we need to request the National Guard?"

"Two former cops should cover it." He started to leave but stopped. "I don't know how my time will go. Have them run you by your office. What about your parents?"

"They'll be back in Atlanta this afternoon. When Grace told them what happened, they switched flights. Do you want to talk to them today since you and I are going back to North Carolina tomorrow?"

"I've decided to drive to Cashiers tonight and return early tomorrow. I'll interview your mom and dad when we get back."

"We're not bringing Savannah here?"

"Sonny and Brenda can handle driving her down in time for the funeral on Thursday—two p.m., right?"

"Right. Phil's secretary is emailing me a file with the entire funeral plan."

"I'm not sure how long I'll be this morning. If you have any spare time, when you finish your errands, start looking through the files I emailed you last night. I'm looking for anything that shows a potential for creating hostility between Kingsley and another party and any suspicious activity or relationships surrounding him. Keep an eye out for foreign names, particularly Russian."

"What kind of files? From Scott's computer?"

"No. Files I received from the Bureau—investigations and dossiers."

Her eyebrows pinched. "They gave you files?"

"FOIA—Freedom of Information Act."

With Fury's help, Scarlett's shopping went quickly. Using her smartphone, she sent choices for Savannah's approval.

By half-past two, Scarlett had completed the shopping expedition and arrangements for her professional obligations. As Mike O'Quinn drove Fury's SUV onto the driveway at the MacGregor house, Scarlett's cell chimed. When she saw it was Jake, she tapped the green icon.

"Jake. What's going on?"

"Thought I'd touch base. Got a call from Weston."

Scarlett's eyebrows furrowed in a puzzled expression. "Who?"

"Deke Weston—from the surveillance team at the Kingsley house in DC."

"Really?"

"The chiefs want a meeting at the field office. He wouldn't elaborate, but I smell something going on. Don't count on me getting back before late afternoon but have everything ready to leave when I get there. I'll text or call when I'm on the way."

"Do you need me to pack for you?"

"I'm cool. I stay travel ready—old routine from the Bureau."

As she reached for the door handle of the SUV, Scarlett hesitated. "Mike. What do you think of Jake Shepherd?"

Fury's dad smiled. "He's a sharp one—a feckin keen guard."

Scarlett's expression betrayed her lack of understanding.

"Translation: a good cop," Fury said. "Pardon Dad's Irish. He's only been in America for thirty-five years."

Scarlett smiled. "Yeah, but I love his accent." Addressing Mike, she said, "Good to hear it from a pro."

CHAPTER TWENTY-TWO

Jake checked his Glock and surrendered his driver's license at the security checkpoint of the federal building. The guard scanned a list on his clipboard and then motioned Jake through. As he walked toward the elevator, through the empty reception area, memories flooded his mind, evoking the feeling of visiting an alma mater. *Life doesn't always play out the way you want applies to you too, Shepherd.*

When he reached the target floor, an escort led him to the ASAC's office.

"Have a seat, Jake," Cameron said, beckoning him.

Before Jake could respond, Deke Weston and Sylvia Blake walked in. Each greeted him with a handshake.

"What have you got?" Jake asked Cameron. "Something turn up at the Kingsley house?"

"ERT is still working on it, but we want to talk to you about a couple of things. I'll let Weston fill you in on the latest development," Cameron said.

As the three agents took seats, Jake repositioned the remaining chair to allow visual contact with all.

"Kirby contacted us right after we landed with information he said to pass along," Weston said.

"That figures. He tries to avoid talking to me. Does it have something to do with surveillance on a woman in DC?"

"It does. Hal had the MPD do a welfare check."

"And?"

"She wasn't there." Weston turned to his partner, breaking eye contact with Jake.

Jake tensed. "And the apartment? Did it look like she moved out?"

Sylvia Blake spoke up. "There were signs of foul play."

"Damn!"

Weston shook his head. "No sign of relocation. But there were signs of a struggle, traces of blood."

"Kirby wants to know what you know about her and how she ties to Senator Kingsley," Blake said.

Jake rested his forehead in his left hand, rubbing his temple, and muttered under his breath. "Damn, damn, damn. Loose ends."

"Care to tell us more?" Weston said.

Jake raised his head. "Yeah. I care to tell you more. I care to tell you that I hope Kirby didn't drag his feet when I asked for surveillance, and I hope what happened to the woman occurred before I talked to him."

"Who is she, Jake?" Weston asked.

"Who is she, or who *was* she?" Jake tossed his portfolio on Cameron's desk. "I'll tell you who. She's the sister of the Kingsley nanny, who you guys better take into protective custody, or her life isn't worth a Colombian peso." Jake looked down at the floor and then back toward Weston. "What did they find in the apartment— purse, phone, keys?"

"No phone or keys, but they found what appears to be her purse. Several drawers appeared to be emptied. Are you going to tell us the complete story?" Weston asked.

Jake stood, looked from one agent to the other, walked toward the door, and stopped. After taking a deep breath, he pivoted. "I have cause to believe Maria Garcia is a victim of sex trafficking by one of the syndicates—likely Eastern European."

"Maria is the missing woman?" Weston asked.

"She is."

"How do you see the senator fitting into that picture?" Blake asked.

"I'm still fitting the pieces together. If I knew all the answers, I'd put the evidence in a box, tie a ribbon around it, and hand it to you so you guys could solve the case. What is Kirby doing to investigate her disappearance?"

Blake spoke up. "We don't know it's a disappear—"

"Don't even go there with me."

Weston raised a palm, attempting to temper the escalating exchange. "He's ordered the usual: background check, surveillance videos, a canvas of the neighbors, a trace on who pays the rent. Be fair, Jake. There's not enough to mount a major investigation. No sign of forced entry. She might be a lousy housekeeper who cut herself and went for medical attention."

"Leaving her purse behind? More likely she's at the bottom of the Potomac."

"Where is the nanny?" Weston asked.

"I have her covered. This new information reinforces my concern for the widow's welfare and potentially her family."

"Where is Mrs. Kingsley?"

"She's safe."

"That's not what I asked. Don't you think it might be wise to let us interview her? Or do you plan to handle the investigation by yourself?" Blake asked as the other two agents stared at Jake.

"You guys have got to know an interview is not my call. Where is our assurance that you've eliminated her as a suspect? If you can't give that, Phil is never going to unleash you on her."

"Checkmate," Cameron said.

"If you don't cooperate, Jake, Kirby may charge you with obstruction," Weston said.

"Never happen. Who says I'm not cooperating? Kirby's bluffing—likes to yank my chain. I know where the line is, and I'm not crossing it. What's the latest from the ME?"

"Nothing new," Weston said. "Apparently cause of death was an allergic reaction, enhanced by a blow to the head."

"Hard to believe he could die that quick of an allergy," Blake said.

Cameron spoke up. "Peanut allergies are treacherous. A thirteen-year-old in California died after taking a bite, spitting it out, and receiving three epinephrine injections."

"What about the head injury? Any conclusion as to how it was sustained?" Jake asked.

"ME says it was likely caused by a bronze Lady of Justice figure falling from a free-standing shelf unit, which impeded his ability to access the epinephrine. Theory is, he began choking, went for his Epi, and bumped into the unit, causing the piece to fall."

"Hmm." Jake squinted an eye. "Lady Justice?" *Maybe poetic justice.* "Not sure I see why the ME ruled the cause of death a homicide when ingestion could have been accidental."

"He found peanut traces mixed with dairy in the vic's stomach," Weston said. "The evidence response team found what appears to be the source item on a plate in his office, which his secretary identified as an appetizer called cheese straws—apparently popular in the South and frequently homemade. The snack is *not* known to contain peanuts. The secretary said the senator was particularly fond of them, but she had no idea where the contaminated ones came from. It doesn't look good for your lady."

Jake shook his head. "Novel MO for murder—not the usual weapon of choice for a hit but doesn't necessarily point to Mrs. Kingsley."

"You may not like it, but it screams wife—opportunity, means, and likely motive," Weston said.

Jake gave him an icy look. "Nope. Not her."

"Is it your theory that Kingsley's murder was an organized crime hit?" Blake asked, her tone dripping with sarcasm.

"I don't have a theory. I see more options than on a Cheesecake Factory menu—most unidentified. I don't know who, I just know where to look."

"If you have leads, you have to furnish them to us," Blake said.

Jake glared at her.

"Chill out, Sylvia. You don't know Shepherd as well as Cameron and I do. He's an annoying son-of-a-bitch, but a straight shooter, and almost as good as he thinks he is."

A tight smile came across Dan Cameron's face as he glanced down at his watch. He then stood and made eye contact with each party. "Now, that we have all that out of the way. Let's get down to the funeral plans." He focused on Jake. "Security coordinators for Atlanta PD and the Capitol Police are in the conference room. Let's take a walk."

CHAPTER TWENTY-THREE

Jake and Scarlett arrived at the North Carolina house shortly before nine p.m. Savannah and Brenda were watching a sitcom with Kai lying nearby. Seeing Jake, he sprinted across the room to meet his master.

"Sonny's taking a nap before taking over the watch," Brenda said as Jake and Scarlett came in. "Do you want me to wake him?"

"No. I'll be up early and talk to him then," Jake said. He glanced over toward Savannah. "I need to ask you some questions. Do you want to do it tonight or early tomorrow?"

"How early?"

"Five or five thirty."

She rolled her eyes. "Tonight."

He nodded. "I'll be back in a minute or two." With his and Scarlett's small bags in hand, he bounded up the stairs, two at a time, Kai following.

Carrying a lightweight garment bag, along with a sack containing a shoebox, Scarlett walked over to where Savannah sat and handed her the items. "You owe me three seventy-five."

As she accepted the items, Savannah said, "Do you think I should wear one of those chiffon type veils over my face?"

"No. You'll be fine. You're not Jacqueline Kennedy."

"Since Jake is going to talk to Mrs. Kingsley, he'll want privacy. I'll go upstairs to the sitting area," Brenda said.

As the security guard left, Savannah laid the clothing over the back of the couch and motioned for Scarlett to come closer.

"What does he want to talk to me about?"

"He doesn't update me, Savannah. It could be anything. He talked to your children, your nanny, Scott's law associates, and others. It might have something to do with what he learned."

Scarlett barely finished speaking when Jake entered and walked toward the kitchen end of the great room. Dropping his portfolio on the long table dividing the seating area from the cooking area as he passed, he asked, "Cold drink, anyone?"

"I'm good," Scarlett said.

Savannah shook her head.

After taking a drink from the refrigerator, Jake waved Savannah over to the table, as Scarlett started toward the staircase. "Scarlett, I want to be on the road by six a.m. Should put us back in Atlanta by nine thirty."

She nodded and continued on her way.

As Jake took a seat across from Savannah, he glanced at an incomplete jigsaw puzzle spread out at the end of the table.

"Where did you get the puzzle?"

Savannah followed his gaze. "On a shelf in the laundry room. Brenda found three, and we've worked them a dozen times. There's nothing to do here."

He smiled as he scanned notes in his portfolio. "I know people who would kill for a week in a place like this."

"Not if they weren't allowed out the door. When is this going to end?"

"It's barely begun."

"You've got to be kidding me. I can't take it. Can't you do something?"

Jake looked up, assessing Savannah's demeanor. "I'm not your fairy godmother and have no training in magic. The best I can do is apply the training I do have to make sure it doesn't worsen and that the right resolution is found. Now, can we get started?"

She heaved a sigh while defiantly pushing away stray puzzle pieces. Several fell to the floor. "I have told you everything I know. Why do you keep interrogating me?"

With a huff of disgust, Jake said, "Let me simplify it for you." He ripped a blank sheet from his legal pad and drew a large circle. "See this? In the center, he drew a small oval. "This is you, occupying the prime suspect throne." He then drew a ring around the bullseye, dividing the remainder into two parts. Pointing to the inside ring, he said, "Here is where close relations, along with past and present lovers, reside." Pointing to the remaining section, he said, "Here is where business, political, social associates, disgruntled strangers, and other potential enemies camp out." It's my job to identify all and to eliminate each as a suspect. The FBI knows that a tidbit called a cheese straw, contaminated with peanut matter, set your husband's death in motion and ultimately killed him. What do you know about that?"

Savannah's face turned appliance white—her pupils expanded to consume the irises.

As Jake tipped his chin, one eye squinted, his brows pinching into a frown. "Talk to me."

She opened her mouth but couldn't speak for a second. Shaking her head, she whispered, "He really liked cheese straws."

"Where did he get them?"

She shrugged. "I don't know."

"Did you make them?"

"No. At least not recently. My mother made them all the time. She would send a box for Scott because he made such a fuss about them when we went home for holiday events." Savannah looked Jake in the eye. "Surely, you don't think my mother poisoned Scott?"

"I don't think. I dig for information. Has your mother sent any lately?"

"Not that I know of. You know she and Dad were in Europe. She couldn't have sent them. Besides, she would have no reason to harm Scott. Mom thought he was wonderful, and I couldn't bear to tell her the truth. Scarlett would come closer to sending him poison than my mother."

"You mentioned in one of our meetings that you employed a chef."

Savannah stared at Jake for a few seconds. "If you're thinking André could have made the cheese straws, he couldn't. He took a month off to visit family in Italy—not that he ever made them."

"Were you cooking for the family during that time?"

She stood and then sat. "No. A catering service provided our meals. You can check that." Tears began to stream down her face. "The FBI thinks I killed Scott, don't they? And if they find out about our horrible marriage, they'll arrest me."

"You are currently their favorite person of interest. The magic elements fall directly on you—means, motive, and opportunity."

Savannah began to shake. "You're scaring me."

"You need to be scared. Not because you're going to prison, but because whoever killed your husband may have reason to harm you. While it may take me time, I'll prove you didn't do it."

"What if you can't?"

"I can. If I doubted your innocence, I wouldn't be here. Believe me. It would make at least one person at FBI headquarters happy to see me fail, which is no reflection on you. Fairly sure there's a pool in place with high odds. But it's not going to happen."

With a shaky voice, she asked, "How do you know you can prove it?"

He smiled. "I'm good at what I do. But you can't get in my way by refusing to follow my instructions or otherwise fail to cooperate— even if it means things coming out that are embarrassing." He pulled out some photos from his portfolio and presented them to her.

"Oh, my god." She covered her mouth for a moment. "Where did you get those?"

"Your computer and cell phone." He then took out several cards and letters, fanning them out. "Do these look familiar?"

"Has Scarlett seen them?"

He shook his head. "No. That is you, right?" he said, pointing to a photo of a nude woman in a provocative pose, reclining across a bed—the one in Savannah's Georgetown room.

She looked away. "Tear that up, please."

"It's not going away, Savannah." He then pointed to photos of a nude male, facing away from the camera. "Who is he?"

"Oh, no. Oh, no. I should have deleted that."

"Who is he?"

"I can't tell you." Desperation, bordering on hysteria, blanketed her face and distorted her tone. "Please."

"Are any of these letters or cards from him?"

Tears gushed down her cheeks as she nodded. "Some. Not all. It's not what you think."

"I'm paid to investigate—not judge. Who is he?"

She stood and walked across the room and back, trying to compose herself. When she sat back at the table, she looked Jake in the eye. "I'll tell you after the funeral. I just can't talk about it now. But please don't let Scarlett see those."

"What about the cards and letters that are *not* from mystery man number one? Who are they from?"

"Someone I had an affair with."

"But not Darren Warner?"

She shook her head, staring down at the table. "Not Darren."

"I need to know who he is, Savannah."

"He couldn't have been involved in Scott's death. I don't want him brought into this."

"It's too late for that. Anyone you were involved with needs to be brought in." Jake took out an explicit email. "Is this from your lover?"

Her head moved up and down, but she refused to look at Jake.

"I need his name."

No response came.

"Savannah, the FBI will track the IP number that it came from."

Her head popped up. "No. They can't. I'll tell you everything on Friday. Please. Give me until Friday. I promise. I'll tell you everything."

"All right—until Friday." He then took out a copy of the note Scarlett found in Scott Kingsley's jacket. "Have you ever seen this?"

Savannah wiped her face with the hem of her shirt and took the paper from Jake. "No. Not that one."

"Am I to take that to mean you've seen similar ones?"

She nodded. "Notes. Wrong color lipstick on his shirt. Wrong fragrance on his clothes. Phone calls he had to leave the room to take. Unexplained absences. Scott cheated. You know that."

"Do you have any names to go with what you just told me?"

"No."

"Savannah, this isn't my first rodeo. In my experience, wives want to know who the other woman is. I believe you know."

"I quit caring."

"But you knew."

"Okay, okay. One was named Anne. Anne Franklin. She worked on his campaign in Atlanta, but I think it ended when we came to Washington. Another was named Phoebe something or other. I think she worked in his law practice. You don't have enough paper to write them all down."

"That's a start. Can you think of anyone else?"

Her gaze went to the puzzle and quickly back to Jake. "Oh! There was a June, or Jeanne, or Jen. She worked on his campaign staff and came to Washington."

"Good. Thank you. Let me know if you think of any others. Moving along. How was life in your bedroom?"

Her head snapped up. "That a rude question."

"I know. They'll carve 'Rude, Arrogant Bastard' on my headstone. Please answer the question. How was your sex life?"

"Is this relevant to your investigation or for your personal enjoyment?"

He laughed. "Just answer the question, and don't tell me Friday."

"I hate to disappoint you, but I don't have any juicy tales to tell. It was nonexistent. When he came home, he reeked of cheap perfume and sex he had elsewhere. Some nights, he spent time locked in his office on his computer."

"Pornography?"

She nodded. "He liked the rough stuff."

"I want you to continue giving thought to the names of women Scott Kingsley toyed with. Come up with as many as possible." He flipped the page he had been writing on. "Now. Let's talk about Manuela."

"Manuela?" Savannah appeared confused. "My nanny?"

Jake nodded.

"What do you want to know? She took care of the children. You know that. Scarlett said you talked to Manuela at my sister's house."

"Did she work for you in Atlanta?"

"No. We had a maid and yardman, but my parents and Grace helped with the children when I needed it."

"So, you hired Manuela in DC. Who found her and how?"

"What do you mean?"

"Did you find her through a service? On Craigslist? Someone recommend her?"

"Oh. Someone recommended her to Scott."

"Who?"

She responded with a puzzled expression. "I don't know."

"He didn't tell you?"

"If he did, I don't remember. Why is that important?"

"Please don't make me remind you again. I ask the questions." He glared at her. "What do you know about her sister?"

Savannah shook her head. "What should I know?"

"Did you ever meet her?"

"No. Why would I have? It's not like we were friends. Manuela is an employee. She took care of Victoria and Colin. Did she say something bad about me?"

"Why would you ask that?"

"You talked to her."

He nodded. "I did."

"What did she say?"

"What she said is not important for us to discuss. Was there ever anything about her that struck you as unusual?"

"No. She hardly spoke English. She took care of the children."

"Did she do any cooking?"

"No. Not really."

"She never cooked?"

"I didn't say never." Savannah picked up a puzzle piece and twirled it between her fingers. "She made lunch for the kids when they were home. She probably cooked for herself."

"Did she ever make cheese straws?"

Savannah appeared taken aback by the question. "You're not suggesting?"

"I'm investigating. Did she ever bake for the senator?"

"Not that I know of."

"Did she know about his allergy?"

"I suppose. I'm sure at some time I told her we couldn't have anything with peanuts in the house, including peanut butter."

"Do you have a recipe for the cheese straws? You said your mother made them."

Savannah nodded. "I have a recipe box with a lot of Mom's recipes. I'm sure it's in there."

"And she had full access to your kitchen, right?"

Savannah nodded.

"Did you ever notice any unusual behavior from Manuela when visitors came to the house to meet with your husband?"

"I don't remember."

"Think about it. Try to picture some of the times men came to visit with Scott."

Savannah closed her eyes, shaking her head. After a couple of minutes, she looked up. "The only thing I can tell you is she never seemed to be around. But then I always went upstairs. Scott made it clear his meetings were private."

"Do you recall any names of men meeting with your husband?"

"No."

"Were any foreign nationals?"

"How would I know? I didn't ask for ID."

"Did any have a foreign accent?"

"Like what?"

"Spanish? Russian? Italian?"

"Maybe. There were three men who had thick accents. Scott never told me their names. He said he couldn't pronounce them. They would always go to his office to talk. But Scott knew people from a lot of places. We were supposed to go to Europe this weekend on a second honeymoon. What a joke. Some of Scott's contacts helped him make the arrangements. It was a photo op for him, but I would get to shop."

"Well. That's interesting. You didn't mention it before."

"I didn't think it was important."

"Everything is important, but I'm going to stop here." Jake laid his pen down.

"What's going to happen on Thursday? I feel left out of the picture."

"Brenda and Sonny will drive you to Atlanta where they'll meet up with Scarlett, Phil, and me. My people will provide security for you to the church where a team from the Capitol Police will take over. I would have preferred my people guard you, but I was outranked. When the service is over, the Capitol guys will drive you to your parents' home where Brenda and Sonny will pick you up to return to North Carolina."

"Will you attend the funeral?"

"We'll all be there. Do not engage in conversation with the Capitol guys. You might as well be talking to the Bureau as they will be debriefed. Phil will tell you to stay silent as anything you say can be used against you. Also, try to appear a little grief-stricken. We both know how you feel, but not a good idea to let the public or the FBI know."

"If I was able to act like I was happy with Scott, I can act sad now."

Jake grinned. "Don't overplay it. Be aware that the media will be there in force, putting you under a microscope. From the minute you step out of the car, cameras will be on every breath you take. Don't consider anything you say private whether anyone can hear or not. The Feds will have lip readers translate any conversations you have. Limit your statements to appreciation for support and concern. Do you understand?"

CHAPTER TWENTY-FOUR

Thursday morning, Scarlett showered, dressed, and went down to the breakfast room at five a.m. for a cup of tea and aspirin. To her relief, she made it back to her room without seeing anyone. Sleep the night before had been difficult, and daylight had not mitigated the boxing match in her stomach caused by thoughts of Scott's funeral. Adding to her misery, a severe headache arose during the miserable night. She and Jake had returned to Atlanta the morning before and met with her parents, which turned out to be as stressful as expected. Susan Kavanagh made no effort to restrain her emotions.

After learning nothing of use from the senior Kavanaghs, Jake agreed Scarlett had correctly predicted the outcome of the interview. By mutual agreement, she did not accompany him to the hotel where Scott's parents were staying. According to a brief phone conversation between Scarlett and Jake the afternoon before, he told her the Kingsleys offered no more information than the Kavanaghs. He then said, he would meet with Phil Madison at the latter's hotel and likely return late.

"Give Fury and Gray my regrets for dinner. Don't bother to wait up for me."

By the time he returned to the MacGregor mansion, Scarlett had been in bed.

As she kicked off her sneakers and scooted back onto the bed with tea in hand, she tried to relax, hoping the headache would respond to medication. Both cats joined her. Casper, taking over her lap, almost caused the cup to spill. Setting the vessel on the night table, she pulled the Persian close. "How I wish I could skip today—stay here with the two of you."

Once the initial shock of learning of Scott's death had passed, meeting Jake, searching Savannah's house, traveling to North Carolina, and the activities in Atlanta had consumed Scarlett's attention. However, the reality of the funeral renewed her shock and disbelief. She shivered at the idea of being in the church with Scott's body, plus TV cameras, dignitaries, emotional family members, and a multitude of law enforcement. For seven days, his death had been abstract—a headline, a sound bite. With the service, it became concrete. *Thank God the casket will be closed.*

"I can handle it," she whispered, leaning over to put her cheek against Casper's head. "Grace, Rob, and Dad can take care of Mom and Savannah. It would be nice if Fury could sit with me." Jake had made it clear that even though the MacGregors would attend the funeral, to protect the confidentiality of their location, he did not want the association to go public.

"Gray is high profile. We don't need the attention," he said when Scarlett mentioned it. "Too easy for the press to locate his properties."

As if the day's schedule did not paint a gray mood, heavy rain began pelting the Atlanta area shortly before six a.m. Scarlett grabbed the remote and turned on the TV, seeking a weather report, but she missed the local prediction. Leaning back against the headboard, she mulled over the prospects of coping with the bad weather at the church. With use of her smartphone restricted, she felt helpless to check before remembering she could look on her laptop. As the weather screen loaded, Scarlett realized her hand was shaking. *I'm coming apart. Can't do that. One neurotic Kavanagh sister is all this day can bear, and who knows how Mom will react?*

Draped in cats, Scarlett dozed off. At nine thirty, a soft knock on the door woke her.

Jake? She moved the cats and eased off the bed, not bothering to put on her shoes.

"Hey, honey. I hope I didn't wake you, but I was worried," Fury said. "You're usually up early."

"I didn't sleep much last night and woke with a headache. I think the whole thing is getting to me."

"That's understandable." Fury's forehead wrinkled to convey a sympathetic expression.

"Come on in." Scarlett backed up to allow Fury to enter.

"Don't you want something to eat or something for your head?"

With a shake of her head, Scarlett rejected the offer. "I had a cup of tea earlier, and I think I would choke if I tried to consume anything else. The headache is much better. Is Jake gone?"

Fury nodded. "He left about six thirty but said he would be back for you around noon. He expects Savannah to be here by then."

"Where did he go? Do you know? I didn't see him last night."

"From the conversation I overheard between Jake, Gray, and Dad, I think he is picking up Phil Madison."

Scarlett nodded. "Makes sense. Madison is to ride with us to the church. I think he wants to make sure Savannah doesn't do or say something stupid." Despite her resolve, a tear strayed down Scarlett's cheek. She instantly wiped it away. "I'm not going to give in to this."

Fury put an arm around her friend. "If there's anything I can do."

Scarlett patted the hand on her shoulder and then pulled away. "I'm fine. You and Gray have done so much. I can never thank you enough."

At one fifteen, Scarlett, Savannah, and Madison occupied Jake's SUV. "Good the weather cleared," Phil Madison said, leaning forward to look at the sky as Jake drove toward Atlanta. However, despite cessation of the rain, clouds hovered. Sandwiched between an SUV containing Brenda and Sonny in the lead and one with Mike O'Quinn and an associate behind, the interior of the Lexus had remained predominately silent during the forty-five-minute ride.

The closer the vehicle came to its destination, the muscles in Scarlett's stomach grew tighter. She glanced across at her sister, wondering what Savannah was thinking. The widow gazed pensively out the tinted window on her side. Savannah's hands lay relaxed on her lap. *If she's nervous, it isn't showing.*

Since arriving in Georgia, Savannah had said little but did talk with Scarlett for a few minutes about her children before Phil Madison whisked her into Gray's study for a private conversation. Scarlett assumed he provided last-minute reminders on how the widow should handle herself.

When Jake made a right turn, Scarlett switched her focus. From her position behind the front passenger seat, she had a clear view of him and noted how good he looked—clean-shaven and wearing a black suit, white shirt, and dark-gray tie. Although he had worn the same suit the day they met, in his haste to strip to comfort level, she had missed the Yale attorney image. *Grace is right. He's pretty cool. Probably has a significant other.*

Her attention quickly returned to Savannah and memories of their youth when curious acquaintances had asked if twins had ESP. *Not hardly. I've never known what you're thinking. I'm not even sure you weren't involved in Scott's death.* Scarlett blinked her eyes and took a deep breath. *Dear God. I hope you weren't.*

As the large church came into view, Jake said, "I'll alert your security we're about to enter the property. They'll meet us on the west side and escort you inside."

"I know," Savannah said, staring blankly at the windshield. "We'll all gather in the big room behind the sanctuary."

"Are you going in with us?" Scarlett asked Jake.

He shook his head. "No. I'll be in the crowd, keeping an eye out. Phil and the Capitol Police will stay with you until after the graveside service, but I'll be close."

Scarlett felt the knots in her stomach shift. "You don't think anyone will try anything, do you?"

Phil Madison and Savannah looked at Jake.

"There's been no word of potential threats, but anytime there's a large gathering with high-profile participants, security goes on high alert. Don't worry. There's more security on the scene than for a presidential visit."

People were filing into the church as Jake made a turn toward the side entrance. Atlanta PD secured the side road, prohibiting entry of any unauthorized vehicles. As he brought the SUV to a stop, two men in dark suits, accompanied by uniformed officers of the Capitol Police, walked down to meet the occupants. After assisting the two women from the car, the shorter man introduced himself and his companion while Jake and Madison stood by.

"Mrs. Kingsley, I'm FBI Assistant Special Agent-in-Charge Dan Cameron of the Atlanta Field Office, and this is Assistant Special Agent-in-Charge Hal Kirby of Washington." Kirby nodded.

Hearing his name gave Scarlett a start. *Jake's? Oh, my gosh!*

"We wanted to extend our deepest condolences and to let you know we're here should any need arise," Cameron said.

Savannah stared at Dan Cameron without any show of emotion, gave a slight nod, and began walking toward the building, leaving the men to speak to Madison and Jake.

"Nice to see you, Madison," Kirby said, shaking hands. "Jake."

Scarlett stared, fascinated by the exchange of the two men, connected by marriage to the same woman.

Seemingly unfazed, Jake shook Kirby's hand. "Kirby."

While Savannah proceeded up the walk, flanked by the Capitol Police, Scarlett remained frozen in place, almost holding her breath as if expecting trouble. It ended quickly with Madison ushering her to the building while Jake returned to the vehicle to relocate it to a designated parking spot.

Was that an awkward moment? As she entered the church, the muffled sound of Handel's "Largo" from *Xerxes* set the tone for the service to come, and the familiar smell of the old building rekindled memories from her childhood. Scarlett sang in the church choirs from elementary school through her college graduation. After the breakup with Scott, she chose to attend a small church in Decatur but never joined the choir.

"Scarlett, are you okay?" Grace said as the family greeted one another with hugs. Savannah's children, overjoyed to see their mother, jockeyed with their grandmother for her attention. As Scarlett embraced her youngest sister, she noticed Scott's parents occupying a sofa on the opposite side of the room. Once greetings were completed with the Kavanagh family, Joe and Carolyn Kingsley stood, approached Savannah, and then Scarlett.

"Thank you for coming," Carolyn said. "It's been so long since we've seen you, Scarlett."

Scarlett smiled weakly. "I'm so sorry, Carolyn. I don't know what to say."

A tear cruised down the gray-haired woman's face. "I know. Maybe we can talk later."

Despite her negative feelings about Scott, Scarlett pitied his mother as she gazed into Carolyn's sad eyes. *You have no idea who your son was, and I hope you never have to learn.*

A low drone of conversation continued in the room generally used for assembly by the choir before services, for vestry meetings, and for small receptions. Little change had occurred in the years since Scarlett last stood there.

At one forty-five, the family organized for the procession into the sanctuary. Savannah and the children would enter last.

This is it. Scarlett inhaled and mentally rehearsed her role. *Shoulders back, careful steps, inscrutable face.*

Seven minutes later, Scarlett stood in the second pew with Grace and Rob. She watched as Savannah entered and then paused by the casket. In a gesture of tenderness, the pretty widow placed a hand on the polished wood and bowed her head. *Well played.*

A seat in the first few rows precluded an opportunity to see the crowd once Scarlett took her place. However, on the short journey, she caught a glimpse of the huge crowd and what she suspected were plainclothes law enforcement persons positioned in the aisles. The family sat on the right side, VIPs on the left. Scarlett wondered where Jake was, disappointed she didn't see him before taking her place. *Could the killer be here?* The thought sent a shiver down her spine.

The service went smoothly. Politicians offered formal eulogies, praising Scott's work and lamenting his untimely demise. After an hour, which felt like ten, the cleric pronounced the benediction, the recessional hymn began, and officials escorted Savannah and the children back to the prior chamber. The remainder of the family and the high-ranking attendees exited down the middle aisle behind the casket, clergy, and choir, which provided Scarlett a view of the congregation. However, she never found Jake in the crowd.

Outside, limousines and SUVs lined the street, waiting to transport the family as they assembled. Uniformed police lined the area. "Where's Savannah?" Susan Kavanagh asked.

"A limo is picking her up at the side door and will drive her around to follow the casket to the cemetery," Madison said. As if reading Scarlett's mind, he said, "Jake is picking you and me up. He's in the line." He pointed toward Jake's vehicle.

"At least the sun is finally out," Scarlett said, looking up at the sky.

Groups had formed while waiting for their respective transport to reach the walk. Those without drivers disbursed to the large parking lot.

"What's taking so long?" Grace said as she joined Scarlett and the attorney.

"Savannah's probably redoing her hair and makeup. No one can go until her limo comes around," Scarlett said. "Is that your car behind Jake's Lexus?"

"Yeah. Rob and I are riding with Mom and Dad. The Kingsleys are riding in the limo behind Savannah and the children."

Scarlett opened her purse, took out a tissue, and blotted the small beads of perspiration on her nose.

"This is ridiculous," Grace said. "Savannah left the sanctuary long before we got out, and we've been standing here for nearly twenty minutes."

"Typical, don't you think," Scarlett said, turning her head so her face could not be seen by the bevy of TV cameras lining the area. "Be careful what you say. Media is everywhere."

Grace twisted her mouth and raised an eyebrow, giving Scarlett a dubious look, and then went to the vehicle containing the rest of the Kavanagh family.

Five minutes later, as Phil Madison checked his watch, Jake exited his vehicle and approached them.

"What's going on," Madison asked.

Jake leaned in. "We've got a problem," he said, tight-lipped.

Madison's jaw tensed. "What kind of problem?"

"Client is MIA."

Scarlett could barely hear but caught the MIA and couldn't resist interrupting. "What do you mean MIA?"

"Keep it down," Jake said, his brows meeting and his eyes flashing a warning. "Your sister disappeared after going into a bathroom at the back of the church."

Scarlett leaned toward Jake, covering her mouth. "How could she disappear? Weren't there security agents with her?"

"Seems they cleared the room but were forced to give her privacy since they were both male. When she didn't come out, they reached out for a female officer from Atlanta PD to check. The bathroom was empty."

"Oh, my god." Alarm rose on Scarlett's face.

"Watch your expression. *Meet the Press* is everywhere."

"Any sign of foul play?" Madison asked.

"Not that they've found. Dan Cameron has called in all available law enforcement to help, but the first question is—does the service continue?"

Scarlett looked from Jake to Madison.

"I say, yes. We need to keep a lid on this until we know more," Madison said.

"How does the service go on without Savannah?" Scarlett asked. "What if she's been kidnapped?"

Ignoring Scarlett's question, Madison said, "We make an announcement that she became ill but wishes the service to proceed." He looked around. "I'll handle it with the clergy."

"Can you brief your family when you reach the cemetery, Scarlett?" Jake asked. "They should know before any public announcement is made. Don't let them know she's missing. Use the same cover story— she's not feeling well."

Although bewildered, Scarlett nodded. "Yes. I'll tell Mom and Dad Savannah wants us all to go through with the graveside prayers." She looked at Jake, a plea for understanding in her eyes, but after glancing around at the TV crews, she chose not to ask questions.

"One more thing, we need to arrange for the Kingsley children. They are in the choir room with the Capitol Police," Jake said.

"I think they should go to the cemetery. The fewer changes we make, the fewer questions will arise," Madison said. "Have them brought out here. We can fit them in our car. Jake, you should hang out with the Feds as much as they'll let you. I'll drive your car and pick you up later."

Scarlett looked from lawyer to investigator and back, trying to process the shock of what had happened. Her mind raced, but she knew the importance of remaining calm in the face of the circumstances. "It would be better, Phil, to have Colin and Victoria ride with my parents and my youngest sister. I hardly know them."

"Not a good idea, Harvard," Jake said. "That would send shock waves and likely set off a firestorm. We'll tell them when we reach the cemetery, right before the official announcement."

"I can tell you've met my mother." Taking a deep breath, she exhaled and then said, "I get it, but won't someone in their car likely see the children coming toward us? Their vehicle is right behind us."

"True, but arousing curiosity won't necessarily create alarm. It's our best shot." Jake pointed to his watch. "We've got to get this moving." He looked around. "People are getting restless, and the media is ready to attack."

"Agreed," Madison said and proceeded toward the limousine transporting the clergy.

After Madison spoke with the officiating priest, he returned to the pair.

"Jake, reach out to your FBI contact. Say the family wants the service to continue as planned. The widow's limousine, with curtains drawn, will take its scheduled place behind the hearse without her. Have them bring the children to us."

"Won't the public resent being deceived when they find out?" Scarlett asked, struggling to keep her face stoic for the benefit of onlookers.

"Possibly, but it's a risk we have to take. Keep in mind they're here to pay respects to Senator Kingsley, not your sister. Do you think anyone would choose to skip the final portion of his funeral because she wasn't present?" He glanced over her shoulder. "I'll head to the back. Look sharp, Harvard. They'll be bringing the kids out as soon." He looked Scarlett in the eye. "Better take your place near the car. They may spit out questions when they see you. Conversation needs to stay inside the SUV."

Scarlett's heart raced; her palms grew damp. "What do I say if they ask where she is?"

"Play it by ear. There's no manual for this situation."

Scarlett blinked, took a deep breath, and walked to the Lexus.

Dear God. Don't let me blow this.

CHAPTER TWENTY-FIVE

"I hope this isn't a stunt orchestrated by you," Hal Kirby said as Jake reached the two ASACs.

"I'll do you a favor and ignore that." Jake gave his former supervisor a look that could slice a diamond. "Need I remind you guys who kicked my security team out of the picture? This is on your people. Couldn't take care of her for ninety minutes?"

Dan Cameron raised a hand to quell the tension. "Jake, what do you know?"

"Other than this was a botched job of security—not much. How the hell do you lose a woman in closed quarters with more scrutiny and security than at an inauguration?"

Ignoring the question, Cameron said, "I think we need to determine whether she's a victim or a fugitive?"

"I don't see Shepherd in that equation," Kirby said, "but my money is on the latter."

Jake cut his eyes toward Kirby, his jaw tense. "Typical rush to judgment. Don't even try to cut me out." Jake glanced at a text on his phone from Phil, asking if he had connected. He hit the thumbs-up emoji and said to Kirby, "You need me as much or more than I need you. And, by the way, those are not the only possibilities. Ever occur to you she might be a scared rabbit on the run?"

"Afraid of being arrested," Kirby said.

"More like afraid of the sketchy dealings her husband may have been involved in. Have you forgotten you have a woman missing in DC and a dead politician who lived like Jeff Bezos on one seventy-five a year?"

"Okay, boys, have your debate later. How is the funeral to proceed with the widow missing?" Dan Cameron asked. "Who's in charge?"

"As the widow's legal representative, Phil Madison is on top of it," Jake said. "He wants the media kept in the dark until they reach the cemetery. No sense creating public chaos." He slid his phone back in his inside breast pocket. "Have an escort take the children to Madison at the front of the church—and try not to lose them. Then send Mrs. Kingsley's limo around to join the procession, curtains drawn."

Cameron gave a slight shake of his head, an okay sign with his hand, and then typed a text on his cell.

"What are you guys doing to find her?" Jake asked, drilling down on Kirby, who began to sweat from the heat of the sun.

"I'm deferring to Cameron on this one," Kirby said. "He's got the Atlanta manpower and can reach out for backup from the other agencies. His people have already locked down the area where she was last seen and are doing a thorough search of the premises. I assume you had her on a throwaway cell." He shifted his stance and adjusted his weapon through his coat. "Save us some time and give me the number."

"I'll trade you the number for your guarantee to provide me with what you get from a trace."

Hal Kirby gave a disgusted snap of his head. "Why would I do that? I don't need you getting in the way."

"You really want to play it that way when I've got attorney-client privilege in my back pocket and don't have to share a damn thing with you?"

"Cool it, fellows. Play nice. For the moment, I think we're all on the same team," Cameron said. "Since she's gone missing in my jurisdiction, I'm coordinating the investigation along with the Capitol Police and Atlanta PD." He made eye contact with Jake. "You've got *my* word."

Kirby growled under his breath as Jake pulled out a small pad, scratched down the number, ripped off the sheet, and passed it to Kirby.

"I want to check the area where she was last seen and talk to the Capitols assigned to her," Jake said.

"We've already talked to them. They're clueless," Kirby said.

"Humor me."

Cameron glanced over at Kirby and then tipped his head in the direction of the church. "Follow me."

As the two men walked inside the building, Kirby trailing, Jake asked Cameron, "What's the status of surveillance cameras on the property?"

"Inadequate. Probably installed by *Bob the Builder*. Front is covered, but back has big gaps."

"Damn. As if thieves never enter through the back door." Jake turned toward Kirby. "I know you have data on her bank account and credit card activity. I'd like a look at that as well."

"What makes you think we can pull it so fast?"

Jake's brows pinched together. "Cut the BS. We all know you've been monitoring the family financials since the ME pronounced homicide. Probably had the warrant drawn up before they picked up the body."

"As smart as you think you are, Shepherd, you should know they went silent after she withdrew a substantial bankroll the day the senator was discovered—which could have been to finance a getaway, use for a payoff, or pay your fee. How much do you charge?"

Jake gave him a dirty look. "Get a subpoena."

When they reached the combination conference room, lounge, and family waiting room, FBI agents Weston and Blake were standing at the door, along with two male officers of the United States Capitol Police.

"Find anything?" Kirby asked.

"No sign of Mrs. Kingsley, but we found a possible means of exit," Deke Weston said.

"A window?" Jake asked.

"No. A door."

"An exit door in the bathroom?" Kirby asked, a dubious look on his face.

"Come on. I'll show you." Deke Weston gave a nod toward Jake as if to ask, "Is he allowed?"

Catching Weston's nonverbal question, Dan Cameron spoke up. "Shepherd's working with us."

Inside the restroom, there were three stalls on the right and a long counter with three sinks on the left. Cameron walked to the back wall. Next to the last stall, an open area created a hall, which led to a door, slightly ajar. After putting on a pair of latex gloves, he opened the door to reveal a long, narrow closet with choir robes hanging along the right and shelves on the left with various supplies. Pointing through the storage area, he said, "The door at the other end opens into a room that has an outside exit."

"They leave this unlocked?" Kirby asked.

"Not routinely. That's the rub. Whether she fled or was forcibly taken, there's a question as to how. Was the door left unlocked? Did someone have a key?"

"Close it and give me a glove," Jake said and pulled out his wallet. The two Federal agents looked at him.

"Go ahead. Close it."

When Cameron complied, Jake slipped the glove on his right hand, leaned around Cameron, and slid a credit card in the jam, releasing the lock. "*Voila.*"

Kirby and Cameron both shook their heads. "Score one for Shepherd," Cameron said.

"Look, fellows. This is a church—an old church. Their locks are designed to keep out honest people. They don't anticipate the criminal element."

"I think this proves she fled of her own volition," Kirby said.

"I beg to differ," Jake said. "How hard would it have been for an armed abductor to gain access to this area when everyone was in the sanctuary, wait for the widow to come in, which would be a reasonable assumption, and then force her out? Maybe a female operative."

"The fallacy to your theory is John Q. Cop out there supposedly cleared the room before the subject entered."

"Yeah? Like you, John Q. Cop probably assumed the door was locked and therefore the space secure. I'm not saying that's the way it happened. I'm saying that's one possibility. I suggest you err on the side of caution and treat this as an abduction."

"Isn't that a change from your position this past week? You did a *damned* good job of keeping her whereabouts unknown," Kirby said.

"The threat of foul play trumps my previous position. I'm forced to yield to your resources to solve an abduction."

"If you expect us to cooperate with you, I expect reciprocity. You give us any leads you develop in the murder—full disclosure."

"Why wouldn't I? You have the authority to make an arrest."

CHAPTER TWENTY-SIX

Madison left Scarlett on the passenger side of the vehicle to wait for the children while he circled around to the driver's side.

Colin came dashing toward Scarlett as she steadied herself, breathing in the aroma of wet grass and continuing to pray for the right words to convey to the fatherless, possibly motherless, children. A warm breeze brushed her face, drying the perspiration beads on her nose.

"Aunt Scarlett. Where is my mom?" Like vibrant blue marbles, the seven-year-old's eyes pleaded for reassurance as his golden bangs clung to his damp forehead.

The innocence tore at Scarlett's heart. *If you've run away, Savannah, leaving these children, I could kill you myself.* Scarlett felt instantly guilty when the alternative flashed through her mind.

"I'm not quite sure, sweetie, but we need to get in the car. Okay?"

The little brow creased as if he were experiencing difficulty in processing the situation.

"Can you do that for me?" she asked, glancing past him at Victoria. *She could be my daughter—hair, eyes. What is that child thinking?*

A woman dressed in a classic black suit walked beside Victoria. When close enough, the woman extended her hand.

"Special Agent Sylvia Blake, FBI. I'll be riding with you to the cemetery."

"Nice to meet you. I'm—"

"You don't have to tell me. You're Mrs. Kingsley's sister. The hair may be different, but I see the likeness."

"Interesting. Most people don't. I assume you'll sit in front."

Blake nodded, opened the door, and introduced herself to Phil Madison.

No one prepared me for the FBI riding with us. Best keep quiet.

Victoria looked up at Scarlett but didn't speak as she climbed into the SUV and slid across the seat. Colin followed, leaving Scarlett a place by the window.

The limousine, with curtains drawn, pulled around the SUV. Madison cranked the Lexus and shifted into drive.

"Is Mommy in that big car?" Colin asked.

What do I say? What do I say?

"It's her car, honey." *How are these children going to take the news their mother is missing? There's no way to shield them.*

The explanation appeared to satisfy the boy, but before the procession started, he leaned across Scarlett, pointing out the window. "There's Kyle." He turned to Scarlett. "Can Kyle ride with us?"

Caught off guard, Scarlett hesitated, staring out the window at a six-foot, young man who looked to be in his late teens. *What did I hear about Kyle? He's a handsome kid.*

No one in the vehicle spoke.

"Please, Aunt Scarlett. Let Kyle ride with us."

Victoria gave him a dirty look, rolling her eyes, but did not comment. "Please."

"Colin, I'm so sorry, but we can't do that."

"Why not?"

Scarlett glanced at Special Agent Blake, who sat rigid, eyes forward. *Okay, Scarlett. How are you going to deal with this?* Glancing toward the driver, she thought she saw Madison's lips curl. *Don't look so smug, Madison, or I'll tell him to ask you.* Turning toward the boy, she took his hand and rubbed it gently. "We can't invite Kyle to ride with us because it's against the rules." *I'm going to Hell for this one.* "Maybe you can see Kyle at the cemetery—after the service." She wanted to seek clarification as to Kyle's identity, but glancing at the back of Sylvia Blake's head, she thought better. *Not the time to open up a dialogue.*

CHAPTER TWENTY-SEVEN

By six o'clock, the entire Kavanagh family had settled into the home of Alan and Susan. Rob Burton took the children for pizza. The tedious afternoon had taken a toll on all the family. When the priest announced at the gravesite that Savannah had taken ill and would not attend, Susan Kavanagh had maintained her composure. It wasn't until they returned to the house that Madison and Scarlett broke the news that Savannah was not ill but had disappeared. Even then, although distressed, Susan managed to contain her emotions to Scarlett's relief.

"She's been kidnapped," Susan said, her body rigid, color absent from her face.

"We don't know that, Mom. She may have felt she had to get away." *I can't let her see my fear.*

Grace covered her mouth, her eyes betraying her shock. "The private investigator must have been right. She *was* in danger."

"Everyone, please try to avoid assuming the worst," Phil Madison said. "The FBI is on top of this. They haven't found any evidence of foul play. While no one is ruling out abduction, there's also no reason to believe that's the case."

"Where is that investigator?" Alan Kavanagh asked. "He was here yesterday, asking Grace and me questions about Scott and Savannah."

"He's working with the Federal agents," Madison said. "Trust me. He's good at what he does. You couldn't have a better source working for you."

"I believe him, Dad. I've been with Jake since last Friday. He can be a bit abrasive, but he's smart and remarkably intuitive. He's a former FBI agent."

"Jake wasn't just an FBI agent," Madison said. "He was a member of the elite HRT."

Scarlett snapped her head around toward Madison, her brow furrowed. "He was a member of the HRT?"

"He was."

"What's that?" Grace asked.

"I don't know exactly," Scarlett said. "But Bud Wilson talked about wanting to join the FBI and be part of it."

"It's the FBI's Hostage Rescue Team," Madison said. "They are the Navy SEALs, the Army Delta Force of the FBI." Madison looked at his watch. "I'd better take off. I need to pick up Jake, stop at my hotel, and pick up my bag. My flight takes off at nine thirty."

"Do you need a ride to the airport?" Alan asked.

"Thank you, but either Jake will run me out, or I'll take a cab. You need to be with your family."

After Madison left, Susan took a Valium and went to her room.

"Should she be alone?" Grace asked.

Alan shook his head. "I'll check on her."

When he left the room, Scarlett turned to Grace. "I'll stay if you think you need me."

"We'll be fine. You've been helping Jake, haven't you?"

"As much as I can. I understand the FBI is taking the nanny back to DC. Did they tell you?"

"I think so. I've been so upset, I can't remember who told me what." She rubbed her forehead. "You know those children are virtually orphans if they don't find her."

"Don't go there, Grace."

Later that night, Scarlett lay on the edge of her bed in the MacGregor guestroom, eyes wide open. She had wanted to escape for solitude but found it lacking in comfort. Although exhausted, neither TV nor reading delivered sleep. She had not seen or talked to Jake after leaving the cemetery, although she thought she heard him pass her room about eleven.

After trying every trick in her insomnia catalog, including self-hypnosis, at twelve forty-five, she remained awake. Multiple images of horror tumbled around in her head: Savannah being forcibly taken by a weapon-wielding abductor; Savannah's mangled body being found in some ditch or shallow grave; Alan and Susan being told Savannah was dead; the children orphaned.

Scarlett's nerve endings tingled with terror. She needed reassurance, Jake's confidence—his strength—his protection. Climbing out of bed, she donned her silk caftan and slipped out of her room and down the hall

Softly tapping on Jake's door, she waited, her heart pounding. *I won't knock harder.*

The door opened, revealing Jake pulling a well-worn tee shirt down over his washboard abs. The tight garment bore the letters FBI. His bare feet, disheveled hair, and unbuttoned jeans indicated he had been in bed.

A seductive smile slid across his face as he saw her clutching the lapels of her robe with a shaking hand. "Scarlett?"

For several seconds, the hallway was silent as his hazel eyes engaged hers.

"May I come in?"

A moment more passed in silence, and then he said softly, "Of course, you may." Taking her trembling hand from the garment, allowing it to fall open, he led her inside.

CHAPTER TWENTY-EIGHT

Friday morning, Scarlett barely acknowledged Jake as she passed through the breakfast room on her way to the terrace. Gray shifted his gaze back and forth between the two, settling on Jake.

"Anything you want to tell me?"

"Nothing I can think of."

"Come on, Shepherd. The look she just gave you tells me you either had a hell of a fight or a hell of a delight last night."

"Turn your radar off, pal. Relationships between investigator and client are off-limits."

"She's not your client."

"Close enough. Don't you have a corporation to take over today or a small country to buy?"

Gray laughed. "Ouch! Did I strike a nerve? Surely not with the intrepid Jake Shepherd."

Jake rolled his eyes, shook his head, and then stood. "I need more caffeine." He approached the buffet, filled his cup, and added a spoonful of instant granules to strengthen it.

Gray watched, shaking his head. "If I consumed coffee that strong, I'd be able to fly to DC without a plane."

Jake sat back down at the table, using his free hand to adjust the holster clipped to his belt. "I know. Hazard of the job—too many long hours doing surveillance. But, you're right. I need to wean myself." He took a sip. "Listen up. About Scarlett. All kidding aside. She's on the edge. Can you and Fury pay a little extra attention tonight while I'm in DC? She's too proud to admit it's getting to her."

Gray set his coffee cup down. "We're on it. First murder and now the disappearance—a lot to handle." He watched Jake for a few seconds. "Sounds like you've gotten to know her pretty well."

With one brow cocked and the opposite eye squinting, Jake shot him an admonishing glare.

Gray raised his hands in a sign of surrender. "I know. I know. Go raid a corp—mind my own business." With that, he stood. "I do have to get to the office. But she is a stunning woman." He winked.

"I hadn't noticed, but I'll warn the Exchange you're off your leash."

Gray laughed, slapped Jake on the shoulder, and left.

For a few minutes following Gray's departure, Jake sat, staring at Scarlett through the window. After draining his coffee cup, he stood, considered a refill, and then changed his mind. Instead, he went out to the terrace.

With her chin resting in one hand, her elbow on the garden table, Scarlett glanced up but quickly looked away.

"Did I do something to offend you last night, Harvard?" he asked, sliding onto a chair opposite her.

She took in a deep breath. The aroma of gardenia bushes beneath the veranda filled the air.

"Scarlett. Are you not speaking to me?"

"I don't know what you're talking about. Nothing happened last night."

A twinkle flickered in his eyes as the corners of his lips turned up. "Nothing happened last night?"

"Nothing. If you think it did, you must have been dreaming."

"Okay. If I was dreaming, bring on the Ambien because it was one hell of a dream."

"Nothing happened." She glared at him. "Do you understand?"

"I do. Nothing happened. Whatever you say."

"What did you tell Gray?"

"What could I have told Gray? As you say, 'Nothing happened.'"

"Stop that."

"Stop what?" He scrunched his eyebrows in an expression of confusion.

"Stop answering a question with a question. You do it all the time. That's the cop in you, isn't it?"

"Maybe. Probably." He reached across for her hand curled around her teacup. She pulled it away.

"Scarlett." He grabbed her hand and held it firmly with both of his. "We are working together. Whatever buyer's remorse you are suffering, deep-six it. If you say nothing happened—nothing happened. You write the script and direct the scene. I serve at your pleasure."

"Ohhh—that was a terrible choice of words." Despite herself, Scarlett's resolved faded, and a smile lightened her scowl.

"It was, wasn't it?" He released her hand. "But what can you expect from a rude SOB like me?"

A male cardinal swooped down and landed on the fountain in the center of the nearby flower garden, momentarily distracting Scarlett.

"It's beautiful here, isn't it?" she said. "Peace and tranquility. No sign of the dark and evil elements of the outside world."

"It is, but from what I understand, Gray had his demons like the rest of us—only his were stuffed with diamonds, gold-plated, and packed in large bills."

"Fury really brought him out of his inferno."

"I can see she's good for him, but back to our situation. Are you okay with my going to DC tonight?"

"Of course. You can't disappoint your daughter."

"There will be other ballets. These are extraordinary times for you and your family."

"I've got it together, Jake. I know what you're thinking. I did fall off the train last night, but I'm back onboard today. Besides, you're my sister's private investigator—not my babysitter."

"That's my line, Harvard."

She smiled. "Yeah. I know."

He stood. "So, we're good."

"We're good."

"Then, I'd better take off. Meeting with Cameron and his team this morning. Kirby and company flew back to DC last night with the nanny. If you feel like it, work on those files. I know you'll spend some time with your family today. Let Brenda know what time you want to go."

"Are you coming back before you fly out?"

"Definitely. I'll shower and change here." He reached over and patted her on her shoulder. "Call or text if you need me."

She nodded. "Let me know if anything comes up about Savannah."

He gave her a thumbs-up and started for the French door entry, passing Fury as she came outside.

"Take care of our favorite attorney," Jake said. "There's a marshmallow buried at the core of that steel exterior."

"For sure." Fury's gaze followed as he disappeared into the house. Turning back to Scarlett, she said, "That's one sexy guy."

Scarlett made a face. "I don't believe you said that."

Fury dropped into the chair Jake had vacated. "Chill, my friend. I'm just thinking he would be a good model for the love interest in my next novel. You've got to admit he's hot."

"I thought you weren't writing romance now."

"I couldn't stop completely. Once a romance writer, always a romance writer. As my agent says, I built my tribe and shouldn't desert them. Being around Jake for a week, don't tell me you haven't noticed that muscles-in-all-the-right-places body and that animal sensuality?"

Scarlett shook her head, scowling. "Easy to tell you're a romance writer."

"Okay, okay. I'll drop it. How are you?"

"Fine."

"Be honest. You've been through hell this past week, and now Savannah—missing. This is brutal. What does Jake think?"

"He and Phil Madison say don't assume the worst. Not easy after a week of living on the edge with armed security. Last night my imagination went wild. I kept seeing horrible scenes and thinking about the children. Mom is convinced Savannah would never leave her kids voluntarily."

"I don't know your sister, but I have to agree she would have to be pretty cold to leave them. For a long time, I wouldn't travel without the boys—afraid a plane might crash, and who would love them as much as I do?"

"I have no idea whether Savannah is a devoted mom. I hope she is, but then I don't want to think she was abducted. However, right now, I'd better go upstairs and work on the files Jake is expecting me to review. I'm going to my folks' house before lunch, which I dread. Mom held it together yesterday—better than I expected—but I bet it will be chaotic today."

"Is there anything I can do?"

"Thank you for offering, but no. It's wait and see, which is torture. I'm thankful for Grace. She is a saint—so much patience with Mom and great with the children." Scarlett stood, circled the table, gave Fury a hug, and went inside.

After combing through the case files all morning, Scarlett, along with Brenda Lassiter, arrived at the Kavanagh home in Ansley Park at noon. Grace Burton met them in the front yard. "I need to talk to you before you go in."

"Okay." Scarlett glanced around at Brenda, who was surveying the quiet street.

"Not here." Grace pointed to the side of the house. "The backyard."

Scarlett raised her eyebrows and gave Brenda a shrug.

"I'll follow you," Brenda said.

As the trio wove their way through the abundant shrubbery, Scarlett yelped.

"Damn."

Grace stopped, turned, and put her finger to her lips.

"A rose bush got me." Scarlett rubbed her arm.

When they reached the wooden gate, Grace unlatched the metal clasp and held it for Scarlett and Brenda to pass. Across the yard, the Burton and Kingsley children were taking turns on a refurbished trampoline, a holdover from the Kavanagh girls' childhood. "Stay here by the gate. I don't want the kids to hear us," Grace said.

"What's with the cloak and dagger routine?" Scarlett asked.

"It's Mom. She's out of control, and I wanted you to have a heads-up."

"You couldn't have just said that out front?"

"Scarlett, she wants to call the media. She thinks the FBI is screwing up the search for Savannah and the abductors are going to kill her. She tried to call your investigator, but Dad jerked the phone away before she could finish dialing. She went berserk. I thought she was going to attack him. We can't handle her."

"And you think I can?"

"We convinced her to wait until you got here, but once you go in there, I'm not sure what's going to happen. She's upsetting the kids."

Perplexed, Scarlett looked at Brenda. "Any ideas?"

"Maybe."

Grace stared at Brenda. "I'm sorry. I don't think we've met. I know you're one of the bodyguards."

"Brenda Lassiter. My husband and I work for Jake—security for Mrs. Kingsley in the safe house."

"What are *you* thinking, Brenda?" Scarlett asked.

"Let me introduce myself to her and explain that I am a former Baltimore PD detective and my husband is former FBI. I'll try to convince her it's vital that she follow the instructions of those leading the investigation because they are trained to deal with this type of event."

"I'm not sure she'll listen to you," Grace said.

"I'll lay it on the line. Inform her if she interferes, she could be putting her daughter's life in serious peril."

"I wish Jake were here. He wouldn't put up with her hysteria," Scarlett said.

Brenda smiled. "You've gotten to know him, I see."

Scarlett nodded and looked at Grace. "What now? Go back to the front door?"

"No. We'll go in through the back. I'll just tell her you wanted to see the kids first."

"If that's the case, I'd better give it some validity." Scarlett walked toward the trampoline. "Hey, guys. You having fun?"

"Aunt Scarlett." Colin came running to Scarlett, a big smile proclaiming his excitement. "Is my mommy with you?"

Damn. What do I say? Scarlett crouched down to his level. "I'm sorry, Colin. She's not."

His small face fell. With a quivering lower lip, he appeared close to bursting into tears. But he didn't. "Did you see her?"

She took his small hands in hers. *I can't lie. It will be all over the media.* "No, sweetie, I haven't."

"Where is she?"

Scarlett swallowed, wanting to avoid giving an answer as his eyes silently pled for good news. "I'm not really sure. She didn't tell me."

"My daddy's dead." He spoke with a vacant expression as if she were not aware.

Although the little boy's tone sent a chill down her spine, Scarlett nodded. "I know, honey." Staring at his wide-eyed face, his innocence tore at her heart as she thought of how his life had forever changed in a matter of days.

Colin pulled his hands away but moved closer. Cupping a hand to the side of his mouth, he leaned near her ear, pushing her hair out of his way, and whispered in her ear, "Can you take me home?"

Scarlett choked on his pitiful plea, helpless as to how to comfort the child. *What if Savannah never returns?*

"Please, Aunt Scarlett. Take me home. Mommy might be there. She might be sad."

Scarlett reached up and brushed the blond bangs off his sweaty forehead. "No, baby. She's not at your house. That I do know."

"She could be at the other house. Please."

Neither Grace nor Brenda made a sound. Scarlett took a deep breath and glanced around at them, frantically seeking help. Tears teetered on Grace's lower eyelids. Even Brenda's eyes were glassy. Returning her focus to Colin, Scarlett said, "I wish with all my heart I could take you home—maybe soon. Aren't you having fun here? I saw you jumping on the trampoline."

"It's okay, but I don't have any of my toys or anyone to play with."

"You have your cousins."

His little head shook in disagreement. "Kat's older than me, and she's a *girl*. The twins are babies. They don't know how to play video games. If I could go home, Kyle could come over and play *Fast and Furious* with me on the tablet and take me bike riding—like he does when Mommy's not home."

"Kyle is the young man you saw at the funeral?"

"Uh-huh."

Wonder why a teenage boy pays attention to a seven-year-old? "Tell you what. If you give me a list of your favorite toys, kinda like a list for Santa, I'll make sure you have some new ones by tomorrow. Would that help?"

"Really?" A wide grin flipped his expression one hundred eighty degrees and revealed his dimples. Catching himself, he frowned. "I'd rather have Mommy, but new Hot Wheels and Legos would be awesome."

Scarlett smiled, stood, and pulled him close with a hug, thinking, *Amazon, here I come.* "You've got it." Releasing him, she said, "Now, I need to go inside to visit Grandma and Grandpa. Can you play outside a little longer?"

He raised his little hand for a high-five and then scampered back toward the trampoline.

Watching him, a maternal feeling came over Scarlett as she craved a way to ease his pain. Catching a glimpse of Tori, she realized her niece was suffering as well. *She's internalizing the pain. I have to see what I can do for her.*

As the three women moved into the house, Scarlett's mind wandered. *If I hadn't gone to Harvard, would I have a Colin—a Tori? One thing is sure. I wouldn't be a widow because I would have divorced the bastard.*

Passing through the kitchen, the women met Alan Kavanagh.

"How is she?" Grace asked her father.

"On the edge of the abyss." He set his glass of tea next to a platter of sandwiches covered with clear plastic and hugged Scarlett. "I'm glad you're here, Scout. But I'm not sure you can talk sense into your mama." He glanced toward Brenda.

Reading his thought, Scarlett said, "Dad, this is Brenda Lassiter. She works security for Jake. We think she should talk to Mom."

With a look of doubt, he shook his head but said, "Might as well."

Susan Kavanagh sat alone in the walnut-paneled den with the drapes drawn. While she appeared focused on a TV screen, the empty look in her eyes suggested her brain was not engaged. When the group entered, she sprang from her chair, an anxious expression replacing the zombie look.

"Where have you been? I've been waiting all morning for you to get here. Do you have any news?" she said to Scarlett.

"Hello to you, too, Mom. I told you last night that I would be here around noon." Scarlett walked over to give her mother a hug, but Susan barely reciprocated. "No. I don't have any news."

"You've got to call the FBI and find out what's going on."

"It doesn't work that way, Mom. They will call if there's anything to report."

"Then, I'm calling Channel 2 and CNN."

"Bad idea." Scarlett turned and beckoned Brenda forward. "This is one of Jake's security agents. She's a retired police detective and can explain the procedure to you."

"I don't want an explanation. I want action. My daughter is out there"—her hand shook as she pointed to a window—"enduring who knows what. Maybe dying or dead. No one is helping."

"Mrs. Kavanagh, the Federal agents are working the case. Unfortunately, it doesn't always happen as quickly as everyone would like."

"I want to talk to the agent in charge. I know my rights. If he refuses to listen, CNN will. Savannah is the wife—widow—of a United States senator."

"Don't even think of doing that, Mrs. Kavanagh. You could spook an abductor and force his hand. The Bureau knows the best procedure—the best timing of a press release."

"I want to talk to the man in charge. Scarlett, call that private investigator. He'll know how to get in touch with the FBI."

"We're not going to do that, Mom. You have got to be patient."

Susan's nostrils flared. Fiery rage shot from her eyes. "How can you stand there and say that? Right this minute, some monster could be torturing your sister—murdering her. You've always been jealous of her. You blame her for your breakup with Scott."

Scarlett closed her eyes for a second and took a deep breath. "Considering the circumstances, I'm going to pretend you didn't say that." She turned and walked back toward her father. "I can't deal with her."

Grace stood frozen, glancing from one member of her family to the other. Without warning, she stepped forward. "That was uncalled for, Mom. Scarlett has been doing everything she can to help Savannah. Ms. Lassiter is a law enforcement professional. Her husband is a retired FBI agent. She knows what she's talking about. If you don't get a grip, I'm taking the children and leaving. I expect Scarlett will do the same."

"You wouldn't."

"I would. Your spouting out all the horrible things that may be going on with Savannah is terrifying for my children and atrocious for Savannah's. Either pull yourself together, or I'm out."

Did I hear her right? Grace confronting Mom? Scarlett made eye contact with her father and shrugged. She was about to speak when her cell buzzed. Checking the ID, she saw it was Jake.

Scarlett ducked into the kitchen for privacy. "What's going on?"

"Touching base to give you an update. No evidence of foul play yet. Also, no evidence of how she left the scene. They're reviewing all the surveillance video available and recording plate numbers. Under Cameron's orders, the Bureau videoed every vehicle at the cemetery. A comparison should ID any cars at the church that were not at the graveside. A team is combing through the guest list and setting up interviews. How's the family holding up?"

"Most of us are coping. Mom is a disaster. I knew yesterday was too good to be true. She wants to talk to the agent in charge of the investigation. She thinks the Bureau is not adequately working on the case."

"Have Brenda talk to her."

"We're ahead of you. It didn't help. But I think Grace just put the fear of God in her."

"Good for Grace. I need to give you a heads-up. Cameron is releasing the story on the evening news, nationwide. They're calling it a missing person case. The announcement will say that after leaving the church service because she wasn't feeling well, Mrs. Kingsley disappeared. While there is no sign of foul play, all possibilities are being considered."

Scarlett looked around to be certain no one had followed her into the kitchen. "Jake, I think she had to have been abducted. Savannah isn't smart enough to pull off this kind of disappearance."

"Can't agree with you on that one, Harvard. She's smart enough to pull it off but not smart enough to realize how stupid it is. Listen, I'd better get back and do what I can to help the team. I'll see you around four if you're at the MacGregor house. If not, I should get in between midnight and one if you need company."

"I don't think I will, but I'll keep that in mind."

CHAPTER TWENTY-NINE

At half-past midnight, Scarlett leaned against her bed pillows at the MacGregor house, watching a movie on cable. When hearing a light tap, she flicked the TV off, threw on her robe, and went to the door. Before opening it, she stood still for a few seconds, wondering if she had heard a knock or had imagined it. Easing the entry open, she found Jake standing, one hand shoulder-height against the side jamb. Although he still wore his trademark black suit, his tie was loose, and two shirt buttons were unfastened.

"Heard your TV and took a chance you were awake. You okay tonight?"

Scarlett pressed a finger across her lips for a second, suppressing a smile. "I am fine. I dozed off earlier, but now, I'm wide awake. How was the ballet? I hope you got there on time."

"At one point, thought I might have to fast-rope it but made it with a few minutes to spare." Brushing back his jacket, he hooked the thumb of his free hand inside his belt. "According to my kid, it was a good performance."

"I'm glad you were able to take her." She stared at him for several seconds. "Do you want to come in for a minute?"

"Are you sure?" He squinted, his eyebrows slightly pinched. "Might not be a good idea."

She gave a sweep of her hand toward the interior of the room. "Need I remind you I crashed *your* space last night?"

"Haven't heard any complaints, have you?" He gave her a smug smile and then stepped inside. As he crossed the room to a pair of chairs under the windows, he removed his coat, draped it over the back of one, and sat.

A memory of his taking off his coat on their first meeting flashed across her mind but quickly vanished as she claimed the other chair.

"How did your family react to the press release?"

"It satisfied Mom for the moment. Although she had calmed down after Grace threatened to take the children and leave."

"Disappearances are hell on the family, especially mothers."

"I know. I guess we all need to be more patient with her, but she is so busy feeling sorry for herself she leaves no room for our sympathy. I don't suppose you've heard anything more?"

"Not about Savannah."

She pulled the sides of her robe over her knees. "So, what are the odds?"

"Odds?"

"You know. Odds she's okay."

"I get what you want to hear, but I can't make the call. That said, my gut says she wasn't abducted."

"Just your gut?"

"Look at it this way. If a crime boss wanted to ambush her, making a move in the middle of a funeral with an army of law enforcement and media on-site would be a kamikaze action. He'd likely order a Dallas-type hit. Organized crime doesn't grandstand unless sending a message. None of this fits the MO for those boys. Why would they kidnap her? If she has incriminating knowledge, why not just take her out? Even the senator's murder doesn't fit the profile. Allergy?" He scrunched his face. "Too lame—too unreliable."

"Then why are you looking into the mafia types if you're sure it wasn't a mob hit?"

"I'm not sure of anything—yet. I'm just not leaning that way. However, I do believe major crime and corruption were in play, which leaves a potential for continuing danger on the table and needs to be addressed. Did you find anything of interest in the files?"

"There were three organized crime cases with Atlanta ties, involving persons with Eastern European names. One was an anonymous tip about extortion sent to the media, one a drug case, and the third was a money-laundering charge that didn't stick. I sent them to Liz as you instructed. Have you heard about any new developments in the homicide investigation?"

"I spoke with Kirby when I dropped Sabrina off. They've got Manuela Garcia in protective custody for now. Begrudgingly, he gave up that the senator had been on the Bureau's radar. His lifestyle didn't pass their sniff test. Kirby wouldn't say if they were looking at any particular connection but said the pieces went back to the beginning of the senator's political career. Despite that, they are not willing to take your sister off the suspect list."

"Jake. I'm probably overstepping, and if so, you're free to tell me. But what is it with you and Agent Kirby?"

He broke out in a laugh. "Pretty pathetic, right? What can I tell you? He was my supervising agent at the Bureau, took a fancy to my wife, and now they are raising my daughter."

"But you . . . you talk to him about the case. Can't think of any of my clients who maintain a relationship with the party who broke up the marriage."

"Détente."

She frowned.

He fiddled with a pen lying on the table between them. "Hal Kirby hates my guts. Can't say I'm too fond of him. But he knows he owes me. I trashed my career and didn't make trouble for him. Add in the trickle-down effect of keeping peace with his wife, who wants our child to have a happy, stress-free lifestyle. They're both smart enough, mature enough, to get the picture. Therefore, they need to toss in a little *quid pro quo*. Kirby won't break any rules for me, but he'll cooperate. In this case, he stands to benefit from the relationship as much as I do. He won't admit it, but he knows I'll solve it, and he'll get the credit."

"Why will he get credit for what you do?"

"Did you ever read where a PI solved an FBI case?" Jake gazed at Scarlett for several seconds. "You look beat. I'd better let you get some sleep. I'm heading back to DC tomorrow."

She gave him a quizzical look. "Why the change in plans?"

"The disappearance expedites the need to identify all the players. My instincts tell me the leads are in DC, not Atlanta."

"Does that mean you're going alone?"

He nodded.

"You don't want my help?" A knot suddenly developed in her stomach.

He leaned forward. "It's been a good ride, having you along, but it's probably better you stay with your family."

"But . . . I can help."

He reached over and took her hand. "I'm a solo act, Harvard, and your folks need you."

Her back straightened. "I really want to be involved, Jake. Grace is good with placating my mother and caring for the children. My patience isn't much better than yours."

Jake released her hand. Propping an elbow on the chair arm, he rested his cheek against his fist and stared at her for several seconds. "You want to leave your loved ones, Harvard, to play detective with an arrogant, narcissistic bastard?"

"I do. I've got my law practice covered. Trust me. It would be a relief to get away from my mother." She raised an eyebrow. "Repeat that, and you're a dead man."

Jake laughed, stood, and patted her on the shoulder. "Your secret's safe. This is probably a mistake, but sleep in, and we'll get away mid-morning."

"You're letting me go?"

"With reservations. I'm probably drunk on jet lag. We'll stop by your parents' house on the way out after I pick up Kai from Sonny. I have a few questions for your sister."

She glanced toward the bed where her cats were ensconced—one on the pillows, the other on the corner. "What about Casper and Ebony?"

"Best they stay here. From what I've seen of Fury, she'll have no problem." He grabbed his jacket and started for the exit. Scarlett followed.

When Jake reached the door, he opened it and then turned toward her.

Before he could speak, she said, "About last night."

He put an index finger to his lips. "Shhh. There's nothing about last night. Remember?"

She blinked, took a deep breath, and said with a tight grin, "Right. Nothing."

"See you tomorrow. Get some sleep." He put a hand on her shoulder, smiled, and then left her standing in the doorway, a dozen questions spinning around in her head.

CHAPTER THIRTY

"You can turn your smartphone on," Jake said as he made a right onto the access ramp of I-85. "No reason to worry about being tracked by the Feds now, and there's a chance your sister might try to get in touch with you."

"Great. I can sync with your Bluetooth and play my music."

Jake threw his head back and groaned. "Damn. I hoped you'd forget."

"Not a chance, Sherlock. I had to listen to country for nine hours; you're going to get a taste of quality music."

"This is going to be a long trip." He glanced over at her as she powered up her iPhone.

As Josh Groban's "You Raise Me Up" resounded from the speakers, Jake shook his head. "No sing-along there."

"Come on, Shepherd. Soak up a little culture. It'll be good for you—like vegetables."

"One man's culture is another man's torture."

She grinned and ignored him. After a dozen songs by Groban, Andre Bocelli, Sarah Brightman, and Il Divo, "Shallow" from *A Star is Born* filled the SUV.

Jake glanced around at Scarlett. "Damn, Harvard. Did someone hack your phone?"

She grinned as he joined in with Bradley Cooper on the verse. When Lady Gaga's part began, Scarlett followed suit. Their voices blended well in the duet section. When it finished, the device continued with "Take Me Home, Country Roads." Jake donned a dubious expression as if to say, "really?" before joining in on the John Denver classic.

As the song ended, he said, "You've been holding out on me, Harvard. I might just have to marry you after all."

She gave him a thumbs-down. "Not a chance, Sherlock. One of us would be dead and the other in jail within a month. By the way, don't let it come as a shock, but you were listening to a cover by The Texas Tenors. They also sing opera, which you probably don't know how to spell."

With a smug smile, he gave her a patronizing glance. "Might surprise you, Harvard. I've seen them live, but don't let it get around."

"Well, aren't you a bundle of surprises?" She reached down to her cell and hit the off icon. "But, now, I think it's time you did some talking."

"Do you? Any particular subject?"

"You have the most annoying way of acting obtuse. You know what I'm talking about. I've been patient, letting you feed me tidbits of information when I know there's a lot you're not sharing."

"Got it all figured out, have you? Must be your Ivy League diploma."

"Let's be serious. I'm not the girl who gets your coffee, Jake. I may not have criminal law experience, but I know how to investigate, collect evidence, and build a case. But how can I help when you keep so much to yourself? If you're worried I'll speak out of turn, try to remember, I know how to maintain client confidentiality, which has attached with Savannah."

"You think I've underestimated you?"

"You have."

"Looks like I'm not the only mega ego in the car. You're more like me than I realized—just prettier and nicer. Okay, Harvard. What do you want to know?"

"What you're thinking. What you've discovered you haven't shared. Grace said you grilled her about Savannah's boyfriend. Why are you so sure she's innocent? Why don't you think she was abducted? What did Manuela Garcia tell you? What did you find at Savannah's house you didn't let me see?"

"Whoa. Slow up. Bet you are hell in court on cross."

She laughed. "I am. Better hope I never have you on the stand."

"Since you're a divorce lawyer, I'm safe. What's your *first* question?"

"I guess it's about the murder. What are you thinking now, and are you still sure Savannah had nothing to do with it?"

"Nothing has changed. I'm still in the fact-gathering phase of the investigation. If my opinion about Savannah's role had changed, I would have pulled out. As I told you the day we met, I am not interested in assisting a guilty party avoid justice. While she has not yet been fully honest—and you should know that few clients are—based on observation, information, and intuition, I've found no reason to reverse my original conclusion. Body language speaks louder than words. The lips have a lot easier time lying than the eyes." He paused while changing lanes. "One of the tricks to detecting lies is to ask mundane questions at the beginning of an interview or interrogation. Put her at ease; make her trust you. It gives a baseline of the witness's body language and expressions when answering innocuous questions. If it deviates when you hit the hard ones, you've nailed her. Savannah lied and withheld information, but she did not blink, look away, or tense when talking about the senator's death in any of my interviews."

"Have you ever been wrong?"

He glanced over at her, a smirk on his face. "Of course not. Question number two?"

"I should have known you'd say that. So, what did Savannah lie about in your *expert* opinion?"

"Her extramarital relationships, which brings me to another of your queries. Yes, I found compromising evidence of indiscretions in her room and on her phone. Will I share those with you? No. You don't need to see the images. Knowing they exist is enough." He turned on the windshield wipers as they drove into a heavy drizzle.

"I don't want to see them. Do you know who the man is? Is he the one she named when you first interviewed her at the hotel—the bodyguard?"

"No. Don't think so. But there was more than one. My top priority is identifying her lovers, followed by identifying the senator's. What else do you want to know?"

"What information did you get from Manuela that upped your security concerns, and why is she in protective custody?"

"Strictly classified." He looked over at her. "Understand?"

"Yeah, yeah."

"She has a sister, who mysteriously disappeared after the murder. From what I could piece together through Manuela's broken English, the two sisters were brought here for the sex trade. The sister is apparently younger, prettier, making her a better asset. Your brother-in-law seemed to have dealings with the broker who brought the two from Colombia and was a regular customer. That, combined with the unexplained lifestyle, equals an affiliation with organized crime. It also invites both sisters into my pool of suspects."

When Scarlett remained silent, Jake glanced over. "I'll let you digest what I've said. It's obvious you're overwhelmed."

"You're right. It's giving me chills and causing me to think Savannah did not leave on her own, even though you don't agree."

"Actually, there's a little more to my opinion. I had a feeling she might bolt."

Scarlett shook her head back and forth. "Why?"

"When I interviewed Savannah on Wednesday, she dodged questions about her love affairs again. When I pressed, she said she would give me answers after the funeral. I believe she had the disappearance planned."

"Then, why didn't you try to stop her?"

"My hands were tied. I also underestimated her skill and overestimated the competence of her security team. I wanted my people on the job, but the heavyweights pulled rank."

"Couldn't you have warned them she might run?"

"Not without breaching privilege and potentially strengthening the FBI suspicions. Couldn't very well go to the Feds and say, 'Watch out. My client may run.'"

"So, you believe she managed a successful escape all by herself?"

"Didn't say that. If she ran, she had help."

"Who?"

"That, Harvard, is what we're going to find out."

Despite a lunch break and two pit stops for gas and dog walking, by seven o'clock, they crossed the North Carolina-Virginia border. Scarlett took out her tablet and began research. "Is Alexandria very far from your office?" she asked after about five minutes.

"Not too far. Why do you ask?"

"I'm looking for an extended-stay hotel with kitchen facilities, and I see a possibility there."

"What for? *You* don't need a hotel."

Her head snapped up—a frown on her face. "What do you mean by I don't need a hotel? I'm not sleeping in the car."

"You're staying with me."

"Ohhh . . . I don't think so."

"It's not up for debate."

"You're right. No debate. It's not happening. We've already blurred too many lines."

"Let me put it to you this way, Harvard. You either stay at my apartment, or I call for an escort and drop you at Reagan National for a trip back to Atlanta. You wanted to come with me, which means I'm responsible for your safety, and I don't plan to stay at a hotel. What'll it be?"

She stiffened, sitting silent for several minutes.

"Relax, Scarlett. I have two bedrooms with locks on the doors, one on either side of the apartment. Are you still having trouble trusting me?"

She closed the case over her tablet. "Maybe trusting myself. But for the record, Jake Shepherd, you are abominably bossy. Please note, I'm giving in under duress—contingent on your agreement we will not cross lines. Right?" She gave him a stern look.

"If it makes you feel better, I'll pick up chalk and draw you a line."

She exhaled with a vengeance and then gave his shoulder a slight punch. Kai snapped to attention, uttering a warning growl.

"Whoa, babe. That's a guard dog behind you. He has a problem with aggression toward me."

"Sorry. I couldn't help it. You are so damned infuriating."

At five to nine, they walked into Jake's apartment. "Drop the food on the bar. I'll put our bags away, yours in my room, and then we'll eat."

Scarlett glanced around the large, open living space. "Your room? No. I'll take the other one. It's senseless for you to move out of your space."

"It's not a problem. I'll grab a few things and move into Sabrina's room. It's the larger one if that makes you feel any better. I think she'd be more comfortable with me sleeping on her bed than someone she doesn't know."

"Whatever. No one wins an argument with you."

He grinned. "This relationship might work."

"Where is the bathroom? I'd like to wash my hands and freshen up before eating."

"There's one in here," he said as he took her things into his room. "Second door, next to the closet. I'll get my things and Kai's bed after we eat. I'm starved."

As she proceeded into the bedroom, they met in the doorway. Each hesitated until he stepped back, allowing her to pass.

"Make yourself comfortable. Give a shout if you need anything."

Scarlett breathed deep. *This is a new experience.* She looked around the masculine room and noticed another guitar in the corner, next to a large dog bed. There were several photos on his rustic dress-er—most of Sabrina at different ages, but one of a dark-eyed, gray-haired woman. *Must be his mother.*

A tall chest rose nearly to the ceiling, topped with three cowboy hats. In the corner, she noticed a freestanding safe. *Cash? Important papers? No. Probably guns.* Glancing up at the high windows, she wondered if he had chosen the apartment because of the security they afforded. Lifting her suitcase, she placed it on top of the safe and opened it. After pulling out her cosmetic case, she went into the bathroom.

As Scarlett waited for the water to grow warm, her peripheral vision spotted movement. She froze for a second, afraid to look. When she eased her head around, something dark darted behind a waste-basket. A head emerged from the other side almost instantly. Beady brown eyes stared up at Scarlett. She stifled a shriek, her eyes grow-ing wide, and for a moment she froze, locked in eye contact with the alien. After a few heart-pounding seconds, she darted out to the living room.

Startled by her rapid appearance, Jake dropped the stack of mail he had been flipping through. "What's the matter?" Instinct drew his hand to his holster.

"There's a . . . rat—a big rat—in the bathroom."

Relaxing his hand, he burst out laughing.

"Why are you laughing? There's a rat in there. Do something. Shoot it."

"Calm down. I should have told you about Romeo."

"You name your rats?"

"He's not a rat, Harvard. Damn, woman. Don't you know a rabbit when you see one?"

"Of course, I know a rabbit. That's not a rabbit. Why would there be a rabbit in the apartment?"

Jake walked into the bathroom and picked up the floppy-eared, brown creature and brought him into the living room. Thrusting the three-pound bundle of fur in her direction, he said, "Meet Romeo Rabbit. Totally harmless."

"That's *not* Bugs Bunny. Rabbits have standup ears." She formed a V with her fingers and held it to her head. "And they are bigger."

"Shhh. You'll hurt his feelings. Of course, he's a rabbit. He's an American Fuzzy Lop."

As Jake drew Romeo close, gently tucking the little body under his arm like a football, Scarlett said, "Do you know how bizarre that *rabbit* looks next to your Glock? Did he come with the apartment?"

"Very funny. No. He's Sabrina's. Kirby won't let her keep him at their place. Claims he's allergic, which I sure as hell don't believe. Probably doesn't want to pay the monthly pet deposit. But keeping him scores points for me. He's my kid magnet."

"How is he as a chick magnet?"

"You know." He made a mock expression of confusion. "I never tried that." Changing to a serious look, he said, "I don't bring chicks here, Harvard."

"Really? That's hard to believe. And what about Kai? He's never considered having Peter Cottontail for lunch?"

"Nope. Romeo rules."

"That skill he probably learned from you."

"Has your smart mouth ever landed you in trouble?"

She pointed her finger at him. "That's classified."

With a smirk, he said, "I'll keep Romeo in the other room. His litter box and crate are there."

Scarlett's eyes followed, a small smile on her lips, as Jake passed.

What an enigma you are Jake Shepherd. Guns, guitars, and a weird rabbit.

CHAPTER THIRTY-ONE

"Nice jeans," Jake said, as he unlocked the front door of his office.

"I figured as long as I have joined the Shepherd team," Scarlett said, "I should wear the uniform."

With Kai trailing, she passed by him, her subtle fragrance catching his attention and causing him to grin. *Keep your focus, Shepherd. You're on the job.*

Once the trio assembled inside, Liz Glover looked up from an array of documents covering her desk.

"You remember Ms. Kavanagh, don't you?" Jake said, reaching for mail stacked in the bottom tier of a pair of wire baskets.

"Call me Scarlett, please."

"Of course, I remember her, Jake." Liz smiled at Scarlett. "Welcome back. I'm so sorry about what has happened in your family. Has there been any word about your sister?"

Scarlett shook her head. "No—but thank you."

As he flipped through the envelopes, Jake asked, "Anything I should be aware of in this batch or any important phone messages?"

"Other than a voicemail from Lila Stonebridge and an impressive check from Washburn and Batson, nothing that can't wait." Liz took a zippered bank bag from her desk drawer, opened it, and held up the check.

Jake's face lit up. "Nice. I like the zeros to the left of the decimal point. What's up with Stonebridge? Does she have a new case for us?"

"I think it was more along the line of a personal call." A twinkle in her eyes suggested insider knowledge.

He cocked a brow, forming an expression somewhere between confusion and annoyance. "She can wait."

"Ooookay." Liz returned his look with a smug one of her own before continuing. "One other thing. Phil's runner brought over a package of USBs with videos from the surveillance cameras. Do you want to start reviewing them today?"

Jake rubbed his beard as if mulling over the question. "No. I think we need to finish up with the media material you've pulled. I also have photos and video taken by Sonny and Brenda at the funeral. Looks like we're going to produce a pool of suspects large enough to sell out Yankee Stadium. You and Scarlett can start work on the video tomorrow. I plan to interview witnesses, starting with Kingsley's office personnel. Were you able to reach his personal secretary and his chief of staff?"

"It wasn't easy since they're not cleared to go back into the office yet. I have an appointment for you with Lavinia Corson, the secretary, in the conference room at Phil's office. Still working on Clyde Register, the chief of staff. His assistant has been stonewalling—trying to push me off on the communications director. As if you want the sanitized version of the story."

"Keep pushing. We need names to go on the top of our suspect sheets."

"In delving through Mrs. Kingsley's emails, I did find one for you," Liz said. "It may shock you."

"Nothing shocks me. You ought to know that."

Liz looked toward Scarlett with a dubious expression as if unsure whether to continue.

"It's okay. Scarlett knows her sister engaged in a couple of indiscretions. Shock me. What's the name?"

"Senator Arnold Manchester."

Jake put the envelopes he held on her desk. "Well, well, well. Not quite enough to shock. But it puts an interesting curve on the ball. What evidence did you find to implicate him?"

Scarlett's eyes grew wide. "You think Savannah was having an affair with another senator? Why aren't you shocked? I am."

"Because your sister is not the type to go for the pool boy unless he was extraordinarily hot. Liz, how did you come up with Manchester?"

"Mrs. Kingsley codes the files in her email account. Most are vanilla, but a couple, maybe three, are suspicious—ambiguous and provocative. The illustrious senator is the only one of the group I've identified."

"Did you crack her code?"

"I see what she's doing but not how she comes up with the code names. She uses geographic locations, probably representing something about the subject. For Manchester, she used Mississippi, which is where he was born. I can't take too much credit for the ID because he slipped up once and used his official email account."

"They always screw up once."

"Check out the exchanges I printed out for you. He had it pretty bad for her, but she seemed to have cooled it off. Not many recently."

Scarlett cringed, her shoulders lurching upward.

"I'm sorry, Ms. Kava—Scarlett."

"No. Don't be. It's fine. Savannah is Savannah. I assume no responsibility for her behavior."

Jake tipped his head, raising an eyebrow. "Then it looks like I'll have to add the senator to the list of interviews I need to schedule. Make him a suspect sheet."

"Will you be able to get to him?" Scarlett asked.

Before he could answer, Liz said, "If anyone can, Jake can."

"Get me the name of his personal secretary. She's the key."

Scarlett looked puzzled.

"Was easier when I carried a badge, but if I drop the right hint as to why I need an appointment, she'll make it happen. Odds are, she knew about the affair." He turned back to Liz. "Have the Feds executed a warrant on the Kingsley house?"

"Yesterday, according to Phil's office. The security company alerted him."

"That starts the clock running. Hope the Bureau hasn't found an analyst as good as you are to sit at your old desk." He turned to Scarlett. "Liz was the best. I'm damned lucky she came with me when she retired."

"Somebody has to keep you alive." Liz winked at Scarlett. "I'm sure you've learned by now Jake has a gift for offending people."

Scarlett chuckled and then said, "I've definitely noticed."

"I've also put the summary of the financials on your desk," Liz said, redirecting her attention to Jake, "along with the murder book. Mrs. Kingsley's bank statements and credit cards look mundane, but you'll want to take a close look at his—sketchy deposits and a conspicuous absence of expected withdrawals."

Jake turned toward Scarlett. "Bet you've examined your share of financials in your practice."

"Oh, yeah. And phone records. I think I can guess, but what is a murder book?"

"What we call the case file—photos, reports, interviews, notes, suspect workup sheets." He glanced over at Liz. "If you haven't finished with the phone records, let Scarlett help you. She'll know what to look for." As he opened the padded envelope of video recordings, he frowned. "Did I understand this is not all we asked for?"

"They're dated," Liz said. "The cover letter said the rest would be forthcoming within the week."

"Damn. I knew there would be a lot," he said, holding the box up to Scarlett. "Appears you're in for a tedious assignment with the months of footage. I hope the cameras were motion activated."

"Where were they positioned?" Scarlett asked.

"Inside and outside of the Kingsley houses, plus any others Phil's office managed to coax from neighbors." He turned his focus to Liz. "Did you get hold of the networks for review of their recording of the funeral?"

Liz nodded. "It's coming."

"How did you get the recordings from Savannah's houses?" Scarlett asked.

"The footage is stored in the Cloud. I took the provider names from the panels and sent them to Phil. He ordered copies."

"They release data to anyone?"

"Remember the documents Savannah signed? One was a general release and one a power of attorney for us to obtain any records needed. You witnessed them."

"Gotcha. I didn't pay much attention. Just thought it was a retainer agreement."

"Liz can show you how we do it. You'll have to log the USB drive, date, and time of any relevant footage." He turned to Liz. "You have blank logs?"

"Of course. I'll email the template to Scarlett along with blank suspect sheets."

"Yeah. Let's get the show on the road. Any coffee made?"

"What kind of girl Friday would I be if I didn't have coffee ready for the boss?"

He shook his head. "In no universe does that describe our relationship." He turned to Scarlett. I know you don't want coffee, but can I offer you a water or a cold drink?" Glancing back to Liz, he said, "Or, do we have any teabags? Scarlett's a tea drinker." He reached over and put a hand on Scarlett's shoulder.

Liz followed Jake's action but did not comment. "Sorry. We don't, but I'll pick some up tonight."

"I'm fine," Scarlett said. "A water will work."

Other than a thirty-minute break to eat delivered sandwiches, the trio spent the day pouring over press clippings and videos of interviews and appearances featuring Scarlett's brother-in-law. At five o'clock, Jake stood. "I'm burned out and starved. Ready to call it a day, ladies?"

"Past ready," Scarlett said. "I've had about all I can take of Scott Kingsley's disgusting grin. How many thousand media photos and sound bites was he in?"

"As I recall, you once liked his grin," Jake said with a mischievous look on his face.

She glared at him. "Watch it, Shepherd. I have a gun and know how to use it."

He laughed. "Yes you do." Holding up his hands in mock surrender, he said, "I was off-base."

Liz looked from one to the other, frowning.

"His little dig referred to the fact I was once engaged to Scott Kingsley."

A look of surprise appeared and then vanished on the analyst's face. "Say no more. I get the picture. But before we close up shop, you need to look at this, Jake." She pointed to printouts of several clippings positioned next to a blowup of a photo of a gray-haired male.

Scarlett and Jake circled the worktable to look over her shoulder.

"Looks like a match. You might have found the pot of gold. Got a name?"

"He's got several, but Vladimir Petrokov caught my attention."

"That's definitely the same man standing behind Scott in the photo on the far left." Scarlett pointed to one of the clippings. "Look at the one in front of the theater marquee. But the caption says, Walter Peters."

"Walter is the English translation of Vladimir," Jake said. "And he fits the description the nanny gave."

Scarlett's face lit up. "His name came up in the money laundering case—it was a film company—Idalv Retep Productions."

Liz slid out of her chair and went out to her desk as Jake and Scarlett examined the photos.

"Write that out in reverse," Jake said.

"Oh, my god. It's Vladi Peter."

"Sometimes, they make it too easy. Now we need to know just who Vladimir alias Walter is."

"Suspected Yurisevskaya," Liz called out from her desk in the front room.

"Aha. Bratva."

"I don't speak Russian," Scarlett said. "Can you translate?"

"Yurisevskaya Bratva is a Russian crime syndicate—currently the largest and most powerful. What are they bringing in these days, Liz?"

"Last I heard, the estimate was eleven billion a year."

"The pieces fit—description, connection, entertainment industry, entertainment attorney. I knew Kingsley had friends. If we research Vladimir, my money says Boris will surface."

"So, what now?"

"I'll turn what we have over to Kirby and company. Maybe they can get more out of Manuela. They can certainly track the financials down the chain."

"Does this change your opinion about what happened to Savannah?"

"I'm not eliminating the possibility of Bratva involvement in both the murder and the disappearance, but I tend to doubt it. However, the investigation may create a potential threat. Make up a suspect sheet on Vladimir."

CHAPTER THIRTY-TWO

After dropping Scarlett and Kai at his office on Tuesday morning, Jake drove to Phil Madison's office. Lavinia Corson was there, chatting with Madison's receptionist. A middle-aged woman with her hair immaculately coifed although dyed too black, she appeared nervous when Millie introduced Jake.

"I don't know why you want to talk to me," Corson said. "I'm not even sure it's appropriate. Should I talk to a lawyer?"

Jake smiled. "Not unless you've done something wrong. However, there are at least two in this office if you think you need one."

"But, you're—"

"I'm kidding, Ms. Corson. I just want to ask you a few questions about the late senator. And by the way, I want to offer you my sincere condolences. I'm sure the loss has been hard for you."

She seemed to relax. "It has been, Mr. Shepherd."

"Can we offer you something to drink? Millie, would you mind?"

"Of course. Ms. Corson, we have coffee, tea, water, soda."

"Maybe a soda. Anything."

"My usual, Millie." He turned to Corson. "Come on back to the conference room." Jake swept his arm in the direction of the hallway. "This won't take long."

As he escorted the woman to their destination, they passed Phil Madison headed to court. Jake made the introductions while Madison apologized for being in a hurry. Once in the room, Jake pulled a chair out for Corson and then took a place adjacent to her.

"Have you been given a timeline for when you'll be able to go back into the office and wrap things up?"

"No. Clyde Register, Senator Kingsley's Chief of Staff, is taking care of all that. He just returned to Washington last night."

"Really. I've been trying to set up an appointment with him."

"If you like, I'll pass that on."

Jake reached into his shirt pocket for a card and passed it to her. "I would appreciate your asking him to give me a call." *We both know he won't.*

She took the card and tucked it into an outside pocket on her purse as Millie came in with the beverages.

Jake took a swallow of his coffee, took out his pen, and opened his portfolio to a clean legal pad. "Let's get started, Ms. Corson—or may I call you Lavinia?"

"That's fine."

"And I'm Jake. I'm sure my assistant told you, Phil Madison, who you just met, represents Mrs. Kingsley's interests, and I'm his investigator."

"I'm so upset about Mrs. Kingsley. Do you think she's okay? Do you know where she is?"

"I wish I had answers, but I don't. The FBI is working the case."

"What exactly do you want from me? The FBI is also investigating the senator's death. Two of the agents asked me questions."

"They are, and I have been in touch with the team. Actually, I'm a former agent."

His statement caused her eyes to open wider. "Oh. I didn't know that." She seemed to sit a little straighter.

"What I would like to know first is, are you aware of any enemies the senator had? Had anyone threatened him that you know of? Had there been any disagreements, misunderstandings, confrontations?"

Her head turned in denial. "All politicians have enemies. But none would do something so terrible."

"How long have you worked for Senator Kingsley?"

"About eight years. I worked for him when he was in the Georgia legislature and came to Washington with him."

"So, you knew him pretty well."

"I would say so."

"You know, they say a man's secretary knows him better than his wife and spends more time with him."

A flush came across her face. "You're not—"

"No. Absolutely not, but spending five days a week with someone, you probably know the people who were positive and ones who were negative in his life. Right?"

She hesitated. "Right."

"Did you know he was highly allergic to peanuts?"

She looked at him for several seconds. "Yes, I knew. I had to make sure none of the snacks we kept on hand contained peanuts. I don't know how he got hold of peanuts that night. There was nothing in the office with them." While she seemed to become agitated, she never broke eye contact with Jake.

"It was likely the cheese snacks he ate before he died. Do you know where they came from?"

"No." She started to tense but did not look away from Jake. "Are you asking if I had anything to do with those, those cheese straws?"

"Did you?"

"I did not." She started to rise.

Back off, or she'll bolt. "You'll have to bear with me, Ms. Corson. Those who know me will tell you what a jerk I am. In fact, they'll use language I won't offend you with. Let's change the subject."

She stared at him for a few seconds, but Jake could see the tension in her shoulders relax.

"Let's talk about the senator. Keep in mind you can't hurt him now. I have reason to believe he might not have been faithful to his marriage. Tell me what you know about that."

Her brow pinched. "I didn't intrude into Senator Kingsley's private life."

"I'm sure you didn't. But, I'm also sure that as close as you worked together, you couldn't help but know or suspect things that might be going on. I'm assuming you cared about him and would want whoever was responsible for this tragedy to be accountable."

She looked down at her lap. Jake could tell she didn't want to answer his question but agreed with his theory.

"Who was she, Lavinia?"

Lavinia picked up her glass of soda and took a long drink.

She's struggling. She wants to tell me.

"Lavinia. Who was Senator Kingsley having an affair with?"

She took another drink.

"I get it. I know you feel a sense of loyalty to Senator Kingsley, but you can't hurt him. You can't destroy his marriage or his career, but you can help me get to the bottom of what happened. You might be doing yourself a favor as well."

"What do you mean?"

"The FBI will be looking at everyone who had means and opportunity."

"No. Why would—"

"They won't be as concerned about why. They'll look at how you had unlimited access to the office, knew he was allergic to peanuts, and, as a Southern lady, probably know how to make the offending cheese straws."

Lavinia did not speak—did not move. Jake waited; his steely gaze appeared to weaken her defense.

"What if they find your fingerprints on the container the cheese straws were in?"

Panic set in as her pupils dilated and her breathing grew rapid. "Jeanne Abbott."

"Jeanne Abbott? Who is Jeanne Abbott, Lavinia?"

"I don't have any proof. I never saw them doing anything."

"But you knew there was something different. Describe that for me."

"She worked on his campaign. I suspected something back then, but she was only nineteen and supposedly going away to college. But when we moved to Washington, she came as a staff assistant to his director of communications."

"Is she still in that position?"

Lavinia nodded, took a deep breath, and said, "Shouldn't you Mirandize me?"

The question caught Jake off guard, and he smiled.

"I'm not an officer working under the color of law, and this is not a custodial interrogation—no deprivation of your freedom. We're just chatting. I'm like a reporter gathering information for a story. Would you like another soda?"

She hesitated before responding. "Yes. May I use the restroom?"

Keep her under pressure or . . . ? "Of course." He stood, walked to the door, and pointed the way for her.

While Lavinia was gone, Jake buzzed Millie and requested the beverage. When Lavinia returned, he waited until she had taken a drink of her fresh soda.

"Now, where were we?" He paused, giving her time to respond, but she didn't. *You know I remember, Lavinia.*

She glanced around the room, avoiding eye contact.

"I believe you were about to describe the Senator's relationship with"—he glimpsed at his pad as though he had forgotten the name—"Jeanne Abbott."

Lavinia's focus flitted from one direction to another, obviously dodging connection with Jake. "I'm very uncomfortable talking about this."

"I know you are. Look at me."

She flinched but complied.

"Remember, it's to help solve the homicide, and you can't injure the senator."

She took one more sip of soda and said, "I had started to think they had broken up. He seemed to avoid her. I saw her crying in the bathroom one day. She didn't notice I had come in at first and was mumbling to herself. All I heard before she became aware of me was, 'I gave up everything for him, and he—' That's where she stopped."

"When was the last time you know Jeanne Abbott had contact with Senator Kingsley?"

"I think it was the day before he died. She waited to talk to him in the hall. I passed by them, but I didn't hear what was said. She looked upset, and he looked angry. Oh, she regularly dropped sealed envelopes, addressed to him, on my desk. I assumed they contained personal notes or letters. He never talked about it, but he wouldn't have shared his personal life with me."

Jake spent about an hour questioning Lavinia but did not uncover any additional information relevant to his investigation. When she rose to leave, she paused.

"Mr. Shepherd, you don't think Jeanne killed Senator Kingsley, do you?"

"Do you?"

She shook her head. "I don't think so. I might have believed it the other way around."

That's interesting. "What makes you say that?"

She immediately pulled back. "Forget I said it. I don't know why. Can I ask you a question?"

"Fire away."

"If the FBI questions me again, should I ask for a lawyer?"

Jake stared at her for a second. *Means and opportunity but no obvious motive.* "Ms. Corson, I am a lawyer. I would have to err on the side of caution and advise anyone to have a lawyer present. Strange things can happen during investigations."

On Tuesday morning, Jake entered the Capitol Building at eight twenty, wearing his usual black suit, a white shirt, and a burgundy tie. Earlier, when he had exited Sabrina's room at the condo, Scarlett looked him up and down and said, "You clean up well, Shepherd, but

I've got to ask. Why are all of your suits black? Did you work in a mortuary?"

With a huge grin on his face, he tapped her on the shoulder as he passed on the way to the kitchen. "Nothing wrong with your powers of observation, counselor. Yeah. I have a couple of black suits—all left over from my days at the DOJ and the Bureau. Just simpler."

His fifteen-minute appointment on Senator Arnold Manchester's agenda had been obtained by using Phil Madison's reputation and a bit of flirtation.

When he reached the chambers of Senator Manchester, Jake walked to the reception desk and presented his identification. Although he was ten minutes early, he was immediately sent to the private office and greeted by the six-foot-two, gray-haired legislator.

"Come in, Mr. Shepherd. What can I do for you?"

First clue—he's anxious to know what this is about.

"Just a few questions for you, Senator. As I'm sure your secretary told you, I work for Phillip Madison, who is representing Savannah Kingsley in matters concerning the unfortunate death of her husband."

"That was tragic. It caused a great deal of anxiety for everyone here on the Hill. But I don't know why you think I have any information. I barely knew the senator, and I'm not sure I've ever met Mrs. Kingsley. Have they found her? What did you say her name is, Sandra?"

Jake stared at the man. *So that's the way you're going to play it.* "Savannah. She hasn't been found. May I sit?"

"Oh. Of course. Would you like a cup of coffee?"

"No. I'm fine." Jake sat in a high-back leather chair in front of the senator's massive desk and opened his portfolio. "You say you never met Mrs. Kingsley?"

"Right. Not to my recollection."

"How well did you know Scott Kingsley?"

"Not well at all. Maybe to pass in the hall. I think I would recognize him."

"Did you attend the funeral in Atlanta last week?"

"I did. Formality. You know."

Jake glanced around the office at the richly appointed furnishings and expensive artwork, his eyes landing on family photos on an etagere. "Your wife and children?"

"Yes. My oldest is serving as a page in the House this term. Do you have a family, Mr. Shepherd?"

"I have an ex-wife and a daughter. So, tell me. How long have you been in office?"

"Oh, my. It's going to be nineteen years. Seems like my entire life. I hate to rush you, but—"

"I understand. You're a busy man, so I'll get right to the point. Isn't it true that you had a personal relationship with Savannah Kingsley? In fact, an intimate relationship."

Righteous indignation flooded the senator's face. "Absolutely not. Where did you get such a preposterous idea? Is this some kind of shakedown?"

Jake smiled. "Hit a nerve, did I? Come on, Senator. Don't try to bullshit me. You and Mrs. Kingsley got it on, and you don't want your wife, the media, or your constituents to know."

"I'm going to have to ask you to leave."

"Really?"

"Do I need to call security?"

"I wouldn't do that, if I were you." Jake reached into his portfolio and drew out a copy of the email with the senator's official signature. "You might want to look at this before you throw me out."

The senator's hand shook as he took the paper from Jake. After appearing to study it for a few seconds, which Jake guessed was not reading time but composure time in preparation of a response, he tossed it back toward Jake. "That's a fake. I never sent any such thing. I don't know the woman. If she says otherwise, she's lying."

"It bears your official signature, and a trace will show it came from your IP address."

"It's not authentic. Someone could have hacked my account. That's done all the time. I'll have the authorities look into it."

"Senator, you can lie all day, but we both know you and Mrs. Kingsley had an affair. That's not the only evidence I have. Which brings me to the final question. Did you have anything to do with Senator Kingsley's death?"

"Get out of my office. I'm calling security."

"You really want to do that? The media will want to know why you threw me out." He closed his portfolio. "But, don't worry. I'm leaving. You've answered my question."

Jake stood up, tossed the email back on the desk. "You can keep this one for a souvenir. I have more. Thank you for your time."

"Wait a minute. Does anyone else have a copy of that?"

"If you mean the FBI, Senator, I don't know, but I expect they will. They have access to the same computer I pulled it from. Better work on your story a little more."

When Jake returned to the office after his confrontation with Senator Manchester, he found Scarlett and Liz buried in review of surveillance tapes and financial documents.

Breezing by Liz on the way to his office, he said, "A word," and tilted his head in the direction of his private office.

She put a sticky note to reserve her place on the document she had been scanning and followed him.

As Jake dropped his portfolio on his desk, he said, "We've got to nail down Savannah Kingsley's primary lover, and it isn't the senator."

"You talked to him?"

"I did. I'm not taking him off the suspect list, but I'm bumping him down to level two. I don't think the guy's got the balls to arrange or execute a hit. He's a typical politician—all talk—no action."

"Did he physically match up with any of the male photos from her file?"

Jake tilted his head, squinted, and made a quizzical facial expression. "Maybe. But it would be a stretch. He's not a bad-looking guy and has a decent frame, but the personality is off. Savannah Kingsley's not the type to settle for second chair, and he's not the kind to leave his wife. He likes to play around and may have had a real hard-on for her, but I don't think he would wreck his family, possibly his career, to make it permanent."

Liz smiled. "You don't like him."

"I don't. Enjoyed making him squirm."

"There's an evil streak in you, Jake Shepherd." Her smile grew broader. "I love it."

"That makes you the one and only member of my fan club. Kidding aside, I want you to track down Darren Warner and set up a meeting. He works for a local security firm. How's Harvard doing?"

"I can hear you," Scarlett called out from Jake's combination work-conference room.

"So, then, how are you doing?"

"Bored. My jeans are stuck to this chair."

"You volunteered to play."

"Yeah. Well, I thought it might be a little more interesting than glaring at a TV screen for hours. I need a road trip."

He glanced down at his watch. "Looks like lunchtime. Want to grab a bite?" He looked toward Liz and tipped his chin, raising his eyebrows as if to invite a reply.

"Yes, dang it," Scarlett shouted, clicking off the TV and standing.

Liz shook her head. "I'm good. I'll just call the sandwich shop and order in. You two take a break."

When Scarlett and Jake returned after lunch, Liz was giving Kai fresh water. "Located Warner. He's coming to meet with you at four thirty."

Jake gave her a thumbs-up. "How'd you pull that off? Coming here. Today."

"He works for that big rent-a-cop company on the northside. I told the gal who answered you were looking into the murder of Senator Kingsley, want to talk to those who knew the family, and understand Warner to be in the group. Got a call from him within fifteen minutes. He is on a night job and said he would stop by on his way. I think he was nervous."

"We'll see if he shows. Since that locks me down for the afternoon, I'll take a look at the financials you've tagged until he arrives."

At four twenty, Kai rose from his favorite corner of Jake's office, the fur on his back bristling. Just as he commenced a low growl, Jake gave him the quiet sign. "I think we have—" The doorbell sounded before he finished his sentence.

Liz glanced at the image from the security camera app on her iPad, opened the audio, and said, "May I help you?"

"Darren Warner to see Jack, I mean Jake, Shepherd." He held a driver's license and a business card up to the lens.

Liz buzzed him in as Jake made it to her desk.

Slightly taller than Jake, Warner looked to have spent an hour too long on weights at the gym.

Jake quickly assessed the man. *Competition bodybuilder. Probably his only qualification for the job.*

Kai stood next to Jake at full alert, drawing Warner's attention.

"You carrying?" Jake asked.

Warner, a man in his late twenties, had a face for radio—a mouth too large, a crooked nose, matching teeth, and a comb-over hairstyle. He wore khaki pants, a white dress shirt, and a jacket with his company logo. To the eye of a layman, there was no sign of a weapon.

"The dog doesn't like firearms."

The security guard pulled back his jacket to reveal a shoulder holster with a small semi-automatic.

"Tell you what. If you don't mind, leave the gun here on Liz's desk." He patted the corner. "Accept the assurance of one pro to another; you're in no danger in this building."

Without protest, Warner complied.

"I'm Jake Shepherd. Appreciate your coming." Jake extended his hand, and they shook. "Can I offer you a cup of coffee, soda, or a water?"

"No. I'm fine. Not sure why you want to talk to me, but here I am."

"Come on back to my office. This won't take long."

Jake closed the door once Warner and Kai were in the room. "Have a seat. Make yourself comfortable. I'll try to make it quick." Jake grabbed a legal pad and pen from his desk and sat on the corner, directly in front of Warner.

"Is he a certified K-9 police dog?" Warner asked, pointing at Kai.

"He is—several certifications. Don't worry. He'll stay quiet as long as you don't make an aggressive move on me." Jake smiled. "So, tell me, Darren. How long have you been doing security?"

"Three years. Mostly retail."

"You're former military?"

"How'd you know?"

"Just a hunch. Combat?"

"Afghanistan."

Jake nodded. "Thank you for your service."

Warner gave a quick nod, signifying acceptance of the appreciation. "Guys at the office said you're former FBI. Is that right?"

"For what it's worth."

"They say you're good."

"I am." Jake smiled.

The response caught Warner off guard. "That's an honest answer if I've ever heard one."

"Well, we're not here to talk about me. Let's get on with it. I know you have a job waiting. Give me a rundown of your history with the Kingsley family."

Warner shook his head. "No history. I barely know—knew—the people."

"Did you ever work for them?"

"If you mean, did they ever cut me a check? No."

"Ever work indirectly for them?"

"It depends on how you define that. I worked a couple of VIP parties they attended."

"Did you ever have an affair or even a one-night stand with Mrs. Kingsley?"

"What the fuck?" Warner's hands curled into fists and then relaxed.

"Want me to repeat the question?"

"No. No to both. You don't need to repeat it, and I never—you know. Why the fuck would you ask me that?"

Jake studied Warner's face for several seconds. "Given your answer, can you explain why Mrs. Kingsley would allege you were lovers?"

Warner stood up, a flush emerging on his cheeks. "I don't know what the hell you're talking about or where you're going with this. You are so far off base that you're not even in the ballpark. I doubt that woman would know me if she walked through that door right now." He pointed to the entry to Jake's office. "Does anyone know where she is? Bring her here. Let her say that to my face."

"Take it easy. Relax. It's just a question. Sit down and describe for me *any* contact you remember having with Mrs. Kingsley."

Warner remained standing for a minute or more, staring at the floor and then at Jake. Finally, he calmed enough to take a seat. "All I remember about her is working a party where a call came in that one of the Kingsley kids was sick. The senator didn't want to leave, and she didn't want to wait for a cab."

"So, you took her home?"

"Yeah. We hardly exchanged five words. She was upset about the kid."

"Did you give her your name?"

"Yeah. She asked for it and wrote it down. I waited around in my car at the house until she came back out and gave me the all-okay sign. Stayed in case she had to make a run to the ER. A few days later, I got a thank-you card with a C-note." He held up his right hand as though taking an oath. "That's it, buddy. I swear. That's it."

Jake made notes on the pad and then stood. Extending his hand to shake Warner's again, he said, "Thank you once more. I appreciate you stopping by." Grabbing one of his cards from the holder on his desk, he added, "If anything comes to mind you think I need to know, give me a call."

As soon as Warner left the building, Jake turned to Liz. "Scratch him off both the list of lovers and the list of suspects. Savannah Kingsley never slept with that guy."

Scarlett had come out of the workroom and heard him. "You're sure he's not the one?"

"I was sure the minute I saw him. Actually, I felt sorry for the guy. I think he was terrified of being pulled into a murder investigation." He turned back to Liz. "Tomorrow, start canvassing all the security companies for male employees on vacation or otherwise not on the job since the funeral."

"What are you thinking?" Scarlett asked.

"That our mystery guy works in the business and may be with your sister. Just a hunch based on Savannah's using Warner to muddy the waters. She didn't want me to know who her lover is, but her first thought was to name someone in the profession."

Jake spent the next two days interviewing other members of Scott Kingsley's staff, neighbors, service providers, and social acquaintances. On Wednesday, he questioned Clyde Register, the senator's Chief of Staff, at length. As expected, Register stonewalled but finally admitted to Kingsley's affair with Abbott. When questioned about the senator's private finances and campaign fund, despite denials of any knowledge, his body language confirmed Jake's suspicions. However, Register displayed no reaction at the mention of Senator

Manchester. The minor staff members Jake interviewed offered no new information. His efforts to interview Jeanne Abbott failed. She had not returned to the office since the Atlanta service, and no one seemed to know where she might be.

"Does her disappearance push her up the suspect ladder?" Scarlett asked Jake Wednesday evening.

"Jury's out on that one. She could be hiding out of guilt or fear, but she could be in seclusion out of grief. No way to know until I find her."

"Is there any possibility she has been abducted?"

"Harvard, anything is possible. But I have no reason to believe that at the moment. No one has reported her missing. I need Liz to track down her family."

Six suspect sheets and one wild card graced the bulletin board in Jake's workroom. As Liz created a sheet, she made a copy for the board and filed the original in the murder book.

Jake touched base each day with Dan Cameron's team to learn of any developments in Savannah's disappearance, but the investigation remained stalled.

On Thursday afternoon, Jake interviewed Regina and Martin McClellan. When he told Scarlett, she asked, "Aren't they Kyle McClellan's parents?"

"They are, but he wasn't home. The wife said he had practice for his school's tennis team. In fact, Regina McClellan and your sister played tennis together on a country club team. She volunteered that the kid worked out with them occasionally. I asked for an opportunity to question the boy later since he seemed to have spent time in the Kingsley home. They were willing but could change their minds."

"Colin talks about him all the time, which made me wonder why. The common interest in tennis could explain it."

Jake thought about it for a few seconds. "Maybe. I'll put it down to explore fur—" His cell interrupted. "Sam. What's up?" Jake walked into his office, leaving Scarlett and Liz in the reception room.

"I wish I could tell what he's thinking," Scarlett said to Liz.

"If you're around long enough, you'll get used to him. Jake gathers all the information before forming a theory. He's ruling out possibilities as he goes. He may have suspicions, but he'll never point a finger until he's sure. When he does, you can trust he'll be dead on."

"I can't tell you how often I've told a client to be patient, and I'm doing the same thing—wanting answers before there's been time to find them."

"It's normal."

"How would you like to have an evening out?" Jake said as he walked back in.

"Is there a catch?" Scarlett asked.

"I take it that was Sam Bryant on the phone," Liz said.

"It was. His act for tomorrow night canceled."

"And he wants you to cover."

"He does."

"Cover what?" Scarlett asked, her gaze moving from Liz to Jake and back.

"He hasn't told you?"

"Told me what?"

"Jake sings at a country-western bar periodically."

"You're kidding." Scarlett looked to Jake. "You perform? For real? Not just carpool karaoke?"

"I do. Only perk of leaving the Bureau. Might even let you join me on stage for a number. You've got a good voice, Harvard."

She wrinkled her brow and then shook her head back and forth. "Shepherd, you are . . . you are—" She took a deep breath. "Damn, I don't know what you are. But there's no way I'm going on a stage."

He walked over to Scarlett, put his hands on her shoulders, and gave a little shake. "Loosen up. Take a little R & R. It'll do you good."

Liz cut her eyes from one to the other, grinning.

CHAPTER THIRTY-THREE

Friday night, Jake pulled the Lexus into the roadhouse parking area. Earlier, he had taken Scarlett shopping for an appropriate outfit, including a pair of boots and a cowgirl hat.

"I can't believe I let you talk me into wearing this costume," she said as he exited the SUV. And get this straight, I'm not going on a stage."

"Come on, Harvard. You've never sung karaoke in a club? Don't lie."

"Not the same. Everyone singing was an amateur."

"You consider me professional?"

"A lot more professional than I am."

Once inside, Scarlett looked around as the regulars greeted Jake. He seemed to know all the staff and quite a few of the patrons. A cliché country-and-western establishment, the place had a long bar, a mechanical bull, pool tables off to one side, about thirty patron tables, and a small dance floor in front of an elevated stage at the center back of the large room.

A short woman with long, gray hair walked up to the pair. "Thanks for saving the day, Jake."

"Happy to oblige. Myrtice, this is Ms. Harvard. Can you look after her while I'm doing my thing?" He turned back to Scarlett. "This is Myrtice Bryant. She and her husband, Sam, own the place."

"You've got it. What can I get you, Ms. Harvard? Your usual poison, Jake?"

He gave a thumbs up and turned to Scarlett. "Myrtice brews the best coffee in Virginia."

After settling Scarlett at a table bordering the dance floor, Jake took his place on the stage, introduced by Sam Bryant. He immediately opened with a Garth Brooks cover.

It didn't take long for Scarlett to fall into the upbeat mood of the club. The crowd loved Jake, and she could see he was in his element.

After the first set, Jake joined her at the table.

"I'm impressed," she said as he took a seat. "Been doing it long?"

"My dad taught me to play the guitar. He used music to balance out the dark side of his job. This gig came as an accident." He took a swallow of water from a bottle he brought to the table. "One night after my divorce, I came here with a date. She talked me into the karaoke thing. Sam liked what he heard and asked if I would consider becoming a regular. Since I was just getting the PI practice started, the extra money sounded good. Now, like Dad, I do it for stress relief."

On his way back to the stage after the break, he stopped to speak with Sam, as Scarlett watched. During the exchange, he pointed in her direction.

As he was about to begin the second set, he said into the mike, "Anyone here like Kenny Rogers?"

Cheers and applause filled the room.

"Well, how about I cover 'Islands in the Stream'?"

Another round of applause came forth as Scarlett felt her stomach lurch. *He wouldn't.*

"Only trouble, guys, is I need a Dolly to do it up right. Wait a minute."

Scarlett started shaking her head.

"There. I see Dolly. Fellows, can you escort her up here?"

Two of the club's bouncers walked up to Scarlett's table as she gave Jake a dirty look but made the trek to the stage where Jake extended his hand. The crowd cheered.

"I'm going to kill you, Shepherd," she said in a low voice.

"He grinned. It's been tried. Relax. Have some fun."

The number went well. The crowd loved them, and Scarlett survived—even appeared to enjoy the moment.

After leaving the stage, she went to the bar for a fresh soda while Jake continued with another Kenny Rogers hit. After getting her drink, Scarlett walked back toward her table. As she started to sit, out of nowhere, an arm went around her neck.

Scarlett's scream stopped Jake in the middle of a line of lyrics. Almost simultaneously, a shout bellowed.

"No one move, or she dies." A rangy man with an odd gun had a stranglehold on Scarlett. He held the weapon over his head and fired into the ceiling, immediately repositioning the semi-automatic at Scarlett's temple.

Jake's guitar fell. He sprang to his feet, weapon drawn almost faster than the eye could see. Instinct kicked in as he took a shooter's stance, aiming his gun toward the armed man and shouting, "Drop it, you son-of-a-bitch. Release her."

"No way. You drop."

A woman in the club gasped. Scarlett stood frozen, staring at Jake, her face drained of color, her eyes screaming for help.

Jake's glare shot across the space between him and the assailant. "Let her go and talk to me. What is it you want?" With his weapon trained on the assailant, Jake's grip remained steady. "I'm sure we can work something out." His tone dropped a notch as he said, "Just put the gun down. My name is Jake. What yours?"

"Not your business," the gunman said, looking around the room.

"*Look* at me. Keep your eyes on *me*." Although calm, Jake's tone projected unwavering confidence. "No one has to get hurt." Not a muscle in his body moved. "I don't know what this is about, but you need to listen to me. You have no other option. If you don't put the gun down, you give me no choice but to shoot. Trust me. As a former FBI sniper—I won't miss."

"What are you? Negotiator or something? You won't shoot. I take her with me." The gunman tried to position Scarlett in front of his body as a shield.

"Wrong. You'll be dead before you take another breath. You do not want to do this. Understand. I don't want to, but I can and will take you out."

With a sneer, the assailant said, "You theenk you keel me before I keel her, Mr. Negotiator?"

"I'm as far from a negotiator as they come. I don't compromise. And you, my friend, do not want to go up against me. Now put the gun down before it's too late."

"Not believe you."

Jake slowly shook his head. "Now, that's a mistake."

The man's hand started to shake.

Her head not moving, Scarlett's eyes cut to the side and then back toward Jake.

"Where are you from?" Jake said, striving to keep the assailant talking. "Did you bring the *Gyurza* from home?"

"Not know what you say. Me—American."

Like hell you are. "I don't think so, bro. I hear Eastern Europe, and I'm looking at a weapon made in Russia."

"I show you," he said through clenched teeth.

Seeing frustration build in the gunman, Jake knew he had to act. "Time's running out, Ivan or whatever your name is."

Scarlett squeezed her eyes shut for a second and then looked back up at Jake.

"Drop the Vektor!" Jake's gaze remained fixed on the Russian. "Last chance. Drop the fucking gun before I count to three."

The assailant stretched the fingers of the hand around Scarlett's neck, but his arm retained a tight grip on her.

"One." Jake's voice echoed through the silent room. "Two." His eyes flashed as he silently hoped the assailant would not force his hand. "Three!"

A shot rang out, followed by the shrieks of several women and then silence.

CHAPTER THIRTY-FOUR

The Russian crumpled, his weapon hitting the floor with a resounding crash. Scarlett stood in place but crossed her arms across her chest, clutching her shoulders. Not a patron moved for what seemed like an hour.

The round had barely left the muzzle when Jake leaped from the stage, looking around the room and shouting, "Sam. Lockdown." Passing an empty table, he grabbed a napkin. "No one out until the cops get here."

The bullet had found its mark. Using the napkin, Jake scooped up the pistol with a flourish, stuck it in his belt, and then knelt, putting two fingers to the man's neck.

Still holding his weapon, he stood, pulled out his cell with his free hand, and tapped in 911. When the dispatcher answered, he said, "This is Jake Shepherd, PI, at the Bucking Bull. There's been an attempted abduction. I'm assuming a call has come in and officers have been dispatched. I want you to alert the responding units that I am armed because of a possible accomplice, but not, repeat not, holding hostages. I will surrender my weapon upon their arrival. The assailant is dead. I will continue to secure the premises until your people take over." He then tapped Hal Kirby's number.

"Kirby, you need to get your team to the Bucking Bull before the locals mess up the crime scene. There was an armed attempt to take Senator Kingsley's sister-in-law hostage. I took out the main assailant. There may be accomplices."

"Fuck, Shepherd. You know how to mess up a weekend."

Jake terminated the call without responding and approached Scarlett, looking around as he moved. "Are you okay?"

"Great. Considering I just had a gun at my head." She shook her body with an exaggerated shudder. "You let me win at the range, didn't you?"

"Good god, Harvard. Is that what you're thinking about right now?" Although talking to Scarlett, Jake continued to assess the room.

"Better than thinking about my brains splattered all over this floor." While her demeanor appeared strong, Scarlett's hands trembled.

"Have to admit I am impressed with how cool you were. No hysterics. If I didn't know better, I might think you trusted me."

"I didn't have a choice."

As Jake put a hand around her shoulder, his gun still drawn, Sam Bryant approached.

"Heads up." Jake pointed toward the man on the floor. "The SOB may not have been alone."

Twenty minutes later, the Metropolitan Police were on the scene, taking statements from witnesses, when Deke Weston sauntered up to Jake.

"Damn it, Shepherd. Why'd you have to kill the guy? You know how much paperwork you've caused? I should take you in based on the grief my wife is going to give me. We had weekend plans."

"Do what you've got to do. But keep in mind"—Jake swung his arm around, pointing out the crowd of customers—"there are at least fifty witnesses in this room, plus how many surveillance cameras? I think you won't have any trouble seeing it was a good shoot. Only questions you have to answer are: Who is this bastard? Was he operating alone or under orders? And was Ms. Kavanagh or her sister the intended target?"

"That's in the works. Where's your weapon?"

"Officer Friendly over there"—he pointed to where two uniformed police officers stood—"has both mine and the perp's Gyurza. Getting them away from him will take the force of the AG."

"Holy shit. The guy had a Russian SR-1 Vektor? Those things shoot through concrete and steel."

"And just about anything else. Where do we stand?"

"Kirby's on his way. He can figure it out. By the way, he said for you to stand down. We're taking this."

Jake's face took on a scowl.

"Relax, man. I told him the only way you'd stand down would be to put you in lockup or a body bag. So, what's the story?"

"Ms. Kavanagh can give you the best description. She's over there." He pointed toward the end of the bar where Scarlett was talking to a local detective. "I was on the stage, doing my thing, when she screamed. I looked her way, saw the gun at her head, and drew my weapon. Did my best to talk him down, but he wasn't buying. Gave me no choice. His finger, intentionally or accidentally, could have pulled the trigger. It would not only have killed her but would have killed anyone in the line of fire after the shot went through her head."

As Jake finished speaking, Special Agent Sylvia Blake walked up. "See you've been busy, Shepherd."

With a tip of his head and click of his tongue, Jake said, "Where is a cop when you need one?" He glanced around the room and then said, "I saw you talking with the ME. What do you know so far?"

"Very little. No ID. ME estimates the perp was no more than twenty-one or two. The accent, the Russian cannon in his possession, and the resumé tattooed on his torso point to Bratva. With no tear drops or skull and dagger in the artwork, he might have been working on his coronation."

"Any sign of a vehicle or an accomplice?"

"Not so far. But the locals found a media photo of Mrs. Kingsley in his pocket. Maybe he thought he had the widow. The sisters look enough alike if you change the hair color."

"What's your take, Shepherd?" Weston asked.

"I'm going with mafia wannabe trying to abduct the target to gain traction with the bosses."

"You don't think he planned to kill her? Committing a murder is a prerequisite for membership in some chapters," Weston said.

Jake sucked air through his teeth. "Right, but I'm betting this guy aimed to grab and go. What I don't know is whether the SOB thought he had Mrs. Kingsley or her sister."

"So, you're not thinking it was an ordered hit?" Blake said, adjusting her holster.

"Nope. News may have circulated through the dark circles that the senator's high-ranking connection had concerns about what the widow could tell you guys."

"He must have thought he had Mrs. Kingsley." Blake scowled. "I see no reason to kidnap the sister."

Jake shook his head. "I disagree. If Mrs. Kingsley is in hiding, taking a close family member could be an attempt to flush her out or keep her quiet."

"I'm with Jake," Weston said to Blake. "And I don't see the bosses sending a green recruit to do a job this blatant, especially within range of a sharpshooter." He turned toward Jake. "He obviously underestimated you."

Jake grinned. "Yeah. Most people do."

"As much of a pain in the ass as you are," Weston said, "even Kirby has to admit it's better to have you in the loop than going rogue. What's your latest theory on the senator's murder?"

"He slept with the Yurisevskaya, but they didn't kill him."

"How did I know you were going to say that? Do you always take the road less traveled?"

"I aim for the right one."

"If you didn't have a nose like a cadaver dog, I would argue. Tell me why you're convinced organized crime did not kill a guy flying on the wings of their dirty money—especially after tonight. You have your eye on another suspect?"

"No primary yet."

"Bullshit. You know something you're not telling. If you have to insert yourself into the investigation, at least play fair," Weston said.

Before Jake could respond, Scarlett walked up. He immediately put an arm around her shoulders. "You okay?"

"Tired. It's about to catch up with me. How long do we have to stay?" Fatigue had drained Scarlett's face of its normal color as she curled her lips inward and rubbed her forehead to cope with the stress.

"It's up to—" Jake dropped his hand and looked back toward Weston. "Who is it up to? Are you guys taking jurisdiction or letting the Met run it?"

Weston nodded to Scarlett and then said to Jake, "You called Kirby, so we've got to wait for him to get here and do the talk. Fairly sure he'll claim a piece of the action on the grounds it's connected to the senator's homicide. You might try not to antagonize him. Give him a tidbit so he'll make life easier for us all."

"I'm closing in on some solid leads. I know I'm going to have to solve it for you guys. But right now, I plan to sit down at the bar with Ms. Kavanagh, have a cup of coffee, and wait until you guys free us to leave. Fair warning. If you take too long, I'll have to drag Madison down here. You should keep in mind"—he cut his eyes toward Scarlett—"a civilian suffered significant trauma here."

"I'm sure Kirby and the locals will want to avoid your reaching out for Madison. You're both like stepping on a wad of gum." Weston turned his focus to Scarlett. "Please accept my apologies, Ms. Kavanagh, for the red tape and my condolences for the ordeal you experienced. I'm extremely glad you weren't injured."

Two hours later, Jake pulled up in front of his apartment building. "What the frigging?" He swerved the Lexus into a parking space next to a Mercedes, jolting Scarlett.

"My gosh, Jake." She grabbed the armrest to brace herself. "What is it?"

"Jackie's car." He pointed toward the black luxury sedan.

"Jackie? Your ex-wife? Are you sure?"

Without answering, he exited the vehicle almost before the motor died.

Both front doors of the Mercedes popped open. In the light of a nearby lamp, Scarlett watched a willowy, young brunette run toward Jake.

"Sabrina, what the—"

"Daddy! I was so scared. Are you okay? She threw her arms around him."

Jake grasped her in a tight hug. "I'm fine, baby. I'm fine. What are you doing here? It's after midnight." He looked up at his ex-wife as Scarlett rounded the Lexus. "Jackie? What the hell? How did you get through the gate?"

"I showed the guard ID. We're on your list, remember?"

"Yeah, right. Do you know what time it is?"

"And do you think your daughter could sleep after you called the house and told Hal you'd been involved in a shooting? She had to see you."

He nodded. "I get it." He rested his cheek against the top of his child's head. "I'm absolutely fine, princess. Remember, I'm a super-hero. You can't kill a superhero."

"I'm not in kindergarten, Daddy. You're human."

He lifted his head and turned his attention to his former wife. "Didn't Hal think to let you know I wasn't hurt?"

"Of course. But do you think Sabrina would believe him?"

"Yeah. Right. But you shouldn't be roaming around this time of night."

"Hal's going to meet us out front and follow us home."

"Good for Hal. Come on up and wait in the apartment." He turned around and noticed Scarlett. "Scarlett, this is my daughter, Sabrina, and her mother, Jackie Kirby."

"You're Senator Kingsley's sister-in-law," Jackie Kirby said.

"I was."

"I'm sorry for your loss. Tonight must have been terrifying. I'm thankful you weren't hurt."

"Thank you." Scarlett gave her a weak smile.

"My dad saved you, didn't he?"

Scarlett's smile broadened as she nodded. "Indeed, he did."

As the foursome rode the elevator to Jake's unit, Jackie's phone pinged, notifying her of a text. She read it without comment.

"The hospital or Kirby?" Jake asked.

"Hal. He'll meet us in front of the complex in about thirty minutes."

As they entered the living room, Scarlett said, "If you'll excuse me. I've got to take a shower and change. I feel so—so—"

"Certainly," Jackie said and glanced at Jake as Scarlett went into his room.

Shooting a warning look toward his ex, Jake turned and said to his daughter, "Sabrina, why don't you check on Romeo. He's in your room. I'm using it while Ms. Kavanagh is here." He looked back toward his former wife. "Save your comments, please." Tipping his head toward his bedroom, he said, "Her safety is my responsibility."

"I didn't say anything."

Forty-five minutes later, Jake and Scarlett were alone as he rinsed and tucked two wine glasses onto the dishwasher rack. When done, he turned. "How you doing?"

Scarlett didn't respond.

Jake waited, watching until she finally spoke.

"I wish I knew how to answer that. The wine helped."

"You want to talk about it?"

She shook her head. "I don't think so." Raising her eyes, she connected with his, her brow furrowed. "Don't leave me alone."

He stood silent for a moment and then put his hands on her shoulders. "That could be a problem." His fingers tightened. "I'm still human, Harvard. We're both revved up. If I stay with you, I can't promise nothing will happen between us."

She blinked and took a deep breath. "I know." Glancing at her feet and then at him, she said, "Stay."

Silence filled the space between them for several seconds.

"Are you sure?" He took her hands in his.

"I'm sure."

"You may regret this tomorrow."

"Right now, I need . . . I need proof I'm still alive. Can you make that happen?"

"You are alive—thank God, and I can damn sure make that happen." Dropping Scarlett's hands, he took her by the shoulders. Pulling her closer, Jake rested his cheek on the top of her head, holding her tight. After several seconds, he lifted her chin and pressed his lips to hers.

Scarlett's knees went weak. The prickly stubble of his beard scratched her face as the gentle warmth of his kiss quickly escalated into a fiery rage. When his hands began to explore her body, Scarlett surrendered.

With his breath warm on her ear, he found the buttons on her shirt and whispered, "You are way overdressed for what I have in mind." When the last fastener came free, he slipped his hands inside the garment and caressed her bare skin.

His touch sent waves of passion over Scarlett. In succumbing to the moment, she allowed the surge of desire to erase the peril of hours before—purging her memory of the fear and horror—lifting her from darkness to euphoric pleasure. When a pang of conscience tried to emerge, she shut it down. *Seize the moment. Don't care about tomorrow or if this is wrong.*

With a flourish, he swept her up as though she were weightless and carried her to his room. When the ultimate moment came, she clasped her arms around him as though life depended on it.

Afterward, he lay next to her, silent for a while and breathing heavy. Rising onto an elbow, his free hand caressed her face as he whispered, "You are a beautiful woman, Scarlett Kavanagh. . . . Are you okay?"

"I am."

"No regrets?"

"No regrets." A streak of moonlight poured through the window, illuminating his chest and exposing a scar on his left shoulder. Scarlett's finger traced the imperfection. "What happen? A bullet?"

He rose higher and positioned himself over her. After gazing at her for several seconds, he lowered his body and kissed her. Their bodies touching sent another wave of exhilaration coursing through Scarlett, almost causing her to forget her question.

Rising, he said with a slight shake of his head, "Just a flesh wound. Forgot to duck."

"Sure you did. Who are you, Jake Shepherd? What have you seen?"

He emitted a light snort. "A lot I'd like to unsee." He threaded his fingers through one side of her hair. "Should I go back to the other room?"

"No. Stay. Please. Just for tonight."

A smile crept across his face. "Just for tonight—unless you change your mind."

CHAPTER THIRTY-FIVE

The next morning, Jake stood in the kitchen drinking coffee with the morning paper spread out on the counter.

Scarlett stared at the headline as she slid onto a barstool.

He glanced up, smiled, and said, "How are you today? Speaking to me?"

"Of course, I'm speaking to you. I'm fine."

"Just checking." He reached over and tapped the microwave dial. "You still okay with last night—the part after we got home?"

"Do you have to ask?"

"And the rest? How are you handling the trauma?"

"I'm fine." She pointed to the paper. "Is that about us?"

"Unfortunately. I suggest you don't read it. At least not today."

She moved her head affirmatively. "Jake. About us. I'm not attaching any meaning or thinking we're a couple—just so you know."

He grinned, took the cup of tea from the oven, and put it in front of her. "Now, why would I make such an assumption about an independent, strong-willed Harvard lawyer?"

"It was a one-time thing."

He cleared his throat and raised an eyebrow. "One time? I think your math is a little different from mine."

She shook her head. "Okay. Two-time thing. But it won't happen again. You sleep with Kai and Romeo, and I stay in the other room. When Savannah's case is over, we may never see one another again."

"That would be a shame. But I told you before, Harvard—you're in charge."

Lowering her eyes, she said, slightly above a whisper, "It was good."

Jake broke out in a broad grin. "It was." With his head bobbing, he said, "Yeah. It was *definitely* good." He walked around the bar dividing his kitchen and great room. With a devilish expression, he patted her shoulder. "I'm clear. We're not a couple, but I hope I don't have to fill another body bag to earn an encore."

She drew a fist and started to sock him playfully on his shoulder, but he intercepted the blow, pulled her close, and kissed her. Pulling away, he released her hand. "Definitely not a couple, right?"

"Right. Absolutely right." She tilted her head to one side. "But after sharing a near-death experience with you, I do have a plan."

He stepped back, with a quizzical expression on his face. "A plan? Enlighten me, Harvard."

"Nope. Not ready. But, if you play your cards right, one day, you might find out. Now, go feed the rabbit while I have a piece of toast. I know you're going to want to leave for the office in a few minutes."

Thirty minutes later, as they drove toward Jake's office, he glanced over at Scarlett. "A plan, huh? Just what kind of plan, Harvard?"

Her eyes sparkled as she said, "For me to know, and you to find out."

"Gonna play it that way, are you?"

"I am." She curled her lips in, fighting a grin.

"Interesting you mention this plan while you're disclaiming couple status."

"It is, isn't it?"

Liz stood when Scarlett, Jake, and Kai entered the office. "My god, Jake—Scarlett. What a night the two of you had. Why are you here?" She looked from one to the other. "Are you both okay?"

"I'm fine," Scarlett said.

"She's lying, but we'll humor her," Jake said.

"I am not lying. It's over. I'm fine."

"He's right, Scarlett. An experience like that plays with your head." She turned to Jake. "And what about you, cowboy? And don't give me the macho-guy response. I know the psychological effects of shootings. You both should talk to someone. Jake, you know very well it's required protocol with most all law enforcement. Just because you're private sector now doesn't mean you don't need to continue the routine."

"Relax, Mom. I've done my time on the couch and know the script. I'm booking appointments for both of us."

"You are?" Scarlett gave him a startled, wide-eyed look.

"Yeah. It's my plan."

A smile crept across her face. "It's eating you up, isn't it?"

Liz appeared puzzled.

Scarlett tipped her chin and winked in Liz's direction. "He can't stand it because I told him I have a plan and won't tell him what it is."

Liz grinned and gave her a thumbs-up. "Good for you. Give him a taste of his own medicine."

"Careful. No double-teaming allowed."

Scarlett laughed. "Don't dish it out if you can't take it, Shepherd."

In jest, he shot her a reproving glance. "Moving on. Where are we with identifying Mrs. Kingsley's mystery lover? When we left yesterday, Liz, you were making calls."

"Yep. I checked with every security service in the area, and no one is missing an employee. Your instincts might have misguided you on that one."

"I don't think so. I'd bet my next fee he's in security work. Savannah spit out Warner's name without hesitation, which tells me Warner and the mystery guy have some type of connection."

"Well, it's not being a bodyguard."

"Maybe not private. Maybe law enforcement?"

"The Metropolitan Police?"

"I'd start there."

"Without a subpoena, we're not going to pry that kind of info out of them," Liz said.

"Good point. On Monday, have Joyce, over in Phil Madison's office, call the Met HR and say Phil is planning a high-profile event and needs security. Have her ask for their list of members who moonlight, especially those who cover—" He stopped, appearing to think for a minute. "Wait. Better idea. Cameron has the list for the Capitol Police team covering the funeral. I'll give him a call." He took out his phone and typed in a reminder. "The more I think about it, the more I see our mystery man as one of that crew. I wondered how the hell they lost Savannah." Giving a flick of his head in Scarlett's direction, he raised an eyebrow. "Shines a new light on the picture."

Scarlett stared at him, the corners of her lips curling upward—admiration streaming from her eyes. "Damn, Shepherd. That would make sense. You're good."

"I know."

Liz put her fingers to her lips. "Don't feed his ego. He's already hard enough to live with."

Scarlett nodded. "You're right."

Jake grinned. "I was going to say we'd take the weekend off, but I'm going to change my mind if the two of you don't stop ganging up on me."

"I like that idea," Scarlett said, her eyes lighting up. "After last night, I'm not sure you can glue me to that tedious computer today."

"Tell you what. We'll take a drive to Ocean City Beach—it's about three hours. Be a chance for Kai to get some exercise. Want to go with us, Liz? We can pick up here on Monday."

"Thank you for the invitation, but my place could use some attention. You two enjoy the day. The weather's perfect."

Jake was on his cell before she finished speaking. "Hey, Coop. How about a day at the beach? Do you and Doris have any plans that can't be changed?"

Scarlett watched as Jake appeared to be waiting for an answer.

"Ten-four. Pick you up in thirty, and I'll fill you in on last night." He glanced over at Scarlett and winked. Before ending the call, he said, "Yeah. Be prepared."

When he terminated the call, Scarlett gave him a quizzical look but didn't comment.

"What?"

"Who did you invite? And be prepared for what?"

"Pete Cooper—my partner in the security company. After last night, you don't think we're going to roam around without a little backup, do you? Just a precaution."

CHAPTER THIRTY-SIX

As Liz entered the office on Monday morning, Kai met her at the door. "Aren't you the early bird today?" After stowing her purse in a lower desk drawer, she started to sit as Scarlett came out of the work-room. "Good morning. What time did you and Jake come in?"

"A little before seven. Jake's talking to his friend in the Atlanta field office about the list of officers guarding Savannah at the funeral. He wants to meet with you and me to go over what we have on all the suspects."

"Thought he might. How is your family holding up through all of this? I assume they know about the assault on Friday night."

"I'm afraid they do." Scarlett exhaled, shaking her head. "But, on a positive note, I was able to tell them Jake believes the attack reduces the likelihood Savannah was abducted. My mother latched right onto the idea. But I'm worried about my niece and nephew. Those little guys are suffering."

"Of course, they are, but how did the weekend go for *you*? Any nightmares?"

Scarlett brushed a stray strand of hair from her forehead. "No night-mares but, once or twice, I had flashbacks that sent shivers through me. Jake's making appointments for both of us to talk with a coun-selor today. I think I'm fine. It's not like I've never felt threatened. Family law attorneys make enemies. People don't like interference with their kids and their money."

"Never thought about it, but I see what you mean. Well, gal, we'd better get our stuff together before he"—she pointed toward Jake's office—"comes out huffing and puffing."

Scarlett laughed. "Well, Sherlock doesn't scare me. I've seen his secret side."

Liz gave her a dubious look and then grinned. "I don't think I'm going to touch that one."

Once the trio had notes, documents, and forms spread out on the worktable, Jake said, "Let's start with Vladimir Petrokov and possible associate, Boris."

Liz flipped through a small pile of forms, pulled out one with photos attached, and handed it to him along with the rest.

"What do we know about Mr. Petrokov?"

"Definitely organized crime," Liz said. "Appears in a few press clippings with the victim, and some of his known businesses made substantial contributions to Kingsley's campaign chest. Plus, he fits the nanny's description of the man who recruited her sister for sex trafficking."

Jake pinned the form to the far right of a large bulletin board mounted to the wall. "Have we been able to tie him to our victim's lavish lifestyle?"

"Nothing concrete yet," Liz said, "but I'm still chasing the paper trail of shell corporations that begin with the one holding title to the DC house and the one leasing the apartment where the Garcia woman resided."

"How about the MMO?"

"All uncertain," Liz said, "but not impossible."

"I'm going to bump him down to tier three. While murder is equivalent to shoplifting with those guys, unless Kingsley stepped out of line, the murder doesn't seem plausible. Why dispose of a valuable asset? Getting a US senator in your pocket is gold and takes a big investment of time and money."

"I don't see a clear means or clear opportunity," Liz said. "What OC guy sends food, which may or may do the job, when they can shoot, stab, strangle, and torture?"

Scarlett watched and listened, soaking in the way Jake and Liz analyzed the circumstances.

"What about the cameras? Any sign of Petrokov on video? Scarlett?"

"Yes. Just a minute." She checked through her notes. "There were two recordings of a man fitting his description coming to the house in DC. No sign of him at the funeral."

"Any recent dates?" Jake asked.

"No. Both were at least six months ago. He came in a Rolls with a couple of big guys who waited in the car. I have the exact times, dates, and where they are on the recordings."

"When we finish, plug that info into the notes section of his sheet."

"I assume there's been no word on the missing Garcia sister," Scarlett said.

"No. But I have a theory."

"Care to share?"

He leafed through the sheets and pulled out one for each sister. "Mind you. It's just a theory—no hard evidence. But I suspect both sisters are in protective custody—maybe WITSEC. Kirby won't or can't say. It's not his department, but he would have privy since his team is investigating the murder. The Organized Crime unit would be lead on that investigation."

"So, the sisters are off your suspect list?"

He shook his head. "Not yet." He pinned the two sheets under the second column of suspects. "They score on all three elements: motive, means, and opportunity. So, I can't cross them off. However, Manuela doesn't appear to have the backbone. Can't speak for the other one since I haven't met her. But I'll keep them on the second tier. Can never eliminate a suspect strictly because of a weak appearance. I've seen cases where a coward morphed into a cunning killer."

Jake pulled out another suspect sheet with a photo of the grinning Senator Manchester attached. "This one is also second tier. While lover and motive are opposite sides of the same coin, and his opportunity is a short walk from one office to the other, I doubt the pompous phony has the ability or courage to kill." He looked over toward Scarlett. "Did you see him on any of the home videos?"

"No. Just at the funeral, along with his wife, and he acted like everyone else—shaking hands with other politicians and smiling at the media. I didn't see him pay any attention to Savannah on the footage taken during the service. Can't believe she slept with him. He must be twenty years older and looks superficial."

Jake smiled. "Politics breeds strange bedfellows. If it's any consolation, I don't think the affair lasted long, which brings us to her mystery—"

The office phone rang, interrupting Jake. Liz held up a finger to indicate pause and then went to her desk to answer the call.

Jake turned to Scarlett. "We'll hold a place for Savannah's mystery lover. Cameron's info should be on the fax machine by the time we wrap. Just for the hell of it, I'm going to put him in the primary list along with Jeanne Abbott. If he's a Capitol cop, cruising the halls of all the legislative offices would go unrestricted and unnoticed."

Liz appeared in the doorway. "It's Lila, Jake."

"Did she say what she wants?"

"She wants to talk to you. She saw the article about last night."

"Tell her I'm tied up."

"Jacob. You can't avoid her forever." Her eyes narrowed. "You want to lose the account?"

Tossing the remaining sheets on the table with a flourish of annoyance, Jake started for the door. "Okay, okay. I'll talk to her. She's been blowing up my mobile."

Scarlett watched the exchange with interest, wondering who Lila might be. *Lose the account? Must be a client. Why does he want to avoid her?* Curiosity urged Scarlett to ask Liz about Lila, but discretion held her back. To fill the pregnant pause, she flipped through her notes on the video footage.

Jake returned within three minutes. "Where were we?"

"I hope you were diplomatic, Jake," Liz said with a cautionary expression.

"You know I'm dangerous when I'm diplomatic. But don't worry, it's all good. Let's get back to work."

Scarlett suppressed a smirk but remained silent.

"You mentioned listing Jeanne Abbott and Mrs. Kingsley's mystery lover as primary suspects before you took the call," Liz said, drumming her pen on the table.

"Right." He picked up the two sheets and pinned them to the far-left side of the board, Abbott on top. Neither had photos. "Liz, what do we know about Ms. Abbott?"

"She'd worked for the senator since his days in the Georgia House, beginning as a volunteer, probably stuffing envelopes." Liz flipped a page of her legal pad. "By the time Kingsley moved to DC, she had worked, or slept, her way to his communications team."

"When did they meet?" Jake said.

"Apparently while she was in college. I found an article where she told the interviewer that during her sophomore year as a political science major at Shorter University, he visited the campus and gave a speech. Abbott waxed on with how he impressed her with his platform. She managed to finagle a face-to-face at the reception that evening. It ended with him inviting her to intern on his campaign staff."

"Probably slept with her that night," Scarlett said. "What was she? Nineteen? Twenty?"

While neither Jake, nor Liz, commented, he failed to mask an amused grin.

Liz did not appear to notice. "According to the article, he encouraged Abbott to change her minor to communications, which led to her staff position in DC."

"Married or single?" Jake asked.

"Single. She's from Valdosta, Georgia, but moved to Atlanta after graduating from Shorter. In DC, she lives in a pricey apartment outside the perimeter."

"Bet Kingsley was paying the rent. See if you can get a copy of her college yearbooks, maybe high school as well. We may need to look to her friends for leads as to her whereabouts."

"I know you haven't interviewed Abbott, but from what you know, how is she scoring on your MMO test?" Liz asked.

"Pinging all the buttons. As a staff member, free access to the office gave her opportunity. Being a Southerner and longtime lover suggests knowledge of his allergy and the snack food. As for motive, with illicit affairs, motives are a penny a truckload. Case in point: Savannah mentioned a European trip—a second honeymoon. That would be enough to incite any lover to take aggressive action."

"If her boyfriend is Capitol Police, looks like the same analysis applies," Liz said.

"Yes, to opportunity and motive, but the means? First, poison, even by allergy, is a female MO. A trained cop, and much as I hate to admit it, we're all shot full of testosterone, would go for a macho method of extermination."

"Nice to hear you admit it," Liz said, grinning.

Jake gave her a mock evil eye and continued, "To get a peanut ingredient in the tidbits, they'd have to be homemade. Right, Harvard?"

"True. I don't think you can buy any with peanut content. I bake a similar snack with pecans."

"Really?" His expression suggested the revelation shocked him. "You bake the deadly treats, which equals means, had good reason to dislike the bastard, which equals motive." He pinched his eyebrows together. "Should we create a suspect sheet for you?"

Scarlett's eyes flashed daggers. "That's not funny."

"Jake, you should be ashamed," Liz said.

"Okay. Bad joke. Duly noted. Moving on. I'm putting Abbott at the top, but not ruling the others out. Have either of you turned up anyone else we should look at? Anything in your review of the evidence make you pause? Created a question in your mind?"

Liz shook her head, but Scarlett thought for a minute.

"Scarlett?"

"I'm sorry. I need to recheck something." *Should I?* No. Her pulse raced. *That can't be relevant.* Scarlett looked at Jake for several seconds before asking, "Do you have a photo of Jeanne Abbott?" *They'll think I'm ridiculous.*

"Liz. Can we pull a photo of her?"

"I'm on it." She made a note on her pad.

"That'll do it for today. Scarlett, you keep on the video. Liz, you and I are going to follow up on the list Cameron sent. It should be on the fax by now."

"Are you leaving the office today?" Scarlett asked.

"You want to get rid of me?"

"Be serious."

"I'll be here most of the day. Clyde Register, Kingsley's chief-of-staff, promised to email a batch of records on contributors, staff, and the like. I plan to take a run at Kirby, tomorrow, if we can't track Abbott through our resources."

"You think he can or will help you?" Scarlett asked.

"He can track her credit and debit cards to suggest the area she's in. If she has a cell, which is likely, he can run that as well."

"But will he?"

"Only because it pertains to his case."

"And if I know Jake, he'll play the trump card if Hal balks," Liz said.

Jake gave Liz a faux frown. "I better be careful. You know me too well."

"What's the trump card?"

"The media," Liz said.

"You would do that?" Scarlett said.

"That's classified. Even Liz doesn't know. So far, I've never had to, but it's good to have it in my pocket."

It did not take Liz long after the meeting ended to find photos of Jeanne Abbott for Scarlett. "Here you go. I should have pulled these before."

"My. She's very pretty. Of course she is. Otherwise, Scott wouldn't have given her a second glance."

"Have you seen her on any of the recordings?"

"I believe she's on the funeral tapes. I'll have to go back and compare, but there was a blonde who was very emotional. She wore dark glasses but kept dabbing her face with a tissue. I made a note."

"Maybe you could review my file on her while Jake and I work on the boyfriend. Abbott was active on social media. That's where I found the images, but she went silent after the murder. Track the friends who have posted on her Facebook page. You might find clues as to places she might go or people she might contact for help."

CHAPTER THIRTY-SEVEN

At ten o'clock, Wednesday morning, Jake walked into the FBI offices, greeted by a warm reception from his former colleagues. Jeanne Abbott's location remained unknown.

"Where've you been hiding?" one agent said, while another shook Jake's hand and asked about Liz. Several of the support staff greeted him with enthusiasm as well.

Deke Weston and Sylvia Blake rose from their desks and approached Jake. "Hal's expecting you," Deke said. "He wants the three of us to meet with him in the conference room. You know the way. I'll let him know you're here."

As Weston walked toward the private office of Hal Kirby, Agent Blake said, "Can I get you something to drink before we start?"

"As a matter of fact, I could use a water." Jake glanced around the busy room, spotting his old desk with a new face occupying his chair. Flashbacks of his tenure with the Bureau flickered in his mind.

The moment of reflection crashed when Kirby and Weston beat Blake back to where Jake waited.

Extending his hand, Kirby said, "I see you brought a file. Let's move down the hall and get started."

As they approached the corridor, Blake joined them, handing Jake the water bottle.

Upon entering an austere meeting room, another wave of nostalgia washed over Jake as he looked at a large plaque of the FBI seal hanging on the wall. Kirby pointed toward one end of the table, suggesting Jake take a seat. The supervisor took the chair at the opposite end, while Blake and Weston sat on either side of him.

"Why do I feel like I'm on the stand, about to be grilled?" Jake said.

Kirby laughed. "Not intentional. So, what is it you want? You asked for this sit-down."

Jake noted Kirby's pleasant tone and wanted to look around to see if he was speaking to someone else. *Did Jackie sprinkle play-nice powder on his cereal?* "I need your help in locating a woman."

"Who do you need to locate and why?" Kirby asked.

Where is the egocentric, snarky Kirby? "Name's Jeanne Abbot. She may have come up on your radar."

Kirby looked at Weston and then Blake. Both shrugged.

"She worked for Kingsley, and they allegedly shared an off-the-clock relationship."

"Wait a second," Blake said. "I saw her name on a couple of lists but haven't gotten down to checking her out."

"You're suggesting Ms. Abbott and the senator were warming the sheets?" Kirby said.

"That's what I hear. Not that they were exclusive."

"That could explain the two half-filled wine glasses with a plate of caviar, crackers and—what do they call those cheesy tidbits?" Weston said.

"Cheese straws," Blake said.

"Someone want to tell me what you're talking about?" Jake said.

"The wine and goodies were on a console in his office," Kirby said. "But you need to keep it to yourself. If what you're telling us is true, she could have been the unidentified guest, leaving the question of whether she attended the little rendezvous. You've got her on your suspect list?"

"Right. What about prints on the glasses? I know your people dusted."

"Clean but for Kingsley. Couldn't you take a run over to his office and talk to her? They haven't cleared it out."

"I could if she were there. No one has seen her since the funeral."

"Ohhh. Another missing lady from the senator's harem," Kirby said.

"You said that. I didn't. But funny, isn't it? So many going MIA. And as long as we're on the subject of missing persons, what is going on with the Garcia woman?"

"Let's finish with Ms. Abbott, and I'll give you what I can when we're done. What are you planning to do when you find Ms. Abbott?"

"Sit down for a chat."

Kirby mulled over Jake's response, squinting his eyes with a slight frown on his face. "Explain for me why we should find the lady but allow you to conduct the interview?"

"Simple." Jake stared Kirby down with a robust air of confidence. "I'm good at it. Plus, I don't arrive pulling the United States Government behind me in a little red wagon. I can get her to relax and trust me." He paused but not long enough to relinquish the floor. "No one reads people better than I do."

"And no one has a bigger ego. So, you'll use that supposed ESP of yours to parse out her guilt or innocence?"

Jake took a second to respond. "I like to think it's more about paying attention than mystical power. So, what do you say, Kirby? Are you going to run the cards and the cell and help me locate her?"

"I think we can do that—provided you keep us in the loop about what you find."

Didn't expect it to be that easy. "Not a problem. I think we're allies in the same war."

"You're convinced Mrs. Kingsley had nothing to do with her husband's demise?"

"I think you know me well enough to be aware I wouldn't be representing her interests if I thought she was guilty."

"Our personal issues aside, Shepherd, I don't have to like you to respect your ability and your code. You worked for me."

Blake's eyes cut from Kirby to Jake in what appeared to be fascination.

"Likewise, I'm sure. Even you'll have to admit, it's more effective if we pool our efforts."

Kirby nodded. "While I know your answer, I've got to ask. Do you have the widow stashed somewhere?"

"Hate to disappoint you, but I don't."

"Would you tell me if you did?"

"Maybe not. But I don't."

Kirby gave his head a shake. "If she took off on her own, you know it makes her look guilty."

"Haven't we had this discussion? I continue to disagree. With the senator's shady connections, she could easily fear for her life. Wasn't Friday night enough evidence of that for you?"

"She's not in danger, Jake. And neither is the sister—the one I understand who is calling your place home these days."

With a slight cock of his head, a broad grin crossed Jake's face. "My, oh my, how word gets around. Jackie tell you that?"

Deke Weston covered a smile with his hand, a twinkle in his eye, while Sylvia Blake shot a quizzical glance his way.

"As a matter of fact, she didn't. It was Sabrina—your daughter."

Jake shook his head. "Kids. I'll have to talk to her." Cocking an eyebrow, he said, "What do you know, Kirby? You act damned sure there's no threat, and where *are* the Garcia women?"

"You've got to realize I'm not free to tell you much. The Organized Crime Unit is running that investigation. They've got it under control and claim the dots don't connect between the Russians and the murder. We've been given orders to stay away from the Bratva. OC is afraid we could mess up their case. Cameron's been told the same. The Atlanta house was hit, looking for a wad of cash. We beat them to the Georgetown house."

Jake studied Kirby's face, his wheels turning. *Bet they were looking for the stash we found in Kingsley's house, and you guys found it with your warrant, which should keep Bratva from going after Savannah.*

"I *am* able to assure you that reliable intel reports no interest by the syndicate in your client, much less her family."

Yep, Vladimir knows the Feds have the cash.

Kirby continued, "The Friday-night shooter was a maverick on an unauthorized mission. If you hadn't killed him, they probably would have taken him out for potentially bringing them unwanted attention."

"Good to know. Sounds like OC has an undercover planted or a trusted CI. But I'll keep my guard up a little longer. Can you tell me anything about the Colombian sisters?"

"Other than OC suspects the trafficking asset is either dead or was taken out of the country the minute Kingsley's death went public. We turned the nanny over to them for their investigation. She'll probably go into WITSEC or back to Colombia. Is the Abbott woman your only suspect?"

"I'm narrowing the field."

"Care to share any other theories?"

"Not yet. I need to do a little more digging."

Kirby leaned forward, lowering his voice. "Can I trust you to keep us informed?"

"Why wouldn't I? The last time I checked, I have no authority to make an arrest. You guys can take all the credit. I'll settle for my fee."

Kirby nodded. "As long as you're clear that we're playing on the same team, give Blake all you have on your suspect, and she'll run the data you need. Don't make me regret it."

"And destroy our brotherly love? Not a chance."

Weston almost choked in an effort to avoid laughing.

Kirby gave the table a slap, stood, and said, "I'm done here. You people finish up." He made eye contact with Jake and said, "Give Liz my best. Don't know how she puts up with you." Without a fare-thee-well, he exited the room.

As the door closed behind the supervisor, Jake looked at Weston. "Almost as important as he thinks he is."

"As well as the two of you appear to be getting along, it's like old times," Weston said.

"Far from it, pal. Far from it. There's a huge difference between working with Kirby and working for him. As much as I miss all this, I would *never* report to the SOB again."

Blake seemed absorbed in the exchange but stood. "I'll let you two old partners catch up. Send me your info on Abbott, Shepherd, and I'll get started pulling the data."

Jake reached into his document holder, took out a manila folder, and handed it to her. "You should find everything you need in there. If anything is missing, give my office a call."

Eying the case, Weston said, "Nice leather, partner. Haven't seen one like it at Walmart. PI work must be paying well."

Jake rolled his eyes with a smirky smile. "Gift from a client for a good verdict."

With a click of his tongue and a thumbs up sign, Weston said, "Gotcha. Have time for a drink?"

Jake looked at his watch. "You're on."

CHAPTER THIRTY-EIGHT

After a full day of effort by Jake and Liz to track the names provided by Dan Cameron, Savannah's mystery lover remained unidentified. But on Thursday morning, Liz hung up from a phone conversation and shouted, "Bingo. Found him."

Jake came out of his office, followed by Scarlett emerging from the workroom. "You've got a Capitol cop, who's been absent since the funeral?" he said.

"I do. His name is Randall Cummings, Lieutenant Randall Cummings, officially listed as 'on vacation.'"

"A lieutenant. Interesting." Jake circled the desk and patted Liz on the back. "Good job. Now, let's find out more about Lieutenant Cummings. Run a background, a social media, a Google search—all the usual resources. Build me a dossier."

"You want to hit Hal up for another phone and financial search?"

Jake shook his head. "No. Still premature. We'll do our homework, and depending on what we find, I'll touch base with Cameron. The disappearance is his case, and he's a hell of a lot easier to work with."

"But Hal has his people working on Jeanne Abbott for you," Liz said.

"No guarantee he won't balk at another request. I'm still not sure he wasn't on drugs, Monday. He was almost decent."

Liz rolled her eyes while Scarlett followed their conversation with intense interest.

"Have the records on Jeanne Abbott come in?" Scarlett asked.

"Liz?" Jake said.

"Nothing yet. She—what's the new agent's name?"

"Blake. Sylvia Blake," Jake said.

"Sylvia Blake may be holding it up until she has everything." Liz tore a sheet of notes off a legal pad and stuck it in a manila folder. "What's that new one like, Jake?"

"Young. Eager. Full of self-righteous ambition and willing to suck up to Kirby."

"Got the picture," Liz said. "I'll call over and give her a nudge."

"Let me run a social media search on Lieutenant Cummings," Scarlett said. "It'll give me a break from the video review."

Jake gave her a thumbs-up. "I'll make some calls to see if any of my people know the guy, and, Liz, you can get to work on the standard background search after you light a fire under Agent Blake."

"Wait," Liz said. She moved her computer mouse while staring at the screen. "We've got an email from the Bureau with attachments. Looks like Blake came through after all."

Jake gave a hearty fist pump. "All right. Now, we've got the day's work cut out. I'll postpone the work on Cummings and review the Abbott data. Order lunch for us, and about four thirty, we'll convene in the workroom and put together what we've found. Both of you see if you can find any photos of Cummings."

As planned, Scarlett and Liz took seats at the long table in the workroom at the appointed time. They could hear Jake's muffled voice from behind the closed door at the end of the hall.

"He must be on the phone," Liz said, tipping her head in the direction of his office.

The words were hardly out of her mouth when the talking ceased, and within seconds, Jake entered, carrying a legal pad and several manila folders.

"How'd the two of you do?" he asked. "Any photos of the Lieutenant?"

"I found several," Scarlett said, extracting three images from one of the files fanned out on the table. She handed them to Jake, who remained standing in front of the suspect board. He spread them on the table and then took an image from one of his folders. Comparing his photo with the ones Scarlett presented, he shook his head while the women watched intently.

"Not him."

"Not who?" Scarlett said.

Thumping the corner of the photo with his middle finger, he said, "Not the Chippendale in the photo I pulled from Savannah's texts."

"One you wouldn't let me see?" Scarlett said.

"Yep. But you can look if you don't mind triple R rated."

Scarlett nodded, and Jake slid the photo to her. As she stared at the image of a nude male, his back to the camera, her eyebrows pinched together. "This guy has dark hair. Cummings is a blond, almost the same as Savannah. Why would a guy send a photo of his rear—I mean back view."

"Must be proud of it. By the way, there's a frontal, but it's cut off at the waist. I don't think you have one to compare with that angle. I can show it to you if you like." He gave her a devilish expression.

She returned his look with a sardonic smile. "I'll pass."

"So, that means there's another mystery man?" Liz said. "Assuming that's not Kingsley or Manchester."

"Pretty sure it's neither. Manchester hasn't been that fit in thirty years," Jake said. "Scarlett, what are the chances of it being Kingsley?" When she didn't respond, he said, "Scarlett? Earth to Scarlett."

She flinched. "Oh, I'm sorry. I was just looking at that guy's leg. What's that?" She pointed to the photo.

"Best I can tell, it's a tattoo. I can have the image enlarged and enhanced to better identify it."

"That's not Scott. He thought tattoos were disgusting. No way would he ever have one."

"Nothing is that definite," Jake said. "But for now, we'll assume it isn't the deceased."

"What in the world was my sister all about? Three men?"

"She was miserable in the marriage. Probably just trying to survive," Jake said.

"You're more sympathetic than I am. She should have left him."

"Out of the mouth of a divorce lawyer," Jake said.

Scarlett scoffed. "No. Someone who plays by the rules."

"Could she be with that guy in the photo instead of Cummings?" Liz said.

"Maybe—but doubtful. The escape was much too smooth not to have been assisted by an expert. So, unless body beautiful, here"—he tapped the photo—"is a pro, I'm hanging tough with Cummings." He scooped up the pictures Scarlett produced and pinned them under the corresponding suspect sheet and then tucked the other one back into his file. "So, what do we know about Cummings? Liz?"

"Background clean. Age forty-seven and comes from Kentucky."

Jake turned and made a note on the suspect sheet. "Might be where he would take Savannah. He would know the area—maybe have family or contacts to harbor them."

Scarlett put an elbow on the table and her hand to her chin as she listened.

"Give me the rest."

"Been with the Capitol Police fifteen years. He came from the Metropolitan force. Looks like he went into law enforcement directly out of college. Graduated from American University with a degree in Public Affairs."

"That brought him to DC."

"He started law school at NYU but dropped out after the first year. Sound familiar?" She smiled at him.

"Yeah, but I finished."

"So far, he sounds like a decent guy," Scarlett said.

"I didn't find any red flags in my research," Liz said. "He is recently divorced. According to the Final Judgment, he has three teenagers who live with their mother. No nasty allegations in the pleadings."

Jake appeared to process the information for a minute before speaking. "What financial information did you find on him in the divorce docs?"

Liz flipped through files on her laptop. "Here it is. He reports on his financial affidavit an income just north of six figures with overtime and off-duty pay."

"And the final judgment. Does it squeeze him?"

Liz nodded. "Yeah. It looks that way. He's got alimony and child support obligations."

"The sister I know would never trade a senator with eyes on higher things for a cop with financial obligations," Scarlett said. "No offense, Jake."

"None taken. But your point is valid. However, if she collected on Kingsley's insurance, she could afford a working stiff. Could give him a motive. What else do we know?"

Scarlett shook her head. "He doesn't have a social media presence, but I located pages for two of his kids. That's where I found the photos." She tapped her fingers on the table. "From what I saw, he has a strong bond with his children. I have to admit—he's a handsome guy. Except for the money angle, he fits the profile of a man my sister would find attractive."

"Professionally, he's received several official commendations," Liz said. "And appears admired on the job. Jake, what do you think the fallout would be of an officer fooling around with a senator's wife he was supposed to be protecting?"

"I'm not sure whether there's a written policy, but the risk of it going bad with a potential complaint for sexual harassment or assault would make it frowned upon."

As she made a note, Scarlett said, "I don't know about you two, but I'm thinking this guy's not a killer."

"Anyone can snap, Harvard, but he's not at the top of my list. I don't see a cop playing around with a victim's allergy. More likely to go for a sure kill with something like cyanide." He gathered his files and pad into a neat stack. "Unless either of you has any other info we need to discuss, we need to get home and pack."

Scarlett did a double take. "What?"

"We're flying south *early* tomorrow. From the data I assembled with the financials and phone records, Ms. Abbott is probably still in the general vicinity of Atlanta. I need to get to her before she decides to move on. Liz, I need you to see if you can track any friends or family she may have in the area and their addresses. Find out everything you can about her. What she likes; what she hates; hobbies, pets, awards, all of it."

"Are we going back to the MacGregors'?"

"For a day or two, unless you want to stay with your family."

"I do have a condo there."

"True. But I'm not quite ready to let up on your security. I prefer to know you're safe while I'm working."

CHAPTER THIRTY-NINE

Jake turned to Scarlett as he ended a call on his cell phone. "Liz is pretty certain she has Abbott's location pinpointed." He glanced at his watch as they waited in line for a rental car in the Hartsfield-Jackson Airport. "She's emailing the data."

"That was quick." She shifted her handbag from one shoulder to the other.

"Looks like she's north of Atlanta in the Chattahoochee National Forest. By identifying the phone numbers in Abbott's log, Liz connected a sorority sister from the college yearbooks and followed up with social media. The sister's family owns a cabin near a lake there." He slid the cell into his shirt pocket as they moved forward in the line.

"I've been thinking, what if she won't talk to you?" Scarlett said. "You're a total stranger. Why should she? Especially if she gave Scott the cheese straws."

He smiled. "Guess I'll have to be persuasive—use my best Oklahoma charm."

"Right. Maybe you could sing to her." Pressing her lips together, she pulled them inward in a mischievous grin.

"Maybe. Hadn't thought of that technique."

"Seriously, Jake. You're an unknown male. I wouldn't talk to you." She stopped, appearing to mull over a thought. "Maybe I should interview her—at least to break the ice."

He squinted with a dubious expression.

"Don't look at me like that. I'm a lawyer. I know how to question a subject. Do you have any idea how many lovers of cheating husbands I've cross examined in court?"

"Accusing a witness of adultery is not the same as pressuring a murder suspect—not to mention, you're also the sister of the woman Abbott has to resent."

"How stupid do you think I am? I wouldn't tell her I'm Savannah's sister."

"Try looking in the mirror, Harvard. You're twins. I'll get to her. This isn't my first rodeo."

"When you strike out, don't say I didn't warn you. In this day and age, no woman is going to talk to a strange man, much less one asking questions about a murder."

"You wouldn't underestimate me, would you?" He tipped his chin and raised his eyebrows.

She gave him a disgusted look and muttered under her breath.

"I didn't hear you."

She stared him in the eye. "I said, 'You're an arrogant control freak.'"

He laughed. "And you're right." After a quick glance at his watch, he said, "If traffic doesn't delay us, I should be able to drop you at Gray's and head over to the Bureau in an hour or so. With luck, I can make it to the Chattahoochee Forest by early afternoon, do the interview, and return to the MacGregors' by dinner."

"No comment," she said as the customer in front of them completed his rental.

"Our turn," Jake said, stepping up to the counter.

Once he completed the paperwork for a car, he took out his cell and rang the FBI office as they walked out of the terminal. After ending the call, he turned to Scarlett. "So far, the stars are aligned. Cameron's in the office and will see me at eleven."

When she didn't answer, he said, "Not speaking? Don't tell me you're pouting because I won't let you do the interview."

"I don't pout. But I could do the interview. And I don't like being underestimated either."

"Touché."

"She's not going to talk to you."

He did a double take. "Care to make a little wager?"

Jake checked his watch as he parked his vehicle for his appointment with Dan Cameron. By the time he cleared security and reached the ASAC's office, it was eleven o'clock on the nose.

"Shepherd, good to see you. How was your flight?" Cameron said, as they shook hands. "Come on back and show me what you've got."

Once in the agent's private office, Jake sat, opened his case, and took out a file. As he handed it to Cameron, he said, "I'm pretty sure I've put together what happened at the funeral, specifically, my guess as to how Ms. Kingsley gave her security the slip."

"Have you? You've ruled out abduction?"

"I think we all doubted abduction from the beginning. According to Kirby, there's no noise coming from the Russians."

"Yeah. We got the memo from OC. But, what about the assault on the sister?"

Jake shook his head. "Not a hit. From what the organized crime team learned, the assailant acted on his own, trying to score points."

"So, you're convinced Ms. Kingsley slipped away despite all the surveillance around."

"If what I believe is true, it would have been easy. I'm looking at Lieutenant Randall Cummings, United States Capitol Police. I have good reason to believe he and Mrs. Kingsley are—you know, an affair. He was there and could have facilitated the whole thing, with or without the help of anyone else on the team. He's been on vacation since the funeral. No contact with his office. Only question remaining is where are they now? That's where you come in."

"I'd like to close this one out, especially with a good conclusion. If I'm reading you right, you have evidence of their relationship, and you want us to track him."

"Exactly. His cell number is in that file. Her bank and credit cards have been silent, but Cummings probably feels safe using his plastic and his phone since they don't think anyone knows about the relationship. She played coy with me."

"Do you think he's involved in the murder?"

"I haven't eliminated him. He certainly had opportunity, possibly motive, but he doesn't fit the profile for me. Everything we have on him is in there." Jake pointed to the manila folder Cameron held.

As the agent opened the file and flipped through the documents, he said, "You know, we've treated this incident the same as we would a child abduction, implementing the Rapid Start program. We've followed every lead while trying to keep it under the radar." He closed the folder and addressed Jake. "The Evidence Response Team came up with nothing significant, nor did the canvas of witnesses. We have taps on all the relevant phones, but no ransom calls or claims of abduction yet."

"Sounds like we're on the same page," Jake said.

"I admit, our team suspects a voluntary disappearance, but we've been scratching our heads as to how she could pull it off. This info helps. Good work, and thanks for bringing it to us. I'll follow up and be in touch."

"Fair enough." Jake stood, reached over Cameron's desk, shook his hand, and then took several business cards from a brass holder. "Appreciate you keeping me posted. Before I go, I have one more favor to ask."

CHAPTER FORTY

It took Jake ninety minutes to reach his destination. The quaint, redwood cabin belonging to Jeanne Abbott's sorority sister stood nestled in the woods overlooking a ravine. A Toyota Corolla was the sole vehicle on the property. He parked beside the car, exited his rental, and approached the steps leading up to a wrap-around front porch. Cliché rockers and a hanging glider completed the setting. The barking of a small dog pierced the quiet tranquility of the picturesque scene. As he walked, the sound of his sharkskin boots crunching the gravel competed with the incessant yapping. *Chihuahua or poodle?* As he reached the top step, the barking suddenly ceased.

Jake knocked on the door and waited. When no one answered, he knocked again, resisting the urge to pound.

When the door cracked open, restricted by a security chain, an unseen female voice said, "Who's there? I have a gun."

"Ms. Abbott? My name is Jake Shepherd. I'm a private investigator from DC. I'd really prefer you didn't shoot. Would you consider answering a few questions to help unravel what happened to Senator Kingsley?" He eased his boot into the crack in the door, his portfolio under his arm. "I know you don't know me and have every reason to be apprehensive." He took out his wallet and removed several cards. "Here is my business card, my driver's license, and the official card of FBI Assistant Special Agent in Charge Dan Cameron."

A small, trembling hand came through the opening and snatched the cards.

"I mean no harm. Please give Cameron a call. He will vouch for me. I'll wait here on the porch."

"You want me to call the FBI?"

"Yes, ma'am."

"Why would the FBI vouch for you?"

"Because I'm a former agent. I understand your reluctance, Ms. Abbott. Discussing the senator must be difficult. I am sincerely sorry for your loss. But talking to me today could reduce the likelihood of investigators from the Bureau showing up at your door."

"Please move your foot."

"I have no intention of forcing my way in. I just want you to listen. See, I'm removing my foot. Make the call to Special Agent Cameron. What do you have to lose?"

As soon as Jake's foot cleared the door, it closed. He heard the deadbolt click. Stepping back, he waited, hoping she would follow through. *Do your stuff, Cameron.*

Several minutes later, Jeanne Abbott opened the door wide, a golden Pomeranian in her arms.

"I called. The Assistant Special Agent in Charge said you are who you say you are, and I can trust you." She extended her hand to return his ID. "Come in, but you're wasting your time. There's nothing I can tell you."

After accepting the three cards, he returned his business card. "Keep this in case you want to reach me in the future."

Abbott took the card and then put the dog on the floor. The fluffy creature immediately went to Jake, sniffing his boots.

"Bambi, no. Come here," Abbott said.

Jake leaned over and held his hand, palm up, for the dog to sniff. "She's okay. She's just doing her job."

Abbott stared at him for a second. "You must know dogs. Most people try to pet her, and she doesn't like being touched until she gets to know you."

Jake smiled. "I like dogs. May I sit?" He pointed to a round table with four chairs near the kitchen area of the great room.

Abbott nodded.

After taking a seat, he removed a legal pad from his zippered case and clicked open his rollerball.

Abbott watched, not moving to join him.

"Won't you sit? I promise I won't invade your personal space."

"I'm not accustomed to being alone in an isolated cabin with a totally strange man."

"I respect that. You do realize you've notified the FBI I'm here. If I were to make an offensive move, I would be in big trouble." Jake tipped his chin in a partial nod. "Right?"

"I hadn't thought of it that way. Why is a private investigator looking into Sco—Senator Kingsley's death? Aren't the police—the FBI—doing that?" She took a step closer to the table with Bambi jumping up against her leg, vying for her mistress's attention. Abbott leaned over and again scooped up the canine.

"Knowing you worked for the senator for a considerable amount of time, I'm sure his death has been hard for you. Can you imagine how hard it is for his widow and the children?" He paused, observing Abbott's body language at the mention of Savannah. *She flinched. She tried not to react, but her emotions prevailed.* "I've been hired to help speed things along. Just another set of eyes and ears."

Without responding, she eased closer to the table, avoiding eye contact with Jake. She appeared to fixate on the gold cross hanging around his neck, exposed by the unfastened buttons of his white dress shirt.

"Sit, Ms. Ab—may I call you Jeanne?"
His words seemed to startle her as though for a moment her mind had drifted. She nodded and sat, still holding Bambi.

"To start, Jeanne, tell me a little about yourself. I understand you're a Michael Bublé fan."

She raised her eyelids, making direct eye contact with him. He recognized an element of surprise in her expression and a trace of fluid on the lower rims of her eyes.

"How did you know I like Bublé? And what do you want to know?"

Jake smiled. "Google knows everything. I also saw where you love Paris."

She smiled. "It's magical. But I don't understand why you worked so hard to find me. I'm nobody—just a low-level staff member. Shouldn't you be talking to people like Clyde Register or Lavinia?"

"I have spoken to both. But let's talk about you. Where are you from? How long did you work for the senator? What was your job?"

She eyed him for several more seconds. "What has all that got to do with him?"

He didn't answer but smiled as if to agree.

"If you were able to find me here, you know everything about me."

She's not dumb. "I'm busted. You're right. I know you're from Valdosta, here in Georgia, attended Shorter University in Rome, and worked for the senator since you were in college. Why don't you tell me something I don't know?"

She remained silent.

He allowed his gaze to drift, first to the dog, which Abbott firmly grasped, and then to her other hand. Her fingers spread across her stomach as though massaging it. "You're pregnant, aren't you?"

An involuntary gasp escaped from her mouth. "Why would you say something like that?"

"You're pregnant and don't know what to do." He switched to a sympathetic tone while engaging Abbott in eye contact. "Are you contemplating abortion?"

She frowned. "You are . . . you are—"

"Presumptuous? Rude? You're right, but I'm not judging you. I get it. You loved him."

Her reserves failed, bringing forth a flood of tears. "I don't know what you're talking about."

"I believe you do, Jeanne." From his file, Jake extracted a photocopy of the note Scarlett found in Scott Kingsley's clothing and presented it to her. "Do you recognize this?"

Abbott's face flushed, and she looked away.

"It's okay, Jeanne. He's gone, and you no longer need to protect his reputation. Did he know about the baby?"

"I haven't said there's a baby." The dog began squirming, and Abbott put her on the floor.

Jake laid his pen down, laced his fingers, and looked her in the eye. "Let me give you my take on this. Senator Kingsley was the father of your baby. You told him you were pregnant, and he told you to abort. But you're growing older and tired of waiting for him to make good on his empty promises to leave his wife."

As he talked, Abbott's eyes opened wider and wider, telling him he was on target. "You don't need to answer. I can tell I'm right so far. You confronted him. Drew a line. I would hazard a guess this wasn't the first time he got you pregnant, but desperation made you stand your ground this time."

Abbott began shaking.

"It's okay. Like I said, I'm not judging you. Kingsley was a bastard. You're not the only one he hurt. What I don't know is whether you had anything to do with his death. I wouldn't blame you if you did. Maybe you didn't mean to kill him."

She shook her head, her hands trembling, her chest heaving.

"Jeanne, I'm sure you knew about his allergy to peanuts, and being from Georgia, you are no doubt familiar with cheese straws. Am I not right?"

She nodded.

"But I can see you're a good person. You were Scott Kingsley's victim. Men like him reach out and take what they want without regard to the consequences to others. Were you with him the night he died?"

She stared straight ahead, not moving, her hands clasped tight in her lap.

"You want to tell me. You've needed to talk to someone, and you couldn't. Were you there when he ate the tainted tidbit?"

She continued to stare, a vacant look in her eyes.

"Did you give him the wafers?"

She shook her head but remained silent. The only sound in the cabin came from the dog lapping water from a bowl near the sink.

"Tell me the whole story. I'll do whatever I can to help you. If you were involved, it's only a matter of time before the FBI puts it together—fingerprints, DNA. Their labs will find it all."

She put her elbows on the table and buried her face in her hands.

"You were there when he died."

Without looking up, she shook her head.

"Talk to me, Jeanne. Let me help you."

"He was dead when I got there. He was on the floor—blood around his head—I thought someone shot him. It was horrible."

"And you were scared—probably terrified. What time was that?"

"I don't know. Eight thirty, maybe nine. I didn't kill him." She looked him in the face. "I loved him." Her tears saturated her cheeks.

"Okay. If you didn't, help me figure out who did." He paused, giving her time to collect her emotions. "Did you see anything unusual in the room? Anything that could have been used as a weapon?"

"There was his bronze statue and some books on the floor."

"Did you touch anything?"

"No. I just ran back to my office. I was afraid whoever hit him might still be there and would kill me."

"Did you call for help?"

"No. I was afraid. I hid and waited for about thirty minutes and then left. The guard must have been on a break because there was no one at the security desk when I passed."

"Why haven't you come forward and told what you saw that night?"

"Fear. I didn't want the media clamoring to talk to me. I was afraid they would ask why I was there that late. I didn't think anything I knew would be relevant." Her hands began to tremble. "What am I going to do?" Her voice cracked. "How am I going to take care of a baby with no husband, no job?" The dog, reacting to her tone, trotted over to Abbott. Standing on her hind legs, the Pomerania pawed at her mistress.

"Don't you have family?"

"I can't tell them." Her head drooped forward. "My parents are extremely religious and would disown me if I have a baby without a husband." Raising her head to face Jake, she said, "How did you find out? No one knows."

"I didn't. I just know how the story goes with guys like Kingsley. Are you aware of any enemies he may have had? Anyone threaten him? Anything you noticed or heard that did not compute?"

"No. I worked down the hall with his public relations team. My job was to set up photo ops, research for any mentions of his name in media, stall reporters. That night, I went to his office after everyone went home." An expression of alarm came over her face. "Is the FBI going to question me?" She covered her face with her hands.

"I can't promise you they won't. The best way to avoid that happening is if the person who did it is found. Look at me, Jeanne."

She did as he asked.

"Were you aware Mr. and Mrs. Kingsley were planning a trip to Europe—a second honeymoon?"

She cringed, a stricken look on her face. "No."

He paused, analyzing her reaction. *She's telling the truth.* "One more time, Jeanne. Did you have anything to do with Senator Kingsley's death?"

Without hesitation, she said, "I did not, Mr. Shepherd."

Despite the tears flowing down her cheeks, Jake noted her calm tone, the unwavering expression of her eyes, and stillness of her body as she spoke. "I'm inclined to believe you. So, I'm going to leave it at that today. But I want you to think about who could have hated him enough to cause his death or had reason to benefit from it. If anything comes to mind, no matter how small or insignificant, contact me."

Jake arrived back at the MacGregor house shortly before six p.m. and was met in the game room by Scarlett as he and Gray entered.

"You made it in time for dinner," she said. "How was the trip? She wouldn't talk to you, would she?"

He dropped his portfolio on a side table and gave her a smug smile. "Hate to rob you of the told-you-so moment, Harvard, but I had a successful interview. I'll let you read the transcript when it's typed."

"You're kidding. She let you in?"

"Of course."

"Was anyone else there?"

"Just a little yappy dog, far as I know."

Gray took a beer out of the fridge under the bar and offered it to Jake.

As Jake moved to accept the drink, she put her hands on her hips with her face scrunched in a frown.

"What did you do, Shepherd? Hypnotize her? Or seduce her?"

"Trade secret. However, I'm flattered you think I have sufficient sex appeal to seduce a suspect into talking."

"Did you two get married while you were in DC?" Gray said. "You sound like an old married couple."

"Not hardly. I'm sorry, Gray. It's my fault," Scarlett said. "I didn't think the woman would let a strange man into her house."

"Good point, Jake. How did you pull it off?"

"Used a friend. Dan Cameron at the Bureau vouched for me." He turned toward Scarlett. "See, Harvard. You underestimated me again." He held up a palm. "No sneaky tricks."

Gray laughed.

"Well? Did she do it?" Scarlett asked. "Did she kill him?"

"Don't think so."

"You're kidding. If she didn't, all we have left is the guy with Savannah, assuming there is a guy with Savannah."

"I didn't say I've cleared her. I said, I don't think so. What we have to do is go back and look at everyone a little closer—everyone."

"What did your friend at the FBI say? Is he going to run down the name you gave him?" Scarlett said.

Jake took a swallow of his beer and nodded. "He'll let me know how that goes. I suspect he'll send a team out when he pinpoints a location. If he's successful, we could know where your sister is within the week."

"Can I tell my parents?"

"Tell them there's a lead in the case. We're hoping she is in seclusion and not being held against her will. No names. No labels. Tell them just enough to provide a little assurance."

"I'll go make the call." She crossed the room and headed out in the direction of the staircase.

"Where do you go from this point?" Gray asked as he sat on a brown leather couch.

"Hang around here tomorrow so Scarlett can have some time with her family. After last week, she can do with an R and R day. Then, back to DC on Sunday. Take another look-see at the other suspects and hope something pops."

"Want my plane to take you?"

"Thanks. We'll be fine with commercial. Sundays are light travel."

As Jake finished speaking, Scarlett reappeared.

"How'd it go with your family?" Jake asked.

Scarlett held out a hand, twisting it in the so-so sign.

"That good, huh?"

"Mom likes hearing Savannah wasn't abducted, but she doesn't quite buy it. She still says Savannah would never leave the children."

"What do you think?" Gray asked Scarlett.

"I don't know my sister—not as a mother. When we were young, she didn't have an unselfish bone in her body, but she wasn't a mom." She shrugged. "I don't have a clue."

"Take Jake over to your parents' house. He can use his cowboy charisma to reassure your mom."

Jake made a face and shook his head.

"You can't mean the duke of diplomacy standing there?" Scarlett said, pointing toward Jake.

"Of course. If his good-cop charm fails, he can use his bad-cop persona to bully her." Gray grinned from ear to ear.

Scarlett laughed and then said to Jake, "Would you?"

His brow furrowed. "Would I what?"

"Try to reassure my family."

He ran his fingers through his hair, took another swallow of beer, and then said, "Why not? We'll stop by on our way to the airport."

Scarlett smiled. "I see your strategy. Time will be limited."

"Hard to fool a Harvard lawyer."

Gray stopped in the middle of taking a swallow. "Careful, Shepherd. Have respect for the superior school."

With his hands in the air, Jake feigned surrender. "Damn. How could I forget being outnumbered?"

Back at work on Monday, Jake left Scarlett and Liz to meet with Hal Kirby for an update on Jake's interview of Jeanne Abbott.

Although bored with the tedious job of reviewing the various surveillance tapes, Scarlett stayed the course and was near what seemed like an endless supply of footage. At two thirty, she glanced at her watch and considered closing down the computer. She had a hair appointment, arranged by Liz, for three o'clock. Just as she was about to cease the review, she abruptly pushed pause, enlarged the view, and stared at the screen. *What's he doing?* After hitting pause, she ripped a clean sheet of paper off her legal pad and jotted down the tape location. *Jake's got to look at this. Maybe my gut wasn't off base.* She took the message to his office and laid it on his desk chair. As she returned to the workroom, Liz buzzed.

"Pete's here."

It was nearly four thirty when Pete Cooper dropped Scarlett off. Liz was preparing to leave for the day.

"He's in his office. I've got errands to run, so I'm going to slip away. See you tomorrow."

At the end of the hall, Scarlett could see Jake's door standing open. Before seeking him out, she stopped by the workroom to drop her purse where Kai greeted her. "Hey, big guy. You ready to go home?" After petting the dog for a second, she proceeded to Jake's doorway and tapped the jamb to get his attention. "Did you read my note?"

He looked up from the array of papers spread out on his desk and then shuffled them around until he pulled out the one she had left on his chair. "This it?" He gave the message a quick glance.

"Yeah. You haven't looked at it, have you?" She crossed her arms, assuming an annoyed stance.

"Not yet. I've only been back a few minutes and wanted to recheck a couple of facts. What's it all about?"

"Just come look at the video."

"Yes, ma'am." He grabbed the paper and passed briskly by her, tapping her shoulder as he went.

When they reached the workroom, he stopped. Want to boot it up for me?"

"You only need to wake it. I left it on for you to see."

"Okay." He sat and hit the enter key. The computer took a couple of seconds but came up.

Scarlett moved behind him. "Start the video."

"As it began running, he said, "What am I looking at, Harvard?"

"It's Savannah's kitchen in Washington."

A male figure appeared on the screen, looked around the area, and then disappeared from view into a walk-in pantry.

Jake glanced up at Scarlett. "Is that what you wanted me to see?"

"Just hang on a minute."

After a brief period of no movement on the display, the subject emerged, carrying a wooden box covered with colorful flowers.

"Do we know who this is?" Jake asked without taking his eyes off the screen.

"I'm pretty sure it's Kyle McClellan."

"McClellan? The son of Savannah's friend?"

"Yeah. The one Colin likes."

"And why is this important?"

"Watch the damn video, Shepherd." Scarlett's pulse raced.

"Calm down. I'm watching."

"Do you see that? He's taking a picture of a recipe."

"I see."

"That's a box Mom made in her art class. She gave all of us one. If we enlarge the image, I bet he's photographing her cheese straw recipe."

Jake nodded. "Holy mother of Satan, you might be right. You may have found a smoking gun, Harvard." He moved his face closer to the screen.

Scarlett squeezed her hands into fists, displaying her excitement. "Yes, yes, yes. I knew it. I knew it. Something didn't ring right. Why would a teenage boy pay so much attention to a seven-year-old? You've got to talk to him." She rested a hand on Jake's shoulder. "You've definitely got to talk to him. You didn't see him when you interviewed the parents. Do you think? Could it possibly have been this kid? No. Why would he kill Scott?"

Jake stood up, turned, and put both hands on her shoulders. "Steady, counselor. Good work. You have found a good lead—maybe the key to solving the case."

"You think? Really?"

"Hold on." He walked down to his office, dug through a stack of manila folders, and took one out. Returning to the workroom, Jake pulled out the photo of the unclothed male and held it to the paused screen. "Could definitely be a match." He then clicked the browser icon and brought up Facebook. Kyle McClellan's page produced more photos.

"Oh, that's disgusting. Savannah had an affair with a minor? That's sick—illegal."

"Slow up, Harvard. One-sided sexual obsessions gone bad are common. Case in point, John Hinckley Jr. and Jodie Foster."

"But a teenager? A teenage killer?"

"Try Googling teenage killers. There's no minimum age on murder."

"Should you call your brother—I mean husband-in-law?"

"Let's not get ahead of ourselves. You've uncovered a viable suspect. But put your lawyer hat on. We don't have enough for an arrest, much less a conviction. What do we have? His hormones are in overdrive and aimed at your sister. He indulged in the dumbass sexting to impress her. But Manchester and her other paramour, AKA the cop, had the same idea but used words instead of images to convey it."

"But he took the recipe. Why would a teenage boy want a recipe for any other reason?"

"Harvard, you're jumping the gun. If you were representing him, what would you say to a jury about that?"

She went silent. After nearly a minute, she said, "That his mom asked him to get the recipe for her?" She made a face. "But, Jake, you've ruled out everyone else, except Cummings, and none of us think he's likely."

"We can't make someone guilty just to solve the case. My gut is telling me the boy is a hot suspect, but we've got work to do."

"You interviewed his parents."

"Well, it's time I paid another visit."

"If they believe you suspect him, they won't let him be around you."

"Which is why I need to visit when they're not at home."

"He won't let you in."

"I've got an idea about that." He studied her for several seconds. "Think you're up for a little undercover work."

She looked at him, stunned. "Really? You would let me go?"

"Provided you agree to wear a blond wig."

"What?"

"I want you to look like Savannah, and I doubt you want to dye your hair, which by the way, looks very nice."

"Thank you. Why do you want me to look like Savannah?"

"You'll see."

"Can we go tomorrow?"

"Patience, Harvard. We've got to set it up. Discover when his mom is not home. The dad should not be a problem during the day."

"Can you legally question a minor?"

He switched the screen back to the video. "I'm not law enforcement. Just a citizen having a conversation. I'll put Liz and Coop on determining the best time."

CHAPTER FORTY-ONE

On Thursday morning, Jake coached Scarlett on her role in his interview of Kyle McClellan. After a late lunch, she donned a blond wig, styled to resemble the way Savannah wore her hair, and they headed toward the McClelland home.

Shortly before they reached the neighborhood, her phone pinged, indicating a new text. Glancing down, she silently read the brief message.

Savannah found. She's fine. Call me.

A huge grin crossed Scarlett's face as she closed the app. "Jake. Savannah's okay. I just got a text from Grace. The FBI must have found her."

"Sounds like I was right. Good to hear." He gave a thumbs-up signal, and said, "I'll catch up with Cameron for details after we're done here." Within minutes, he pulled up a circular drive and parked in front of the McClellan home. "Ready to get the show started?"

"Ready."

"One more thing. For our purposes, let's keep this new info to ourselves for the time being. Got it?"

"Got it."

Moments later, the two stood at the entry to a two-story, red-brick house. Jake took the initiative and banged the heavy brass knocker. When the door opened, Scarlett immediately recognized the dark-haired boy as the same one Colin pointed out at Scott Kingsley's funeral.

"You must be Kyle," Jake said. "How ya doing? I'm Jake Shepherd." He handed the young man a card. "I'm a private investigator, working for Savannah Kingsley. You know Mrs. Kingsley, right?"

The boy's pupils enlarged as his eyes went to Scarlett. The sight of her seemed to render him speechless.

"Kyle? Did you hear my question?"

He snapped his face back in Jake's direction. "Yeah, right. Sure. I know Mrs. Kingsley." He returned his gaze to Scarlett. "I thought you were her."

Scarlett smiled. "We're twins."

"Kyle, this is Scarlett Kavanagh. As she said, she's Mrs. Kingsley's twin sister."

"Yes. No. Yes. I knew she had a sister. Colin mentioned his Aunt Grace—not Scarlett." The handsome young man's face flushed as he manifested signs of agitation.

"I'm the other sister."

Apparently unable to take his eyes off of Scarlett, he said, "Was it you the guy tried to kill at that bar?"

With a furrowed brow and patronizing tone, she said, "I like to think he intended to abduct me—not kill me."

He turned to Jake. "You're the one who shot the guy."

"Unfortunately."

"Jeez."

Jake disregarded the boy's awe. "Can we come in, Kyle? I would like to chat with you for a few minutes. I won't take too much of your time. We're trying to find Savannah Kingsley and hope you can help."

"Aren't the cops working on that?"

Jake scrutinized the young man, taking care not to intimidate him. At the sound of Savannah's name, Kyle had sucked in air, appearing to struggle to control his reaction.

"They are, but sometimes it helps for a civilian investigator to assist, which, in this case, would be me."

"Yeah. I heard about you from my mom. But why do you want to talk to me?" Kyle kept sneaking looks at Scarlett and then quickly back to Jake as if to avoid being caught.

"It's my job to speak to everyone in order to develop a clear picture as to what happened. May we come in?" Jake observed the boy's demeanor. *Bingo. He can't resist a chance to be near Scarlett.*

"Yeah, sure." He stepped aside, allowing Jake and Scarlett to enter.

"Is there somewhere we could sit? Maybe a table," Jake said, looking around.

"The dining room is over here," Kyle said, pointing to the right side of the large entry hall.

"As each took seats toward the end of the long, fruitwood table, Kyle said, "I don't know anything about where Mrs. Kingsley is. My mom will be home soon."

"I've already spoken to your mom, Kyle. Unfortunately, there's more to my investigation than looking for Mrs. Kingsley. She is not only missing, but she's also number one on the FBI's list of suspects in the murder of her husband."

"That's dumb. She didn't kill him." His eyes kept cutting back toward Scarlett.

Jake made no comment but studied the teen's face.

Shifting his focus back to Jake, the boy said, "She didn't. They've got it wrong."

"I agree with you, Kyle. I believe you can help me figure out who killed the senator, but first, tell me a little bit about yourself."

Kyle eyed Jake with a slight frown. "What do you wanna know about me?"

"For openers, how old are you?"

The young man stared at Jake without responding.

"It's not a trick question, son." Jake maintained a calm demeanor, returning the boy's stare but keeping his expression sincere.

"Whatever. I'm sixteen."

Jake sensed resistance. "I would have guessed eighteen or nineteen. So, you're in high school?"

Jake's ploy worked as Kyle's attitude began to thaw. "Yeah. Gonna be a junior."

"Bet you've got big college plans."

With a bit of hesitation, Kyle nodded.

"Any school picked out?"

"Not sure. It's a while."

"What's your best subject?"

"Study hall."

Jake chuckled. "What a coincidence. That was mine too."

Kyle broke into a smile for the first time. "I like science. Guess it runs in the family. My dad's a doctor. He owns a chain of primary care clinics."

"Impressive. My alma mater has a great med school."

With obvious interest, Kyle asked, "Where's that?"

"Connecticut—Yale."

"Really. You went to Yale?"

"Law school."

"Wow! Did you graduate?"

Jake smiled. "You're wondering why I'm a private investigator if I went to Yale. The answer is yes. I have a law degree—even a license to practice. I just don't have the personality for it. But tell me, what do you like to do for recreation?"

"The usual. Video games, TV, tennis." As Kyle spoke, he adjusted himself in his chair and pulled his cell phone from his hip pocket. After holding it for a second, he set it on the table, covering it with his hand.

Jake glanced down at the device. "Nice phone. Which one is it?"

"An iPhone 10."

"Bet it takes good photos. Mind if I try it?"

Kyle gave him a what-the-heck look but said, "Why not?" and slid the phone toward Jake.

Jake looked it over and then opened the camera app. "Smile, Scarlett."

She complied.

"If you don't mind," Jake said with a nod to Kyle, "I'll send the photo to myself and then delete it."

Kyle scrunched his face in a befuddled expression but shrugged as if to say whatever. "You don't have to delete it."

Jake tapped the screen several times, while Kyle seemed distracted by Scarlett, and then returned the device. "I heard you are quite a tennis player—even coached Mrs. Kingsley." As he spoke, Jake opened his portfolio, took out a stack of photo enlargements, and fanned them across the table in front of the subject.

Kyle looked down at the pictures and then back up toward Jake while Scarlett remained silent.

Trying not to give away your interest in the photos, aren't you, kid? "I'm interviewing everyone who knows the family. I understand you spent quite a bit of time with the children—babysitting. Colin told me how much he enjoyed playing video games with you. He misses you."

Kyle's eyes once again wandered toward Scarlett.

She nodded, smiling at the boy.

"Yeah. Colin's a sport."

"I also understand you played tennis fairly often with Mrs. Kingsley—that you're an ace player."

"I do okay." Kyle's focus shifted again but to the photos on the table.

"Didn't you win an important junior tournament?"

"No big deal."

"Looked like a big deal to me. How often did you play with Mrs. Kingsley?"

With a smile, Kyle looked at Jake. "Once, twice a week. She's good. Better than my mom." Once again, his eyes cut back to the images of Savannah. "Why'd you put all those pictures out?"

"Are they bothering you?"

"No. Just don't know why you need to do that to ask me questions."

"You want me to put them away?"

"No. They're fine."

Of course, you don't. "I brought the photos, Kyle, because I find looking at photos often sparks a person's memory. What do you think when you look at Colin?" Jake picked up one of the images of the child and centered it in front of the teen.

Kyle didn't react. "Nothing special. Maybe Xbox."

Jake shuffled the images around to include one of Colin and Savannah in swimsuits beside a pool.

Kyle took a deep breath.

Getting aroused, kid? "Was there some reason you didn't want to meet with me when I came here before?"

"I don't know what you're talking about."

"I think you do. When I met with your parents, you were conspicuously absent."

"I had tennis practice."

"Not true, Kyle, I checked. So, why were you avoiding me, just like you're avoiding looking at these?" Jake shoved three photos of Savannah and Scott Kingsley directly in front of Kyle.

Kyle instantly turned his head away.

"Look at them, Kyle. Or would you rather look at this one?" He pulled a photo of Savannah in a bathing suit at the beach from under the stack and held it up in front of Kyle's face. "Tell me more about you and Mrs. Kingsley."

The boy squirmed in his chair. "What do you mean?"

"You and Mrs. Kingsley. Do you have a special relationship with her?"

"I don't understand. She's Colin's mom."

"I think she might be a little more than Colin's mom where you're concerned." Jake's stare locked the teen's eyes in a contact he appeared unable to break. "She's a beautiful woman, isn't she, Kyle?"

The boy's pupils dilated as panic appeared to set in.

"Did you and Mrs. Kingsley ever get close?"

"I don't want to talk to you anymore."

"I understand, Kyle. But do you want Mrs. Kingsley to go to prison because of you?"

Kyle's body jerked. "She won't. They don't put innocent people in prison."

Got him! "Unfortunately, that's not true, son. It can happen. Maybe there's something you would like to tell me."

The young man shook his head. His eyes flitted between the photos and Scarlett, appearing to avoid eye contact with Jake.

"Let it out, Kyle. You have a thing for Savannah Kingsley, don't you?"

Silence saturated the room.

Jake pressed relentlessly. "Look at me Kyle. You think you're in love with Savannah Kingsley—maybe obsessed."

"I don't know what you're talking about." The boy's hands trembled. Trying to steady them, he moved them to his lap.

"Yes, you do." Jake's eyes flashed. "You know exactly what I'm talking about. Did Senator Kingsley find out?"

Kyle's chin quivered for a second.

"Was Mrs. Kingsley planning to leave the senator for you? Or, did she tell you she wouldn't leave the senator?"

"We never talked about that."

"But you had a relationship, didn't you?"

"No. Yes. I like her, and she likes me."

"Tell me about that, Kyle."

"No. I don't think I should."

"But you want to. Tell me. Were you sleeping with Savannah Kingsley? Was it a hot, steamy relationship?"

Scarlett flinched.

"Stop it. You don't know what you're talking about."

"Oh, but I do, Kyle. Did you and Mrs. Kingsley make love when the senator was away?"

"She kissed me once."

Scarlett squeezed her eyes shut and took a deep breath.

"She kissed you once?"

"Yes, she did. She likes me."

"Am I to take that to mean, the only physical contact you had with her was a single kiss?"

Kyle sat frozen for several seconds before nodding.

"Describe for me how that kiss came about. Was it on the mouth?"

"I found a gold necklace in the yard when Colin and I were playing catch. When I gave it to Savannah, she grabbed me, hugged me, and kissed me on the cheek."

"And that was your sole, physical contact?"

"Yes. But I knew how she felt from the way she hugged me. Afterward, she was always so sweet. I know she cares about me. She just couldn't show it while Senator Kingsley was still her husband. He wasn't a nice man. He treated her awful."

"How do you know that? Did she tell you?"

"No. But Colin said things, and I could tell he was mean from the way he was when he came home, and I was there."

"It was you, wasn't it, Kyle? You made the cheese straws with just a little ground peanuts and sent them to Senator Kingsley."

The young man sprung to his feet.

Before Kyle could speak, Jake said, "Sit down." He hit the table with his fist. "It's over. We know what you did." Softening his tone, Jake said, "But I don't believe you meant to kill him."

"You're nuts." Panic caused Kyle's voice to rise an octave and slightly crack.

"If you tell the truth, you can probably work something out with the U.S. Attorney."

The teen attempted to take a defiant attitude. "You're full of crap. You don't have any proof, and you can't arrest me. You're not a real cop."

"You are absolutely right, Kyle." Maintaining control, Jake said, "I don't have a badge, but I know plenty of people who do. Don't make it worse on yourself."

"You can't prove anything."

"Actually . . . I can." Jake took out his phone and brought up a video. "Take a look at this. Recognize the young man in the Kingsley kitchen?"

Kyle's chin twitched, and beads of sweat appeared on his forehead. "That's not me."

"Oh, I think you're wrong. Trust me, son. The FBI tech team will enlarge and enhance the image until there would be no question in the minds of a jury. They'll even be able to identify the recipe you photographed. It's you all right. You in the Kingsley kitchen, going through Mrs. Kingsley's recipe box and taking a photo of the cheese straw recipe. I'd bet a year's pay that the image of that recipe is among the photos I sent to myself a few minutes ago from your phone."

Adjusting his position in his chair, Kyle stared at Jake like a doe in the headlights. "I don't believe you. You didn't have time to look through my pictures, and even if you did, you couldn't do that. You don't have a warrant."

"You're a pretty smart kid, Kyle, but not quite smart enough. I didn't have to look through them. I sent them all. As for the warrant, I'm not a cop as you pointed out, so I don't need a warrant. And you waived your expectation of privacy when you handed me your phone and agreed to let me send the photo."

Kyle's eyes appeared to glass over.

Jake reached into his portfolio and took out an enlargement of the nude male found on Savannah's phone. "Recognize this photo, Kyle?"

"No."

"It won't do you any good to lie. Look at the tattoo on the leg. I bet if you rolled up your pant leg, I would find the same tattoo. I'm sure we'll find the original shot among those photos on your phone."

"That still doesn't prove it's me."

"Don't play me for a fool, Kyle. This photo is also on Savannah's Kingsley's phone, complete with time, date, and number from which it was sent. In an attempt at anonymity, I'm guessing, you took the image with this phone, sent it to a prepaid, and from there forwarded it to her. Smart move, but not quite smart enough. The FBI will track the throw-away, track where it was purchased, and probably find your image at the checkout counter purchasing it." A tell-tale blaze of color spread across the boy's cheeks as Jake, with a fierce look of certainty, drove home his message. "We both know the truth, Kyle."

"So." Kyle took a deep breath, attempting to regain his composure. "What does that prove? It doesn't prove I had anything to do with the murder."

"It proves you had a real thing going for Senator Kingsley's beautiful wife, which is a powerful motive for murder. You probably knew there was a trip to Europe planned for a second honeymoon. You wanted to throw an obstacle in the way. Don't get me wrong. I don't believe you're evil. You didn't think it would kill him. Right? If you confess, tell your side of what happened, you will improve your chances of avoiding a charge of first-degree murder. Stealing the recipe, making the snack with peanuts—that proves premeditation, Kyle." Jake slapped his hand on the table, causing the teen to jump. "That carries a life sentence, son—possibly the death penalty if they charge you as an adult."

Scarlett flinched at the sound of the death penalty.

Kyle began shaking. "You're crazy. I didn't touch him. All I did was make some stupid cheese things. They said on TV he had a blow to his head."

Scarlett looked at Jake, but he remained stoic.

"So, all you did was send Senator Kingsley cheese snacks that had peanut content?"

"That's all. I was never in his office, so I couldn't have hit him." The boy did not appear to realize he had confessed.

"The head trauma did not kill him, but it probably prevented him from reaching his EpiPen. In reconstructing the scene, the theory is he ate the cheese straws, began choking, and in a compromised state, bumped into the piece of furniture causing the heavy bronze statue to fall. Regardless of which caused his death, the food you furnished with knowledge of his allergy set the crime in motion."

"I want my parents."

Jake ignored Kyle's statement. "I've got just one question, Kyle. I know you are in love or lust with Mrs. Kingsley. I know you made the cheese straws Senator Kingsley ate. What I don't know is how did you get the snack to the senator?"

"I'm not saying anything else."

"Then, let me give you my best guess. While you could have given him the container, I don't think so. Too risky. You could have left them in the Kingsley kitchen, but that's also too risky. Which leaves me with only one possibility."

The boy's demeanor wavered between an attempt to be aggressive and moments of childlike fear.

"I'm guessing you mailed the food to the senator. The post office photographs every item. Were you aware of that?"

The teenager flinched and looked away.

"A review of the tapes for the time period will give the authorities the image of any packages addressed to Senator Kingsley." Jake paused, allowing the impact of his words to soak into the boy. "The FBI has handwriting experts, Kyle, who will have no problem identifying who addressed the package, and they have search teams who can track down discarded trash and sift through it to find microscopic evidence—DNA, fingerprints. They're probably on it now."

The boy appeared near tears. "I said, I want my parents."

"No problem. Call them. We'll wait."

CHAPTER FORTY-TWO

Regina McClellan arrived first, still wearing her tennis dress and athletic shoes. "What's going on, Kyle?" Scarlett caught her eye, causing her to do a doubletake before addressing Jake. "What are you doing here, Mr. Shepherd? My husband and I told you everything we know, which is basically nothing about Scott and Savannah Kingsley. You have no right to come into our home, behind our backs, and interrogate our son, scaring him."

"Let's wait for your husband, Mrs. McClellan." Jakes words had barely fallen when the front door burst open, and Martin McClellan stormed in.

"What the hell is going on here?" the father said, anger blazing in his eyes. "Why are you trespassing on our property and talking to our son without permission?"

Jake stood. "I appreciate your position, Mr. McClellan, but I suggest you hear me out. Your family has a problem—a very *big* problem. Don't make it worse."

"What the fuck do you mean? You need to get out of my house. Regina, call the authorities."

"I wouldn't make that move if I were you. You'll be igniting a fire you won't be able to contain." Jake returned the man's glare. "I can leave, and I will, but you'll be making a mistake if you don't listen to me."

Kyle stood by the door leading to the back of the house—his face devoid of color.

Scarlett watched the drama, slid her hand into her purse, and wrapped it around her phone.

"Kyle said you accused him of having something to do with Scott Kingsley's murder. Where do you get off upsetting a minor with such a preposterous statement?"

Jake could tell by the man's balled up fists, tone of voice, and hostile expression that he was about to lose control.

"There's substantial evidence backing up my accusation, Mr. McClellan. You'd be wise to hear me out. What you do, how you react, can have a strong impact on Kyle's future."

Scarlett pulled out her phone and pressed 9-1-1 but did not tap send.

As if seeing her for the first time, Martin McClellan glanced toward Scarlett. "What are you doing here, Savannah? I thought you were missing."

"She's not Mrs. Kingsley, Dad. She's her twin sister."

"Mr. McClellan, I want to help Kyle," Jake said. "I don't think he meant to cause what happened."

"Who are you? You're nothing but a private dick."

"You're absolutely right. Although you won't believe it now, I've done you a favor. You have a chance to get in front of this before the badges do show up. Kyle isn't under arrest right now. But the FBI will be coming, and his options will quickly disappear."

"He has a video and pictures of me that make me look guilty, Dad."

"What the fuck? Does the FBI have those?" McClellan said.

"They don't know it, but they do," Jake said. "They have everything I have, and in time, they *will* get to it. They always do. The best thing for your son is to turn himself in. Get ahead of this thing. As I said, I don't believe he meant to kill the senator, but the more he hides, the guiltier he looks. Get him a lawyer ASAP—a good criminal defense lawyer—not one of your big-ticket corporate guys. Get intent off the table."

The man's shoulders seemed to drop, the muscles in his face relaxed, and his hands opened. "I've got to process all this. If there's any truth to what you're saying, this is going to ruin his life."

Regina McClellan leaned against the wall, tears flooding down her face. "What have you done, Kyle? What have you done?"

"Believe me," Jake said. "I feel your pain—both of you. I'm a father. Unfortunately, lives are ruined by hormones. Help Kyle salvage what he can at this point. There's no statute of limitations on homicide. Even if he runs, it will be with him for life. Be smart. The Feds *will* get him. Take my word for it."

"You knew all this when you interviewed us, didn't you?" Regina said.

"No. No, I didn't," Jake said.

"Are you going to turn him in?" the father asked, his hostility waning.

"If he doesn't turn himself in, I have no choice. But even if I don't, they have all the evidence I have. It's just a matter of time. Kyle had it bad for Mrs. Kingsley and didn't want her going on a so-called second honeymoon. It's tragic what immature judgment can do to a young person's life."

"How did this happen?" the distraught mother said. "My son's not a murderer."

As he turned toward her, Jake said, "I don't think so either, Mrs. McClelland, but, trust me, this is a high-profile case. Even if the prosecutor assigned to the case is sympathetic, too many eyes will be on him to permit him to show sympathy. I repeat, get a good attorney— now." He looked Kyle in the eye. "If the FBI or U.S. Marshals show up, Kyle, you immediately say, 'I want a lawyer,' and do not, I repeat, *do not*, say another word without your lawyer present."

CHAPTER FORTY-THREE

As they drove away from the McClellan house, neither Jake nor Scarlett spoke for at least three miles.

"What happens now?" Scarlett asked, breaking the silence. "Are you going to turn him in? What if they run?"

"What I hope happens is the parents take my advice and retain the best defense attorney available, and he or she arranges for Kyle to turn himself in."

"And if they don't. Couldn't they run with him?"

He glanced over at her with his smug smile. "They're not going anywhere that the Feds don't know. They're under surveillance as we speak."

"You knew that? You already reported him?"

"Not quite. I let Kirby know the boy was a suspect, but I didn't have enough for an arrest. Trust me, Hal knows me well enough to know I had cause. He immediately assigned a surveillance team and started digging. I'll hold off giving him all I have until the family has a chance to obtain legal assistance but there will be eyes on them if they try to pull anything."

"I'm drained," Scarlett said when Jake stopped for a red light. "There were times while you were interrogating Kyle when I wanted to scream out, 'Stop, he's just a boy.'"

Jake neither responded nor looked her way until the light changed and he accelerated. "If I'm honest, I'll admit I hoped we were wrong. Trust me, Harvard. There were times I wanted to pull back."

"It's supposed to feel good to catch the killer, but I feel sick." She reached up and pulled off the blond wig, shook her short hair loose, and ran her fingers through it.

Jake nodded. "Hard case and one of the rare times I was glad I didn't have a badge—both when I hijacked his camera and when I wasn't the one to take him into custody. I'd have much preferred taking down a crime lord or the pompous senator. The boy is just a heartsick teen who made a stupid error in judgment. Kids being kids commit serious acts."

"You were a U.S. Attorney. What do you think they'll go for?"

"I hope second degree—reckless endangerment. His defense will turn on his mens rea. He can't deny intent to do harm, but I don't think he wanted to kill the bastard."

CHAPTER FORTY-FOUR

"When they reached Jake's office, he gave Liz a nutshell version of what had happened, and she handed him a message to call Dan Cameron. Scarlett went into the workroom and began straightening up the files while Jake went to his office to make the call to Cameron.

As she worked, a strange feeling flooded her body, settling in her stomach. She looked around the room and felt a letdown similar to when she opened her last Christmas present as a kid. It's over. *This crazy life I've been living for four weeks with this brilliant, unpredictable, rude, sexy cowboy is finished. I should be happy. Why do I feel like a loved one just died?*

After Scarlett finished the housekeeping, she went to the tiny kitchen and took a cold drink from the refrigerator. As she poured it into a cup, Jake came in. "Want one?" she asked.

"I'm good."

"Did you find out more about Savannah?"

"Cameron had Cumming's credit cards and bank account flagged. When he got a notification from the credit card company that Cumming's card just been used at a Walmart in Kentucky, he sent a team out. From there they were able to determine Cummings had a sister living on a horse farm outside Lexington where he and Savannah are staying. Savannah's fine. Claims she sent a letter to your younger sister, explaining why she left."

Scarlett's lips formed a tight smile. "Right. My first guess is she's lying. But if not, she probably got the zip code wrong, and it's in the dead letter box. Did either of them give an explanation as to why or explain how they did it?"

"Your sister claimed she had no knowledge of what the senator was involved in, but Cummings figured out he had some type of illegal deal going on and thought it best to take her into a do-it-yourself WITSEC. He parked his car behind the church, in one of the surveillance dead zones, and left it unlocked with a cover in the back to conceal her. He distracted the other members of the team long enough for her to slip out, get into the car, and cover herself. When they searched the parking lot, Cummings made certain he was the one to clear his car. No one had reason to question a member of the security team or to question his leaving the scene."

"You nailed it. While I hate that the McClellan boy turned out to be guilty, I'm kinda glad it wasn't Cummings—even though I don't know him. He must care a lot about Savannah to risk his career."

"You're not going to go all mushy on me are you, Harvard?"

She balled her fist and punched him playfully on the arm as she walked out of the room.

CHAPTER FORTY-FIVE

Two days after the interrogation of Kyle McClellan, Jake tapped on the jamb of the master bedroom of his apartment, the door being halfway ajar. "Have a rabbit in there by any chance?"

Scarlett chuckled. "As a matter of fact, I have a dog and a rabbit. You can come in."

When he pushed the door open, Kai looked up from where he sat watching Scarlett pack. Romeo hopped around the bed out of sight. "The little bastard slipped out of the room when I was cleaning his pen. I see you're getting ready to travel south."

"I do have a couple of cats who may have forgotten who I am, plus a law practice to address. But I'm going to miss Romeo. The little rascal has a way of charming his way into your heart."

"Can't believe I'm going to say this, Harvard, but I'll miss that smart mouth of yours giving me a hard time."

Scarlett grinned. "It's been an unexpected, crazy time. I can't believe it's over even though I'm relieved. I guess for you, it's been just another day in the life."

"Not quite. So, you're back to Georgia and divorce court?"

"Not exactly."

A puzzled frown arose on his face as he tilted his head and eyed her. "Not exactly? What does that mean?"

"Well. . . . There's something I need to tell you."

"Please." He hooked his thumbs in the pockets of his jeans. "You have my full attention."

"I've put a deposit down on a one-bedroom in this building."

"You've what?"

"I've put a binder on an apartment."

"Why would you do that?"

"I'll need a place to live when I move up here."

He sat down on the bed, a frown on his face. "When you move up here? What are you talking about?"

"I told you I had a plan."

"Oh, yes. The plan. Your mysterious plan. Are you finally ready for a big reveal of your *plan*?"

"As a matter of fact, I am. I want to buy into your agency."

"Excuse me. Did I hear you right? You what?"

"Don't look so shocked, Jake. I didn't say I'm pregnant. I want to become an investigator—buy into your business. I can afford it."

"Let me get this right. You want to invest in my agency?"

"Yes. I want to be your partner."

"I know I didn't hear *that* right. You want what?"

"I want to buy into your business as a partner and become a private investigator."

"Oh, no." He shook his head violently. "Hell no. There are so many reasons why that's a bad idea that we don't have time for me to list them. For openers, I don't play well with others. You've got to have figured that out."

"You and Pete are partners in the security operation. You and Liz work like two parts of a precision instrument."

"Yes, but Coop stays on his side of the fence, and I stay on mine. You are not the type to stay on your side. As for Liz, we come from the same place. We fill in each other's blanks, and she is not my partner. Why would you even think of giving up your law practice?"

"You gave up yours."

"That wasn't the same. I never wanted to be a lawyer."

"Well, I'm tired of it. I don't see arguing over who gets the kids on Halloween for the rest of my life. On the day we met, you asked how family law was working out for me. It resonated. The past weeks, I've felt so alive seeing you work a case—finding that definitive piece of evidence—solving the puzzle. I'm good at interviewing people and researching. I know how to use a gun."

"It's not a board game, Harvard—and not like TV. If you're serious about changing careers, and for the record, I think you've lost your f-ing mind; you need to go back to school and get a degree in criminal justice. Better yet, go to a police academy. You could open a nice little operation in Atlanta."

"I'd rather learn from the best, and that's you. I know you're the best because you've told me—quite a few times."

"Ouch. Never thought that would come back to bite me like this. Scarlett, this job can be dangerous—not all the time but it can be. You, of all people, should know that."

"Which tells me you don't know much about family law. More family law attorneys and judges are shot than in any other area of practice. Google it. I need a change. I've worked with the bleak side of love for too long. Come on, Jake. It would work. I know it would. Remember, I was the one who first zeroed in on Kyle McClelland."

"I'll give you that. You're observant, intuitive, and detail oriented. But what about the personal side of the equation? All I've heard from you is, 'We're not a couple.'"

"That's right. We're not. Business and pleasure don't mix. You know that. I want to be your business partner."

He eyed her, putting his hand on his chin. "My business partner? Never happen. I might consider hiring you—might. But partner—not a chance."

"Really. You're hiring me?"

"Do you have a hearing problem? I said, 'might.'"

"You're not going to regret it."

"Wrong. I already do, but what the hell?"

"You're going to wonder how you ever got along without me."

"I wasn't finished. If I decide to give it a try, and hear me, I said, 'if,' it'll be conditioned on you taking a self-defense class, some police practice classes, and an advanced firearms class. I'm assuming

Harvard gave you an education in criminal justice. And we're *not* partners. You're the employee. I'm the—"

"Boss?"

"I was going to say employer. But—yeah. Boss works fine."

"I prefer partner."

"I'm sure you do, Harvard. But you're going to have to settle for employee and follow my orders. You'll sit that gorgeous you-know-what at a desk until—make that *if*—I think you've learned enough for field work."

"Can't you teach me what I need to know?"

"Hell, no. First of all, I'm not a teacher; and second, me teaching you would be like a pit bull training a wild cat. Personally, I think our best arrangement would be couple. That would be a challenge—but one I think I would enjoy. So far, we're batting zero at keeping personal out of business."

"We'll have to work on that."

He stood, moved close to her, and slid his arms around her waist. "Yeah. We *definitely* will." Lowering his voice, he said, "How much time do we have before we have to leave for the airport?"

JUDITH ERWIN is the award-winning author of seven books, including the Shadow of Dance Series, three standalone novels, and Book 1 of the new series, Shepherd & Associates. She won an FAPA gold medal for The Studio, which was also a finalist in the international Reader's Favorite Contest. Her romantic novel, Shadow of Doubt was a Royal Palm Literary Awards finalist. A retired attorney and freelance writer, her work has been published in numerous periodicals. A native of Atlanta, Georgia, she lives and writes in North Florida.

Subscribe for announcements, giveaways, and more at:
www.juditherwinofficialwebsite.com
Visit her on Facebook at Judith Erwin Books

Neat stacks of sealed boxes stood in the center of Scarlett's Atlanta living room while furniture lined the walls, waiting for transfer to Virginia. As she handed her younger sister a can of soda, a cell phone chirped.

"Mine or yours?" Scarlett said, setting her Coke down.

Grace pointed to the table. "Yours. Mine's in the car."

When she grabbed the device, a smile crept across Scarlett's face. "It's Jake." She held up her index finger. "Give me a minute."

Not waiting for a reply, Scarlett navigated a course between the boxes to exit the room.

"No problem," Grace said, unheard. "I need a break anyhow."

As soon as out of earshot, Scarlett turned her attention to the caller. "What's up? I didn't expect to hear from you."

"How soon can you be here?" he said.

Scarlett tipped her head, a quizzical expression on her face. "What do you mean how soon? You know I'm moving there next week. Grace is here, helping me pack."

"Need you yesterday. That is—if you want to work."

"Of course, I want to work. What's so urgent?"

"Critical case. Madison wants me on it. I'm swamped, plus this one needs a woman's finesse."

"And your finesse is in storage. Right? I thought you weren't going to let me work a case until I improved my skills."

"Do you want to debate or work, Harvard? I have a job for you. Coming? Or should I get Brenda?"

Wrinkling her brow, she held the phone out, staring at it for a second while shaking her head, and then brought it back to her ear. "Well, that's the Jake Shepherd we all know and love. Yes. Yes, I'll come. Of course. But I'll have to arrange for the cats and my car. And by the way, Shepherd, please don't trouble yourself with common courtesy."

"Sorry. Guess I was a little—"

"Abrupt? You think?"

"Said I was sorry. We'll cover the details from here: car, cats, and flight. Gotta go. See you tomorrow."

"Yeah. See you tomorrow." She slid the phone into her jeans pocket, took a deep breath, and returned to the living room.

"What did he want?" Grace said.

"Me—in DC—tomorrow."

"What? Why? Surely, you're not going. Does think he can snap a finger, and you run?"

"Why does he want me? Or why am I going?"

"You're going? Darn it, Scarlett. Are you making this move because you want to change careers or because Jake Shepherd rocks a tight pair of jeans?"

"Wow. Don't mince words. You're about as subtle as he is."

Grace dropped her chin and then glanced up with a contrite expression. "I guess that was pretty blunt. I apologize. But it's all crazy and totally out of character for the smart, sensible Kavanagh sister. Giving up a successful law practice to move seven hundred miles away to become a private investigator? It's insane."

"You sound like Mom. I've told you. I'm burned out and want a change."

"Change is one thing but come on. Going from lawyer to detective seems to me like going from doctor to nurse. I give you Jake Shepherd is easy on the eyes and apparently almost as competent as he thinks he is, but I can't believe you, of all people, would drop everything and run when he calls."

Scarlett gave Grace a dubious look.

"Don't give me that expression," Grace said. "He is a sexy guy— if you can get past his arrogance and rough edges. And you're both single."

"Cut it out. What you see is confidence, not arrogance. There's another side. And the answer to your question is I want to change careers—not seduce Jake Shepherd. You've got a beautiful marriage, but marriage isn't right for everyone. So, give up on the matchmaking—okay? We're friends, and I admire his skill. That's all."

"I'm not convinced." Grace rolled her eyes. "Did your friend tell you why you have to fly up there tomorrow?"

"He didn't have time. I'll find out when I get there. By the way, I'll need a favor. Can you oversee the movers for me next week? If you can't, I'll hire someone to do it."

"Of course, I will." Grace walked over and threw her arms around Scarlett. "I'm going to miss you, honey. I'm being selfish, but it's hard losing both of my sisters to the Capitol. At least when Scott was alive, Savannah still had a house here." She dug down in her pocket, took out a tissue, and wiped her eyes. "Don't be mad. I want you to be happy. I just hope you're not making a huge mistake."

As Grace released her, Scarlett wiped her eye. "I'll come back to Atlanta often. And any time you need me, call. As for making a mistake, the only permanent step I've taken is selling the law practice to Jennifer, and she said I have a job anytime I want it. You know I'm holding on to the condo and my Bar license. I may even take the Virginia Bar Exam."

Grace shook her head, her eyes glassy.

Later that afternoon, Scarlett opened a text from Liz Glover, Jake's assistant.

> *All in place. Flight departs 7:35 a.m. Paperwork available on Delta website. MacGregors picking up cats and car keys tonight. Cats to travel on MacG plane Monday. Shipping service transporting car. Looking forward to having you back.*

After replying with a thumbs-up emoji, Scarlett leaned back against the headboard and stroked the cat lying next to her. "No flight in cargo for you guys. You're flying private to our new home."

When Scarlett deplaned the next morning at Reagan National, Jake waited at the passenger boundary line, wearing his usual jeans, boots, and a leather jacket. As she approached him, her heart rhythm raged. Think professional, professional, profess—"

When she reached Jake, his arms spread wide to welcome her with a hug. "Looking good, Harvard. How was the flight?"

Scarlett smiled, adjusting the shoulder strap of her purse. "Pretty smooth. How's DC? Have you been keeping it on track since I left?"

"Doin' my best. Do we need to go to baggage claim?"

"Nope. This is all I brought." She pointed to her rolling carry-on. "Everything else is scheduled to ship next week, including my wardrobe."

"He leaned forward and grabbed the handle of her case. "I've got it."

"Did you think to book a hotel room for me?"

"No reason for that. Our prior arrangement worked fine."

"Jake!" She hit him on the shoulder with her fist. "You know that's not a good idea. We agreed. No more mixing business and personal. Me in your apartment? No—doesn't work."

"I beg to differ, counselor. I honor your boundaries—your rules. Will be a hell of a lot more convenient since your car won't arrive for a few days."

"Damn it, Jake. Who taught you to live on the edge? Yale or the FBI?"

He laughed. "DNA, which is probably responsible for this nutty idea of you working for me."

She blinked, shaking her head. "Okay, okay. You win, but—no cheating."

"I never cheat. Told you when you came up with your—plan." He slapped a hand down on her shoulder. "In all things business, I'm boss. All things personal, you are."

"We'll table that issue for now. So. Tell me. What's the case?"

"Let's get to the truck, and I'll lay it out for you."

When they reached his SUV, Jake loaded her bag in the back and then climbed into the driver's seat."

"So, bring me up to speed," Scarlett said, fastening her seatbelt.

"Child disappeared from school. Five-year-old girl. School says mom picked her up. Mom claims an impersonator signed her out. Authorities aren't buying it. She's their primary suspect."

"Oh my gosh. Are we working for the school?"

"Nope. The mom."

Her face registered surprise. "She's your client?"

"Our client, Harvard. Yep. She's the one."

"Do you know what they have on her?"

"Apparently, a body of compelling evidence indicating the child was last seen with Mom, and she can't or won't give the whereabouts of the little girl."

Scarlett frowned, shaking her head. "What kind of evidence?"

"CCTV footage, signature in logbook, eyewitness."

"My gosh, Jake. Sounds open and shut. But you don't work for guilty people. Is that why you're letting me take it?"

"Are you assuming she's guilty? What's wrong with you, Harvard? That Ivy League law degree didn't teach you to collect all the facts first?"

"Point taken. When do I meet her?"

"That's a bit complicated. She is being held in a psychiatric facility on an involuntary commitment order. If not found by the shrinks to fit the criteria for retention, Phil believes she will be charged with child neglect for openers and transferred to the local detention center."

"What is being done to locate the child?"

"All the usual, but Phil has the feeling they're not expecting a happy ending."

Scarlett winched.

He stopped to pay for parking but continued talking. "There's an AMBER Alert, and the Feds have been called in. But only because Phil threw a fit and insisted the locals notify the CARD team."

"CARD?"

"FBI team. Child Abduction Rapid Deployment."

"What does the mom say about the evidence?"

"That's the rub. She doesn't. She shut down after a maniacal show at the school where she screamed 'impersonator.'"

As Jake pulled out onto the main road, butterflies swarmed in Scarlett's stomach. "Where do I start?"

"By treating the subject as you would in one of your domestic cases. Didn't you always begin with quizzing the client? Think you're up to an interview?"

She looked at him with squinting eyes. "You know I am."

A broad smile spread across his face. "That's my gal. You'll do the intake and front-run. I'll back you up."

"So, you haven't met with her?"

"Nope. Right now, Phil is the only one who has seen her, and he got nowhere. Said all she did was cry."

"How did a high-priced lawyer like Phil get involved?"

"His wife, Christine, got a call from their church, which is where the woman works. Chris pressured Phil to help, pro bono. He's covering us. But regardless of what is going on, time is of the essence. That's why I wanted you ASAP. If the mom has done something with or to the child, maybe you can get a bit of info from her. If she wasn't

involved, maybe she knows something about who might have abducted the little girl."

"What if she did harm the child, maybe by accident? Are you still
going to take the case?"

"Do the interview and brief me."